Wolfmother

BY THE AUTHOR OF

Torn Apart
Blood Bound

Wolfmother

Book 3 of Convergence

J. M. Riddles

Cover Design by Seventhstar

ISBN: 978-0-9994476-5-9
ASIN: B08MMP5GTK

Library of Congress Control Number: 2020949891
J.M. Riddles, West Saint Paul, MN

jmriddles.com

Dedicated to my wonderful nerdy husband, Dickie, and my two best friends who have supported my writing through all the years: Natalie and Kat. I love you guys.

ACKNOWLEDGEMENTS

I want to thank everyone who beta-read the first drafts of this story for me and especially those who helped me with my summary because, for me, there is no pain greater than having to summarize my work.

Special thanks to my two best friends, who are like the sisters I never had, and who have been with me through all the many years of my writing and have offered unconditional love and support. Kat, thank you for all the times you've ever helped me edit. Natalie, thank you for suffering through the more risqué chapters of my work. I'd like to promise you there won't be more of them, but there will probably be more.

Lastly, I would like to thank my husband, Dickie, who has supported me during this entire project. He has been my rock during all the years we have been together, and I know he has always been happy to see me write. He always has a million ideas for me, and he's always loved discussing my work with me. I know he wants all the credit, but I will at least say, yes, you helped push me along...a little.

Wolfmother

By J.M. Riddles

CHAPTER 1 – BEYOND THE DARK MIRROR

"Are you in there?"

Nothing.

Was it going to be another one of those days?

Some days he would respond and almost be coherent, speaking of a mysterious voice that tormented him before his capture. Other days were worse, and though he was there, he could not focus or respond to any direct questions. Mad ravings and jumbled memories would pour out and drain away all her hopes.

And then there were the silent days.

"Please. Please, say something," she pleaded while wringing her hands in her lap.

The mirror remained dark. Only the faint outline of her reflection graced the surface, but beneath, there was nothing.

"Lord Anshar, please say something. I need to hear your voice," she tried again in despair as tears threatened the corners of her eyes.

"Halea?" came the voice in the mirror, and pity wrenched at her heart. He sounded so tired. So very tired.

"Yes! Yes, it's me, Lord Anshar. How are you feeling today? Please show yourself. It's been weeks now, and I just want to know that you're okay."

"Why won't you come to me, Halea?"

She bit her lip in frustration. It was going to be another bad day.

"I can't, Lord Anshar. You're in the dark mirror, and I can't reach you, but I can see you. Please let me see you."

"They're tearing me apart. My blood! I can smell it. It's everywhere. Their blood. Their eyes. It's on my hands. I can't get the smell of their blood off my hands. I need you. Where are you? Please, I need you!" he called, and with every word, his voice grew louder, more frantic, more unhinged.

"Shh. Shh. I'm here. I'm here. I'm with you. It's okay. No one is hurting you. Please let me see you. There's no blood. I know there isn't. Please, just let me see you."

Something moved beneath the surface of the mirror, and a form came into view.

It was him.

"Halea?"

"I can see you! Yes, I can see you. You're okay. See, no one is hurting you. You're safe."

"There is blood."

1

"No. No, there is no blood. Don't you believe me?"

His vacant eyes looked up from his trembling hands. Within the mirror dimension, a shimmering surface reflected his surroundings. Usually, it only showed his own morose visage, but now he could see her looking back at him, and his face hardened at what he saw.

"Don't look at me like that, Halea! Please. I can't stand your pity!" he growled as he recalled why he couldn't bear to show himself. He was hurting her. He was making her sad, and it was his fault.

He began to step back.

"No! No, please don't leave, Lord Anshar! Stay with me. We can talk about pleasant things. We can talk about..." she paused, struggling to dredge up some happy memory from their past.

"Do you remember before I became a priestess when everyone was gathered for the New Year prayer, and I was running so late because I fell asleep after our training? Gods, you wore me out, ya know? I mean, really, it was kind of your fault. I came running into the chapel and slammed into Senior Cleric Edgar and knocked him over, and then he knocked over the whole back row of devotees. Everyone was staring at me, and I'm sure my face was red. Mama Dragon was trying so hard not to laugh, and Grandfather was embarrassed and trying to pretend like he didn't know me. You just gave me this exasperated look and shook your head, and High Priestess Maven jumped up and dragged me back out of the chapel by my ear and scolded the life out of me."

"Everyone was trying so hard to keep a straight face, even me," he added, and his voice sounded lighter as if the threat of joviality were tempting him from the shadows. "I heard her slap you from the hall."

And with that, their moment of mirth shattered.

"She hurt you. I remember. You were still just a girl. You couldn't heal yet, and Maven didn't know her own strength. Your face was bruised for a week," he recalled, and his face grew dark with anger.

"It wasn't that bad, really. I did deserve it," she anxiously backtracked as the fond memory soured.

It was no use. He remembered it all. He remembered the smell of tears on her face as she was dragged back into the chapel in shame. He remembered taking Maven aside after the services and admonishing her for being too harsh on someone who was still just a child and not yet a priestess. It was an accident, and Senior Cleric Edgar should have known better than to stand so close to the chapel door. He remembered trying to comfort Halea the next day and asking her to spar again to cheer her up. She loved fighting with him. She was so happy when they were outside together in the gardens. Her eyes would glow. He missed those days.

He missed her.

"What happened to us, Halea? We used to be so close. I've never been as close to anyone as I was with you. You were the only one who saw me for what I was, and yet you never hated me for it. Why?"

"Lord Anshar, please. You didn't deserve to be hated."

"That's not true!" he shouted. "I failed everyone, including you. My weakness is why your mother is dead, Halea. That was me! That was all my fault because I couldn't stand to do my duty. I hate what I am, Halea. I hate what I was forced to be – a servant. My whole life, that's all I've ever been, and I hated every damn moment of it. And you! You knew! You knew the truth. You should have turned from me when you had the chance. You should have hated me as I deserved. Instead, you made me love you. Is this my punishment? To be denied the only thing I've ever loved. I could have endured anything else."

"Lord Anshar," Halea sobbed as unrestrained tears shed from her eyes.

"I know why you're here! You think you can convince me to serve again. You want me to stop the next convergence, but I will not. You know what would be required of me. I see clearly now where I am, trapped in this accursed dimension of Tiamet's own creation. Caged like an animal. But within this cage, no one can control me. No one can bend me to their will. Here, I'm no longer compelled by Tiamet or the voice from within the Chaos. Here, there is only silence and my tortured mind. As long as I'm trapped here, no one can use me against my will again, not even you. Go! I can't bear the sadness in your eyes."

"But I don't want…"

"Listen to me, Halea. I swear upon the gods, I shall never again perform a sacrifice. Now, go!"

Halea jumped to her feet and stormed out of the room, slamming the heavy wooden door behind her.

Lord Anshar watched her flee from within the mirror and clenched his fists in resolve.

"*Whether it remakes the world or utterly destroys it, let the convergence come. I can't save you, but at least I will not be the one to kill you. I'm sorry. I know you think there might be another way, but there isn't. I tried,*" he thought as his image faded from the surface of the mirror.

CHAPTER 2 – WINTER'S END

Halea dried her eyes on the sleeve of her green robe as she stood just outside the tree-dwelling door and struggled to compose herself before climbing down and making her way back.

Varg had reluctantly agreed that she could close their bond during her interrogation sessions with Lord Anshar. It was never a pleasant experience, and there was nothing her mate could do to help her except be there to comfort her when she was through.

Opening their bond was like being allowed to breathe again after the suffocating time spent within the isolated tree, and she could sense that Varg was coming.

"Did you get him to speak this time?" Varg asked as he approached, seemingly from nowhere, and she could tell that he had grown impatient and came to collect her. Even though Lord Anshar was trapped, Varg still didn't trust the dragon and had insisted that the mirror be kept as far away from the den as possible.

She nodded and leaned against his muscular chest for comfort, and he wrapped his arms around her, his warmth a soothing balm on her jangled nerves.

"He seemed better today."

Varg regarded her with a raised eyebrow, her emotional distress suggesting otherwise.

"I mean, he talked. He really talked to me. He showed himself, too. His wound has healed, and he looks okay…just…sad."

"What's wrong?" he asked, sensing a dark cloud over her thoughts.

"He said he's not going to help us. He swore to the gods that he would never sacrifice again."

"Then we don't need him. The next time a priestess comes, send him back with them and be rid of him. He's only tormenting you."

"I can't do that, Varg. Tiamet wants me to save him. Maybe it's just the madness talking. One moment he's there, and the next, he's gone again. He says the voice that used to torment him hasn't spoken since he's been inside the mirror, but he's clearly still not well. Whether he hears it anymore or not, it's left a lasting effect, and I have to try and snap him out of it. He's our only hope."

As much as Varg wanted to argue that the dragon had made his vow, and it did not matter whether or not Anshar still heard from his imaginary friend, he couldn't. Halea wanted hope. Her Goddess had not spoken or appeared before her since the day the dragon was caught, but Halea was convinced that Tiamet's intervention was a sign that something could yet be done. He wasn't sure if he believed that or not, but he

4

forced himself to remain optimistic for her sake. As much as he disliked having that accursed object within his lands or that bastard around his mate, if believing that Anshar could change gave her hope, he would endure it.

She looked up at him with eyes imploring for him to understand, and he was defeated.

"If you really believe there's a chance, keep trying. Things have been calmer. I'm sure we'll hold out," he said while running his fingers through her dark golden hair.

Winter had only begun when they brought the mirror to the lycan territory, and now the season was almost over. A few melting and muddy piles of snow littered the ground beneath the trees, but spring was not far away. During the long winter, Varg and Halea had taken out a group of their best warriors every time a demon threatened their lands and swiftly eliminated them. They had only seen two tears in all that time, and thankfully, there were no injuries from dark weapons. The Chaos Dimension's activity seemed to be diminished, but Halea suspected it was only the calm before the storm, and Varg hoped that she was wrong.

Mama Dragon had left their territory with the coming of winter, taking her therian companion with her. She would not return until later in the spring, but Halea was more than capable of protecting the lycan lands in her stead.

"I guess you're done working on the house for today. How is it coming along?" she asked, hoping to change the subject to something more pleasant.

Varg's smile revealed his gleaming white fangs as he detected her eager curiosity. He hadn't allowed her to see any of his construction efforts. He wanted the completed treehouse to be a surprise, but his secrecy also made her nervous. She was always accusing him of going overboard, and she wouldn't have been wrong, but he was confident the finished home would win her favor. Keeping the rest of the pack quiet was the real challenge. Against his orders, many had peeked, and he knew they were gossiping. His only concern was that someone would spoil the surprise for Halea, but thankfully, most knew better than to risk his anger by ruining his plans.

"Wouldn't you like to know?" he teased with a deep laugh before leading her back towards the den.

"Yes, damn it, I would! You're up to something terrible. I just know it."

"Of course, I am, but you'll love it anyway. You'll just have to be patient. Spring is nearly here, and better weather means I can make faster progress."

"I'm sorry if I'm impatient, but you've got me so wound up, plus after a long winter of living almost entirely in caves and caverns, I'm dying to see what the sky looks like again," she grumbled.

"It looks like that," he said while pointing up, but she slapped his arm.

"You know what I mean, you mangy wolf," she laughed as Varg wrapped one arm lovingly around her shoulders.

When winter set in with all its freezing winds and harsh snow, the lycans abandoned their outdoor fire pits and retreated into the mountains' vast caverns. The caverns also had fire pits and were cozy in their own way and beautiful with their veins of gold and shimmering stalactites but being enclosed all the time got tiring after a while. Halea longed for soft spring grass and fresh green leaves, wildflowers,

5

and skies as blue as Varg's eyes. Batsuba's medical training was far more boring during the winter as well. Without fresh herbs to study and gather, Halea was left with lectures, musty tomes, anatomy lessons, and house calls. The house calls were not so bad. Alongside Batsuba, she had finally managed to help deliver three new cubs, and she had cried each time. Giving birth was difficult, and the male mates were unbearable, but to see a new life come into the world filled her with unparalleled joy. She understood why Batsuba never grew tired of it, and her heart ached with unspoken longing.

"I suppose I'd better hurry," he continued. "I'd like to get our home finished before the Spring Moon Festival. There's going to be a lot of work to do between now and then."

For lycans, the first full moon after the spring equinox symbolized the birth of a new year. The entire week before the full moon was one long celebration, and everyone would gather outside and make huge bonfires. Ale and wine would flow, and there would be song and dance and storytellers recounting histories and epic tales of days long past. Prayers would be offered to the wolf gods, asking them to bless the hunts for the new year, and there were also sports and games. After being cooped up inside after a long winter, many lycans longed to stretch their legs and exert themselves. Among the activities, there would be wrestling matches, refereed fights, races, and archery competitions, and for the entire duration of the celebration week, lycans would compete in hunting challenges to see which hunters could bring in the most fresh meat for the festival feasts.

Varg had overseen the preparations for the festival every year since his father died, but all the lycans pitched in to help. Halea knew this and had been waiting for a good time to discuss the matter with him.

"Varg, let me manage the festival this year. Please."

He was a little surprised by her request. Typically, it was the wolfmother's duty to orchestrate social functions, but he had never wanted to force the responsibility onto his human mate. He had hoped that she would come around to performing some of the roles expected of her position, but if not, he wouldn't ask it of her. Halea had struggled to be accepted by his people and earning her place in the pack hadn't come easy. When he first mated her, he had tried to shelter her from the brutal ways of wolves, but his overprotective nature had caused her more harm than good. In the end, Halea was forced to fight and exercise the might of her will against those who opposed her, and at long last, she seemed to command the respect she truly deserved. He was incredibly proud of how far she had come and how much she had accomplished. Even her healer training with Batsuba served to make her a valuable and revered wolfmother. He wouldn't have dared to ask for more, but now she was freely offering to share the burden of alpha leadership, and his heart swelled so much it almost choked him.

"Are you sure? It's a lot of work. You don't have to force yourself to do anything if you're not ready yet."

"I can do this!" she stated with confidence that immediately halted him and made him catch her in his arms. "I've been thinking about it a lot lately. You work so hard for everyone here, and I should support you more. I said before, I want to be a real wolfmother. You deserve a mate who's also a partner."

"Halea, you're already more than I deserve," he argued as he held her close and lovingly looked down on her shining face. The soft light through the bare trees revealed the last charming remnants of her childhood freckles.

She smiled warmly at him. His words couldn't mask the elation she sensed from him through their bond. The pride. The love.

"What, you think I can't manage a party?" she teased.

"You can do anything," he breathed while leaning his face towards hers, drawing their lips close together. Their hands found each other, fingers twining.

"Well, then the matter is settled. I'm in charge. You can just worry about the hunts, and I'll take care of everything else. In fact, I've already recruited several volunteers while you were preoccupied with building our house. We're going to have the best Spring Moon Festival ever!"

"You've been busy behind my back," he said in an amused tone as he nuzzled her nose, and he heard her heart flutter against her ribs.

"I have a point to prove," she confessed with a smile as his lips slowly trailed down her face with the faintest of touches that ignited sparks beneath her skin.

"You don't have to prove yourself to me. The gods couldn't have granted me a better mate. You're everything I've ever wanted and everything I could ever need. I love you, Halea," he huskily spoke before softly teasing her lips with his and savoring how she slowly opened her mouth in response. Her warm tongue met his as passion flowed between them through their bond, and his chest vibrated as a low growl of satisfaction passed through him and ignited her deepest desires. The scent of her arousal permeated the air, and he grew hard with need as the edges of his vibrant blue eyes turned red.

The howl of a wolf cried out from the den, and Varg was forced to break their kiss with a growl of frustration.

"Did they find another demon?" she asked.

"No. It's a runner – from the southern pack. I guess we better go," he grumbled while taking her by the hand, and together they made their way back towards the den.

When they reached the den, many had gathered to greet Ralph, the southern wolf. He had already been escorted to Varg's fire pit and was being offered food and drink after his long run. When Varg and Halea approached, he stood up and bowed his head respectfully, waiting to be acknowledged.

"Halea, this is Ralph," Varg introduced. Ralph had been at the last gathering but hadn't seen Halea since she mated Varg. "Welcome, brother. What brings you this far north?" Varg asked before sitting in his usual seat at the pit and encouraging Halea to join him at his side.

Ralph looked a little uncomfortable at the human wolfmother's presence, but he sat back down across from his king, and another lycan approached and offered them all something to drink. Halea politely refused, but after Ralph's cup was refilled and Varg was given a tankard of ale, the southern wolf got right to the point of his visit.

"Thank you for seeing me, Alpha Varg." There was a slight moment of pause before he added, "And, Wolfmother Halea. Thank you both for your hospitality. It's been a long run, but the gods were merciful and granted me good weather for my journey. I come bearing a message."

"I've been expecting this. So, when shall I expect my cousin?"

"Alpha Raoul wishes to formally request a wolf gathering so that he may present himself before you and the council. The Spring Moon Festival is next month, and he believes this would be the most ideal opportunity to bring all the packs together."

Varg sensed Halea growing anxious beside him, and he swore he heard her heart skip a beat.

"I'm sorry if this spoils your plans," Varg said to Halea. "I know four packs together all at once is far more than you bargained for, and you don't have to manage it if it's too much."

"No," she quickly interjected. "No, I said I want to do this, and nothing is stopping me. You're right. A whole gathering is a lot, but I can do it. It might be more difficult, a lot more difficult, but I'll see it through. My volunteers will help me, and Batsuba will be with me, and besides, you need to finish our house. Don't pretend like you wouldn't just love showing it off to all the other packs, and you won't have time to finish it if you have to manage a gathering and a festival. Please, Varg, let me handle it. I'll be okay."

"If you're sure?"

"Very," she said with a firm nod.

Ralph watched his supreme alpha's interaction in amusement. He didn't know much about humans and had barely caught a glimpse of Halea at the last wolf gathering, but she was undoubtedly an alpha bitch. Suddenly Varg's choice seemed to make a little more sense.

"Then shall I return with a message that the gathering is to be held here for the Spring Moon Festival?" asked Ralph.

"Yes. I'll send runners to spread the news to the northern and eastern packs before they get too far invested into their own festival preparations," confirmed Varg before turning to address his mate. "Halea, there will be more runners over the next few weeks bringing messages from the other packs who will want to coordinate with you for the festival."

"I'll be ready," she replied.

He smiled brilliantly at her and squeezed her hand in appreciation. Any remaining worries she harbored dissipated at his open display of confidence in her abilities.

~~~~✹~~~~

"Are you sure it's safe to come out of hiding?" Priestess Pauline asked while stoking her campfire.

"I don't think Lord Anshar is going anywhere. Tiamet helped Halea seal him within the mirror, and I'm not sure how he'll get back out again. Priestesses have always closed dimensions. I never knew they could open them," Samesa replied as she finished the last of her tea and was grateful for its comforting warmth. Rufus had

8

found her during the winter and delivered a message from Mama Dragon about Lord Anshar's miraculous capture. She had never heard of the Goddess personally intervening before, and deep down, it made her afraid. They were not in a good situation if the gods were getting involved. She had spent most of the winter searching for her fellow priestesses and spreading the news. Mama Dragon was also out in the wilds doing the same thing, and Rufus would often visit with information about the location of the hidden priestesses. They no longer had a base of operation or a leader, and the time might come when they would all be needed.

"If the rangers have taken the castle as you say, there's no point in returning to Antherose. I haven't seen as many demons or tears, but it's probably better if we stay out here to make sure things don't get so out-of-hand again. I'm relieved though, I'm nearly out of that stuff that hides the way I smell, and not much has had time to grow yet."

"I think you can give that stuff a break for a while," Samesa offered with one of her glowing smiles. "I'll pass on your location to Rufus the next time Mama Dragon sends him my way, and if we need you, we'll know where to find you. Well, I guess I better get going. Chaos waits for no one," she said while getting up with a stretch.

"Wait, Samesa!"

"Hm?"

"Have your traps been working? I mean, I know there aren't many demons at the moment, but I swear they haven't been falling for traps the way they used to. I see footprints, but it looks like they know where the traps are and are going around them. You don't think they've learned to read the ancient language, do you?"

Discomfort clouded Samesa's face. She had also noticed this strange behavior. Ever since the last convergence, when Lord Anshar disappeared, the demons had been different. Their forms were less primitive, and they exhibited a heightened intelligence. Where once their senses were dulled by the sunlight, now, they seemed as lethal in the day as they had once only been at night.

"I don't know, Pauline. Things are a little calmer but no less serious. A storm is coming. All we can do is be on our guard. Maybe after spring gets here and things start growing again, you should keep brewing that scent masking potion, just in case. If they really are getting smarter, it wouldn't hurt to stay one step ahead."

"You're right," Pauline conceded with a nod.

The two priestesses embraced in solidarity before Samesa turned and continued on her way through the forest. She had to cover many more miles before reaching the nearest village, and she dreaded the idea of having to spend another night out in the cold. Her thoughts were troubled as she wandered beneath the trees. The future was uncertain. High Priestess Maven had been kept under lock-and-key in the castle dungeon by Favion and Master Uro all winter, and now the rangers were there. They had no leader to guide them. For the first time since she was a child, she felt lost, alone, and afraid.

"Help," a small voice called in the distance.

Samesa snapped out of her brooding thoughts at the shocking sound.

"Please, help me. I'm lost, and it's cold. Please, someone, help me."

"*A child? Out here in the middle of nowhere?*" Samesa thought in horror before rushing through the trees.

There, huddled beneath the trees in a dirty cloak, was a young boy, maybe about seven or eight years of age.

"Hey, kid, what are you doing way out here? Where are your parents?" Samesa asked as she approached.

"I'm lost. Please help me. Please," the boy begged as he looked up at her with tear-filled eyes.

Samesa's heart flooded with pity as she stepped closer. When she reached down to help him up, the moment his tiny hand touched her, something snapped within her.

Her grandmother bleeding from her throat. Her younger brother being torn to pieces as a demon shredded the flesh from his body and devoured it. Incredible pain as a dark blade sliced into her. Screams of terror as flames rose up to the night sky as her village burned to the ground. Sand dunes that stretched on endlessly. The mirage of her family beckoning to her, but always just out of reach. A kind woman with a white face. Seeing endless trees for the first time. Sparring with her mentor. Standing over a grave.

The pain of her memories being violated forced her to scream out in rebellion before the invading presence could reach any further into her mind, and before she knew it, she was lashing out with the white light of her purification.

"Stop!" Samesa shouted as the powers of Tiamet flowed through her, and suddenly she was standing in the forest again and smoldering before her lay a hideous writhing mass of spindly legs attached to a hairy bulbous body. The child's warped humanoid face was on the creature's head, and snapping mandibles stretched out from its mouth. A sharp barb twitched as the beast struggled to move. Without a second thought, Samesa called upon her powers again and purified the hideous creature, which burst into white flame.

A strange green smoke rose from the charred remains, and Samesa watched in horror as it moved through the trees like it knew where it was going, and then it was gone.

CHAPTER 3 – HOME SWEET HOME

"If you cauterize here, and here, you can stem the bleeding," explained Batsuba as Halea prodded through the dead beaver's insides. A few weeks had passed since the wolf gathering was announced, and Halea was scrambling to keep up with her apprenticeship while organizing the Spring Moon Festival. The last of the snow was gone, and small green sprouts were beginning to shoot up from the soil.

"What about a coagulant?"

"It depends on the severity of the case," but before the elder could go on, Halea's eyes glazed over, and her hand stilled in its motion. "Oh, gods, what does he want now?"

"He's excited," Halea said with a smile as Varg's elation and anticipation came through their bond as powerful as a shout. He had been in a good mood all day, and now she could tell that he was coming to get her.

"What, in the middle of the day? Can't you two ever give it a rest?"

Halea's face burned beet red at the old healer's implication.

"Not that kind of excited!" she quickly defended. "I have a feeling he finished it."

Heavy steps thudded up the stairs as Varg entered Batsuba's tree-dwelling, and Halea jumped up without a word as together they went back out and through the den.

"Are you ready?" he asked.

"I thought I was," she said while taking a deep inhalation to calm herself.

The location Varg had selected for their new tree-dwelling was on the furthest southwestern edge of the den. They would still be a part of the community, but with a little more privacy, which Halea had particularly longed for ever since being mated. Lycans had such powerful senses they could see, hear, and smell over vast distances, and while Halea had grown a little more comfortable with her new people, she still didn't relish the idea of everyone in the den knowing all the intimate details of her sex-life with Varg.

As they drew near, Varg stopped, reached into his fur pelt, and pulled out a soft strip of leather.

"Close your eyes," he said.

"Oh, come on! I never peek."

Which was true. Ever since they were mated, Varg had dragged her to all corners of his territory for random surprises, and she had always humored him.

"I'm not taking any chances," he said with a laugh before fixing the blindfold over her eyes. She held out her hands for him to guide her and was surprised when he didn't grab on.

"Where are you?"

"This is very amusing," he quietly whispered into her ear. "I rather like having you at my mercy," he added while stalking around her.

She shivered when she felt his breath behind her ear. "Don't tease me now, you mangy wolf! Haven't you made me wait long enough?"

"My, how eager you are, my puny human," he said from somewhere in front of her, and she frowned in frustration.

He laughed roguishly before scooping her up into his arms, causing her to cry out when the ground disappeared from beneath her feet.

Halea felt a rush of air as they dashed through the forest, and before long, they reached their destination, where Varg gently set her down. Being carried at high-speed while blindfolded disoriented her, and she clung to Varg as a wave of dizziness passed.

Varg placed his hand on her lower back to steady her until he was sure she was settled before finally reaching up and untying her blindfold. Halea's eyes grew as round as saucers as she took in the enormity of the tree-dwelling that towered before her and sucked in one long gasp.

Since Halea had last seen those trees, they had grown their new spring leaves, and the soft green moss that coated their trunks were now dotted with tiny white flowers. Resting comfortably within their mighty boughs was a segmented tree-dwelling with two structures. The largest structure was situated between the three thickest trees and had a railed-off porch circling the entire building, and the smaller structure was connected by a rope bridge and occupied the fourth tree off to the side. Rather than a spiraling stair, as was more common among lycan tree homes, these stairs zigged and zagged between two of the closer trees and were adorned with an ornately carved handrail. The roofs gently tapered on two sides, leaving only the chimney pipes that stretched up far enough to avoid catching the leaves on fire. The larger structure had wide swinging doors and heavily shuttered windows on all sides, and the smaller structure had only one door and two windows.

There was no wiping the grin of satisfaction from Varg's face as his mate stood there with her mouth agape.

"Varg," she finally managed to croak out.

"So, what do you think?"

"I think you went overboard."

He nearly doubled over with laughter. He had expected that much from her, but he sensed no anger, only awe, and giddy excitement despite her comment.

"Time to bring my mate home," he said before scooping her up once again and carrying her up the stairs and into the larger segment of their home. He set her down just over the threshold, and Halea stood stock-still in amazement at the beautiful interior. Everything was bright and airy as warm light filtered through the green leaves from outside, and the entire room smelled of fresh pine and cedar. The room was big enough to entertain at least twenty people, and in the center, the floor was recessed to form a circle lined with benches and covered in soft furs and cushions, and in the middle sat a wood-burning stove. Most lycan tree-dwellings had one to three small rooms, but this one room was large enough to fit an average-sized tree home within it. Outside of the pit, thick and ornately carved structural beams provided support for the high ceiling. Halea admired the carvings that portrayed vines and birds and budding roses. She had never even realized that Varg was such an artistic woodcarver. There were also two doors and an entryway leading to another room.

Varg encouraged Halea with a nod, and she stepped forward and gently pushed open one of the doors to find a modest room containing a single-sized bed, a washbasin, and a window with a lovely view of the mountains. Halea looked through the entryway into the other room and found that it was a kitchen. Not quite a human kitchen. Varg had no idea what one of those would look like. It was one of the more rudimentary cooking stations that some lycans would use for the few meals they did prepare away from the communal fire pits. It was stocked with cooking utensils, dishes, many of her favorite food items and seasoning herbs, and a small stove.

"Don't cook too much food in here; you'll break Ulrica's heart. She's gotten rather fond of preparing most of your meals, but I figured you might enjoy using this on occasion."

"Oh, I will. I love it!" Halea cried as she brushed her hand over a smooth countertop. "Where did you get these stoves? I don't remember you trading for them last fall."

"We had a few extras lying around," he quickly explained, without specifying the devastation of the convergence that had once separated them. Many homes were left without owners, so the items had been repurposed. He did not want to spoil their happy moment by bringing up the worst day of her life.

Halea accepted his explanation without further question before turning to the final door, which opened to the outside and led to a rope bridge connecting the smaller structure. The detached segment was a single spacious bedroom. Because they had their own private hot spring close by, they didn't need the addition of a tub, and there was also a latrine not far outside.

A cozy-looking fireplace was built into the wall, and the two windows were open, letting in the fresh sea breeze from the west. Halea noticed that most of the room's furnishings were brought in from their cave. The same bed, the same chest of drawers, even her and Varg's personal belongings were present. His hunting bow and the spear from her days as a priestess were propped in a corner.

"How did you have time to get all our stuff here since this morning?" she asked.

"Aatu and Faolan moved it in for us while I finished the last few touches. A lot of the decorative carved pieces I worked on this winter. I had some free time between hunts and while you were busy learning medicine from Batsuba. I cobbled together quite a few things around here in a cavern workshop. It made it quicker to get the main structure together once the weather cleared with a lot of the smaller pieces premade and just needing to be installed."

Halea quickly brushed her hand across her eyes and discovered that she was crying.

"Varg, you did all this for me?" Halea asked while choking on her words.

Varg wrapped his arms around her, and she laid her head on his chest. He knew she was only crying because she was happy.

"I'd do anything for you. I want you to be happy, Halea. You deserve it. I know how much you've given up to be here with me and how much you've done since becoming a part of the pack. You deserve a million treehouses. And if there's anything you want to change or add, just say the word."

"Oh, Varg, the gods gave me everything the day I met you. It's so beautiful, and everything's perfect," she said before sobbing again, and he rubbed her back to soothe her.

"You're not angry that it's too big?"

"It is big, but I see what you mean," she managed to say after catching her breath. "I didn't know you could put a fire pit in a tree-dwelling, but I guess as alphas that is good to have. I'm sure we'll have guests eventually. Is that what the spare bedroom is for?"

They had already agreed that when Halea's grandfather came to stay later that spring, he would be given his own private cave within the den. Due to his advanced age and increasing infirmity, a tree-dwelling's stairs would not be agreeable with him. Varg had also not hidden his disinterest in cohabitating with the cranky old human, and Halea could not disagree. The whole reason they had chosen a home located on the outskirts of the den was to have a little more privacy. Her grandfather was used to living alone, but he would still be close enough to not be lonely.

"Guests stay in the caves. That room is for our child."

He had to resist the urge to laugh when Halea looked at him in startled confusion.

"Someday," he added. "I know you're not ready yet, but I figured it wouldn't hurt to be prepared. I've designed this place so I can easily add as many extra rooms as we want."

Fresh tears appeared in her eyes, and he sensed anguish ripping through her. The rune of contraception was still painted upon her wrist.

"What if we never get to use that room?"

He softly cradled her face in his hands and stared deeply into her eyes. "Then as long as I have you, I have enough. I want whatever will make you happiest. If you want children, I'll give you as many as you please. If you're afraid of the future's uncertainty, then the two of us will have each other. Always. All I need to be happy is you."

He was just as concerned about the future as she was, even more so because the threat of the swordmaster's prophecy was still hanging over his head. He did not entirely believe the dragon's vow that he would no longer sacrifice those blessed by the Goddess, and he was fully prepared to destroy the beast if he ever escaped the dimension of the mirror. Halea wished to save Anshar, and that worried him. She was the last chosen sacrifice of Tiamet, and Varg was not about to let anyone take her away from him. She had sworn that she would never offer herself as a sacrifice again, but that didn't mean that if the dragon returned to his senses and resumed his duties, that he would not attempt to complete the ritual and kill Halea. Varg's greatest fear was for Halea to successfully bring the dragon out of his Chaos-induced madness.

Though he never wished to oppose her, he would take any stand necessary when it came to keeping her alive.

Halea was aware that her success came at the risk of both her and Varg's lives. The only known way to stop a convergence was by sacrificing Tiamet's last chosen priestess, and if she died, Varg would die. She had sworn a vow that she would never willingly offer herself as a sacrifice again, and she could not break it, not when it would cost Varg his life too. The possibility was real, and it terrified her, but somewhere deep inside, she couldn't help but believe that there was another way. She wasn't sure how, but something had to change. Lord Anshar had tried to offer himself instead and failed, and now the Chaos Dimension was behaving erratically. Lord Anshar once believed that there was something sentient behind the Chaos Dimension, and he had mentioned that a mysterious voice spoke to him while he was trapped in that dark void, forcing him to act against his will and lying to gain control over him. There was something behind all this. These dimensional tears were not just some strange anomalies of the universe. The real answer was buried somewhere within Lord Anshar's shattered mind. He must have experienced something while he was within the Chaos that held the key to what was really going on. She didn't want to bring Lord Anshar back just to force him to serve again; that wasn't what he wanted or what she wanted. She wanted to bring him back because she knew he was their one hope for the truth, and that small gleam of hope was what kept her going. She would not give up.

Halea returned Varg's embrace as relief and love drowned out her pain.

"I love you so much, Varg. I know you worry about the future too. I know you try to hide it, but it's okay. I'm not giving up. There's got to be an answer to all our problems that doesn't involve either one of us having to die, and once I find it, we can be free to share our lives together however we want. Maybe when that day comes, we can finally make use of that little extra room," she said with a bittersweet smile.

Though Varg hated hiding things from Halea, he was grateful that the severity of their situation was enough to mask his deepest fear – the prophecy. It was not that he did not worry about the threat of the Chaos Dimension, but convergence or not, losing Halea would be the end of the world for him.

"There's one more thing I want to show you," he said while guiding her to their bed.

"I've seen that surprise before," she replied with a raised eyebrow and an impish smile.

He chuckled as they lay together on their bed. "That surprise comes later. I'm referring to this." He pulled a cord hanging over their bed that connected to a series of pulleys attached to the sloped ceiling, and a panel in the roof opened to reveal the clear blue sky above.

"You said you wanted to see the sky again. Well, there it is," he pointed up in amusement as Halea clasped her hands over her elated face.

"I can't believe you," she said while breaking into laughter.

"What? You don't like it?"

"I love it. I love everything here, especially you." She rolled over and wrapped her arms around his neck. He returned her embrace and deeply breathed her comforting scent. The bond they shared thrummed with happiness as they each committed this moment to their most treasured of memories.

"I remember when we were kids, and you once told me that you'd live in a tree if you could. I never forgot it. Even then, your place was in the forest with me." He stroked his hand along the curve of her neck, admiring the mark that bound their souls together.

"I've never been happier anywhere else. The cold echoing marble halls of the castle in Antherose and the overly-manicured gardens – no. I never belonged there. I wanted to be where the trees grew tall, and the grass was untamed, where little creatures made their nests in trees and burrowed beneath the earth, and where streams flowed through patches of ferns and wildflowers. I wanted to live in the same world as you."

Varg could not bear the overwhelming rush of joy that flooded his heart at her sweet words, and he quickly sealed her lips with his as longing echoed across their bond. Her soft flesh grew warm beneath his fingertips, and the tantalizing smell of her arousal fragranced the room. Her scent always called to him, even when she didn't realize it. Sometimes he would catch her looking at him with eyes dilated in appreciation, and the flutter of her heart was like music to his ears. When he was first becoming a young man, he had dreamed that he could affect her as strongly as she affected him. He craved her every time he looked at her. Her eyes shifted from fiercely determined to vulnerable and gentle in a way that made the wolf within him rage to protect her from the world's cruelty. She trusted him with her heart and soul, and he treasured those gifts above all else. When Halea submitted to him, it pleased him, not just because he had the power to possess her but because she trusted him. She could surrender herself completely into his hands, and for that, he would fulfill her every desire.

"Will you trust me?" he asked before pulling out the blindfold once more, and without hesitation, she nodded her head and allowed him to place the cover over her eyes.

He climbed on top of her and straddled her hips while slowly gliding his hands over the front of her robe until he reached the tie at her waist.

He fumbled with the knot only for a second before a rush of cool air caressed her newly exposed skin, and her heart hammered in anticipation. Beneath her ribs remained a faint stripe of scars from her battle with Rafe, but they did nothing to lessen Varg's desire. His hands slowly glided back up her stomach, where he held the small of her waist between his two hands, and his thumbs gently massaged around her navel. A tingle shot up her spine as the edges of his long sharp claws slowly scratched against her skin. There was no pain, just the pleasant sensation of being utterly comfortable and relaxed while also burning with desire from deep within her core.

She gasped as he continued to run the sides of his claws in gentle sweeps and circles along her stomach and up to her ribs. He was not breaking the skin because he wasn't using the tips, though it was slightly reddened from the gentle scratches. He tenderly cupped the underside of her plump round breasts before allowing his claws to rake around their full circumference.

Her lips parted, followed by a sharp intake of breath, and gooseflesh rose along her neck as he moved his thumbs over her nipples and slowly scratched across the rosy-pink flesh, causing them to grow taut and firm. She squirmed beneath him and wound her fists into the fur bedding. The scent of her arousal, the beat of her heart, her breaths coming short and fast, and the flush in her face caused him to strain with need as he sat above her, savoring the feel of her beneath his hands.

He leaned over her, bringing his nose beside her face and teased the lobe of one of her adorable rounded human ears with his lips. "Varg," she moaned, as her hands moved to reach up for him, but he quickly pinned them back beside her head.

"Shh, just submit," he purred into her ear, and he sensed her growing anxious with need.

He moved away just long enough to undress, and then she felt him tugging her robe down past her shoulders. She pulled her arms free of the sleeves as he helped her out of her boots and the rest of her undergarments until she was entirely at his mercy.

His chiseled, strong body lay over hers as his claws continued to roam along her curves and down, where they scraped along her thighs before parting them and slipping his fingers along her soft, wet fold and gently exploring.

Halea was panting in his ear as he slowly tortured her. When he removed his hand to continue scraping his claws further down her leg, she whimpered. A jolt of electricity shot up her back as he dragged a single claw down the back of her calf, and she cried out from the sensation that was so powerful her leg shook. He grinned wickedly as he held her leg to prevent her from accidentally kicking him before leaning in and nibbling along the soft flesh of her thighs and torturously upwards until he delved into her most sacred of spaces. She squirmed and arched her back as wave after wave of hot pleasure pulsed within her while his hands roughly clasped her thighs and buttocks, where again his claws softly scraped along her heated flesh, causing shivers to course through her until she was nearly at the edge.

"Oh, Varg. Varg, please," she begged, but he was already beyond the edge of his limits. The red was seeping into his eyes as the beast within hungered, and at the sound of her plea for release, he moved back up her body and entered her while wrapping her thighs around him and growling in relief to be joined.

He didn't protest when her hands reached up and wound within his hair and then down along his muscular shoulders as he moved against her at a languid pace that he knew would prolong her torment and make her beg.

"Quit holding back, you mangy wolf!" she practically growled, and he chuckled in amusement at her impatience.

"Tell me what I really want to hear," he said while slowly peppering kisses along her throat before scraping his fangs along her mating mark.

"I submit," she professed in a breathy voice and tilted her head back, surrendering herself to her alpha. She could sense how much her words pleased him through their bond, and the wild, untamed beast roared with desire.

17

He wasted no more time before pummeling inside of her and piercing the surface of her flesh with his elongated fangs as he latched onto her mating mark. When they were first mated, he was afraid she could not handle his alpha nature, the untamed wolf that knew only blood and lust, but she never shied away from what he was. She never knew fear or pain or revulsion, only love and desire and need as he claimed her like the beast he was. She wanted him to be free within her arms, to offer him everything he needed, and in that, she never failed. It was he who was at her mercy and a slave to her desire. Even the rage within him crumbled at her whim as she was the only one with the power to truly tame him, and for her, he would surrender body and soul.

They came together with gasping breaths and shuddering spasms as they poured their love and desire into each other through their bond.

"Varg, I love you so much," she confessed while snuggling close beside him as they lay in bed, staring up at the blue sky above.

"I love you too, always," he said before placing a soft kiss on her waiting lips.

CHAPTER 4 – UNANSWERED QUESTIONS

She wept bitterly, and it broke Uro's heart. He could only imagine the depth of such despair if anyone had ever delivered the same devastating news to his granddaughter when she was a young, blessed hopeful.

"But I want to serve," Jennifer cried while wringing her hands in her tunic sleeves. Her messy, sandy-colored hair was stuck to her tear-stained face, and her large brown eyes shimmered in desolation.

"I'm sorry, but Lord Anshar is not with us anymore. He was the only one with the power to bestow the Goddess's gift of oath, and without that, you can't serve as a priestess."

"But she's trained for years," argued Samuel, her mentor cleric. Samuel was in his mid-thirties, with dull green eyes and a long, crooked nose. "Even without immortality and rapid healing, she would be a valuable servant for Tiamet. Just because Lord Anshar is no longer on our side doesn't mean Chaos isn't still a threat. Let her perform the duties of a priestess for what years she can."

"Even a mortal life is worth something. Make me a cleric if I can't be a priestess," the young acolyte begged.

"Clerics were always ordained by Lord Anshar or the High Priestess, but High Priestess Maven has been imprisoned since the beginning of winter. Normally, it would be up to her to make such a judgment call. I may be a senior cleric, but I am still just a cleric. I don't want to overstep my authority."

"Are there no senior priestesses who can give their blessing?" Samuel asked.

"Perhaps I can write to Senior Priestess Gwen in the capital on your behalf. She will be the rightful successor to High Priestess Maven, but she's been so preoccupied with the king's council she hasn't had much time to concern herself with our problems here in Antherose," offered Uro.

"No one is here?" asked Jennifer.

"What's left of our priestesses are out sealing tears in the wilds. Rangers have taken the castle. There's just so few of us now...so few," Uro lamented before his face shifted into a hardened resolve. "Perhaps, in our current predicament, none of that matters. You're here. You're blessed. You don't need a uniform or a title to fight for our world or my permission. I know all about the call, and if you really want to fight, then fight. Who's going to stop you?"

A hopeful gleam dried Jennifer's eyes as she nodded her head. Just because she didn't have an official title didn't mean she couldn't serve Tiamet's will, and though she was disappointed to not be made a priestess as she had always dreamed, nothing could keep her from answering the call of the Goddess. She would fight.

~~~☼~~~

Uro leaned heavily on his rune-carved staff as he marched towards the castle with a sinking feeling of dread. He had been avoiding the home of Lord Anshar since the rangers arrived. The king's servants had a contentious relationship with the devotees of Tiamet, even at the best of times, and he still resented them for turning his son from his calling. He had hoped to avoid them until Halea came to claim him, but now he had no choice. He had to meet with Edmond and Codeon.

He entered the castle's halls and avoided making eye contact with the rangers that wandered the premises. They were used to seeing the red-robed clerics coming and going and paid them little mind. Many clerics had returned to Antherose for lack of anywhere else to turn once the news spread that it was safe to come out of hiding. Many were directionless, panicked, and desperate due to the utter lack of leadership within their faith. They looked to senior clerics and any priestesses who passed through with hopeful eyes, but no one had any answers. No one knew what the future would bring, and everyone was frightened.

The news of Lord Anshar's miraculous capture by Halea was both a blessing and a grave concern. The Goddess had personally intervened, an occurrence that had not happened in ages. Times were desperate if Tiamet had to return to the mortal realm, and many wondered why she had chosen to reveal herself to Halea, who was known to have broken her oath and was no longer officially a priestess.

It was no mystery to Uro. Lord Anshar had always openly favored his granddaughter. It was finally apparent that his interest in Halea went beyond the bond of pupil and mentor that they once shared. The Goddess had come to Halea because she was the only person who had ever been permitted to come close to the stoic head of their faith. That was why they had agreed that it should be Halea who carried the mirror into the wolf shifter's territory where she could try to reason with their wayward lord. Tiamet had given her the power to open the dimension within the mirror, and so the Goddess wished for Halea to save her grandson. If anyone could reach him, it was Halea.

"Master Uro, thank you for coming," exclaimed Codeon, who looked up at the elder's approach.

"Is she here?" he asked, skipping pleasantries and getting right to the point.

"Yes, I'm sorry. I know you didn't want her coming here, but the asylum was overflowing after so many unchecked tears and demon attacks. Edmond tried to secure her place at Weldison, but they insisted that she be transferred."

"Where is Edmond?"

"In the infirmary with Dean. If she had to be brought here, he insisted that Dean be transferred as well."

"I'm in his debt. I didn't want to leave her all alone in that place," Uro said before walking towards the infirmary with Codeon in tow.

20

When Uro entered the infirmary, he found it greatly rearranged. More hospital beds were rolled out, and chairs were lined up along the stained-glass windows where patients who suffered from Chaos Madness sat in a dazed stupor.

And there she was, slouching beside Edmond, who read from the sacred text to both her and Dean as they stared blankly into nothingness.

"Theia?" Uro called, praying for a response, but the catatonic woman only drooled as her eyes remained unblinking.

"She hasn't spoken in a very long time," explained Edmond as he closed the sacred text and rose to greet the senior cleric with a comforting pat on the shoulder.

"Thank you, Edmond. I know you already had your hands full with Dean."

"Does Halea…"

"No! No, I don't want her to see this. There's nothing that can be done. Just look at her. She must have been like this since the convergence that destroyed Ruinac."

"Why did it take her so long to be put in an asylum? Where has she been all this time?" pondered Edmond, who only knew that she was found abandoned on the steps of the Weldison asylum.

"I don't know. It really makes no sense. How has she survived all these years? Someone must have taken care of her, but how she escaped the demon hordes that swarmed the ruined city, I'll never know. It doesn't seem possible. I know of no other survivors from the disaster."

It was a mystery that kept Uro awake at night, but he had to accept that there would never be an answer. Only Theia herself could unravel such a mystery, but no one ever recovered from Chaos Madness. No one.

All Uro could do was keep Theia's survival a secret. Halea would be devastated if she knew that her mother had survived to only live every day trapped in a waking hell from which there was no hope and no relief. It would have been more merciful for Theia if she had died.

"I'll ensure she receives the best of care after you leave, Master Uro," promised Edmond.

"Thank you. Halea told me I should want for nothing when I go to stay with her and the shifters, so I'm leaving the assets of my estate to ensure that Theia will always receive the highest quality of care."

"So, you're going, then?" Codeon asked.

"Yes. Halea should be coming to claim me in a few more weeks. I've seen to my final affairs. There's nothing left for me here."

"What happens if Halea comes to the castle?" questioned Edmond with a concerned expression.

"There's nothing for her here either, and to her knowledge, certainly nothing in the infirmary. There's no reason for her to come to this place again, and I'll ensure that she doesn't. Leave that to me."

Uro left the two clerics with his thanks and gave Theia one final look of remorse before heading into the hall when he noticed Favion up ahead in a heated exchange with a senior ranger.

Though Uro didn't wish to get involved, Favion called for him, and with a sigh of resignation, he approached the two men.

"Uro, my, it's been a while," the ranger exclaimed when he recognized the senior cleric.

"Greetings, Captain Mark. Still a ranger? Shouldn't you be well into your retirement by now?" Uro quipped in irritation. He remembered the Captain well, though he had more hair the last time he saw him, and his face was less weather-beaten. He had been one of Perion's superiors during his years as a ranger.

"Funny, I was thinking the same thing about you, but I'm glad that you're here. Favion has been filling me in about the situation with the High Priestess. I've received a damning statement from one of your other priestesses that she had a hand in your shifter lord's murdering of your people. Would you like to provide your statement before we make the final arrangements to take her to Westvear for trial?"

Uro cast a questioning glance towards Favion, who quickly explained. "Kalee stopped by yesterday. She didn't stay long, but she did speak with the rangers before setting out again."

"I can corroborate everything that has been reported by Favion and Priestess Kalee. High Priestess Maven colluded with Lord Anshar to murder several of our priestesses and kidnapped myself and Favion and threw us in the dungeon."

"These are serious crimes, indeed, but I should have known. No therian is worth trusting. The old gods have long abandoned humans, and it's clear that Tiamet no longer cares for the suffering of mankind. She's no different than the other gods. It was only a matter of time before her shifter progeny turned against us. And where is the Dragon Lord? He can't escape the law forever," grumbled Captain Mark.

Tiamet was honored by many for being one of the few creator gods that had not turned their back on humanity and for her servants who battled Chaos and the threat of the convergence, but many others chose to shun the old gods. Priestesses and clerics were greatly respected by some and distrusted by others. Even Lord Anshar was not immune to scrutiny and hatred. Though he had been a member of the king's council, many other lords and bureaucrats distrusted him and muttered behind his back about the deceptive and inherently evil nature of shifters. His invaluable service as their savior from the Chaos often meant little to mortals with short memories who rarely lived long enough to even see a convergence, which for ages only happened roughly every two hundred years, and, in the past, had always been swiftly and successfully banished. The disastrous convergence that devastated the holy city of Ruinac had blackened the reputation of Lord Anshar and the Tiamet devotees. The recent surge in demon attacks and tear activity and the mysterious lack of intervention from the priestesses left a poor impression throughout the realm. Many in the capital were calling for Lord Anshar's head. Senior Priestess Gwen was forced to confess to the king and council that the Dragon Lord was no longer fit to perform his duties, and the news that he had turned murderous only reinforced a long-held opinion on the true nature of therians – that the only good shifters were dead shifters.

"Tiamet herself has seen to his imprisonment, and only she has the power to free him," defended Uro, who, despite Lord Anshar's crimes, could not help but feel some loyalty and reverence for the great man that his lord had once been.

"And where is this prison?" asked Captain Mark with a scrutinizing glare, but Uro only met his burning eyes with hardened resolve and silence. Interrogating their High Priestess had only yielded an unreliable tale of magic mirrors and shifters, and Captain Mark wanted to know if there was any truth to her ravings. "Aiding and abetting a murderer is also a crime, Uro," threatened the senior ranger.

"I don't precisely know. Lord Anshar is somewhere guarded by a pack of man-eating shifters out in the wilds. Good luck tracking him down. You can count this as my official statement. I must be on my way home," Uro replied with finality.

Captain Mark's face reddened in frustration, but he said nothing more as the elderly cleric took off in a huff.

~~~☼~~~

Batsuba watched in amusement as Halea attempted to listen to her squirming patient's lungs with the strange human object.

"Daisy, hold still for Wolfmother," Ulrica ordered, but the little girl was too preoccupied with wanting to join the other cubs playing in the common area.

"It's all right. I've heard enough. I think she's over that bronchitis now and should be good to go play," Halea decreed as she tucked away her stethoscope.

"Are you sure? I still hear her coughing sometimes," fretted the over-protective mother.

"The residual cough will clear up soon. Her lungs are fine, and she's long over her fever. Let her go play with Fillin," Batsuba interjected.

"But what if she gets the other cubs sick?" argued Ulrica.

"They were the ones who gave it to her," Batsuba replied. Spring colds and the flu were common, especially among the cubs who insisted on running around underdressed for the still chilly season, but being therians, they recovered quickly and usually did not experience as much discomfort as a human would. Daisy was in her third year, and like many cubs her age, she wanted to play with the bigger children and imitate their behavior. Her latest preoccupation was Fillin, who had recently learned to shift into his wolf form. Cubs often learned how to master the ability to change their shape at around four or five years, and once they knew their true forms, there was no containing them.

"Wumah, please?" begged the little girl with large and manipulative eyes.

"She's learning to pull rank, I see," commented Batsuba, who struggled to keep a straight face as the cub pleaded with Halea.

Halea avoided requesting final approval from Ulrica. Though Daisy was Ulrica's daughter, Halea was the wolfmother of the pack and would lose face if she asked for consent from anyone beneath her rank. She had no choice but to give the final word.

"Go play, but don't yank Fillin's fur this time," said Halea, and the young cub quickly toddled off to play with the older children.

23

Ulrica watched her daughter join the others wistfully. "She's getting so big, maybe by next year, she'll learn to change form too. Is it weird that I already miss that she's not a baby anymore?"

"They grow like weeds," agreed Batsuba as they all watched the little girl tagging along after the older cubs. The older cubs knew to not play too rough with the younger ones, and Fillin seemed to enjoy Daisy's admiration.

"Daisy will be such a cute wolf, though," added Halea, who practically squealed with delight the first time she saw Fillin in his newly discovered wolf form. She had been walking to her fire pit when the cutest little wolf cub came running up to her excitedly with its tail wagging and his tongue lolling out of his mouth. Halea had never seen such a tiny wolf before, and though lycans detested being compared to dogs, she couldn't resist thinking of the young wolf as an adorable little puppy. Varg was young when she first met him, but not that young, and his wolf features were somewhat more mature.

Fillin was particularly pleased with his wolfmother's delighted reaction to his changed form, and he would often make it a habit to come running up to her for attention, though Alpha Varg did tend to get annoyed if he did it too often.

Halea was about to get up and leave the common area when Lyall approached. Varg was out on another hunt. The other packs would soon arrive for the gathering, and extra meat was being stored in ice cellars for the impending celebration. Varg had left Lyall with a small band of hunters to defend the den due to the ever-present threat of demons.

"Wolfmother," Lyall curtly greeted with his head bowed.

"You may speak, Lyall," Halea replied. She was used to Lyall being formal and standoffish. He had never approved of Varg mating a human. He had respected her as a priestess and as Varg's mate, but even after all that she did to prove herself, he still didn't quite consider her to be a part of their pack. Lyall would never dare to voice such disapproval, but it was always there in his posture and tone and the way he went out of his way to avoid her unless absolutely necessary. Lyall had once been a close friend of Bledig, Varg's father, and Halea knew he loved Varg like a son and was only looking out for him, but she had hoped that he would set aside his prejudice with time.

Since slaying Rafe, the previous southern alpha, in single combat, none of the lycans openly opposed or challenged Halea's position as supreme wolfmother, and many who had once doubted her had grown to respect her as a valuable member of their pack. There would probably always be a few who were reserved towards her, but as long as no one challenged her authority, she could live with that. To be honest, she was far better received than she had ever hoped, and many loved her and considered her their friend. Not even among humans had she been so welcomed. Though the path to her acceptance hadn't been easy, she felt like she had a home for the first time since she was a child. Soon her grandfather would be coming to stay with them, and thanks to her own time and contribution towards the pack, adding one more human presence to the den would be a little easier. Many disliked the idea of another human coming to stay, but nobody would complain or cause trouble at the risk of their

24

wolfmother's anger. Halea wasn't worried, she knew her grandfather would care little for whether or not he fit in among the wolves, and as long as no one harmed him, he would be fine to go about his business for the remainder of his life among the lycans.

"We've picked up a scent," reported Lyall.

"I'll get my spear and meet you at the edge of the den," Halea replied. It had been a few weeks since they last detected any demons, but she suspected such peace could not last forever. Halea ran back to her new treehouse and grabbed her spear, the weapon she was given for serving Tiamet as a priestess. Though she was no longer a priestess, it was still hers, and if needed, she would not hesitate to take up arms and fight against the servants of Chaos. She raced back to the edge of the den and found Lyall waiting with Hemming, Daciana, and Faolan.

"Let's go," Halea said, and Lyall shifted into his wolf form and led them out toward the scent trail. As wolfmother, Halea would take charge of their little pack after they found their target. In the meantime, she did not mind relying on the powerful senses of the lycans to guide the way.

Through their bond, she could sense Varg's concern, and she did her best to convey that everything would be all right through her emotions. He still disliked the idea of her fighting without him. He could never entirely stop worrying about her. Still, he was better at accepting that she was more than capable and could be trusted to manage any demon that invaded their lands while he was away.

They raced north through the forest, where the tall oak trees grew thick around the edges of their hunting lands. The party came to a halt when Lyall stopped to sniff the ground, and Halea noticed fresh humanoid tracks. Most of the demons they found in the winter were of the weaker bestial variety, and Halea hadn't seen a single wraith since the last convergence. It appeared as if the eyeless humanoids had been replaced with the more dangerous black-eyed demons. These new servants of Chaos were far more intelligent and stronger, and the sunlight no longer seemed to diminish their strength.

Halea and the lycans followed the trail until both the tracks and the scent vanished.

"Did it disappear into a tear?" asked Daciana.

"Demons aren't prone to closing tears. The rift would still be here," Halea replied while tightening her grip on her spear.

A dark shadow swooped down from overhead, and Faolan let out a scream as he was carried into the trees above by a humanoid demon with scale-covered wings. Acting quickly, Halea launched her charged spear into the air, narrowly missing the beast and causing it to falter and drop its prey. Faolan hit the ground with a sickening crunch and a blood-curdling scream as his leg snapped beneath him. Daciana rushed to Faolan's side as the beast dove in for another attack, and she fended the creature off with her razor-sharp claws. Halea raced into the trees to find her fallen spear while Lyall and Hemming circled their fallen comrade, but the winged demon chose to turn its black eyes on the human woman – its true target.

Halea gasped as the demon leaped down in front of her and unfurled its massive leathery wings before unsheathing a dark blade. The creature's shape was unmistakably humanoid, but the face was distorted, and there was something familiar about its wings. Its mouth was filled with sharp silvery teeth, and its eyes were solid black and unblinking. It slashed its sword at her, but Halea jumped back and narrowly avoided getting gutted.

Reaching within her green robe, Halea produced the knife that Varg had given her for extra protection while managing to keep back from her advancing opponent. Charging her weapon, she brandished it, and the white light temporarily blinded the demon, who faltered long enough for her to grapple the beast and prevent it from swinging its sword once again. This demon was far stronger than any she had ever encountered, and she was nearly overcome when a giant wolf leaped onto the demon, tearing into the servant of Chaos with its fangs, causing it to drop its weapon, and brutally ripping off one of its wings as its black blood sprayed the forest floor. The creature let out a high-pitched shriek as it flailed, but Halea seized the opportunity to throw her charged knife straight into the black-eyed demon's heart, causing it to burst into a flame of white that consumed it until there was nothing left.

Lyall shifted back into his humanoid form and spit the foul-tasting demon blood from his mouth as Halea retrieved her knife and spear from the forest floor. "Are you all right?"

"Yes," Halea replied but stopped to observe the severed wing on the ground. Kneeling and using her spear, she turned the appendage over and examined the silvery-white scales. "Let's hurry and get Faolan back to the den," she added with one last cautious glance at the sky.

~~~~☼~~~~

"Will it be healed in time for the Spring Moon Festival?" asked Faolan with a slur as he was still quite heavily sedated.

"You might have to miss the first couple days of events, but you won't miss all of it," was Batsuba's verdict as she packed up the last of her herbs while Halea finished wrapping a bandage around the plaster-covered splint on Faolan's leg.

"More wins for me!" Aatu declared with a smug grin. The beta male had begged to be let in to see his injured friend the moment Batsuba and Halea were done setting the break.

"Don't make me put you out," grumbled Batsuba while giving Aatu a warning glare on her way out of Faolan's cave.

The beta sheepishly bowed his head in submission to his elder before quietly taking a seat next to his friend's bed.

"Just a few more minutes, Aatu. He's falling asleep," Halea advised as she propped up Faolan's injured leg. Faolan only blinked lazily as his friend sat there with him in companionable silence. Once Halea was satisfied that her patient was well and rested, she made her way back outside and squinted in the bright daylight. Varg and his hunting party had not yet returned, but she could sense that they were on their way.

As Halea made her way along the path back towards the common area, Lyall approached and bowed his head.

"You may speak, Lyall."

26

"How is he?"

"Sleeping - or he will be soon. Aatu is keeping him company, and he'll be up and running again in about a week. By the way, thanks for the help with that demon."

"Pack looks after pack," he replied matter-of-factly.

"Lyall, can I ask you something?"

The older warrior nodded his head, but his expression was guarded.

"I'm technically a part of this pack, but you don't treat me like the others. I know you still don't really like me because I'm a human. I suppose you don't have to like me if you don't want to, but is there nothing I can do?"

Lyall frowned and avoided her gaze as he took a moment to carefully gather his thoughts. "You think my dislike for you is personal or because you are human, but that is not entirely why."

"Then what is it? What did I do?" she asked.

"It's what you haven't done. Varg is very dear to me. His father was like my brother, and I want the best for my supreme alpha. I don't doubt that you have an alpha's will, but I doubt that you're capable of being a wolfmother worthy of someone like Varg. When he claimed you, you cared little for this pack, at first. He carried the burden of his leadership alone, and it's not right for an alpha to have a mate who doesn't support him. I must admit that since then, you have come far, and you've learned to contribute and be more supportive of Varg. I was surprised when he told me that you offered to manage the Spring Moon Festival and the gathering. Varg works very hard for this pack - for all our people. I want him to have a wolfmother who is worthy of such a great leader. Perhaps you have that potential, and I see that you are trying, and I know Varg has been more than patient with you, but until you prove that this pack is as important to you as it is to him, as far as I'm concerned, you are a wolfmother in name only."

Anger burned hot within her, followed by bitter disappointment, and she sensed Varg's concern across their bond. She wanted to argue that she cared about the pack and that there were many who she counted as dear friends. She had fought for them and alongside them since before she and Varg were mated, and her choice to become a healer was driven by her desire to help the lycans and to be a contributing member of the pack, and still, it was not good enough. She wondered if there was any female in the world, lycan or not, who could be worthy enough for Varg in Lyall's eyes. But though she hated to admit it, he did have a point. She had not wanted the alpha's responsibility when she and Varg were first mated, which made for a bad initial impression. She had not felt that it was her place to assume control over a people to whom she had not been born, and she had struggled to learn and accept many of their ways and to rise to the expectations of being the mate of their wolf king. It had not been easy, and even now, it seemed as if she still had a long way to go, and she fought back the sting of tears threatening her eyes.

"I see. Thank you for being honest with me. Perhaps someday I will live up to your expectations," Halea said while quickly walking past him before her emotions could betray the depth of how much his words had wounded her.

When Halea reached the common area, she found Varg rushing towards her with an angry frown.

"What happened? Who hurt you?" he growled.

"It's okay, Varg. I'm fine. It was my fault for bringing it up."

"Bringing what up? Is someone in the pack giving you trouble again? You have my permission to beat the hell out of them, you know," he grumbled while taking her in his arms. She did seem a little calmer, but he could sense that she didn't want to discuss it with him, and he suspected the cause of what had upset her.

"Do I have to break his nose again?"

"No!" she cried. "Come on, Varg. Please. Please, just let him be. He does me no harm."

"No harm! I smell dry tears."

"No real harm. Please, Varg. It's been a trying day. Just let it go. There's something more important right now."

Varg narrowed his eyes in irritation. She had always avoided her problems, and it never did her any favors, but he decided to relent rather than upset her further.

"I was told about the demon attack and of Faolan's broken leg. How is he?"

"He'll be fine. It was that demon we fought today - it was different. I mean, they're always different, but this time, it had wings. They almost looked like something you'd see on a dragon."

CHAPTER 5 - DRAGON'S BLOOD

Halea removed the cover from the mirror and sat down. The surface was dark again, but she didn't expect him to be there waiting. Lord Anshar hadn't spoken since vowing to never again perform a sacrifice, but now he had to speak. He was the only one with any answers.

"Lord Anshar, it's me, Halea. I'd like to speak with you."

Silence.

"Lord Anshar, I know you can hear me. Please, I need your help. Something strange has been happening lately. Ever since you disappeared into the Chaos, the demons have changed. They're smarter now, stronger. They're no longer deterred by sunlight and their forms…" She paused while struggling to explain their foes' nature. "They can change shape. They have eyes now. Sometimes their eyes are just black, and other times they're able to pass for human. Today I fought a demon, and it had wings – dragon wings. Why? Why is this happening? You have to know something."

Silence.

"Talk to me!" she shouted in frustration.

"It's because of me, Halea," came his weak voice.

"Lord Anshar, what do you mean?"

Another moment of silence passed before his image appeared from within the mirror. He had taken off his armor and cloak, and as he removed his linen shirt before her, tears poured from her eyes.

His body was mutilated.

Even Varg did not have scars and marks such as the ones she saw upon Lord Anshar's flesh. Lord Anshar had raved about claws tearing into him or the horror of smelling his own blood many times, but she assumed it was all the imaginings of his madness because he cried out as if he were still being tortured.

"Is this what it did to you?" she asked in a shaking voice.

He only nodded his head, refusing to meet her eyes in shame as he pulled his shirt back over his scarred skin. "It took my blood. It took so very much. Even now, I still feel those invisible claws tearing into me. The pain. My blood and life were worth more than my death. I was a useful servant to hunt the blessed where it could not. A puppet. A fool."

"I'm so sorry, Lord Anshar."

"Don't pity me, Halea. I told you I don't want it! I deserve every mark on my flesh and every bit of the suffering that I've endured. Why can't you see that? Everything that's happened is my fault! This all happened because I was too weak to perform the duty that was expected of me. I should have struck Priestess Ami down when I had the chance, but I faltered, and because I hesitated to claim one life, countless others were lost, including your mother. It's my fault she's dead, Halea. Her blood is on my hands! Everyone's blood is on my hands! The weight of the world rested on my shoulders, and I was weak. You should have hated me. Why? Why didn't you hate me?" he asked with a trembling voice.

Halea's hands quivered in her lap as she absorbed his anguish.

"I thought about it," she confessed. "I thought about what my life would have been like if that day had gone differently. I've spent years thinking about that day. Nightmares. Never-ending nightmares of the city being swallowed by the sea and the convergence in the sky. Imagining what my mother must have endured...before she died. Yes, you were weak. Yes, you should have performed the sacrifice, and your mistake cost me my mother. But...it was a mistake. It wasn't your fault. It was Chaos's fault. That attack was planned. I refuse to believe that if those tears had not opened over the Citadel, that you wouldn't have performed your duty. I saw it in your eyes when you sacrificed Priestess Bree - you hated the killing. You hated what you were forced to do. You didn't want to sacrifice anyone, and you fought to protect so many that day, including me. And the more I thought about it, the more I realized that I would have done the same thing if I were in your position. I would have hesitated too. I would hate to be forced to endure what you were made to endure for ages. It wasn't fair that Tiamet put such a burden on your shoulders. It wasn't fair that you weren't allowed to show compassion or mercy. It wasn't fair that you had to endure such an existence for ages without any hope for an end to the suffering. It just wasn't fair. And I felt sorry for you. So very, very sorry. I know you don't want my pity, but I couldn't hate you then, and I can't hate you now. For all that you are, to me, you're just a man, and everyone is weak at times – even you."

Instead of being comforted, he only snarled at her words. "I damned the world for you, Halea. I don't deserve your pity. I risked everything just to save your life. I may have hesitated the first time, but for you, I willingly chose to risk the world. And I'd do it again. I don't give a damn about anything anymore! Either the world will be remade, or we will all perish in fire. And don't think for even one second that if I get an opportunity to make you mine, that I won't take it. At this point, taking one more life won't matter, and I told you that wolf can't keep you."

"I know you're just saying that to make me hate you! Say whatever horrible things you want. I'm not giving up!" she shouted back at him before jumping up and rushing out the tree-dwelling door.

~~~☼~~~

"Wolfmother? Uh...I mean, Halea?" Ulrica said while waving her hand nearly in front of Halea's face.

"Sorry, I guess I drifted off. It's been a long day," Halea finally replied as she shook herself out of her brooding thoughts. She had not even touched her lunch that was still sitting beside her on the fire pit bench.

After her last encounter with Lord Anshar the day before, she had sunk to her knees beneath the tree where the mirror was kept and cried her eyes out. It took a long time to quiet her emotions enough for her to reopen her bond with Varg. Varg hated how she was always so emotionally drained and upset after every visit with Lord Anshar, but despite the toll the sessions with the dragon took on her nerves, she had to persist. Lord Anshar had revealed some vital information to her. There was something, or someone, controlling the convergence. It took Lord Anshar's blood and used it to empower the demons and make them more deadly. It had also used Lord Anshar to hunt the priestesses, and it clearly still had some influence over his mind. Who? Why? What did it want? What did it have to gain by destroying their world? The more answers she received, the more questions remained, and she longed to speak with her grandfather.

She and Varg had agreed that her grandfather would be brought to the den after the Spring Moon Festival. It would be best to slowly introduce him to life among the lycans, one pack at a time, but now more than ever, she needed his wisdom. Her grandfather was one of the most knowledgeable clerics to have ever served Tiamet, and perhaps he could provide some insight into this new information. She certainly wouldn't mind having his help when it came to Lord Anshar. She wasn't sure how much more she could take, and perhaps her grandfather would prove more skilled at extracting the information they needed.

"I was just saying that Ralphina and I have finished cleaning and preparing the caves for the arrival of the other alphas."

"Thank you so much for helping me, Ulrica. I don't know what I'd do without you guys."

Halea had spent the past two weeks working non-stop to prepare for the festival gathering and ensuring that everything would be ready for the arrival of the other packs. She knew it would be a lot of work but had not anticipated just how much until she was in the thick of it all. It made her feel horrible to know how much Varg used to manage all on his own, and that knowledge made her relive the sting of Lyall's words, but it also made her more determined to ensure that the gathering would be a success. She would prove to everyone that she was a capable and worthy wolfmother.

"Please ask Aatu to clean out the north-end cellar to make more room. Varg said the hunting party should be bringing in a considerable amount of wild boar, and it won't preserve well if it isn't kept cold until the gathering."

Ulrica agreed with a nod and was just getting up when Daisy came running over.

"Mama! Mama!" the little girl shouted as she offered her mother a fistful of half-wilted wildflowers. "Pretty! Smell!"

Ulrica knelt to indulge her daughter, who smiled brightly at her mother's attention.

"Are you done playing?" Ulrica asked.

"No!" pouted the toddler while stomping her foot in irritation. It was getting close to her nap time, and Ulrica was already dreading the struggle she was about to have. When Ulrica reached to grab Daisy's hand, the little cub shied away and hid behind Halea with a sulking expression.

"Daisy!" Ulrica called, but the little girl pretended to ignore her mother and instead turned her attention to Halea's plate, which contained fresh fruit and a couple of sweet biscuits. She grabbed one of the biscuits and took a bite.

"Mmm. Yummy!"

Halea watched and tried not to look too amused by the cub's antics. She didn't want to encourage her disobedience towards her mother but seeing the little she-wolf eating human food with such relish was unexpected. Most lycans, even young cubs, preferred raw meat and rarely partook in other foods willingly, and Halea was not entirely able to conceal her surprised reaction.

"Daisy, those are Wolfmother's! I'm sorry. She gets that from her father. Gerwulf was strange too. He liked fruit and especially honey, anything sweet."

"Really? That's good to know," Halea said with a mischievous twinkle in her eye as she imagined spoiling the little girl with sweet treats behind her mother's back. Perhaps she'd be able to make more use of her new cooking station after all.

Ulrica was not sure what shifted her wolfmother's mood, but she did not seem offended by Daisy's antics. Halea insisted that Daisy take the last sweet biscuit with her, and the offering placated the cub enough for her mother to finally carry her away for her nap without further protest.

Halea watched them go with a pang of sadness. She enjoyed the company of children vicariously through the other mothers, but it wasn't the same, and she stared regretfully at her contraceptive rune. She was due to be in heat again soon, and it would be poor timing because the gathering was sure to be in full swing. Due to Rafe's attack in the fall and all that transpired afterward, she had been unable to gather enough of the yellow vine that the lycan females used for contraception before winter set in. She could have asked Batsuba for some dried herbs from her stores but decided to rely on her rune instead. Now that she and Varg had finally settled into their new home, which had its own private hot spring, she had to consider the necessity of backup measures once again, but she was perpetually distracted by the preparations for the impending festival and the demands of her healer apprenticeship.

Before Halea could ruminate much longer, she noticed Batsuba approaching with her medicine bag, and snatching one last piece of fruit from her plate, she went to join the elder for her lesson.

~~~☼~~~

The hunters had just finished gutting the three massive boars and were preparing to carry back the heavy slabs of meat when Varg noticed a shadow overhead that immediately set him on edge. He no longer had to fear the dragon, but with the demons demonstrating the ability to fly, he was extra cautious of threats from above. As he looked up, he spotted something gently floating down on the breeze – an enormous, single black feather.

"Varg, what is it? Is it a demon?" asked Lycurgus.

"No, it's something else. Everyone, go on to the den without me. Let Halea know I will be there soon."

Lyall gave Varg a look of reluctance as he sniffed the air and detected the unfamiliar scent, but the warning in his alpha's eyes left no room for argument, and so he turned and went with the others.

Varg moved further into the trees, into the direction of the shadow, and there he found the crow.

"It's you. Why have you come to the western lands?" Varg asked while putting up a block on his bond with Halea so she wouldn't notice the sinking sense of dread within him.

A massive black crow with unblinking reflective eyes stared down at him from where it perched on high within a tree. The crow shifted into his humanoid form, leaving only his oily black wings, which he used to gracefully lower himself to the ground where he stood before the wolf king.

"A vision has brought me here," Corbin replied.

"I've had enough of those," grumbled Varg.

"It's not for your mate this time, but for an old friend, a friend to us both – Ethelwolf."

"Ethelwolf? What have you seen?"

"A tear is coming, far larger than any you've seen of late. Everyone will be in danger once the demons spill forth, and Halea must be there to seal the rift, or many lives will be lost. In my vision, I saw the eastern alpha swarmed by the hordes. I'm sorry, after that, I cannot say, but I had to come. You may share this prophecy with Halea, but you cannot speak of it with Ethelwolf or anyone else. The knowledge of the gods is forbidden to most for a reason."

Varg's brow furrowed in distress. Ethelwolf was as dear to him as a father, and he was a good alpha and a close friend.

"At the first sign of danger, Halea and I will be there. If we can prevent this, we will."

"You can prevent nothing. My visions are never wrong, but perhaps there is hope that the outcome will not be so grim, though the fact that I was warned by the gods at all does not bode well."

Varg snarled as Corbin's words cut deeper than just the prospect of losing the eastern alpha. He had spoken of the crow's prophecy to no one and hiding the truth from Halea had been nearly impossible due to their bond.

"You don't have to remind me of the accuracy of the gods' cruelty. I've lived every day since your last vision in fear for my mate's life. My only comfort is the knowledge that if the gods take her from me, I can at least be with her in the afterlife - small comfort though, that is."

"Are you so sure of that, Varg?" asked Corbin while quizzically cocking his head to the side.

"What do you mean? Of course, I'm sure! Our spirits are bound as one. Lycans always follow their mates into the next world."

"But she's not a lycan. You have the favor of the wolf gods, who will surely come to claim your soul when you die, but why would they claim Halea? She is not a wolf. If any god has a claim on her soul, it would be Tiamet. Very few are fortunate

33

enough to have more than one god come to claim them in the afterlife, and for those souls, they have the right to choose which god they'll follow into the heavenly realm. A soul can choose whether or not it's ready to be judged and claimed, and by which god, or it can choose to willingly throw itself into the oblivion."

"I've submitted myself to the gods and will serve them as I've promised. All I ask is to be with her, either in this world or the next. And if they will not admit her into the heavenly realm beside me, then I will sooner choose the oblivion of hell than to spend an eternity in heaven without her. If they truly want me, they must take her too!"

Corbin smiled in fond sadness.

"Take comfort then. The wolf gods love their children. Though humans and lycans don't often mix, the bond of love between a mated pair is something even they know they cannot challenge. As long as Halea doesn't offend them, I'm sure they will offer her a place beside you."

The possibility that another god could sway Halea's soul unsettled Vag as he knew the Dragon Goddess still called to his mate, but she had already chosen him over Tiamet the day she agreed to be his. He took solace in knowing that if anyone could impress the wolf gods and earn an honorary place among them, it was Halea. Despite her remaining doubts, he knew that she had everything it took to be a wolfmother.

"One way or another, we'll be together," Varg affirmed.

"The gods have shown me how much you two have overcome together. I know that Halea captured Lord Anshar within the dark mirror and that you were able to stand against him as a true swordsman. This old bird is proud," he said with a dry laugh.

Varg could not suppress the smile that tugged at the corner of his lips at the crow's praise. "I couldn't have done it without Halea by my side, and you knew, didn't you?"

Corbin's creepy thin lips spread in what passed for a smile upon his gaunt face as he merely nodded his head.

"I'm not a fan of your damn prophecies, but I'm grateful that you chose to help me. Both for training me to use the Fang and helping me see what I should have always seen standing there before me; that Halea is my strength. Thank you."

"The gods are wise," said Corbin as he accepted Varg's gratitude. When the young lycan first came to him, he had been ruled by his instincts and ego, but now he stood before him as a wiser and more humble king. "I must return to my duties. There are many souls to be carried. Remember my warning and watch over Ethelwolf for me."

"I will," promised Varg, and with that, the crow spread his wings and transformed as he soared into the air, back towards the east.

34

CHAPTER 6 – SPRING MOON FESTIVAL

Halea rolled over in bed to find that Varg had already risen for the day and slipped out. Being a lycan, he didn't need as much sleep as her, but he always did his best to make sure his morning duties were taken care of as quickly as possible so he could still join her for breakfast at the fire pit. This morning, she had slept in after a restless night of worry.

Varg had told her of his visit with the swordmaster and his prophetic warning about Ethelwolf and that the knowledge was to be kept between the two of them. They agreed it would be best to keep an extra guard of warriors around the den during the festival, and Halea would personally do her best to make sure that she did not stray too far in case a tear should open. If this tear was large enough for the swordmaster to fly all the way from the east to warn them about it, she wasn't confident that she would be powerful enough to subdue it on her own. She wished the other priestesses were there to help her, but without Rufus, she had no way to contact them, and Mama Dragon was not due to arrive back in lycan territory until after the gathering. She had lain awake most of the night, offering silent prayers to Tiamet and asking for her strength as Varg tried his best to comfort her.

Varg got up early to manage the warriors and ensure that everyone could evacuate the den in an orderly manner in the event of a demon attack. Many were concerned with their alpha's precautions, but he would not speak about what had prompted his sudden apprehension.

Halea was just putting on her boots when she heard Varg's voice.

"Halea? Oh, you're awake," he said while stepping through their bedroom door. "Great. The northern pack has arrived. I would have howled to let you know, but I didn't want you to misinterpret the call as trouble."

Halea was used to some of the lycan howls, particularly the ones warning of danger. Almost as if they were a second language, there was a nuance and variety of meanings to the calls that she couldn't always distinguish. After last night's warning, she was particularly on edge about the prospect of hearing howls in the distance, and now she had another stress to deal with.

He sensed a little hesitance and dread from his mate but quickly wrapped his arms around her in comfort. Halea hadn't seen the northern wolves in nearly a year, and she didn't know them as well as the western and eastern packs.

"Everything will be fine," Varg promised.

"I know," she said while forcing a nod and straightening her spine. If she was going to act the part of a wolfmother, she needed to exude total confidence and authority. Such willpower hadn't come easily at first because she had feared it wasn't her place to rule over Varg's people, but when it came to lycans, one could not be timid, and eventually, she had learned to assert herself and stand tall against any who opposed her. To her surprise, it had grown easier. Fulfilling the expectations of an alpha had become second nature to her, at least when it came to the western pack.

As they walked together back towards the den, Halea gradually began to make out the excited commotion that signaled the arrival of the northern pack. Many lycans came out to the common area to greet their northern friends and relations, and everyone was standing around in large social clusters, talking animatedly and sharing warm hugs of welcome and friendly slaps on the back.

Varg led her to Alpha Bertolf, who, much to Halea's relief, bowed his head respectfully before his supreme alphas.

"Welcome, brother Bertolf. It's good to see you again," offered Varg, and Bertolf lifted his head at his king's acknowledgment.

"Greetings, Wolf King and Supreme Wolfmother. Thank you for welcoming my pack into the west."

"Well, enough of this formal bullshit," Varg said with a laugh, and Bertolf's face lit up with a bright smile as the two males warmly embraced and thumped each other on the back.

Halea couldn't help but envy how quickly Varg could go from austere leader to casual chum, but she smiled and relaxed a little at the two male's affectionate display.

"It's been too long since we've all gathered for a Spring Moon Festival. I'm dying to compete in some games and see if you can kick my ass half as much as your father used to."

"Don't worry, I won't go easy on you," Varg replied with an excited gleam in his eye. Alphas loved to compete, and the festival games allowed the wolves to enjoy friendly competition with each other.

"Please join us at our fire pit for some food and ale. I'm sure you would love to relax and catch up with Varg after your long journey," Halea offered with her warmest smile.

Bertolf was not put off by Halea's human presence. He had accepted Varg's choice just as he accepted his own brother's choice to mate with the human woman Jance. Human women were weird, very different from she-wolves, but from what he could tell, no less loving of their mates. He had spent the past few weeks exchanging several runners with Halea, who had orchestrated the festival's details as a good wolfmother should, and he was impressed by her initiative. Bertolf was an old bachelor, and not having his own wolfmother, he had to assume sole responsibility for his pack in preparation for the gathering. Some were left behind to keep watch over the den and those who were physically incapable of making the long journey, but most chose to make the trek from the north to attend the gathering.

With a grateful nod, Bertolf accepted his supreme wolfmother's kind offer and joined her and Varg at the main fire pit where several platters of raw meat were brought out, and ale was poured into tankards. There was no need to light the fire because the day was warm and bright, but the pit was no less cozy.

Rather than sitting in Varg's lap, as he usually preferred, Halea cuddled up close beside him, and he wrapped one of his arms around her shoulder. She was finally growing more comfortable with the public displays of affection so common among lycan mates.

Bertolf and Varg immediately began a lively conversation about the upcoming festivities to which Halea only interjected on occasion, and she was relieved that the northern alpha was far more pleasant than he had been on their first encounter. Bertolf had not been cruel or disrespectful, but he had been far more standoffish and unnerved by her presence the first time they met.

As they sat at the pit, Halea noticed someone waving in the distance to get her attention. The face was hard to make out from so far away, but the flaming red hair was unmistakable. It was Jance.

"I think I see someone who wants to say hello. You two carry on," Halea said while excusing herself from the alphas.

The short redhead came running up to her excitedly the moment she left the pit and threw her arms around her in a big hug.

"Halea, I'm so glad to see you again, or, I guess I should say, Wolfmother, now. Either way, it's good to see you!"

"Halea is fine. We'll let the wolves be formal."

Jance beamed excitedly at the thought of two humans living among lycans who didn't have to adhere to their customs, at least not when around each other, and she laughed in relief.

"I was hoping I could get your attention, but I'm not allowed to interrupt the alphas unless invited. Thank goodness I'm not an alpha. How do you stand it?"

"Not easily," Halea confessed.

"You must be amazing to pull off being a wolfmother! Even Bertolf praised you for managing this festival and helping to bring us all together. I'd be terrified if that was all on my shoulders."

"Where's Alf?" asked Halea.

"Having festival fever with all these other crazy males. I don't care for sports, but Alf hasn't talked about anything else since this gathering was announced. I'm honestly grateful to get a break from it and just talk with another human for a change."

Halea smiled at the other woman's lively banter before escorting her to a small unoccupied fire pit where Jance wasted no time unloading her travel bag of all the delicacies she had baked for the occasion.

Jance had not forgotten how much Halea enjoyed her food the last time they met, and she had outdone herself by bringing sweet cakes, biscuits, tarts, turnovers, and several other treats.

"Wow, you made all these! I don't know if just the two of us can eat them all before they spoil," Halea said while eying one of the mouthwatering tarts.

"We can make a valiant effort of it!" Jance declared, and the two women laughed.

They sat together and talked about their experiences with life among the lycans, and Halea was glad to have found such a dear kindred spirit. There was never a dull moment listening to Jance.

Ulrica approached and offered them some tea to wash down their repast, and Jance squealed in delight when she saw little Daisy peeking out from behind her mother's leather skirt. The cub was watching the new human woman with large and bashful eyes, and when Jance noticed her, she shied behind her mother.

"Oh, she's so adorable. Is that your cub?" asked Jance.

"Yes, her name is Daisy," Ulrica replied with a smile as she was always happy when anyone acknowledged her precious daughter. "Daisy, it's okay. You can say hello."

The bashful toddler only peeked out a little before ducking behind her mother once more.

"Here, offer her a cake," suggested Halea.

"Cake?" Jance cried incredulously, but despite her doubts, she held the sweet treat towards the lycan cub who appeared from behind her mother. Her small button nose twitched as she sniffed the air and took a shy step towards the cake.

To the redhead's amazement, the little she-wolf accepted the confection from her outstretched hand and immediately took a bite. Daisy's face lit up in joy as the sugary food melted on her tongue, and she greedily ate the rest while plopping onto the ground beside Jance and Halea.

"Say thank you, Daisy," admonished her mother, but when the little girl opened her mouth, it was too full of food to make out much more than an incoherent mumble of gratitude.

"Well, I've never seen a lycan cub like human food before!" Jance cried. "But I love it! Oh, please let us feed her some more," she begged Ulrica, who nodded in permission. Ulrica did not know the northern human, but Daisy was more than safe in the care of her wolfmother, and with a gentle kiss to her daughter's forehead, she went along with her duties.

"More!" Daisy cried once she finished her snack and held out her sticky little hand, and Halea and Jance were more than happy to indulge her in a few more biscuits.

"I've never met such an unusual little cub before," Jance declared. "I would love to keep spoiling her, but I suppose we shouldn't give her too much more, or she'll get a tummy ache and won't have room for her dinner."

"Yes, I suppose you're right," Halea agreed as Daisy munched her treats contentedly while wiggling her bare feet in front of her.

"If Alf and I could have had children, I wonder if that's what they'd be like? Having my human sweet tooth, I mean."

"You two haven't had any?" Halea asked. Though made immortal by being bound to her mate's life force, Jance was not exactly young, at least not by human years. She was in her forties, though she would forever be frozen in her twenties.

"I was pregnant once, but I'm not a very strong person, or maybe there's just something wrong with me on the inside. It was a difficult pregnancy. I lost the baby and nearly bled to death," Jance explained as her dark eyes grew moist. "Our healer warned me that another pregnancy could be the end of my life. After that, we decided not to risk it again. Alf couldn't bear the thought of losing me, even though I know he wanted children as much as I did, but I guess the gods have decided that it's not meant to be for us. Even if we can't have children, we have each other."

Halea's heart bled as Jance's face contorted with the memory of her loss.

"I'm sorry. I didn't mean to upset you."

"No, it's okay. That was many years ago, and I don't mind just spending time with the cubs when I can. I even learned the lycans' written language so I could help teach the little ones to read it," she said with a proud twinkle in her eyes.

Infused with an abundance of energy, Daisy ran off to chase Fillin, and the two women chatted together as the day wore on.

Eventually, Halea excused herself to go attend to the preparations for the evening meal. As she passed through the den, she noticed Batsuba looking annoyed as she stood before a tall and lanky lycan male. As Halea approached, the male spun to face her, and she recognized that it was the northern elder, Marrok.

"Priestess Halea! I mean, Wolfmother. Supreme Wolfmother! My alpha. My queen! Let me grovel at your feet!" he proclaimed while trying to get down on his knees, but Batsuba grabbed him by one of his long, pointed ears and pulled him back up.

"Oh, stop it, you old fool!" the healer grumbled.

"It's good to see you again, Elder Marrok," Halea greeted with an awkward smile. Marrok was still one of the strangest lycans she had ever met. He did not usually act as one would expect from an elder. There were moments when his fathomless ancient eyes would grow serious, and his voice would become commanding in a way that instantly garnered the respect of all those all around him, but at other times, he could be almost childlike.

"Batsuba has told me amazing things about you. Simply amazing! I knew you were special the moment I saw you. Didn't I say she was special, Batsuba?"

The she-wolf only regarded him with narrowed eyes and a frown.

"See! She remembers!" he said while nudging the unamused healer with his elbow and earning a growl from her in response.

"If you are quite done, Marrok, you could help me set up the altar in the sacred cave," grumbled Batsuba. Soon the other pack's elders would arrive, and they would all convene in private to hold rituals before the wolf gods to ask for blessings for the festival and the new year.

"They're not here yet! I want to praise our wolfmother. Ow!" he cried as Batsuba grabbed his ear once more and dragged him off.

"You best run along, Halea," Batsuba said over her shoulder. "He's too excitable, and there's work to be done."

Halea did her best not to burst out laughing as the two elders bickered while making their way up the mountain path before she turned to resume her duties.

As the sun sank in the west, the pit fires were lit, and Halea was once again seated with Varg and Bertolf. She listened in grave silence as Bertolf explained the woes of the northern wolves.

"The demons have begun to scatter our herds. A priestess came and sealed the tear we found on our lands, but she said she couldn't stay long. The demons returned the moment we were left on our own, and they're harder to kill now. We lost two pack members to dark weapons."

"I'm so sorry, Bertolf. Many of Tiamet's servants have been slain, and their ability to help everyone who needs them is stretched thin. There are few of us…I mean, them, and priestesses must seek out tears. They can't afford to linger unless they're sure another tear will appear. It's not that they wanted to abandon you," Halea apologized for her former sisters of the faith.

Varg hadn't missed her slip of the tongue. It still bothered him that deep down, in her heart, Halea still considered herself to be a priestess.

"Varg told me of your trouble with the Dragon Lord and that he was slaughtering your people. It seems that dark times are ahead for all of us."

Halea could only nod her head in agreement, and Varg tightened his arm around her as he sensed her sadness across their bond.

Howls suddenly rang out across the den, and Halea's heart leaped into her throat as she jumped to her feet in fearful panic, but she saw no signs of the purple light associated with the presence of a tear.

"Halea, it's okay. It's all right," Varg promised as he quickly clasped her wrist and pulled her close. Sweat was pouring from her skin, and she reeked of fear and anxiety. "They're announcing that the southern pack is here," he explained, and her rapidly fluttering heart calmed as she took a deep breath and nodded in understanding.

Bertolf stared in wide-eyed confusion. Why was the wolfmother so on edge? There was no time to ask as the two alphas quickly set off to greet the latest arrivals.

Halea cursed that she probably reeked of anxiety just before facing the southern wolves and their new alpha. That sort of scent could easily be misinterpreted and might make a bad first impression on the unfamiliar leader.

Everyone cleared a path as Varg and Halea approached the southern pack. It was easy to distinguish which lycan was their new leader as he moved ahead of the rest of his entourage with an undeniable air of authority, and Halea was reminded of when Úlfa had asked her if she could sense the will of an alpha. There were no doubts that this alpha possessed the will of a true leader, and she had to stifle a gasp as she first caught sight of him. His skin was a little more tanned, and his hair was as black as ebony, but his eyes were the same unmistakable shade of blue as Varg's.

"Greetings, brother Raoul," offered Varg after the southern leader gave a respectful but short bow of his head.

"Brother? Don't you mean cousin?" he asked with an even but deep voice as his face remained impassive.

Varg gave a forced smile. "Of course, cousin. It's good to see you again. It's been many years."

40

"I haven't seen you since you were but a cub, and now you're my king," Raoul replied and extended his arms. The two males shared a brief but somewhat unenthusiastic embrace. "You've certainly grown to take after your father. Thank you for welcoming us to the western lands. And I take it this," he said while turning his vibrant blue eyes on Halea, "is our supreme wolfmother?"

Halea stood tall and unflinching under the piercing gaze of the southern alpha.

"Yes, this is my mate, Halea," Varg introduced with pride.

Halea hadn't received many runners from the southern pack since Ralph came to request the gathering on Raoul's behalf. The few inquiries she had received regarding the festival had been brief and were mainly concerned with the state of the local herds, and she had no choice but to delegate those messages to Varg.

"I welcome you and your pack to the western lands," Halea spoke without hesitation. "You must be exhausted after your long journey. Please, come and join us for supper. Alpha Bertolf is also here, but Alpha Ethelwolf and the eastern pack have not yet arrived."

The southern alpha regarded her for a silent moment before finally accepting the offer. With a signal from Halea, several of her western pack volunteers approached the rest of the southern lycans and escorted them to other pits where they would be given refreshments and a chance to rest after their long journey.

When they returned to the main pit, Halea couldn't help but observe that Raoul greeted Bertolf in a somewhat more openly friendly manner than he had greeted her and Varg.

"As soon as the eastern pack arrives, you may present yourself before the council," Varg explained as they ate before the fire.

Normally, Varg shared some of his meat with Halea, which she would skewer and lay on the fire, but she didn't want to run the chance of offending the new southern alpha with her peculiar human diet, at least not on the first night. She had requested that Ulrica prepare her entire meal for her beforehand so the smell of the cooking food wouldn't be an unwelcome distraction. Her precaution didn't seem to work as Raoul quirked an eyebrow at the sight of her eating from a separate plate than her mate, and she suspected the subtle twitch of his nostrils was an indication that he was not pleased with the scent. Lycan mates usually shared food from a single plate as a form of bonding and a display of affection, but she couldn't share that cultural tradition with Varg. She did her best to ignore Raoul's subtle disapproval and kept her eyes focused on whoever was currently dominating the conversation.

"I look forward to their arrival," Raoul replied. "There is one other thing I wish to discuss with the council while I'm here. I'm sure you're aware that demon attacks have been on the rise. They're getting clever and far more lethal, and rumor has spread into the south that the old dragon won't do his job anymore. They say that you were able to best him in battle. I'd very much like to hear how you accomplished such a feat."

"Varg and I went into the east, seeking the swordmaster," interjected Halea, who could tell that Varg was starting to become annoyed with his cousin, who seemed

41

openly doubtful of the rumors. "With the help of the crow and the great wolf gods, Varg was given mastery of the Fang."

Raoul narrowed his eyes at Halea's words, and Varg did his best to suppress a growl.

"I see. If this is true, it would seem that you indeed have the favor of the gods, but I'm not sure if that will be enough to keep me from presenting my claim before the council."

"What claim?" asked Varg, no longer bothering to mask the growl rumbling in his voice.

"I'm not entirely confident about how you and your mate have been handling this crisis. When I appear before the council, perhaps I'll announce my intention to challenge you for the right to be the wolf king."

CHAPTER 7 – LOYALTY

In a flash, the two males were on their feet, snarling in each other's faces. Bertolf quickly jumped in to pull back Raoul, and Halea threw herself in front of Varg to prevent him from falling into a blood rage.

"You dare challenge me?" Varg roared.

"I might, Varg. I just might. It's easy to sit here and pretend like everything's under control and throw a celebration when the truth is that things have gone to shit! Who's going to banish that convergence if it comes back? What are we going to do about these demons and tears invading our lands if her kind can't manage them? The western territory was nearly destroyed the last time a convergence went wrong, and now there's nothing to prevent that disaster from wiping out everything as we know it. Perhaps the gods have chosen you as their champion, but what are you going to do about it? What is her kind going to do about it? Sit around here and wait for our end to come? I want answers, Varg! I want action! My pack is in danger! Your pack is in danger! If you two can't prove to me that you've got a plan, then I will challenge you. I can't sit by and watch our people be destroyed!"

Halea had to lean into Varg with all her might to keep him from leaping forward and going for Raoul's throat.

"You know nothing of what we've endured!" Varg replied. "The dragon has lost his mind, and it was only by the will of the gods that we were able to subdue him before he slaughtered everyone who prays to their Goddess. Don't forget that for the last two convergences, it was the western wolves who stood between the demons and all the other territories. You southern lycans were always the first to abandon us in our time of need!"

"That was Rafe's doing, and you know it!" Raoul growled. "If I had been alpha at that time, I wouldn't have turned my back. All lycans are our people, but Rafe cared nothing for our friends and kin in the other packs."

Despite Raoul's aggression, Halea could find no fault with his words. There hadn't been much open communication between the western and southern packs since the last convergence, and it was easy to understand that things looked dire from an outsider's perspective. It was true that they didn't have much control over the situation, but they were not without hope or a plan.

"Raoul, I understand your concern," Halea interjected. "We're worried too. You're right - we're in a bad situation. We all are. But Varg and I have not been idle. You deserve to know the whole truth about what's been happening. Please, let's just all sit down and discuss this rationally."

43

Raoul raised a doubtful eyebrow at her proposal, but with a reluctant sigh, he sat back down, and to Halea's relief, Varg and Bertolf also reclaimed their seats, though they were both still noticeably on edge.

Halea explained everything from the beginning of the last gathering: Lord Anshar's disappearance and return and his current mental condition. She described their journey into the east after Rafe's attack, and Varg interjected to tell of his experience with the swordmaster and his encounter with the wolf gods. They talked about the current situation with the demons and tears, the few and scattered worshippers of the Dragon Goddess, and the miraculous capture of Lord Anshar within the dark mirror.

Even Bertolf listened with rapt attention as new details emerged about their predicament.

"If the gods have granted you their favor and mastery of the Fang, I can't deny that you're their chosen champion, but if the dragon refuses to do his duty, that still doesn't leave us in a good position," Raoul grumbled after hearing them out.

"There's hope," argued Halea. "Tiamet came to the earthly realm to give me the power to trap Lord Anshar. She asked me to save him. I know most never recover from Chaos Madness, but Lord Anshar isn't like others, he does have his lucid moments, and I know there was something else in the Chaos with him. There's something behind all this, and he has the answers. I just have to get through to him, but I need time, and I know we're running out, but if this is what the Goddess wants, then we are not without hope."

"I don't like gambling on the sanity of a dragon who's already turned his back on his people. If he keeps his vow to never sacrifice, we're lost," Raoul said.

"I don't know the will of the gods, but they're definitely involved," added Bertolf. "The gods are mysterious and work in ways that we can't begin to understand, but I feel like they know something that we don't. Varg and Halea are being guided by their will, and though I don't like depending on the whims of a mad dragon, it would seem that Lord Anshar still has his part to play."

"That's it, then? We're all in the hands of the gods?" Raoul grumbled. "I can't say that's particularly comforting."

"I understand your frustration," Varg said with sympathy. "These are things beyond our control that can't be challenged with claws or fangs. We're dealing with a mysterious force from another dimension with unknown motives and gods that may or may not care whether we live or die and a dragon that's fed up with his lot in life. All I know is that I trust Halea. If the dragon has the answer to our problem, she will find it, and I will do everything within my power to buy her the time she needs. The Fang is a sword of protection, and I will fight for my mate, my pack, and our people, all of our people, because I *am* the wolf king, and that is my purpose. If you still doubt me, then I welcome your challenge."

"I'll think about it," Raoul replied. "I am still undecided. I can't say that I could do any better in your situation, but the wolf gods grant their favor to the strongest. I will wait until the end of the festival to make my decision. If you can prove to me that you are worthy of being my king, I will swear fealty to you, but not until then."

"Fine," Varg conceded.

<center>~~~☼~~~</center>

After things died down, Halea guided Raoul up the mountain path towards the spacious cave reserved for the alpha of the southern pack. Bertolf already knew where his accommodations were, they were the same every time he came to the west, but this was the first time Raoul had ever come to a western pack gathering as an alpha.

To be a good wolfmother, Halea had to play the part of a perfect hostess. Swallowing her nerves and ignoring Varg's concerned glance, she offered to show Raoul to his accommodations.

The walk up the mountain was silent and awkward, but she held her head high. When they reached the heavy iron doors, Halea went inside first to light the lamps with the small torch she had carried from the pit.

"Is there anything else you will need for the night?" she asked.

Raoul avoided her eyes by looking around the cave and nervously scratched the back of his head.

"I do love him, ya know," he blurted to Halea's surprise.

He finally met her gaze, and his vibrant blue eyes grew serious.

"He's my little cousin. At least he was when I last saw him. It's not that I wanted to come all the way out here just to bust his chops, but I also have to worry about my pack. I don't know if a human can understand that."

"I understand just fine," Halea replied in a defensive tone. "I know you haven't seen him since he was a kid…cub…but he's doing everything he can. We both are. And don't make your predecessor's mistake of underestimating me just because I'm a human."

"Ah, suddenly his choice makes sense," he laughed at her ire, not maliciously, but with genuine amusement. "I would have loved to have been the one to challenge Rafe, but it was you who defeated him in single combat, and I suppose if you hadn't, I wouldn't be here. For that, you have my gratitude. I did not condone what he tried to do to you and Varg. I can respect you for being a tough alpha bitch and my supreme wolfmother, despite being human, but as to what I think of you on a personal level, I don't know yet. To be honest, I haven't met or spoken to many humans besides you and that dark-skinned priestess you sent to my lands to close that tear. Your kind has been less than endearing, but I'm willing to give you a chance, at least for Varg's sake. I barely even know him anymore after all these years. I'm amazed he even remembers me."

"He did say he doesn't know you as well as he should," Halea admitted. "He also mentioned that you were unpredictable."

"Well, I guess he does remember something about me," Raoul laughed again before his smile eventually grew sad. "He is my last blood relation. I pray to the gods that he really is everything I'm hoping for in a king."

"Don't worry, he is," she promised with a confident smile before saying farewell and leaving the southern alpha alone for the night.

<center>~~~☼~~~</center>

45

Varg waited impatiently by the dying embers of the fire pit for Halea to return and was relieved when she came back down the path. Her emotions had not indicated any distress. In fact, he detected a sense of hopefulness from her that sparked his curiosity.

When she approached the pit, he motioned for her to join him rather than immediately retiring to their tree-dwelling for the night. She accepted his invitation by snuggling up next to him in front of the glowing remains of the evening's fire.

"You seem to have done pretty well for yourself today, Wolfmother," he said with a pleased smile. "I take it Raoul didn't cause you any trouble."

"He might be an unpredictable hot-head, but I think he's fair – so far. I know as an alpha, you can't stand being challenged, but he's just concerned for our people, and I can't blame anyone for being afraid in these dark times. I know you two aren't exactly close, but I don't think you have anything to worry about from him. I don't know if he wanted me to spread the message, but he said he loves you and that you're his family. He's giving us a chance, which is more than Rafe ever did, so I think we can give him a chance too. He won't doubt you for long. I know it."

"Our people?" he asked with a raised eyebrow. He had always hoped that she would come to view his people as her people.

"Yes. Your people are my people now. I do love them, and I love being here with you. For the first time since I was a child, I have a home, somewhere that I belong. I know I didn't feel like I fit in here at first, and it wasn't easy to adapt, but it's different now. Your people aren't perfect. I mean, some are jerks, but humans can be that way too. You wolves are still a weird and cranky lot, but everyone's grown on me."

Varg's heart swelled with pride to hear his mate finally accepting his people and her place among them. He wanted to give her everything that would make her happy, and a home was more than just a treehouse; it was a place and a people. It was family, even if that family wasn't always blood.

He sighed in defeat.

"I guess I should give my cousin some time. When last he saw me, I was little more than an ankle-biter, and he hasn't had a chance to know me as a man or a leader. Although I wish he wouldn't piss me off."

"To be fair, everyone pisses you off," she added with a laugh.

"Everyone except you," he corrected before leaning in and softly brushing his lips against hers.

~~~✸~~~

"It's nearly good enough to walk on now, see!" Faolan declared as he feebly lifted his injured leg in its cast. "It doesn't even hurt."

"Yes, much better, but you're still not coming out of that cast today," Halea said with finality. Beside her, Ralphina looked disappointed.

"That's too bad. It's hard taking care of two babies." Ralphina had been looking after her brother during his convalescence, and it was a lot to manage on top of caring for Bardolph and her volunteer work with the festival, though Lycurgus helped as much as possible.

46

"Hey!" Faolan grumbled, but his sister only shoved his baby nephew into his arms.

"You can watch Bardolph while I help with the morning meal. I'll be back to nurse him later."

"But what about Lycurgus?" he asked.

"Varg took him on a scouting mission this morning, so you're on your own," Halea added with a grin.

The two females left Faolan to deal with the squirming infant. He protested, but he loved babysitting Bardolph and had a knack for keeping him entertained and getting him to fall asleep.

The meal at the alpha's fire pit was far less stressful that morning. Varg, Raoul, and Bertolf were discussing lighter matters and growing excited about the festival games. Suddenly Halea could understand Jance's annoyance with the never-ending topic, but the sound of a howl interrupted their discussion.

"Guess we're finally all here," Varg announced after Halea gave him a questioning glance.

Everyone rose and went to greet the eastern pack. Halea was happy to see Ethelwolf again, and to her surprise, he brought Úlfa with him.

"Thank you for having us, and we're sorry for arriving so late. Far more of the pack wanted to join the gathering this year because of the festival, and it takes a lot to coordinate the journey of so many wolves," Ethelwolf explained after being warmly greeted by all the other alphas. The eastern pack was by far the largest of all the lycan packs, and after a long winter, many were excited for the prospect of taking a journey to a warmer territory and enjoying the festivities.

"We're so happy you both were able to make it," Halea said in greeting before Úlfa stepped forward and offered an enthusiastic embrace.

"Halea, it's so good to see you again," the eastern wolfmother declared as her dark blue eyes twinkled. Úlfa was the only other lycan wolfmother, and the runners she had sent Halea from the east provided the most useful advice and information about planning the gathering. "I'll help you with anything you need for the festival. Otsana will also be volunteering."

Halea looked over Úlfa's shoulder and noticed Otsana standing back with some of the other eastern wolves and that Fenris was also with them. The younger she-wolf angrily huffed and turned her head to avoid eye contact, and Halea suspected she was more of a conscript than a volunteer.

"Thank you, Otsana. I really…" But before Halea could finish, Otsana stormed off. "Oh, okay, well, never mind," Halea lamely finished.

Úlfa shook her head in regret. "Don't mind her, please. You know how she is."

"Yeah, same as ever, I guess," Halea agreed, but inside she felt an ache of disappointment. She had hoped that the time she and Otsana spent together in the east had softened the harsh feelings between them, but it seemed the eastern she-wolf still hated her.

Halea decided to let it go. For the time being, she had to consider her duties as wolfmother, and she quickly offered Ethelwolf and Úlfa the chance to rest and eat after their long journey while the rest of their pack was attended to by the volunteers. Even though she and Varg had only just finished their meal, they joined the eastern alphas and spent a pleasant morning catching up with them.

Halea couldn't help but smile as she observed the usually stoic Ethelwolf melt in the presence of his adoring mate. She could tell the bond between them was so strong that they subtly communicated with each other without even needing words. It reminded her of the happiness she shared with Varg.

But a dark cloud settled over Halea's heart, and anxiety squeezed her on the inside.

What if something terrible happened to Ethelwolf? The swordmaster's prophecy said he was in terrible danger, and they could not even warn him. What if he died? What would happen to Úlfa?

Varg sensed his mate's emotions taking a dark turn as sadness spread across their bond like a miasma. He gently squeezed her hand, and when she looked up at him, he gave her an encouraging smile.

Ethelwolf's fate was not yet known, but they would fight to protect their friends together.

<center>~~~☼~~~</center>

The next day the games began. Halea watched the vicious wrestling matches between the males and tried not to cringe at the openly violent displays of aggression. She knew there was no malice and that it was all in good fun – for lycans – but it was hard as a human and a healer's apprentice to not worry about her friends' wellbeing.

Aatu suffered from a dislocated wrist after competing against Fenris, and Halea couldn't help but observe that Otsana had watched that match with an unsettled look in her eyes. Fenris had shown an interest in leadership that threatened Otsana's place in her pack, and Halea desperately wanted to ask her if she had kept up with her training, but the eastern she-wolf had done nothing but ignore her since her arrival.

Halea was able to reset Aatu's wrist with Batsuba's guidance, and Faolan watched silently as the two women bandaged up his friend. His cast had come off, and he was permitted to walk, but to his disappointment, Batsuba forbade him from joining the races scheduled for that day.

"Too bad," Faolan teased when the females were done with Aatu and left to help the other injured competitors. Aatu had given Faolan nothing but grief for being laid up and missing out on the start of the games, and now it was his turn to sit out.

"Hey, this will be better in a day. Faster than your lame leg, gimpy!"

"Gimpy! Why you…"

"Give it a rest, you two," interrupted Hemming. "The races are up next, and it's not like either one of you would have stood a chance against Varg anyway."

"Yeah, you're right," Aatu admitted. "At least this will be better in time for the archery competition. That's too bad for you."

Hemming glowered at Aatu's challenge. He was the best archer in the western pack and had won every competition for the past decade, but last year Aatu had come close to beating him, and it was no secret that the two males were putting in extra practice to see who would come out on top this year.

48

A small band of southern lycans stood nearby while waiting for the next wrestling match to begin and overheard the western males' conversation and decided to walk over and join them.

"Too bad about the wrist," Loup commented with a less-than-sincere smile. "I hear that Fenris guy is pretty tough. Perhaps they should put him in a match against your human wolfmother. Supposedly she was strong enough to take down Rafe all by herself. Doubt it was a fair fight, though. After all, she is a witch."

"*Our* supreme wolfmother!" Aatu angrily corrected while baring his fangs.

"Fair? He masked his scent to murder her, which would have killed Varg. I say she had a right to defend herself with any means necessary. There was nothing fair about that fight. Rafe got what was coming to him!" snarled Faolan.

The southern lycans growled as Faolan disrespected their former alpha, and one of their males, Otsoa, jumped forward and snarled in the face of the western lycan, who stood his ground in angry defiance.

"That human bitch is not one of us! She doesn't belong here!" Otsoa barked.

Hemming shoved the southern male away from Faolan and stood with his friends.

"Halea is our supreme wolfmother!" Faolan growled as red seeped into the edges of his brown eyes. "She kicked Rafe's ass, and she could kick your ass too, and if you say one more word, I'll tear your fucking throat out!"

Halea had saved Faolan's life more than once and had more than proven herself as an alpha bitch and a friend, and he was not about to stand by and let anyone disrespect her behind her back.

Without a moment wasted, claws were out, and fists were thrown, and suddenly everyone else in the area was watching in shock as the western and southern lycans brawled. Faolan's leg was still stiff, but he was no less capable as a fighter, and even Aatu chose to ignore his injured wrist as he entered the fray and took a bite out of one of the southern wolves. Hemming broke Loup's nose, but more of the southern lycans piled into the fight in defense of their pack-mates, who were quickly being overwhelmed.

"That's enough!" a voice roared, and everyone fighting froze in horror before turning to meet the fierce gaze of Raoul. "What is the meaning of this?" he snarled in a tone perilously close to rage.

"Your asshole pack decided to insult the supreme wolfmother," grumbled Faolan, though he turned his eyes to avoid the alpha's glare. He had seen those same angry eyes from Varg before, and he was all too familiar with the crushing weight of an alpha's will, and Raoul was no less intimidating.

"Is that true?" Raoul asked his pack-mates, but few would meet his gaze, and only Otsoa was able to muster the nerve to give an answer.

"She's not one of us. She is no wolfmother of mine."

Without hesitation, Raoul launched his fist into the beta male's stomach, causing him to double over and crumble to the ground.

"I've had enough of Rafe's shadow hanging over our heads," Raoul growled as he continued to stare down his own pack. "His hateful ways are why he's dead and why we're still not behaving as brothers and sisters. I will not hear of this again! If anyone else disrespects one of our supreme alphas, you will answer to me. Do I make myself clear?"

The rest of the southern wolves bowed their heads in fearful submission. Even if they disagreed with him, they knew better than to challenge their alpha. Everyone dispersed and went back to their business as if a fierce brawl had not just happened. Raoul remained to ensure that his pack mates moved along and did not cause any more trouble. Despite the southern alpha still watching over them, Faolan, Aatu, and Hemming felt better after letting off some steam, though the rumble didn't do Aatu's sore wrist any favors.

Faolan was surprised when he caught sight of Halea approaching them with concern on her face.

Raoul noticed her too and wondered how much of that spectacle she had seen. His anger had kept him distracted, and it didn't help that her human scent was just about everywhere in the den.

"We're sorry, Halea," Faolan quickly offered when she worriedly examined Aatu's wrist. Aatu tried not to flinch as she made him flex his fingers.

Halea rushed back when she heard there was a fight, but Raoul had already broken it up by the time she arrived. She was grateful for the help as Varg was off preparing for the races that were about to begin.

"Take it easy on this hand, would ya?" she admonished, though it looked like the injury hadn't been disturbed too much. "Be thankful Batsuba didn't catch you," she added, and Aatu's face turned bright red in embarrassment.

"Sorry," he meekly replied.

"You didn't have to do that for me, but thanks, guys," she said after finishing her examination. They could not see it, but beyond her smile, they could smell the saltiness of unshed tears.

"I did promise that if I ever caught anyone disrespecting you behind your back, that I'd rearrange their jaw. And I'd gladly do it again too," Faolan reminded, and Aatu and Hemming nodded their heads in firm agreement.

Halea laughed and smiled brighter as their support and devotion overflowed her heart with joy. She wasn't used to any other lycans than Varg sticking up for her, and it felt nice to know that her pack friends cared.

"You guys run along before the races start. I'll catch up," she said, and the three males reluctantly left her alone with the southern alpha.

Halea turned to find that Raoul had been openly observing their exchange the entire time, and she was curious about the strange look in his eyes.

"I have to apologize for the behavior of my pack. You have my word; they will not be disrespectful again," Raoul promised.

"I heard what you said to them, and it means a lot to me that our two packs get along. I know my presence has been a disturbance, but I do care about lycans. All lycans. Even you mangy southern wolves."

Raoul smiled at her teasing remark and was rewarded with a smile from her in return. Though he wanted to reserve judgment, it was quickly becoming clear that his cousin had managed to find an alpha she-wolf who lived within a human skin.

Perhaps she was a witch to be so powerful, but he could not detect the scent of lies as she spoke, and he was forced to concede that perhaps she really was a wolfmother.

"Yes, I can see that you do care, or the rest of your pack wouldn't have fought so loyally to defend your honor. Minds and hearts don't change quickly, but you managed to get a bunch of, as you say, mangy wolves, to acknowledge you as their alpha, and that's no small accomplishment. Rafe poisoned my people with his hateful ways, and I can only hope that my pack will learn to let go of his wicked beliefs in time. Our people need to be unified once more, especially if we're to survive the storm ahead."

Halea nodded her head in agreement. "Varg and I want this as well."

"I'm still undecided, just so you know."

"The festival has barely begun. You've still got plenty of time to think it over," Halea conceded with a grin, but she suspected Raoul was already beginning to make up his mind.

They parted, and Halea made for the edge of the den and towards the trees. She moved with a lighter spring in her step as hope bloomed within her. No doubt news of the squabble had already made its way to Varg as gossip spread quickly among lycans. She had promised to meet him out on the western hunting grounds in time to see him compete in the races, and she was already running late.

"Your presence stirs up shit even when you're not around."

Halea froze at the sound of a familiar woman's voice and noticed Otsana stepping out from beneath the thick trees.

"Lurking like a creep?" Halea asked.

"I wasn't lurking. I'm on my way to the races too!" Otsana angrily defended. "I saw that fight when it happened and got delayed."

"I would have thought you'd have been the first one to arrive at the races considering you disappeared right after watching that wrestling match with Fenris."

"Watching me like a creep?" Otsana accused.

"Hey, you owe me an explanation about what's been going on with you and Fenris since I left the east! I spent all that time trying to help you, and you wouldn't even talk to me."

"Owe you?" Otsana shouted. "I don't owe you jack shit! You left me in the east after saying you could train with me, but things are just the same. Fenris is still an asshole who acts like he's the next leader of the pack. Did you see what he did to your pack mate? He practically tore his whole hand off! That's what I'm up against, and you just took off. You didn't even care. You just left!"

Halea was surprised to see such hurt in the dark blue eyes of the eastern she-wolf and the subtle glisten of unshed tears.

"Hey, I care! It's just that I didn't have any control over that situation. It wasn't that I wanted to leave you in the lurch, but I didn't have a choice. I had to go."

"Shut up! Whether I live or die or lose my pack, none of it matters to you! Why should it? You already have your pack! You have everything, and I have nothing." Otsana shouted as her face burned red, and she took off through the trees. But it didn't matter how fast she ran; Otsana had already smelled the truth.

CHAPTER 8 – CRACK THE SKY

Halea stood dumbfounded as Otsana ran into the distance.

"*Did I really hurt her?*" she thought, though it seemed hard to believe. Otsana had always acted so reluctant to accept her help and been nothing but contentious the entire time she was in the east. She had assumed the she-wolf did not care that she was there and would have cared even less when she was gone.

"*I suppose I did leave without so much as a goodbye,*" Halea regretfully recalled. Otsana had approached her in anger on the day she left the east, but she had chalked it up to being a consistent part of the she-wolf's nature and not because she hadn't been the one to personally tell her that they were leaving. She didn't think that parting so abruptly would even bother Otsana. The eastern female had always acted as if she couldn't stand her presence, and she had just assumed she'd be happy to see her gone. But maybe she was wrong? Guilt gnawed her from the inside as she realized she didn't handle the situation as well as she should have. She had only callously wished Otsana luck without much thought for whether or not she was actually ready to face the hurdles ahead without her help and support.

Úlfa had begged her to help Otsana, but instead, she made a mess of things. Otsana didn't seem any more confident in her ability to challenge Fenris than when she first discovered the nature of their rivalry and abandoning her in her time of need probably didn't do her any favors.

"*Some wolfmother I am,*" Halea thought in bitter disappointment as she set out once more towards the western hunting grounds. Varg had sensed her tumult of emotions and prodded her with concern, and she dreaded having to explain it to him.

When Halea finally reached the stretch of open plain designated for the races, she found a large gathering of lycans milling about and from one of the clusters, hailed Varg. He separated himself from the crowd and made his way towards her.

"It's okay," she quickly stated at the concerned look in his eyes. "I take it, you heard?"

"The southern pack better watch their mouths," he grumbled. "Though I'm grateful Raoul broke it up before it got out of hand."

"I like him," Halea admitted.

"You know he challenged me, right?"

"I know, but he's not like Rafe. You two are more alike than you realize."

Varg could not help but raise an eyebrow in doubt.

"Then why were you just upset?"

"Oh…that," she said while sheepishly avoiding his searching gaze.

"Halea?" he asked in a stern tone, and she knew if she didn't explain herself, he would pull his alpha rank on her.

"I think I hurt Otsana," she confessed in shame.

"You? How? She's the one who always attacked you - physically and verbally. I rejected her for years, and it didn't even seem to faze her."

"I think she really did need my help when we were in the east, and I abandoned her. I think she thinks I turned my back on her or pretended to care when I was training her. Either way, she's upset."

"That is strange. Perhaps there's a heart under that icy bitch exterior after all," he mused before wrapping his arms around his upset mate. "I'm sure you two can talk it out. Try not to let it get to you. You were doing her a favor, and she could have been a bit more appreciative at the time."

Halea nodded and rested her head on his sturdy bare chest. He had removed most of his armor and fur pelts in preparation for the race that was about to begin.

"You're here now, so we can begin," he said before she looked up at him in shock.

"You weren't making everyone wait for me, were you?"

"Hell, yes! You're my good luck charm. Now, what favour will you give me?"

Varg had held back from participating in the wrestling matches. As wolf king, nobody else would have stood a chance against him anyway. When it came to fighting competitions, the alphas usually refrained, but they rarely held back for the non-violent sports. Varg had been looking forward to this race.

When they were children, they constantly raced to see who was the fastest, and the matter remained somewhat unsettled, but Halea was not interested in participating in this event. She didn't like the idea of being watched by so many spectators, and the lycans would run the course in their wolf forms.

Halea removed the blue crystal that matched the color of Varg's eyes from around her neck and placed it over his head. She had given it to him once long ago as a symbol of her feelings for him, and he carried it until the convergence separated them. She had always meant it to be for him, but after finding it in the wake of the devastation, she had kept it to remember him, and he had insisted she wear it ever since.

In his state of half-dress, he stood before her like a bronzed god as the warm spring light illuminated him through the few clouds that speckled the sky. She hadn't even realized she had stopped to ogle him until he smiled, revealing his gleaming white fangs and causing her face to flush with warmth.

"I guess you should keep it for luck until the festival is over," she said with a hint of embarrassment in her voice before reaching up on her toes to give him a sweet kiss to accompany her favour.

Allowing no brevity when it came to her affection, he wasted no time capturing her lips and holding her against him until the fierce pounding of her heart drowned out the commotion of the gathering all around them.

When he finally broke their kiss, she was limp and gasping for breath in his arms, her face even redder than it was a moment ago.

"You mangy wolf, don't you have a race?" she asked, suddenly feeling self-conscious that they were making a scene.

"I expect an even better prize when I win," he teased with a voracious grin.

Halea wished him luck one last time before heading to where the spectators would be waiting. As she passed some of the northern pack members, she noticed that Jance and Alf were also there. Alf gave his tiny mate one final hug for good luck before he too shifted form and joined the runners.

As soon as Jance caught sight of Halea, she came over.

"What'd you give Varg for his favour?"

"My crystal pendant. Well, our crystal, but it's his turn to hang onto it. What about you? What did you give Alf?"

Jance's eyes nervously shifted around her to make sure no one else was too close before she leaned towards Halea and whispered, "My undergarments."

The two women burst into a fit of giggles, causing some of the other lycans to look their way, but they ignored their judgment.

"I'll catch you later. I gotta go cheer for the north," Jance said with a gleaming smile before joining Bertolf and several other northern pack members.

Everyone gathered around the starting point as Varg and the other lycans participating in the race shifted into their wolf forms. Batsuba was also there, taking a rare break to enjoy the festivities, and Halea went to join her. When the lycans transformed, they were massive, far bigger than common wolves, and menacing to behold. Halea could easily spot Varg because of all the wolves, he was the largest and most intimidating, and his eyes always remained their same distinct shade of blue.

Marrok sounded the start of the race with a whistle, and the runners sprinted forward. It didn't take long for Varg to take the lead, and Halea cheered with the rest of the western pack as they watched the wolves run into the distance. Their course would take them beyond the vision of even the lycan spectators, but referees were stationed along their route and would send out howls to announce the runner's progress.

Marrok came over as soon as he noticed Halea standing with Batsuba.

"Oh, what a day for a race!" he commented as his ancient eyes shimmered with delight.

Batsuba merely nodded her head in curt agreement but kept her attention on the runners as they disappeared beyond the trees.

Halea had lost sight of them long before they reached that point as her human vision wasn't nearly as powerful as the lycan's, but she didn't have to see what was happening out there to know how Varg was doing. She could sense his smug elation.

"Varg's as cocky as ever, so I guess he's still in the lead," Halea said, and as if to accompany her statement, a howl rose in the distance.

"And he's left the competition in his dust," Batsuba confirmed as she translated the referee's announcement. "Well, he'll be even more insufferable now."

Halea laughed while shielding her eyes from the sun and staring out into the distance, hoping to catch some movement through the trees. When she couldn't see anything, and another moment passed, she turned instead to her fellow spectators.

54

Raoul and a few more from the southern pack had arrived in time to see the last half of the race, undoubtedly, to cheer on their own who were participating. Many members of the eastern pack were also there, including Ethelwolf and Ulfa, but Otsana appeared to be absent.

"*I thought she was coming to the race?*" Halea thought but eventually assumed that the she-wolf probably would not be interested in festivities or games after how upset she had just been. Again, guilt squeezed her stomach until it churned.

Batsuba noticed the sudden shift in Halea's expression as if a dark cloud had settled over her and stolen all her light and warmth away.

"What is it, Halea?" she asked.

"It's nothing. It's not Varg anyway. Just something I did."

Rather than dismiss the matter, the old healer continued to scrutinize her with her dark and knowing eyes.

"Now, now, Batsuba. She's still new to being a wolfmother," interjected Marrok before turning to Halea and placing a comforting hand on her shoulder. "You carry many burdens, my child. Don't be so hard on yourself. Mistakes will happen. Don't think about it anymore for just now. Enjoy the race."

Marrok's words proved to be unusually comforting, though Halea couldn't understand why. The elder couldn't possibly know the reason for her worries, but something about how he spoke led her to believe he understood more than it would seem.

Taking his advice, she turned back to the race in time to see small dots running in from a distance.

"Is that them?" she asked.

"Yep, and your mate's still in the lead," the healer replied as a smile tugged at the edges of her usually stern mouth. Batsuba was not without pride for her pack or her supreme alpha, but she would never dare admit it aloud. Varg's ego was already enough to fill an ocean, and she wasn't about to add to it. She was still curious about what was bothering her young apprentice but ultimately decided to let Halea handle it as she saw fit.

Everyone was cheering as the runners drew nearer, and Varg swiftly crossed the finish, followed second by Alf and third by a female from the southern pack. Fenris and two other eastern wolves came next, and everyone rushed forth to congratulate them.

Varg was hardly even winded when he returned to his humanoid form, and he eagerly swept Halea into his arms when she ran out to meet him.

Others rushed to congratulate Varg as well, and Halea could tell he was in his element as he beamed with pride under the praise of the other lycans.

After the commotion died, everyone made their way back to the den, but Varg and Halea hung back, taking their time and holding hands as they enjoyed their walk.

"I knew you'd win," Halea confessed.

"So did I," he teasingly bragged. "I only wish that you could have been there running by my side."

"I was there in a sense," she reminded. They were never truly apart with the bond they shared, and her words were the affirmation that pleased him most. He released her hand so that he could wrap his arm around her shoulders as they strolled back through the trees.

Further ahead, Halea saw that Jance and Alf were also taking their time walking back to the den. Jance was practically hopping around her large mate in excitement from the day's event, and Halea couldn't help but notice the exaggerated difference between them when they were close together. Alf was a big male, almost as big as Varg, but Jance was diminutive in comparison, and suddenly a terribly dirty thought crossed her mind as she tried to imagine what intimacy between those two must be like. Before she could stop it, a laugh escaped her throat, and she quickly tried to stifle herself, fearing Alf might hear her.

Varg sensed his mate's mirth, and her laughter and succeeding embarrassment sparked his curiosity.

"What? What am I missing?"

"Shh, nothing," she dismissed in a low voice, though she was unable to wipe the grin off her face.

"Oh, no, no. Whatever this joke is, I want in."

"I'll tell you later," she promised and tried again to not laugh at the pouting look of disappointment he gave her.

~~~⚬~~~

The next day proved to be a rainy one, but it didn't deter the lycans from enjoying their festival. The first hunting competition began before the crack of dawn, and Halea had wearily wished Varg luck when he set out. Though she wanted to go back to bed, she couldn't. It was going to be a busy day. While waiting for the hunt results, there were more fights to watch, and Halea could not help but feel tempted, but as an alpha, she refrained. Her reputation for defeating Rafe had ensured that almost every lycan took her seriously as a warrior and afforded her the respect due to one of her position.

Most of the fighting matches were males versus males and females versus females, but if they felt up to it, there were mixed matches as well. Faolan, with his fully healed leg, won a few fights against some of the southern wolves but was ultimately defeated by a pretty northern female, and everyone couldn't help but tease him for being too distracted.

The female fighting competitions were particularly interesting to watch, and Daciana brought pride to the western pack, but Halea couldn't help but notice that Otsana was nowhere to be found. The eastern she-wolf had always seemed so invested in putting on a tough bitch image, and whatever her doubts were about fighting Fenris, surely challenging other females wouldn't have been a problem for her.

Halea reminded herself to stay vigilant. She had enough problems without worrying about Otsana. During the gathering, as far as demon sightings or tears were concerned, things had remained quiet, too quiet, and with every day, she grew more and more anxious. She didn't want to seem suspicious, but she tried her best to unobtrusively remain close to Ethelwolf and keep an eye on him. At the first sign of danger, she wanted to be ready to spring into action, and so as the day wore on, she found herself out on the archery field.

Thanks to Aatu's ability to heal at therian speed, his dislocated wrist had already fully recovered, and he was enjoying the feel of his bow in his hands. The day's rain had dissipated to nothing more than a light mist, and the satisfying thwack of another arrow struck its target in the distance.

Everyone congratulated Ethelwolf on his excellent shot, and soon it was Hemming's turn.

Halea stood with Faolan and Daciana, who watched her mate with pride while her rambunctious son tugged her hand.

"Good luck, Daddy!" shouted Fillin, and Hemming's face lit up with joy as he turned back and waved at his mate and son.

Hemming effortlessly shot arrow after arrow, hitting every target, including the moving clay disks that were launched into the air, and everyone erupted into a roar of applause and approval at his spectacular marksmanship.

Aatu came next, and the spectators held their breath as every shot was loosed with perfection, but for one. As one of the clay disks soared into the distance, his arrow just glanced the object, which didn't fully shatter on impact, and the audience cried out in disappointment.

When the disk was retrieved, it was found to be missing a large chip but was otherwise intact. If not for that, it would have been a tie, but Hemming was once again declared the winner.

Though Aatu was disappointed to have lost, he bore no ill will and was the first to congratulate Hemming as everyone swarmed him with praise. Hemming patted his friend on the back and wished him better luck next year. Though he hadn't won, Aatu had come even closer to defeating Hemming than the year before, and so he remained determined. He would keep practicing, and he was sure it would only be a matter of time before he replaced the older male as the best archer among the lycans.

There was no escaping the ribbing that came from Faolan, though.

"Lost by a chip!

"Hey, at least I didn't lose because I got caught staring at some ass," snapped Aatu.

"I don't entirely regret that. I'm having dinner with her later," Faolan laughed, and Aatu couldn't help but join him.

"You've still improved, though," Faolan added. "I'll bet Hemming is going to be sweating from now to next year every time he sees you practicing. Come on, Chips, let's get some ale and catch a few more fights before the hunters return.

Aatu playfully punched his friend in the stomach before they set off.

Halea remained off to the side, watching as everyone slowly went on to other activities. Hemming was standing with Fillin on his shoulders and his mate by his side as Ethelwolf and Úlfa congratulated him on his win. Ethelwolf had come in third, and the males were talking technique while Daciana and Úlfa shared their own private conversation.

Everyone seemed to be having a good time, and while Halea was relieved that the gathering was going well, worry dogged at her every step. The Spring Moon was drawing near, and she couldn't help but hope that maybe things would be okay. Maybe Corbin's vision wouldn't come to fruition, and nobody would have to lose someone they loved, but even though she wanted to believe that, she couldn't.

"Forgive me for calling upon you, wolf gods. I know I'm not really a lycan, but please watch over them. Protect them," Halea prayed.

"I don't think you have to worry about impressing our gods," came a familiar voice, and Halea spun in shock to find Marrok, who evidently overheard her prayer.

"They like you well enough. They gave you Varg, didn't they?"

"Considering I broke an oath, I suppose he wasn't a gift from Tiamet," she replied with a smile.

"You were a gift to him. The gods laid you in his path."

"Actually, I stumbled on him in the woods," Halea corrected with a laugh as she remembered the day she fell in front of a snarling wolf with blue eyes.

"All right, they laid him in your path. Either way, I'm sure it happened for a reason."

"You seem to understand an awful lot about the gods," she observed.

"It's because I'm older than dirt, as Batsuba would say," he replied with a laugh. "I remember the world when it was new, back when the first descendants still walked among us. Most of them have gone dormant, yet I'm still awake. I possess the wisdom of the ages, and the only reason my immortality hasn't driven me mad is because I haven't forgotten the joys of life."

Batsuba had once told Halea that Marrok's eccentricities were due to his advanced age, but she had dismissed it as the healer's annoyance.

"Is that why all the first descendants are gone?" she asked.

"Oh, they're not all gone, though they are very few. I hear Corbin is still hanging around, but he has a duty to his father, Morigan, the god of the dead, and that keeps him grounded. But, yes, for most, their immortality was too much to bear, and so they fell into the sleep of dormancy, and no one knows where they are or if they'll ever awake again. It was either sleep or go mad from watching the ages roll by, the years without number, the turning of the seasons to them as no more than the blink of an eye to a mortal. There is such a thing as too much life. It can make you weary. So very weary."

"But what about all the other immortals? Won't they get tired?"

"Of course, which is why many, as Batsuba says, 'get daft with age' and for others, well; there are those who get desperate enough to take matters into their own hands," he explained.

"Why can't they sleep?"

"Dormancy is a gift from the gods to their first children. For the rest of us, there is no relief."

Halea grew thoughtful as her mind turned to Lord Anshar. She hadn't spoken to him since the gathering began. He was a second-generation therian, and his parents had long been dormant, and she wondered if the toll of the ages hadn't added to his madness. Tiamet had given him the task of overseeing the faith and banishing the convergences, and so bound by duty, he was expected to endure a long life of loneliness and despair with no end in sight. It was no wonder that he had finally had enough.

"Lord Anshar was already tired of it all before he threw himself into the Chaos," she thought out loud. "Maybe his mind was already slipping."

"That may very well be the case. He was given the burden of the world. He carries both Tiamet's favor and her curse."

Halea wasn't sure if that was a comfort or not. She hated to think that she might be the sole reason for Lord Anshar's sacrifice because then she would also be partly responsible for the mess they were in, and the teeth of guilt were already gnawing into her enough as it was. Perhaps it would have been better for the whole world if she had just died in the fire when the Citadel of the Sun was destroyed.

"And now the burden is yours," continued Marrok, who hadn't missed her morose contemplation. "Trust in the gods. Dragons, wolves - whichever you like. We're in their hands now."

~~~☼~~~

As Halea neared the den, howls rang out, causing her heart to nearly seize in her chest. Somewhere across the bond, Varg immediately reached out, attempting to soothe her, and she realized that they were only announcing the hunter's return.

"Damn it! I'm going to have to learn to speak wolf or at least learn to understand it before I have a heart attack," she thought in defeat.

When Halea reached the den, the sun was beginning to set, and everyone was already congratulating the hunters who had returned with an absurd amount of game and were showing off their prizes. There were stags, elks, muskox, wild boar, mountain goats, and even a few bears.

Bertolf, Raoul, and Varg had clearly brought in more meat than any of the other hunters and were waiting patiently as their kills were hoisted onto a massive balancing scale. Whoever brought in the most meat by weight would be the winner.

"Welcome home," Halea greeted, and Varg embraced her the moment she was near. "Wow, that's a ton of meat."

"Two tons! So far. They're still putting mine on the scale," he exclaimed with a laugh.

"I don't think I can eat that many hearts," she bemoaned.

When all the meat was at last weighed, Raoul rose victorious, beating out Varg by only a small margin.

Varg hated to lose, but it was only the first hunting competition, there would be a few more before the gathering was through, and there was always a certain element of luck involved. He harbored no ill will towards his cousin as he offered him his hand in congratulations.

"You made me fight for it. I like that," Raoul conceded as he accepted Varg's hand and extended the gesture into a friendly embrace.

Hope and joy swelled within Halea as the two males hugged with more sincerity than when Raoul had first arrived at the gathering, and she could sense that Varg was warming up to his cousin.

A swarm of volunteers was soon hard at work skinning, gutting, cleaning, and preparing the meat for storage and that evening's meal.

Many gathered around Varg to hear more about the details of the day's hunt, and Halea left them to it as she went to help her volunteers prepare for the dinner feast and celebration.

Úlfa and Ralphina arrived to assist with the preparations when suddenly the rain began to fall.

"Great, looks like we're going to have to move the celebration into the caverns," Halea said to the females, who swiftly went to work clearing out the common area.

The only cavern large enough to hold the entire gathering was high up on the den's northeastern edge. Varg and the other alphas joined to ensure that everyone filed up the path in an orderly fashion as the rain continued to pelt down. Once almost everyone was up the side of the mountain, the massive iron double doors were opened wide, and the multitude filed inside as a bolt of lightning cracked the darkening sky.

When Halea looked back, her blood turned to ice as a tear opened on the mountainside, blocking their path back down to the den. Screams of terror mixed with howls of danger and panic spread at the sound of emerging demons, and all at once, the dimensional rift erupted with the servants of Chaos.

"Everyone into the cavern!" shouted Varg as he unsheathed the Fang.

Halea cursed that she didn't have her spear, and there was no chance for her to retrieve it in time. All she had was the knife tucked into one of the secret inner pockets of her robe that Varg had given her. She would have to depend on the warriors to battle most of the demons while she sealed the tear.

"Úlfa, please, get everyone into the cavern," Halea called.

"Be careful, Halea," the other wolfmother bade as Halea forced her way through the chaotic crowd and the pouring rain, back towards where the rest of the warriors stood to face the demons head-on.

Warriors from all the packs, led by the four alphas, assembled between the advancing demon horde and the lycan families taking refuge within the cavern. Halea was soon by Varg's side, her knife in hand. With only a glance, they knew they could depend on each other.

"I'll use the Fang to make a path for Halea. Once she makes it to the tear, we have to guard her at all costs. She's the only one who can seal it," Varg announced, and the others gave him room as he raised his sword. With a mighty force, he dropped the blade. A blinding white blast shot forth, searing through hundreds of the advancing demons whose shrieks filled the air. Still, the path ahead was not clear as even more of Chaos' servants emerged from the tear.

"What now?" asked Raoul.

"We're going in!" replied Varg before charging ahead with Halea behind him, and the other warriors followed. Again, he swung the Fang, and again the power of the sword demolished every demon in its wake until, finally, a path to the tear was cleared.

Halea raced ahead, dodging demons and purifying any that dared to come near her glowing fists as she made for the swirling purple vortex. The warriors entered the fray all around her, some changing into their wolf forms and others remaining humanoid as they tore into demons with claws and fangs. Whenever Varg shouted the order, the lycan warriors would fall back just enough to give him space to wield the Fang, but there was no end to the demon numbers. Soon another flood of dark servants poured from the tear, blocking Halea's ability to get close enough to seal the dimensional rift. With every moment, the tear was growing larger, and her desperation was rising as no matter how she dodged or where she ran, the servants of Chaos seemed intent on singling her out and separating her from the safety of the pack.

"I'm not wearing a priestess uniform anymore, but they must know that I'm blessed. Is this because of Lord Anshar?" Halea thought in dismay as she recalled how the mysterious entity had infiltrated the Dragon Lord's mind, and it made her wonder just how much the Chaos really knew about her.

Their numbers were too many, and soon the swarm was closing in. Before Halea knew it, she was separated from the pack as she fought to purify every servant of Chaos that came within reach as the rain continued to pour down. A black-eyed demon with a humanoid upper body and the long tail of a snake pulled out a dark sword as it leaped ahead of the others and went straight for Halea. Her knife was no match for the demon's weapon, and she narrowly dodged the swing of its blade when its tail lashed out, knocking her feet out from under her and causing her to drop her weapon. She tried to scramble away, but before she could get back up, its tail wrapped around her leg and dragged her towards its waiting sword. She tried to pull away, but her strength was useless as her fingers could find nothing to grasp and only raked through the slippery mud as it dragged her to her doom.

"Halea!" shouted Varg as he reached her just in time to block the black-eyed demon's sword with the Fang. With him were the rest of the lycans who fought to keep the swarm off them. Halea desperately tried to shake free of the demon's tail as Varg locked blades with the beast, who put up an impressive fight against the wolf king's masterful swordsmanship. As they battled over her, Halea's hand brushed against the cold steel of her knife buried in the mud beside her, and grasping the hilt, she called upon the Goddess as she stabbed the demon's tail, causing it to explode in the white light of purification. Varg quickly helped her to her feet.

"Are you okay?"

Though covered from head to toe in mud, Halea nodded as the battle raged around them.

"Get behind me!" Varg shouted to his people, and the warriors ducked or braced themselves, as again, the destruction of the Fang was unleashed.

In that one moment of silence that succeeded the shrieks of the demons as they were wiped clean from the earth, Halea raced for the tear only to be blocked as more demons emerged. Time was running out. If the rift grew much larger, it would be too much for her to seal alone, and soon she found herself outnumbered.

She readied her knife for one last desperate charge and called upon Tiamet when a massive shaggy grey wolf leaped between her and the advancing horde and mercilessly tore into the demons, biting off heads and limbs and swiping them down with its massive paws.

"No, don't, you're too close to the tear!" she shouted through the rain while narrowly dodging the flashing dark weapon of another wraith before purifying it with her charged knife.

But it was too late. The wolf was swarmed, and it let out a piercing howl that ended in a whimper as the servants of Chaos fell upon it and repeatedly stabbed it without mercy until it struggled no more.

"Damn you!" Halea shouted as her entire body burned with Tiamet's light, and she raced ahead, slashing down every demon that fell in her path and striking them with her purified fists until they burst into white flame. Varg and the other warriors were close behind her, holding back the rest of the servants of Chaos until Halea finally reached the tear, and raising her hands, she called upon the Goddess.

"Tiamet, give me strength," she prayed as her power surged forth. The sounds of battle filled her ears; the clashing of swords as Varg fought against the wraiths, the screams of pain mixed with shrieks and howls, and the sickening splatter of blood as the lycans fought to defend her.

She kept her eyes closed to avoid seeing into the Chaos. Instead, she focused on Tiamet's power that flowed through her body and enveloped the swirling purple vortex that slowly began to shrink. Sweat beaded on her brow only to be washed away by the rain, and her hands shook - the tear was too big. It had grown too fast, but she had to be strong enough. She couldn't let them down.

"Tiamet, please," she begged, and just as her strength was about to falter, the tear snapped closed, and thunder rolled in the sky.

Her body violently trembled, and despite the cold spring rain drenching through her robes, she was burning hot. She struggled to remain standing as the world swam before her eyes, and just when she felt that she would collapse, strong arms encircled her waist and lifted her from her feet.

"It's okay, Halea, I've got you," Varg promised as he held her close. The battle's commotion carried on as the remaining demons were slaughtered or chased into the trees where they escaped. Without the tear to defend, they fanned out, and if not quickly caught and eliminated, they could eventually open more dimensional rifts.

"Track them down! Don't let them escape!" Varg commanded, and several dozen warriors broke off and chased after the fleeing demons.

"The injured?" she asked.

"There's a few, but worse...Halea, it's Ethelwolf. He's gone," he replied with strain evident in his voice and a glistening in his eyes that was not from the rain.

He shuddered against her as his emotions tore through their bond, and his anguish caused tears to spill from her eyes. It was more than the loss of a comrade or someone he deeply respected, Ethelwolf had been like family to him, and now he was gone.

Halea's tears were not just because of her empathic link to Varg; Ethelwolf had been kind to her. He had given her a chance. Though it was tenuous between them at first, in time, the eastern alpha had come to accept her, and she had admired his nobility and his obvious devotion to his people, his family, and to Varg.

They had both desperately hoped that they could prevent the swordmaster's prophecy, but they failed. There was nothing they could have done that would have changed the unfortunate fate of the eastern alpha, and this revelation struck Varg the hardest as he clutched his mate in his arms.

As Varg and Halea openly wept for the loss of their friend, many others joined them as they gathered around the fallen body of the eastern alpha, and keening howls of mourning rose into the air amidst sobs and laments. Ethelwolf had reverted to his humanoid form, his lifeless eyes staring blankly into the heavens. Raoul reached down and gently closed them before several members of the eastern pack approached and hoisted their fallen alpha up from the muddy ground.

Though weakened and feeling ill to her stomach, Halea insisted on tending to those injured by the dark weapons. It took almost every last ounce of her strength to rid the two injured southern males, and one of the northern females of the last remains of the evil poison of the dark weapons, and Varg had fretted over her the entire time as she grew noticeably pale. Once the job was done, she wanted to be sick, but she struggled to contain herself as Varg lifted her in his arms once more. The injured were taken back to the den, but the eastern wolves carried Ethelwolf's body back up the path, and Varg followed behind with Halea.

As they approached the top, Halea heard the frantic wailing and sobbing of someone in unbearable pain. As everyone parted to make way for the returning warriors, it was then that through the darkness, Halea saw who was crying – it was Úlfa.

The eastern wolfmother had ushered everyone to safety within the cavern, but after the doors were shut, she could focus on nothing but the bond she shared with her mate, who was out there fighting to protect their people.

And then the bond was broken.

Her scream of unbridled pain echoed throughout the cavern, and everyone knew. In desperation, she threw open the doors and tried to run out to find him, but Otsana and several other members of her pack restrained her. It was too late. There was nothing she could do for her beloved mate. Her soul was rent. Broken beyond repair. Defeated, she collapsed to her knees as her daughter held her, and the two wept without restraint for the lost patriarch of their family.

Halea's tears renewed at the display of grief before her. She knew that pain, that loss, she had felt it once before when the swordmaster severed her bond with Varg to carry his soul before the wolf gods. But Varg had returned. For Úlfa, her mate would never come back.

Ethelwolf was gently laid upon the ground before his pack and family, and everyone wept and hung their heads in sorrow.

Úlfa's sobs eventually stopped, but the light was gone from her eyes as she rose to her feet and went to the body of her fallen mate. She gazed on his face as silent tears streamed down her cheeks before kneeling to lovingly caress his face.

"Oh, Erish. I'm coming,"

"Mother?" Otsana asked.

Úlfa rose once again and turned to face her daughter.

"It's time. I must join him," Úlfa replied, and her daughter's face turned as hard as stone.

"No! No, Úlfa, don't!" Halea cried.

Lycans were incapable of carrying on without the bond they shared with their mate. Some could hold out for a few years if they had small children to raise, but once their cubs reached adulthood, the grieving parent would join their lost mate in the next world.

Otsana was a grown woman, and with Ethelwolf gone, for Úlfa, there was nothing left.

Úlfa glanced at Halea and offered her a sad smile.

"It's okay, Halea. Wolfmother. Don't cry. Please look after Otsana for me."

With conflict in her heart, Halea nodded and broke into a sob as Varg set her on her feet while keeping her wrapped within his arms.

Varg mourned for Úlfa too, but he understood. He had seen many other lycans suffer this same fate. Even his own father could not survive the grief of losing a mate, and he knew it was unavoidable. Everyone knew. Every lycan there among them silently wept but remained still in the face of what was to come.

Úlfa turned back to Otsana, who stood motionless with her hands balled into trembling fists at her side. The eastern wolfmother wrapped her arms around her shaking daughter and quietly spoke a single word into her ear that was drowned out to everyone else by the noise of the wind and rain.

With lips pursed into a tight quivering line, Otsana nodded her head once and watched as her mother turned and walked towards the mountain's edge.

"No. No, this is wrong," Halea protested when she could bear it no longer. "This is wrong! Stop her! Somebody, stop her, please! Somebody, stop her! Otsana! Otsana, don't let her do this!" she shrieked as she broke away from Varg's grasp and ran to Otsana, taking hold of her furs and shaking her until the she-wolf was forced to meet her gaze, but there was nothing but cold emptiness beyond the dark blue of her eyes.

"Stop her, please! Don't let her do this!"

Otsana said nothing as Halea released her grip.

"Halea, this is the way it must be," Varg said as he reached out and tried to calm his mate, but she spun away from his grasp and raced to catch up with Úlfa, who was approaching the edge.

"Úlfa, no! Stop. You don't have to do this," Halea sobbed, but in her weakened state, Varg caught up to her and tackled her before she could reach the eastern wolfmother. "No, Varg. Stop her! Someone stop her, please!" she screamed while thrashing in Varg's arms until he was forced to pick her up and carry her away.

"Úlfa! Úlfa!" Halea screamed as Varg whisked her back down the mountain, sparing her from hearing the sickening crunch as Úlfa's body plummeted onto the rocks below.

CHAPTER 9 – FIGHT

Even after taking her back to their private hot spring to wash off the mud and carrying her to their bed, Halea was inconsolable.

Varg's chest was soaking wet with tears, but he never let Halea go as she sobbed to the point of nearly making herself sick from hyperventilating. Úlfa's death had broken her, and he felt nothing but torment inside because he knew it was more than just the loss of the eastern wolfmother – it was him.

Halea had known the truth of what happened when lycans lost a mate for a long time, and she knew that Varg would do the same if he ever lost her, but somehow, seeing it for herself made it unbearably real. When the swordmaster severed their bond, it had been only for a moment. Would she have longed for death if Varg's soul had never returned? She was told that because she was human, it would be different for her, that she could live on, but she didn't know if that was true. Humans usually didn't end their lives with the death of a partner, though it wasn't unheard of. But for lycans, it was different. Once mated, they couldn't go on without their bond and would seek to join their mates in the next life by any means necessary. The emptiness she saw in Úlfa's eyes haunted her as she imagined what it would be like if it were Varg. She would have to be dead and gone first for that to happen, but that did not matter. She couldn't bear to think of the light going out in Varg's beautiful eyes because of losing her. She didn't want to imagine him destroying himself, even if that was the only way for them to be together, but inside, the creeping terror brought whispered doubts.

She was still Tiamet's last chosen sacrifice. What if there was no other hope? She was bound to Varg through blood and spirit, and if anything happened to her, he would die, and it would be all her fault. Her very existence had cursed him.

"They were after me. I know they were after me, just like that mimic I found in the forest or that black-eyed demon in the chariot. Chaos knows that I'm the last chosen of Tiamet. It must know. It was in Lord Anshar's head. Ethelwolf and Úlfa are dead because my presence drew the Chaos here, and if anything happens to me, you'll die too!"

"Halea, don't…"

"And what if there is no other way? What if my death is the only solution?"

He wanted to tell her that everything would be okay, that he could protect her, but the swordmaster's prophecy hung over him more ominously than ever before. They had failed to protect Ethelwolf. Despite all their vigilance and best efforts, the crow's prophecy had been inevitable. He could no longer mask the bond as terror and helplessness welled up within him as he realized her fate was sealed – she would die. He would lose her. Someday. Somehow. He would lose her. And she wanted the comfort of knowing that he would never harm himself or suffer if he lost her, but he could not offer her that comfort. He couldn't lie and tell her that he wouldn't follow her into the next world. He knew that she felt guilty for jeopardizing his life, but he could not allow her to feel that way.

"Halea, I won't have you blaming yourself for whatever happens to me. Your Goddess didn't bless you. She cursed you. This is all her fault. None of this should have ever been placed on your shoulders, and to be honest, it shouldn't have been placed on the other priestesses either, perhaps not even the dragon. What good has come of it? If Tiamet wanted to save this world, why can't she just banish the convergence herself? Why kill those who love and worship her? Why torment her own kin? What kind of merciful Goddess is that? I know you think you've doomed me, but I will never regret meeting you and falling in love with you. Never."

She wept silently as he spoke. It wasn't that she wanted to give up, but more with every day, hope seemed to be slipping between her fingers.

"I want to believe that Tiamet can still save us, but if not, then what hope is there?" she asked.

He gently stroked the tears from her cheek as he gazed into her shimmering hazel-green eyes.

"There's me. There's us. You said it yourself; we're a team – aren't we? Whatever the future brings, we need to face it together. You'd fight for me, wouldn't you?"

"Of course, until my last breath," she proclaimed.

"And I'll fight for you – until my last breath. No matter what happens, we'll be together - always. So, no more dwelling on the worst possible scenario because this fight's not over yet. I'm going to do everything in my power to protect you, and I know you'll do the same for me." Though Varg didn't know when or how their end would come, he knew they would fight to save their people and their world together. The wolf gods had given him the power to fight alongside her for a reason, and as their vessel, he would not back down from the storm ahead.

"Oh, Varg, I love you so much," she said as her heart swelled into her throat. His words lifted her up out of the darkness and rekindled the fire of determination within her.

"I love you too, Halea. I swear; I'll never let you go."

~~~~·❍·~~~~

The rain finally stopped, and the air smelled fresh and sweet. In the distance, above the trees, a rainbow shimmered.

Samesa loved the spring and lived for the coming of summer. Everything was vibrant green as she moved through the forest. Things had been quiet, only a few bestial demons, but no new tears. Occasionally, she would encounter some fellow priestesses, who were also reporting a strange lull in Chaos's activity.

But she never dropped her guard.

67

Since her strange encounter with the demon that mimicked a human child, Samesa had become distrusting of everyone she encountered in her wanderings. She couldn't shake an unsettling worry that gnawed at her from the inside. Why did that demon attack her mind instead of just killing her right away? What information could it want?

"Damn it!" Samesa cursed as one of her bootlaces popped, and she tossed her bag and spear down in irritation before finding somewhere to sit where she could perform a mending spell. Her feet were killing her anyway, and it felt nice to pull the boot off and stretch out her toes. She never wore shoes or boots as a child as she had always preferred to run around barefoot and would even put up a fuss when her mother insisted that she wear a pair of sandals for special occasions. There was no escaping the necessity for sturdy footwear in the comparably colder northern lands.

She remembered the first time she complained to Rena, her mentor cleric, about her toes being cold when they finally reached the holy city of Ruinac. Rena had left her alone and disappeared to some random stall in the marketplace, and when she returned, she was carrying a shiny black pair of leather boots with glittering silver buckles running up the sides.

They were beautiful, and the moment Samesa put them on her feet, she felt instant relief from the cold. She had hugged Rena in gratitude for the wonderful gift, and the cleric laughed at her youthful exuberance.

Something wet trickled down the side of her face, and when Samesa brushed it away, she found that she was crying.

It always hurt inside when Samesa thought of her cleric mentor. She had been away on a mission when Rena died, and she never got to say goodbye. She never had the chance to thank her for saving her life or setting her on her destined path. She had always just assumed there would always be enough time to say all those things, but she was an immortal, and Rena was not. She would have to live every day for the rest of eternity, carrying that regret like an unshakable weight.

As Samesa worked the simple spell to mend her broken bootlace, she heard a rustling through the brush. Someone was coming. She quickly dropped her boot and snatched her spear, but she sighed in relief when the familiar, red-hooded robe of a cleric appeared through the trees.

"Gods, you startled me," she declared with a laugh that released the tension from within her.

"Samesa?" the hooded cleric asked.

"Yes, were you looking for me? Who are you?"

"It's me, Rena," the cleric replied while pulling down the hood of her robe.

Samesa's dark eyes grew wide, and she forgot to breathe as she beheld the unmistakable face of her mentor. She looked a little older, a few more gray hairs, but it was her. It was Rena.

"Rrr...Rena? No, it can't be. You died. They said you died when I was on a mission. I saw your grave."

"That wasn't me, Samesa. It was a mistake. I never died. I'm here. I've been looking all over for you. I've missed you so much," Rena explained while stepping closer, and Samesa's heart thundered in her chest.

It seemed too incredible to believe, but it had to be true, and a choking sob erupted from Samesa's throat as she reached out to embrace her lost friend.

Before Samesa could reach Rena's outstretched arms, someone grabbed her from behind and pulled her away.

"Don't touch it!" a man's voice commanded.

"Let go!" Samesa shouted as she struggled within the powerfully strong arms of her captor, but suddenly Rena sprang forward, her face twisting and distorting as her chest split open, revealing a long, spiked appendage that shot out towards her.

Samesa screamed in horror, but the person holding her pulled her to the side in time to avoid the stab of the barb, and before she could react, he produced a dagger.

"Get back, demon!" he shouted while brandishing his weapon, and Rena's deformed face tore open revealing mandibles that snapped as it shrieked, but the man threw his dagger into the creature's throat.

Samesa wasted no time charging her spear and springing in-between the man and the demon, where she struck the creature with all her strength. It let out a horrible piercing wail as it burst from the purification, and an acrid green smoke rose like a cloud from its charred remains and eerily slipped between the trees.

"Are you okay?" the man asked.

As Samesa watched the last of the smoke disappear, she could focus on nothing else, and his words were muffled by the pounding of her pulse within her ears.

"Hey, Samesa, are you all right?" he asked again, and she registered a warm hand on her shoulder, which startled her to her senses.

Finally, turning to address the stranger, she took notice of his appearance.

"It's you!"

She recognized the tall, slender man with the wavy brown hair and the long, thin face and shining black eyes as the mysterious stranger she once met when she was alone in the woods. He must have remembered her as well because he had called her by name.

"Heh. Yeah. Me again. I'm sorry for scaring you like that, but you were in danger, and I had to step in."

"But how? Who are you?"

His glittering black eyes darted around nervously, and there was an uncomfortably long silence before he finally replied.

"Sufur. I'm...a ranger."

"Sufur? That's a terrible name. I don't believe you. You don't sound like you're from around here, and you're not dressed like a ranger. They usually travel in groups. Who are you really?" she interrogated while narrowing her eyes in scrutiny. No ordinary man could hold back her superior priestess strength. There was something strange about him and the way he spoke as if he came from a foreign land.

"No, it's true! I am a ranger," he quickly defended. "My mother and I crossed the sea to come to this country when I was quite young. I guess my name is unusual here.

69

Normally we rangers do travel in groups, but between our usual duties and all these strange demon attacks, most of us have split up to cover more ground."

"And your uniform?" Samesa asked with a raised eyebrow.

"Look, you're not going to believe me if I tell you that it was stolen."

"Stolen?" she incredulously shouted.

"It's a pretty funny story, actually, but I'd appreciate it if you didn't rat me out for it. The others wouldn't let me live it down."

Samesa looked him up and down but still didn't believe him.

"And you're just wandering around in the wilds without any gear?"

"I'm used to it out here and don't need much in the way of gear. I was practically raised outdoors. I don't even need a tinder kit because I'm a fire-caster."

"Prove it."

He held out his hands and spoke a few words in the ancient language, and a tiny flame appeared above his palms.

Samesa could not help but be convinced. Rangers were known for their skill with elemental spells, and she did recall that he had offered her the warmth of his fire when she first met him in the woods. He didn't have any gear then, either. Maybe he had just seemed unusually strong because she had let her guard down.

"I'm sorry for doubting you," Samesa said while gazing jealously at the tiny flame that dwindled away within his hands. She had always wished to have mastery of just such an elemental spell but had never shown any aptitude for magic use beyond what the Goddess had given her.

"Don't worry about it. I can't blame you for being on your guard after what we've both just seen," he said while smiling in relief to finally have her trust.

A wave of nausea seized her as she recalled the horrible demon mimic. It had presented itself as the shade of Rena – a shade mimic. Sufur had distracted her for a moment, but now her mind reeled at the implications of what she had just seen. It was a demon. It was just like the demon that mimicked the child, and when it was slain, it produced the same mysterious green smoke. But why Rena?

"It disguised itself as my cleric mentor. She's dead. Has been for years. But how did it know what she looked like? How did it know my name? And how could you tell that it was a demon when I couldn't?"

"It stank of demon," he replied.

"But I didn't smell anything."

His eyes darted away from hers as he quickly explained. "You must have been too distracted to notice. I was passing through the woods when I heard voices. That's when I saw that you were in danger."

Samesa wasn't sure what he meant by stinking of demon. Some of the more bestial servants of Chaos did have a foul stench about them, but the humanoid demons did not have a noticeable smell unless they were cut open as their blood was noxious. Perhaps she really was too distracted to notice that detail.

"This isn't the first shade mimic I've encountered," she explained. "A while back, I found a little boy lost and alone in the forest. He was begging for help. When I got close, he did something to me. He got into my head. I saw my memories. My childhood. My journey to the north. Rena. I fought the creature out of my mind, and when I came to, it was no longer a child, but a demon, and when I killed it, that same strange green smoke rose from its remains and escaped into the woods. Perhaps it didn't fully die. It just took what it wanted from my mind and passed the knowledge on to another mimic who could use a more clever deception to finish the job."

"If you had any secrets, they might be compromised now," Sufur pondered with a furrowed brow.

Samesa thoughtfully gnawed her lip. There could only be one thing the Chaos would want from her.

"I know where all of our priestesses have been hiding, and I bet the Chaos knows now too. I have to warn them," she shouted while scrambling to get her boot back on.

"Is there anything I can do to help?" he asked with genuine concern in his dark, glittering eyes.

"Yes, if you see any priestesses or clerics in your travels, approach with caution. If they really are servants of Tiamet and not more demons in disguise, tell them to contact me or find me as soon as possible and warn them to trust no one and beware the shade mimics."

"If I see anyone of your faith, I'll spread the word. But what about you, will you be okay?"

Samesa clenched her fist tight around her spear before replying. "I won't be fooled again."

~~~⟡~~~

Halea remained silent as the elders conducted the funeral rites. As a wolfmother, she probably should have offered a few prayers, but she could not speak. The words remained caged behind her lips, and if she opened her mouth to try, her breath would hitch, and her eyes would grow moist.

Varg stood with his arms wrapped around her from behind in loving support as, one by one, the lycans stepped forward to add stones to the cairns, along with flowers and other offerings. These were only temporary graves. When the gathering was over, the bodies of the eastern alphas would be carried home to their own sacred burial grounds, where they would be permanently laid to rest.

When Otsana approached the graves, she knelt and added flowers and a few more stones to the piles, but despite her actions, her face was emotionless, and her eyes were empty and dry. Halea turned in Varg's embrace and buried her face in his chest as she shed the tears that Otsana could not.

The she-wolf turned her dark blue eyes on the alpha pair. For the briefest moment, a shadow of jealous longing passed over her face, but she said nothing and lowered her gaze before slowly trudging back down the path towards the den.

"I should talk to her," Halea said when they were finally all alone.

Varg nodded and gave her one last gentle squeeze of encouragement before releasing her from his arms. Since the attack on the den, warriors from all four packs had set out to find the remaining demons that escaped that night, and many had already been caught and slain, though a few eluded them by fleeing beyond the borders of their territory. With the den's safety compromised, everyone was on edge, and Varg had ordered sentries to guard the perimeter of their lands to ensure that the servants of Chaos did not return.

When Varg and Halea returned to the den, every face was darkened with despair, and the once lively atmosphere had grown sour with grief. Groups of lycans clustered around unlit fire pits and muttered voices spoke of what would become of the eastern pack without its alpha pair.

"Alpha Varg," a voice called, and a lycan male stepped forward and bowed. It was Fenris.

Varg looked down on the eastern male and reluctantly acknowledged him. Beside him, Halea grew tense.

"You may speak, brother Fenris."

"I wish to state my formal intent to battle for the right to be the eastern alpha. Let any who wish to challenge me come forth!" Fenris loudly declared, and the den erupted in shocked voices mixed with shouts of support and dissent.

Halea was about to open her mouth in protest when Varg placed a gentle hand on her shoulder. Though the eastern alphas had only just been buried, this was the lycan way, and she balled her hands into fists as she swallowed her anger.

"I will challenge!" shouted Ivaylo, a male from the eastern pack, and soon one more, Lovel, stepped forward to also announce his claim.

"Very well. Tonight – let it be decided," Varg declared as he raised his voice above the din.

The crowd dispersed as everyone swarmed the challenger of their choice to offer encouragement or praise, but Halea could not help but notice that Otsana was nowhere to be found.

"Her scent trail runs that way," Varg said while pointing out past the northwestern tree-dwellings and towards the edge of the hunting grounds. "Find her."

"I will," Halea promised while racing away from the den.

Years of tracking demons allowed her to easily discern the she-wolf's path as the light footprints of someone walking alone stretched out through the trees and towards where the river flowed before the vantage point. There, she found Otsana sitting upon the rocks at the river's edge, staring absently into the flowing water as the sun set in the west.

"What do you want?" Otsana grumbled without even looking behind.

Halea knew the direction of the wind had betrayed her, but spying had not been her intent, so she approached the eastern she-wolf.

"I'm sorry for your loss."

"Why do you care?" Otsana snapped. "They weren't even your parents…and yet you... Why do you care?" she asked again, her voice quieter as her eyes became glossy.

"I liked your parents. I didn't know them for very long, but they were good people. They were good to Varg, and they were good to me. I didn't want…" Halea struggled to explain but grew silent as she bit her tongue from revealing the crow's prophecy. "I know it's the lycan way, but I didn't want to see your mother go like that. I do care."

Otsana stared at the glistening river and took a deep and shaky breath as the warm spring wind caressed her face. Halea's frantic screams still echoed in her memories, haunting her in a way that she could not forget because, inside, she had been screaming too.

Moments passed, but Otsana seemed to have nothing else to say, and Halea's gut wrenched in guilt.

"I care about you too, Otsana."

The she-wolf's eyes grew wide, and her hands clenched into fists in her lap, but Halea went on.

"I'm sorry. I didn't mean to hurt you by leaving the way I did. I didn't think what I was doing mattered that much to you. You always acted as if you didn't want my help, at least at first. I just assumed you wanted me gone and wouldn't care when I left."

"That's not true," Otsana spoke in a trembling voice as unrestrained tears flowed down her cheeks.

Halea struggled to force back a sob as she was wracked with even worse guilt.

"I was wrong. Your mother told me you needed help, and I left you in the lurch without even so much as a goodbye, but for what it's worth, I liked sparring with you. Varg is such an overprotective worrywart since we mated, he never wants to fight with me anymore, and it felt nice to have someone to train with again. I don't want you to give up on your dream of being an alpha. I know how much it means to you, and your mother knew it too. I think that's why she wanted me to help you...and I let you both down. I'm so sorry, Otsana."

Otsana had finally turned to face Halea as she spoke, and her lips trembled as she absorbed Halea's words.

"She spoke only one word before..." the she-wolf faltered as she choked on a fresh surge of tears. "Fight."

"She was right. You have to," Halea said as she wept, but her determination alighted from within. "She believed in you, Otsana. She wanted you to fight. You have to fight for your right to lead your pack. Right now, the males are getting ready to battle. Fenris has already declared his intentions, and if you don't stop him, he'll take everything away from you. Please, you can't let him do that!"

"I don't think I'm strong enough."

"Yes, you are! I believe in you too! Remember when I asked you to pray? You have strength and control when you calm your mind and believe in yourself. Why should you doubt yourself? You said you're a true alpha! Well, are you, or aren't you? Your mother wanted me to help you because it's not about being a woman, it's about being who you really are, and you're an alpha. Are you going to just sit there and let someone else take that away from you?"

"No," Otsana replied while rising to her feet. Her tears had stopped, and her eyes burned with a new light. "I am an alpha, and I will take what's mine or die fighting."

~~~☼~~~

By the time Halea and Otsana returned to the den, it was nightfall, and almost everyone was gathered in the sacred cave. The elders had already chosen the order of competitors by the ritual of the fangs, and the first battle was about to commence. Lovel and Ivaylo entered the circle, and voices rose in excitement, and howls rang out as the challengers faced each other.

Varg spotted Halea and Otsana as they entered the cave and he hailed them to join him at the best seats in the front. The staffs' pounding reverberated off the cave walls, and Halea's heart thundered in her chest as she recalled the first alpha battle she had ever seen. Varg had won the right to be king in this sacred cave, but it was not Varg who would be fighting this time. Beside her, Otsana sat as taut as a drawn bowstring.

The two males squared off in a brutal match where blood was shed, and bones were cracked. This was not the innocent, refereed fun of the festival wrestling matches; this was a serious bid for power where a life could be taken if defeat was not an option. Ivaylo managed to pin Lovel face-down on the ground with his knee in his back, and seizing him by the scalp, he pulled back his head and pressed his claws into his opponent's neck.

"Submit, or I'll tear out your throat!" threatened Ivaylo.

"I submit!" Lovel growled in defeat.

Halea sighed in relief that the match didn't end in a fatality, but she couldn't help being nervous when Fenris entered the circle.

The sweat and blood were toweled off Ivaylo, but despite winning the last match, he had taken a considerable beating, and it didn't look like he was fit to challenge again so soon, but there would be no delay. The fate of the eastern pack would be decided that night.

Howls and cheers mixed with the pounding of the staffs, and Fenris seemed pleased with the amount of support he was receiving. He wore a cocky smile as Ivaylo stood before him, and with lightning-quick ferocity, Fenris swung a right hook that Ivaylo was unable to dodge in time and was promptly knocked unconscious. The fight was over.

"One hit! Did you see that?" shouted several voices.

Fenris's name was being chanted as he raised his fists in victory. Ivaylo remained prostrate on the cave floor. He was alive but in rough condition, and several volunteers entered the circle and gently carried him away.

Beside Halea, Otsana did not move.

"Otsana?" Halea asked, but the she-wolf only stared ahead in horror. "Otsana, look at me!" she commanded, and her words snapped the female lycan from her trance, and she met Halea's gaze.

"Ask your gods for strength. You can do this!" Halea said as she placed her hand on Otsana's shoulder and gave it an encouraging squeeze.

Otsana nodded once and took a deep inhalation before closing her eyes. The whites of her knuckles faded as she unclenched her fists, and some of her rigidity dissolved as her breathing grew steady. When at last, she opened her eyes, they glowed with a new fire of determination.

Marrok was just entering the circle to congratulate Fenris on his victory when one voice rose above the rest.

"I shall challenge!" Otsana called as she leaped into the circle, and one by one, the voices fell silent until even the pounding of the staffs had grown still.

"A female?" a shocked voice proclaimed.

"A female challenger!" cried another, until more voices joined in an eruption of objection and doubt.

"Silence!" Batsuba shouted over the crowd, and the protests stilled. "A female may challenge. There is no law against it. It has been done before and can be done again. Victory to the strong and power to the brave – that is our way. Is this what you wish?" Batsuba asked Otsana with a gleam in her knowing, black eyes.

"Yes, I challenge for the right to be alpha of the eastern pack," Otsana spoke loud and clear, and voices rose again in a mixture of support and dismay.

Fenris narrowed his eyes in irritation.

"What's wrong? Afraid to fight a woman?" Otsana taunted.

"It's your funeral," Fenris growled as the elders left the challengers' area.

Halea nervously clutched Varg's hand and offered a silent prayer as the two eastern lycans slowly circled each other. From this point on, Otsana's fate was in the hands of the gods.

Fenris waited for an opening and lunged forward with an uppercut that Otsana only narrowly dodged, and with a graceful pivot, she punched the eastern male twice in the ribs before he recovered his stance. Fenris growled in pain and kicked her in the stomach, causing her to fall and roll. She clutched her abdomen and snarled but was quickly up again and leaping in for the attack. They tore into each other with claws that sprayed blood across the fighters' circle and fists, impacting loudly upon flesh and bone. The two lycans bared their fangs and growled as red seeped dangerously around the edges of their eyes, and Fenris's attacks increased in brutality.

Otsana was struggling to hold off her opponent, whose rage was growing with every moment. She took ruthless punch after punch to the face until one of her teeth went flying out her mouth, and her right eye began to swell. She couldn't last much longer, and just as Fenris was about to deliver another blow, she caught his fist mid-flight and twisted his arm, using his momentum against him and sending him flying across the circle. Fenris fell for only a moment but was quickly back up again, and his eyes were entirely red. He charged Otsana in anger, fangs elongated, and claws ready to strike, but again she avoided his attack and managed to knee him in the stomach before elbowing him in the face and sending him to the ground with a low-sweeping kick.

Halea's gasp was drowned out by the sound of the pounding staffs and the shouts of excitement. She recognized that move – the water-dragon.

Again, Fenris lunged for Otsana with intent to kill, but there was no fear in her eyes and no trace of rage as if a strange calm had fallen over her, and with perfect fluid grace, she was able to use the eastern male's reckless anger against him. As he charged, she launched a series of fast kicks into his sternum, causing him to growl in pain and stumble backward. His one moment of imbalance gave her the advantage she needed, and she sprang forward, launching her full bodyweight on top of him and sending him to the ground with a thud. Once he was pinned, she sunk her claws deep into his chest, causing ribs to crack and blood to pour out of his mouth.

"Submit," Otsana snarled, and for one moment, the cavern fell deathly silent, and not even the pounding of the staffs was heard as Fenris tipped back his head, exposing his throat in submission.

It was over.

An eruption of shouts and cheers and howls sounded throughout the cave as Otsana stood, her hand dripping with blood and her eye almost entirely swollen shut. Batsuba and the eastern pack healer jumped into the circle to check on Fenris. A mortal creature could have never survived such a wound, but his therian healing power kept him from the edge of death as the healers quickly tended his injury.

Halea also jumped into the circle, but instead of helping with Fenris, who was already in good hands, she leaped upon Otsana and hugged her as all the lycans shouted her praise and raised howls in her honor.

"You did it! I knew you could!" Halea cried in joy, and though in terrible pain, the new eastern wolfmother returned her embrace and gently laid her head on Halea's shoulder.

CHAPTER 10 - FEALTY

"How are things in Antherose?" asked Mama Dragon.

"I haven't been back since the rangers took Lord Anshar's castle. It's too depressing. There's nothing there for us anyway," replied Kalee as she strolled through the forest beside the motherly priestess.

"What about Favion? Isn't he still there?"

Kalee's face grew as red as her hair for a moment, but she avoided Mama Dragon's questioning gaze.

"Yes, but you know he can go wherever he wants. It's not like it matters."

Mama Dragon pursed her lips. It was for the best. Kalee was an oath-sworn immortal priestess, and Favion wasn't bound by their commitments. She doubted Kalee was entirely honest about her indifference, but it would be best for her to keep her distance. Even with Lord Anshar gone and perhaps the oath not mattering as much, they still had a job to do, and until the world was no longer in danger, they needed the full devotion of every priestess they had. If only Rufus could understand that.

No sooner had the thought of her adopted son passed her mind when Mama Dragon heard a falcon crying out on the wind.

"Rufus is back!" Kalee cheerily stated the obvious. Having a therian for a secret ally amused her, particularly because she was one of the few who knew the truth about Rufus, and that made her feel important.

Mama Dragon could tell by the way he was coming in straight instead of circling down that there was no need for her to extend her gloved hand, and sure enough, the falcon shifted into his humanoid form upon landing.

"Hi, Kalee, Sophia," he greeted, though his large, reflective eyes had a nervous quality that Mama Dragon did not miss.

"Oh, gods, what's happened now?"

"Yeah, that message you asked me to deliver to Samesa. I kind of didn't. But something happened!" he quickly explained as Mama Dragon's face scrunched in disapproval.

"What happened?" Mama Dragon asked again, her tone growing stern.

"Samesa was attacked by a shade mimic. I had no choice but to save her in my humanoid form."

"Rufus, she's a priestess. She can handle herself!"

"No, she had no idea. These new demons can appear as anyone. Anyone! A random stranger, a child, and if they get into your mind, they can appear as someone you know or someone you used to know. They don't really die when you kill them, and what information they gather, they can pass on to others. They're using deception to get closer to the devotees than they've ever been able to before. Everyone's in real danger! Samesa was nearly killed by these things twice already. The second time it presented itself as a cleric that she used to know. This is serious! No priestess is prepared to battle this sort of enemy, and the only way you can tell that they're demons in disguise is by their smell. They don't stink of demon as strongly as the others, so you have to get a bit closer before you notice it, and they don't seem to leave a scent trail. If I hadn't smelled the truth when I passed by to deliver that message, she'd have walked right into its trap."

"This is awful! What are we going to do? The Chaos has never created such creatures before. If we can't tell who's friend and who's foe, we're in trouble!" cried Kalee.

"I'm sorry, Rufus. You're right. This is a serious problem. We're human. We don't have a therian's sense of smell, and if that's the only way to detect these things, we're at a severe disadvantage," added Mama Dragon.

"The lycans!" declared Kalee. "We can go to Halea for shelter. They've helped us before, and she's on our side. Lycans can smell the difference between humans and demons. With them, we'd be safe. We can gather every cleric and priestess and stay with the wolves until we find a way to defeat these things."

"I don't think Varg would be too keen on that," replied Rufus.

"Perhaps not, but the agreement we made before was because he was afraid our presence would draw the unwanted attention of Lord Anshar," recalled Mama Dragon. "With him trapped in the mirror, that concern is over, though I know those wolves still don't particularly care for humans. But as much as they may dislike us, they hate demons even more, and we're on the same side when it comes to battling Chaos. There's nowhere for us in the city, and now the wilds aren't safe. We're out of options. Rufus, can you go and ask Halea and Varg to give us sanctuary?"

"Ugh," he groaned.

"He's not going to eat you!" argued Mama Dragon.

"He might."

Despite the dire circumstance, Kalee giggled at Rufus's reluctance.

"Don't worry. You've helped him out before, doesn't he owe you one? And Halea's there. Please, Rufus, you can get there faster than us, and we don't have a lot of time," Kalee begged.

"Fine," he sighed in defeat while unconsciously rubbing his arm. The broken bone had healed perfectly, and if not for Varg setting it, he could have permanently lost his ability to fly. Though the wolf had been the one to break it in the first place, perhaps it was time to bury the hatchet.

"Thank you, Rufus. We'll start gathering the priestesses and clerics, and as soon as you give us their answer, we'll set out for the lycan territory," said Mama Dragon as she placed an appreciative hand on his shoulder.

~~~✦~~~

The skies had finally cleared, allowing the warm sun to shine down on the last of the games. That night would be the first full moon of spring and the last night of the gathering. A meeting of the lycan council would be called, and then a final feast and celebration.

Raoul was not particularly disappointed that the final hunting competition of the gathering ended in Varg's victory. Varg was no longer the precocious cub that followed the warriors like a shadow, and Raoul had to admit that he had grown into a capable alpha. But was a decent alpha also a worthy king? He had been considering the situation since his arrival.

As far as physical strength and capability as a warrior went, Varg had been well-trained by his father, and his power and will were undeniable. Everywhere the wolf king went, his people treated him with the respect and adoration of a true leader, and Varg appeared firm but fair, as a good alpha should be. His choice of a mate had caused Raoul concern at first. But despite being human, Halea demonstrated the will of an alpha, and at every turn, she had proven her love and devotion to not just her pack but to all their people. She had made a bit of a spectacle of herself at the death of the eastern alphas, but perhaps that was just how humans handled their grief. The fact that she had grieved at all proved that she cared, and she had even supported the new eastern wolfmother in her bid for power. She was also friends with some of the northern pack, which made Raoul regret that his own pack had initially been so unwelcoming towards her.

Then there was the issue of the demon attack, which had significantly altered Raoul's perspective on the alpha pair. They had done everything in their power to ensure the safety of those who could not fight first, then gathered the warriors and faced the danger head-on. Varg had wielded the Fang with the expertise of a true swordmaster, and Raoul knew such skill was beyond him. He had seen the wolf gods' favor for Varg with his own eyes, and though no longer a priestess, Halea still seemed to retain the favor of her Dragon Goddess. Working together with the Fang's ultimate power, the advantage of a former priestess, and the full cooperation of all the packs, they had sealed the largest tear he had ever seen and slain the demon horde. Some lycans were injured, and lives had been lost, but it was not for lack of ability or effort on Varg and Halea's part. They had done all that they could, and all the injured had survived. Varg had even successfully overseen the elimination of the demon stragglers and posted extra guards around their borders to assuage their people's fears.

Even before winning the right to be the alpha of the southern pack, Raoul had worried for his people, and now it was time to decide if he could entrust their fate to Varg. As the sun began to set, the elders and alphas gathered once more in the sacred cave where formal matters would be introduced and settled.

The council began with a ritual of prayers and offerings, and Halea watched with interest as the elders conducted the religious ceremony, asking the wolf gods to bless their hunts and to bestow them with plenty, prosperity, and protection. Batsuba, Marrok, and several other elders took turns offering prayers in the ancient language before an altar at the base of the statues of the wolf gods, whose heads were the heads

79

of wolves, but their bodies were humanoid. After the prayers were over, Varg rose and began the meeting.

"Brothers, sisters, thank you for joining this council. Tonight, we must settle several matters while we are all still gathered here together. Who would like to speak first?"

Everyone waited patiently while small issues were presented first before the king and council. They discussed the migratory patterns of the herds, individuals changing packs for apprenticeships, mating, trade agreements, and of course, demon and tear activity, which, except for the attack at the gathering, seemed to be on the decline.

"There is one matter of great importance, at least to myself, that I must address," added Varg after he finished hearing everyone else out. "We are wolves. We do not deny our nature. We are predators. Hunters. Warriors. We hold the right to defend our lands by any means necessary. Those who invade our territory are subject to our swift punishment. But I would like to make a decree, from this day forth, if anyone is found trespassing in our territory, be they human or therian, they must be issued a warning first. If any refuse to heed this warning, you may deal with them as you please, but under no circumstance are they to be eaten. There is better prey to be had. And, yes, I can't deny that this decision comes from a place of bias," he admitted while casting loving eyes on Halea, who looked back at him with delighted adoration. "Are there any who object?" he asked when he turned his gaze back to the council.

"I support this decision. Humans are hardly our primary food source, and most are foul-tasting anyway," offered Bertolf, and though he didn't mention it, this had already been the practice of the northern pack since his brother brought the human woman, Jance, into their lives.

"I'm fine with issuing a warning. Some humans seem to stumble onto our lands by accident. As long as they leave right away and do no harm, there's no need to slaughter them on sight," added Raoul, who had never liked how unbending Rafe had been when it came to how brutally human trespassers were dealt with in the past. "As for eating them, it's no loss to us. Perhaps it was done more in the past when times were hard and good meat wasn't as easy to come by, but these days we are more than capable of feeding our own without resorting to such means of survival."

"I have no complaints," spoke Otsana, and one by one, the elders voiced their opinions on the issue until everyone was in accord.

"Then this matter is settled," Varg decreed. "And now on to the most important thing that has brought us here today; there are now two new alphas. Alpha Raoul, you may present yourself before the council."

Raoul rose and addressed the other alphas and elders.

"I, Raoul, have won the right to be the leader of the southern pack through single combat. It was I who requested Supreme Alpha Varg to call this gathering, not just to present myself before the council but also to voice my concerns about the situation with the Chaos Dimension. I have seen the destruction of tears and demons, and it was my opinion that perhaps our people needed a leader who was more suited to address these problems. I confess that I came to these lands with the intent to challenge Varg for the right to be king, but after careful consideration, I can find no fault with his reign. Since attending this gathering, Varg has proven himself to be dedicated to the protection and preservation of our people and has fought valiantly on behalf of all, and his mate, too, has conducted herself in every way appropriate for a proper wolfmother. Therefore, I, Alpha Raoul, of the southern pack, do hereby swear my fealty to the true wolf king," he declared while dropping to one knee and bowing his head in submission before Varg.

Halea could sense Varg relax across their bond, and she brimmed with joy. It wasn't that she hadn't been worried, but she was less concerned about Raoul after getting to know him. He seemed to share many of Varg's noble qualities, and she couldn't bear the thought of the two cousins harming each other. Raoul's pledge filled her with relief as well, and instinctively she reached out and clasped Varg's hand and received a gentle squeeze from him in return, though his face remained stoic.

"Thank you, Alpha Raoul. My greatest hope is that our packs can finally come together as brothers and sisters, united as we always should have been. I will not hold on to the bitterness of the past because I can trust in you to succeed in leading your people through these dark times. And to you, I vow that I will do everything in my power to ensure the survival and prosperity of all lycans."

"As do I," added Halea.

Raoul nodded his head in gratitude, and for the first time since arriving in the west, the two cousins embraced as family.

Everyone raised their voices in welcome and support to the new southern alpha, and howls of joy echoed throughout the cavern before Raoul finally took his seat, and order was once again restored.

"Wolfmother Otsana, it is now your turn to present yourself before the council," continued Varg.

Otsana rose and nodded respectfully to the gathering.

"I, Otsana, have won the right to be the leader of the eastern pack through single combat. I can only hope to live up to my parents, who came before me, but I can promise this; I will fight to the death to protect my pack, and I will dedicate my life to my people's prosperity. I do hereby pledge my fealty to you, Supreme Alpha Varg," she confidently stated before dropping to one knee and bowing her head in submission.

"Thank you, Wolfmother Otsana. Your parents were good and just leaders, and I know you will follow in their footsteps. I'm sure they would both be very proud."

Otsana's eyes glistened a little when she raised her head and stood once more. She wore a gentle smile as the council welcomed her, and howls rang out in her honor, but when the cave grew quiet, she spoke once more.

"I also do hereby swear my fealty to the supreme wolfmother, for whom I would gladly lay down my life in her service. Long may she reign!" Otsana proclaimed before dropping to her knees again and bowing her head before Halea, who sat in wide-eyed shock with her mouth slightly agape.

"Otsana, thank you," Halea eventually managed to choke out as the she-wolf raised her head to meet her gaze, and the two smiled at each other as howls and applause echoed throughout the cavern.

Crackling sparks from the fire pits rose, and the air was filled with music, laughter, lively discussions, and songs that were more like chants. Somewhere, a circle of drummers was challenging each other to invent new rhythms while those who played string instruments tried to accompany their tune. At the other end of the common area, a storyteller stood before a cluster of lycans, young and old, regaling them with an epic tale of wolf heroes long since passed.

The first full moon of spring hung bright in the night sky, stirring the inner wolf of every lycan beneath its pale silver light. More lycans were out in their wolf forms than usual. Some roamed the common area, and others took off into the woods in small packs to chase the nocturnal prey that slinked beneath the shadows. Whether in wolf or humanoid form, everyone enjoyed themselves to their fullest as this night was the crescendo to the gathering and the birth of their new year. Though fear and grief had tainted the days leading up to their sacred holiday, they would come together as one people and praise the moon for this one night.

After the council meeting, everyone gathered for the final and greatest feast of the festival, and even the wolves were sampling non-meat dishes reserved for the special occasion. Halea had run off to see to the preparations and left the other alphas to enjoy their last night together around the fire pit. Otsana offered to assist her, as she too was a wolfmother now, but Halea insisted that she relax and recover from her injuries and enjoy the feast with the other pack leaders as it was also in honor of her recent victory.

Ulrica had outdone herself by providing an impressive array of dishes, and when Halea arrived to check on the food, she was surprised to discover that Jance had been helping her.

"Ulrica's just wonderful!" Jance declared. "She said she's been making almost all of your food since you came to live with the lycans. It's so nice to meet a wolf who knows how to make human food, and it's delicious too!"

Ulrica blushed under Jance's praise.

"Cooking for Woflmother Halea has taught me a lot about what humans like to eat. I do like being creative with food and seeing her enjoy what I make is such an honor. Plus, Daisy seems to like a lot of the same things."

Halea couldn't say she enjoyed cooking as much as those two but seeing them bond over a shared interest brought a smile to her face. "You've both done an amazing job. Thank you so much for helping with the festival."

"Actually, um, would it be okay if we stayed a while longer?" asked Jance. "I mean Alf and me. The northern pack can spare him for a while, and I really want to spend more time here in the west with you and Ulrica and sweet little Daisy. I miss humans and cooking for those who appreciate it, and the weather here is so much nicer than the cold north. It's not that I don't love my northern pack, and I'm sure I'll get homesick eventually, but please, may we stay a little longer?"

"Of course, you and Alf are welcome to stay as long as you wish."

"Can I stay too? Batsuba will be heartbroken without me," interjected Marrok, who had overheard their conversation.

"Sure. We'd be happy to have you stay," Halea offered, though she had a feeling Batsuba would strangle her for this.

"But Elder Marrok, won't Bertolf need you?" asked Jance.

"I've made long visits to other packs in the past. He'll get along without me for a little while. And besides, when you've lived as long as I have, it's good to change scenery once in a while. It breaks up the monotony of life, and things are so interesting in the west right now."

Halea couldn't help but suspect that he was hinting about Lord Anshar as he gave her a knowing smile. With the gathering coming to a close, she would soon have to resume her sessions with the former head of her faith, and that thought filled her with dread. She wasn't sure she could face Lord Anshar alone anymore, and she was looking forward to having her grandfather's guidance.

When Halea was sure that Ulrica and Jance had everything well within hand, she decided to make one last round of the common area and ensure everyone was having a good time and that all their needs were being met. Everyone was busy celebrating, eating, and drinking, singing, and laughing, changing form, joining night hunts, and enjoying the company of the other packs. Among the different types of socialization, there were even amorous males vying for the attention of flirtatious females, and Halea could tell which she-wolves were in heat by how large their groups of admirers were. It reminded her that she and Varg had not had much time for each other with everything that happened since the festival began, and she suddenly longed for his attention.

When Varg declared that lycans would never again be allowed to eat humans, it had pleased her more than she could express. He had not told her that he intended to make such a decree, but the fact that he did it just for her filled her with an all-consuming warmth and love for her mate. Somewhere across their bond, he noticed the shift in her emotions and responded in kind.

All around her, couples were pairing off for the night. Lycans were all so bold when it came to flirtation and sex. It made her realize how much she missed Varg's affection.

"I'm an alpha, damn it! Why do I need to be shy about it? He's my mate after all!" she thought with determination.

Now that everyone seemed fine, she would go to him, but as she passed one of the pits, Daciana approached her and handed her a full tankard of ale.

"Here, Halea. Don't think I haven't noticed how hard you've been working. You should eat, drink, and be merry too. You've earned it."

"Thank you," Halea said while accepting the drink. She had tried ale before and occasionally wine but had never overindulged for fear of it impairing her abilities while she was on duty as a priestess. Perhaps it would be okay to let loose for just one night, and so she and Daciana raised their drinks to each other and downed the entire contents of their tankards in several large gulps.

Halea barely had time to catch her breath before another lycan passing by with a pitcher noticed them and refilled both their tankards before they could even refuse.

"Yes, praise to the moon!" cried Daciana before letting out a jubilant howl and chugging her drink. Halea followed her example.

After finishing her second drink, she was starting to feel a little fuzzy. Lycans had a much higher tolerance for alcohol than humans. Most didn't seem to get intoxicated at all, no matter how much they drank. She had once witnessed Varg finish the better half of a barrel of ale after a hunting celebration. His eyes had remained perfectly focused, and his speech never slurred. It had no more effect on him than water.

Halea thanked Daciana for the drinks, and empty tankard still in hand, she set out for the alpha's fire pit.

When she got closer, Halea saw the alphas sitting around the fire, laughing, and enjoying themselves. Even Otsana, despite her badly bruised face, seemed the happiest Halea had ever seen her as Raoul and Bertolf continued to raise toasts in honor of her victory. Varg was lounging in his usual seat, looking relaxed with a gentle smile of approval as he enjoyed the company of the other alphas, though his brilliant blue eyes would occasionally roam beyond the pit - searching. Around his neck, he still wore the blue crystal pendant that she had given him for luck. He hadn't returned it yet, but she didn't mind if he wanted to wear it a while longer. It had initially been meant for him, and it looked fetching where it rested over his muscular bare chest. Halea could sense his longing for her through their bond, and her heart fluttered like a bird trapped within the cage of her ribs. He looked particularly handsome as the firelight danced across his rugged, chiseled features, and filled with liquid courage, she was ready to let him know exactly what she wanted.

Varg was quick to spot her as she approached, and he noticed there was something ever so slightly off about the way she was walking and when she sat beside him, he quickly detected the scent of alcohol on her breath, and he couldn't help smiling.

"What?" she asked him defensively after greeting the other alphas who were chatting while enjoying their feast of bloody, raw meat.

"Nothing," Varg replied with a grin that reflected the firelight off his gleaming white fangs. "You just seem to be enjoying yourself, is all. I like that," he practically purred into her ear, and a tingling sensation ran down her spine and pooled in her stomach. Her face, already flushed from the alcohol, got a little redder.

The other alphas ignored their flirtatious behavior. It was nothing unusual for a mated pair, though Otsana's participation in the discussions grew more reserved as the night went on.

All around them, music played, and more food and drinks were served. Varg tried to ensure that Halea was eating properly because, for whatever reason, she seemed to be consuming far more ale than usual. Not that he minded, but he didn't want her drinking too much alcohol on an empty stomach. His puny human mate couldn't handle strong drinks the way lycans could. It seemed to have a strange effect on her, and as the night wore on, her beautiful hazel green eyes grew a little hazy and unfocused. She would laugh at things that weren't all that humorous, and the rest of the time, she would gaze at him with intense interest, which he certainly didn't mind because he could sense and smell that his presence was arousing her.

84

Eventually, the other alphas decided to go and mingle elsewhere or retire as the night was getting late, and they would have to set out on the long journey back to their homelands the next day.

Once they were alone, Halea, suddenly emboldened, climbed onto her mate's lap.

Varg was pleasantly surprised. Lately, he had been trying to tone down their physical displays of affection, at least on formal occasions. She was usually embarrassed by the typical flirtatious behavior of mated lycans, but it seemed the alcohol had removed her inhibitions.

"My, what's gotten into you, my mate?"

"More like what hasn't gotten into me," she teased before giggling with sudden mortification at her own words.

Varg lovingly wrapped his arms around her and laughed at her unusually forward behavior.

"Well, if that's what you want, you only had to ask. I never did get my prize for winning that race."

"You've been so busy," she pouted.

"I'm never too busy for you," he promised, and she rewarded him with her brilliant smile before leaning in and kissing him, causing him to growl in pleasure.

When their kiss broke, she was panting for breath, and the scent of her desire hung heavy in the air, filling him with a throbbing need that she would undoubtedly notice from where she was sitting. But there was something else to her scent, subtle but present, and it stirred the wolf within him. His beloved mate was going into heat. It occurred to him that he must have lost track of time, and the knowledge that she would soon be even more desirable filled him with a possessive need. He was suddenly quite grateful the gathering would soon be over because, in the coming days, he would not want any distractions getting in the way of him satisfying his mate's every desire.

"I'd do anything for you, Halea. Anything you want," he breathily promised while allowing his hands to roam her warm and responsive body.

"Varg, I want you," she whispered in his ear, and her hot breath on his skin nearly sent the red into his eyes, when suddenly she fell slack against him, her head resting on his shoulder.

"Halea?" he asked, but she didn't move, though he could feel her breathing steadily against him. When he gently pulled her back, her eyes were closed. She was asleep.

He sighed in disappointment and then chuckled despite himself. It looked like he would be in for a long hard night. He gently scooped up his unconscious mate and carried her back to their tree-dwelling, where he tucked her into bed before he went to cool off in a nearby lake.

CHAPTER 11 – SPRING HEAT

Bright sunlight filtered in through an open window, forcing Halea to open her eyes to a pounding headache. When she sat up, she disappointedly noticed that Varg was not there. His side of the bed looked like he had tried to sleep, but the disarray of the pillows and covers indicated he had a fitful night. She struggled to remember the last thing that happened before falling asleep and vaguely recalled downing a considerable amount of alcohol and doing some rather brazen flirting; after that, everything was a blur. It appeared as if Varg had removed her outer robe and pulled her boots off because she had no memory of doing so herself. On the small bedside table sat a tall pitcher of cool water, considerately left by Varg, and a cup, which she refilled multiple times before her thirst was slaked.

The pounding in her head forced her to lie back down, but she wasn't tired, and the sun's low position indicated that it was still early.

She thought on the previous night with frustration. It was clear she hadn't got what she wanted, and there was still a lingering fire burning within her. She could sense that Varg was somewhere off attending to his duties for the morning. The other packs would be leaving in the early afternoon, but she could hardly wait that long as torturous thoughts plagued her of his wavy dark hair and how his blue eyes glowed in the firelight. She could not help stretching out across their bed and breathing deep the masculine scent he left behind and feeling achingly hot.

She removed the last of her undergarments, but it was no use, she needed release, and soon her villainous hand worked its way down between her folds where she softly stroked her sensitive flesh.

The bond came alive with sudden and intense interest. Somewhere, Varg was being made aware of what she was doing, and she smiled wickedly. She could have closed her end of their empathic link, but she didn't want to. If she couldn't have him physically, she at least wanted to feel his growing desire across their connection.

~~~☼~~~

Not far past the vantage point, several of the warriors were standing around congratulating themselves on one last successful hunting expedition. Most of the packs would have long journeys home, and it would be easier to prepare meat for travel before leaving rather than stopping to hunt along the way.

Lyall offered Varg the heart of the elk he had slain with his head bowed low in submission, but Varg declined.

"It's your kill. Enjoy it. I'm still mostly stuffed from last night."

"Aren't we all?" chuckled Bertolf, and many agreed, but everyone's laughter abruptly stopped when Varg's eyes suddenly turned blood red.

Everyone jumped back in panic, not knowing what they could have possibly said or done to set him off, but without explanation, Varg turned and sped off into the southwest.

"Is he okay?" Raoul asked Lyall, who presumably knew Varg the best of anyone there. Lyall could only shrug.

"Halea's in heat," stated Hemming.

"How do you know?" asked Otsana. She had noticed Halea's behavior seemed unusually wanton the night before, to the point where it was uncomfortable to look at the alpha pair without a knot forming in her chest.

"Daciana's done that to me before," Hemming confessed with a slight blush creeping up his neck, and everyone burst into laughter, except for Otsana, who stared into the distance where Varg had just disappeared.

~~~⚙~~~

She was breathing heavily as she continued to stroke the sensitive node that sent jolts of pleasure through her, but it wasn't enough. Varg's desire roared across their bond like a ravenous beast. It was hard to sense anything else but his undeniable want - his need. And before she fully knew what was happening, a flurry of steps rushed into their tree-dwelling, and Varg launched himself on top of her. All she could feel was his hot mouth on hers and his rough hands laying claim to her body.

He seized her hand to prevent her from finishing without him. He wanted to be the one to please her, and his inner wolf was answering her call. His mate had desperately needed him, and his alpha nature demanded that he provide.

"Halea," he called in a voice rumbling and deep, and when he pulled back, she knew his beast had taken control, and it excited her.

"Varg, take me. Please. I need you so much," she pleaded, and he wasted no time divesting himself of his clothes before snatching her into his arms once more and running his hot mouth across her burning skin. He moved up her torso, nipping gently with his fangs and sucking the flesh leaving red marks in his wake as she dug her fingers through his hair and moaned in pleasure. As he moved up, his tongue tortured the taut bud of her left nipple as his hand snaked between her legs and found her dripping wet with need. Her scent was driving him mad. Her arousal permeated the air, mixing deliciously with the fragrance of her intoxicating heat. She was ready, so very ready, and his wolf wanted to claim her.

"Oh, please, Varg," she begged again as he touched her most sacred of places, causing her legs to tremble.

He was beyond restraint as he roughly opened her thighs and plunged inside of her with wild abandon. Her soft moan broke into a sweet cry as his girth satisfied the need within her.

His lips found her mating mark, and his fangs gently latched on as his eyes burned red.

"Don't hold back now, I need you," she cried between gasping breaths, and his sharp fangs reopened the mark filling his mouth with the sweet taste of her blood as

87

her nails raked fire across his back. The bond affirmed that there was nothing but desire and pleasure as she writhed beneath him, repeating his name like a prayer until she came completely undone in his arms, and he snarled in satisfaction as he released his seed inside of her.

They held each other as their breathing slowly calmed, and the red receded from Varg's eyes.

"Huh, my headache's gone," Halea announced, and Varg laughed.

"You know you're adorable when you drink."

"Stop," she pleaded with a mortified laugh.

"Oh, yeah. You were all over me last night. In front of everyone too."

She buried her face in her hands, but he gently pulled them away to see her blushing face.

"Too bad you passed out. Are all puny humans such lightweights when it comes to drinking?"

"Ya know, I think that headache is coming back."

He smiled down on her beautiful face as she averted her eyes in embarrassment, but his smile only grew wider. He loved teasing her.

She was going to raise her hands to hide her face again when she noticed her wrists.

Her contraceptive mark was gone.

Varg felt the crushing weight of panic surge through her as terror filled her eyes and stole away their sweet moment of bliss.

"The rune! It's been days since I've worn it. I think the last time I even had it was before that demon attack. I never repainted it after you helped me wash off in the hot spring that day."

After Ethelwolf and Úlfa died, she was too overcome with fear and grief to even think about intimacy, and every moment since had been one event after another, and repainting the rune had completely slipped her mind.

"Halea, it's okay," Varg tried to soothe, but she jumped out of bed and began scrounging for her ink and brush to quickly replace the missing rune.

Her heart was hammering as she scribbled the mark and chanted the contraceptive spell. When she was done, she didn't feel much better.

"Varg...am I?"

He gravely nodded his head. "Yes, you're in heat. I'm sorry. It completely slipped my mind too."

She came back to bed and crawled in beside him, and he held her close and gently stroked her hair.

"It's okay, Halea. Sex doesn't make a baby every time, even when a female's in heat, and even if it did, we'll be okay. I would take care of you - of our child. There's nothing I wouldn't do for you," he promised.

She nodded and forced a deep breath. She had to remain calm and not assume the worst, but inside she knew that Varg couldn't protect her from everything, and she offered a silent prayer to Tiamet.

~~~✧~~~

88

Later that afternoon, Varg and Halea said their farewells to Bertolf and the rest of the northern pack. Jance and Alf were sad to say goodbye to Bertolf, but they promised to return home before winter set in. Halea had mentioned to Varg that she offered extended hospitality to some of the northern wolves, but he didn't mind in the least. He knew she was fond of Jance, and he wanted her to have as many friends as possible. Breaking the news to Batsuba about Marrok was a little less easy.

"It'll be just like old times again, Batsuba." Marrok had beamed in excitement.

"Like I need another reminder of the past," Batsuba grumbled. Her lost mate had been the alpha of the northern pack long, long ago, and during those years, the two packs had joined, and she had spent many years living between the west and the north.

Raoul embraced Varg as they said their farewells, and Halea smiled as the two cousins spoke as if there had never been a rift between them, and it warmed her heart.

"I still fear for our people, but I will place my faith in you and your mate. If there's anything you need, call upon the southern pack. We'll be there for you."

"I will. Thank you, Raoul," Varg replied.

Halea could sense that Varg would miss his cousin, and she would miss him too. It would take time to influence the hearts and minds of the southern pack, but Halea was confident that Raoul would bring about a positive change for his people.

When Halea and Varg went to say goodbye to Otsana and the eastern pack, they found that her face had fully healed, and she was having a discussion with Batsuba.

"Fenris will not be fit to make the journey home for at least another three or four days," explained Batsuba.

"But he'll be okay, won't he?" asked Otsana with a note of remorse in her voice. She had dealt a severe wound to the beta male, and while she would have killed him if she had to, she didn't want to take the life of any of her pack members, even if she and Fenris didn't get along.

"He'll make a full recovery, and as soon as he's fit, we'll send him home," promised Batsuba before excusing herself and allowing the alphas to have a moment alone.

Several members of the eastern pack had retrieved the bodies of Ethelwolf and Úlfa from their temporary cairns. They were carefully wrapped in shrouds and hoisted onto litters where they would be carried to the east and buried in their own sacred resting place.

"Your parents would be proud, Otsana. I know the eastern pack will be in good hands," Varg offered, and Otsana bowed her head in gratitude.

"We're proud of you too, Wolfmother," added Halea with a smile so kind Otsana's next words caught in her throat, and it took her a moment to gather her thoughts.

"Thank you, both of you, for believing in me, even when I didn't believe in myself."

"I knew you were a tough bitch," said Halea, and Otsana couldn't help but smile despite the ache in her heart.

"If…if you need anything - anything at all. You can always send a runner. None of us know what lies ahead, but if you need the eastern pack, we'll come as fast as we can. You have my word."

"Thank you," said Halea.

"Or…if you just want to send a runner…for any old thing. It would be nice to stay in touch," Otsana said while nervously avoiding Halea's eyes.

"Sure, I'd like that," Halea said and extended her arms to hug the eastern wolfmother.

When Otsana returned Halea's embrace, for a brief moment, Varg noticed a faint scent from the she-wolf that surprised him, and as Otsana turned and led her pack into the east, he couldn't help but raise an astonished brow.

"What is it?" Halea asked when they were finally alone.

"Your scent is just very distracting right now," he replied. He was always far more possessive of Halea when she was in heat, and for that reason, she refrained from hugging the male alphas when they were saying their goodbyes. It was not wise to get too close to other males during that time. It was too much of a temptation and could make for an awkward situation.

Now that the festival was over, the den was once again quiet. The common area looked almost bare, and Halea felt partly relieved that it was over and somewhat sad that she would not see so many friends again for quite a while.

"There will be other festivals and gatherings," Varg promised as he sensed the gloomy turn of her emotions.

"I know. I'm happy this festival went as well as it did, but I also wish it had gone better," she confessed. The demon attack and death of Ethelwolf and Úlfa had soured the event for many, not just because of grief, but as a dark reminder that at any moment, the Chaos Dimension could strike and destroy all that they loved. Coming together to celebrate life and the new year was vital to the morale of their entire people, but Chaos gave them no peace.

They were strolling back through the den when Varg stopped to meet Halea's gaze.

"I wish we could have saved them too. Ethelwolf showed me more warmth than my own father in the years after my mother's death, but their fate was beyond our control. We did everything we could, but besides all the bad that happened, I think it was a successful gathering, and I think I have you to thank for that."

"Do you think I did okay – as a wolfmother?"

"You were the perfect wolfmother," he said, while softly stroking her cheek, and his eyes expressed such love that warmth filled her from head to toe.

"You just do so much for everyone, Varg, and I really want to help you in every way I can."

"You do more than enough. You're the perfect mate. You always have been."

Joy bubbled within her at his praise, and thanks to the bond, she knew he meant every word. He always did so much to please her and knowing that she could help him and support him in the same way meant the world to her.

Eventually, they had to part. They both still had a lot of work to do with cleaning up the den after so many lively lycans had been partying there, and Halea looked forward to finally having everything back in order and restoring some semblance of normality to their lives again.

Her volunteers were also hard at work, and she began by giving them a hand with cleaning up the common area and all the fire pits when, to her surprise, Lyall approached her.

"Wolfmother," he greeted with a polite bow of his head.

"Yes, Lyall," she acknowledged.

"I'm not too proud to admit that with this gathering, you proved me wrong. You conducted yourself in every way appropriate for a supreme wolfmother, and your assistance was vital to Varg. You did well."

"Thank you, Lyall," she accepted with a smile of relief, but her moment of joy was short-lived.

"I hope that he continues to receive the support that he deserves and that you don't forget that being a wolfmother is something that must be lived up to every day and not just for special occasions."

Halea tried her best not to frown in the face of Lyall's continued doubt and merely nodded her head, and with that, the old warrior went on his way.

With the vigor suddenly drained from her efforts, she eventually sat down near one of the fire pits and tried to still her roiling emotions before Varg came and threatened Lyall's life.

Batsuba was keeping a close eye on the human wolfmother's interaction with Lyall from where she sat at another fire pit, boiling water for more of her medicinal remedies, and she shook her head at what she had seen.

"Halea," she called while approaching the crestfallen woman.

"Batsuba," Halea greeted, but before she could stand up, Batsuba sat down beside her.

"Don't!" the elder said.

"Don't what?"

"Don't let that old fart get to you. He's honestly come a long way from how he used to be, but you have to understand, there are some people that you can't please, no matter how hard you try. Nothing you do will ever be good enough, but you can't let one sour apple upset you. You're an excellent wolfmother, and you will continue to excel at being a proper alpha, regardless of what one cranky old wolf thinks. There are always going to be people like that. That's just how life is. You can't win them all. Just carry on as you have been, and don't let it get you down."

"You really are a wise old wolf, aren't you?" Halea asked while mustering a smile from Batsuba's kind words.

"I've had ages to learn to not give a rat's ass what anyone else thinks of me. Respect is important for an alpha, but you also must learn to rise above the naysayers. You're too sensitive sometimes, and you'll have to learn to not take everything so personally."

"I guess you're right. It's just never been easy for me. I've always wanted to be liked and accepted, ever since I was a child, but it never came easy."

"It's never entirely easy for anyone. Focus on those who do love you and don't worry about the rest."

Halea nodded her head as she absorbed Batsuba's good advice. It wouldn't be easy to not let such things bother her, but she would try.

"Now that all this festival nonsense is over, it's time for you to get back to your apprenticeship. We have a lot of medicinal plants in bloom, and there's still much for you to learn."

"I'm looking forward to it, though it may still have to wait until after I get back from Antherose with my grandfather."

Batsuba scrunched her face in disapproval of the delay, but there was no helping it. She was aware that Halea had promised to return for her kin with the coming of spring, and it was best to get it over with.

"Well, it might be amusing to have another human around. You already let the northern redhead stay. What's one more?" Batsuba remarked, then stopped short as if listening to something beyond Halea's hearing.

"That falcon is coming," Batsuba explained.

"Rufus?" Halea asked. Mama Dragon had agreed to keep watch over their territory while she was in Antherose retrieving her grandfather, but she hadn't expected Rufus to arrive without her, and it gave her an unsettled feeling.

The falcon appeared above the trees and came down to land after quickly spotting Halea in the common area.

"Hello, Halea. Hello, old wolf woman," Rufus greeted.

"You shall call me Batsuba," she growled.

"Rufus, how are you? Is everything okay?" Halea asked.

"Um, not quite. Is Varg around? I think he might need to hear this too."

"I'll call him," Batsuba offered, and instead of leaving, she let out a loud howl that was carried across the den and picked up by others further in the distance to be passed along.

The eerie wolf calls sent shivers up Rufus's spine and made him uncomfortable, but he waited patiently as the message was carried.

"What is this? A bird therian? In lycan territory?" asked Marrok, who heard the howls and came to investigate.

Rufus eyed him uncomfortably. He had never met this lycan before and didn't know what to expect.

"Don't be afraid, little birdie. I am no big bad wolf," offered Marrok after detecting the scent of fear.

"This is Rufus, Elder Marrok. He's a friend of ours. He usually carries messages from Mama Dagon; she's a priestess of Tiamet," Halea introduced. "It's okay, Rufus."

"Uh…hi," Rufus nervously greeted, still unsure of what to think of the strange, lanky lycan with the young face and the old eyes.

92

It didn't take long for Varg to arrive, and the moment he saw Rufus, his expression turned grim.

"Hello, Varg. You don't seem pleased to see me," said Rufus.

"That's because you're usually the bad news bird. What brings you here without your priestess companion?"

Rufus's reflective eyes darted around nervously before he finally confessed.

"Bad news."

Varg's only response was to take in one exaggeratedly long inhalation before Halea nudged him to stop.

"Let's not discuss it here. Let's go to our treehouse where we can have some privacy," Halea requested in fear that other lycans would overhear ill tidings and spread panic.

"You're welcome to come, Batsuba," Varg offered.

"Of course," she accepted as if she didn't expect anything else.

"Me too!" declared Marrok, to which no one had any objections, though Batsuba looked like she wanted to protest. It was not her place to invite or uninvite people into the homes of others.

After everyone relocated to Varg and Halea's home and were seated in the recessed seating area for entertaining guests, Rufus began explaining everything that was happening outside of the lycan territory.

"Please help them! They don't have anywhere else to go, and they're dead meat if they stay out there with those things roaming around," Rufus implored on behalf of the priestesses.

"I've encountered one of those shade mimic things too," added Halea. "If Otsana hadn't smelled that it was a demon, it would have killed me for sure. A priestess would have no way of knowing. We…they have never fought anything like this before."

"Chaos is changing, but why? How?" asked Batsuba.

"It's because of Lord Anshar," Halea explained. "Whatever lives within the Chaos Dimension used his blood to make new demons. Stronger, smarter, deadlier demons. Things we've never fought before and things we can barely imagine or understand. Varg, please," she pleaded while placing her hand on his arm.

"Elder Batsuba, is this a matter for the council?" Varg asked, afraid that he would have to send runners to call back all the packs that had already set out for their home territories only a few hours earlier.

"This matter is entirely up to your discretion because it would be the western pack providing sanctuary to the Tiamet worshippers," Batsuba replied.

"I agree with Batsuba. Unless this concerns the other packs, there's no need to call another gathering," added Marrok, and for the first time, Batsuba seemed happy that he was there.

Halea was looking at Varg with those pleading eyes that broke him every time. There was no other choice. Whether he liked it or not, his people and the priestesses' fates were undeniably linked to whether or not the Chaos Dimension could be defeated. The Tiamet worshippers were their allies because few others had the power to stand against the coming of another convergence, and the lycans needed the priestesses as much as the priestesses needed the lycans. On top of that, he was still indebted to Mama Dragon. She and Halea had saved his life after his first battle with the Dragon Lord, and she had also rescued Halea from the dragon's clutches after he first emerged from the Chaos. Mama Dragon had also guarded the den when they were away in the east and had agreed to come and defend it again while they would be away fetching Halea's grandfather. Lycans did not like to feel indebted to anyone outside of their pack, and it would be wrong for him to deny the priestess's plea for help. He owed her too much.

"You may go and tell them that the western pack will give them sanctuary. We may both need each other before these dark times are through," offered Varg.

"Oh, Varg, thank you," cried Halea.

"You have my gratitude as well," added Rufus. "I know I've deceived you in the past, and for that, I apologize."

"Forget it. You don't owe me an apology. You helped me find and save Halea, and for that and all the other help you've given us, I'm in your debt. Let's put our disagreements in the past," Varg replied.

"You set my broken arm, so the debt is paid. Does this mean we can be friends now?"

"Maybe, try bringing good news next time."

CHAPTER 12 – MASTER CLERIC

"Lord Anshar? It's me, Halea. Are you in there?"

Silence.

Halea sighed as she gazed into the dark mirror's surface that revealed only her own faint reflection. She had neglected Lord Anshar during the gathering. There were too many other things occupying her time, and she feared that she had lost the progress that was made.

"I'm sorry I was away for so long. Things have been very busy, and I just wanted to see you before I leave for Antherose."

"Antherose?" a voice softly asked.

"Yes. I won't be gone for long. I'm bringing grandfather here to live with us. I don't want him all alone at his age. It's not good for him."

It had been several days since the gathering ended. Rufus had flown away with the news that the Tiamet worshippers would be given sanctuary. As soon as Mama Dragon arrived, she and Varg would set out for Antherose.

"Alone. I see," said Lord Anshar, who remained hidden within the mirror.

"I was hoping we could talk. A lot has happened. There was a tear, and now new demons are threatening the devotees of Tiamet. I know I'm not a priestess anymore, but they're still my people. I'm going to help them."

"Stop it, Halea! This is not your fight!" he growled. "The dimensions must converge. Everything must end! Don't you understand that you're only prolonging the inevitable? The world must be remade!"

"You know that's all a lie," she replied with raw anger in her voice. He couldn't possibly believe that anymore.

"You're lying to yourself if you think you can save this world. Tiamet will not help you. She doesn't care! The convergence will come, and either the world will be remade, or everything will perish. You're wasting your time!"

"Priestess or not, I'm not giving up, and you can't make me! Maybe we will all die, but I'm going to fight until the bitter end. Tiamet hasn't abandoned us."

"Tiamet wants to continue the status quo, and I told you before – I will never perform another sacrifice. I would rather see the world burn than serve her will again."

"I don't think you have to kill anyone. Just tell me what's in the Chaos. You spoke to it. Tell me who's in there. Tell me what it wants. Please," Halea begged.

Lord Anshar strained his mind to resurface the things he heard, the things he saw, but there was only pain, terror, invisible claws tearing into his flesh, eyes begging, pleading for him to save them, a sword coated with blood, a foul metallic stench, and dead bodies strewn at his feet. And then the memory of the voice that had tormented him from the shadows.

Remake the world.

"Stop it! Stop it! I can't!" he screamed in anguish.

A single tear rolled down Halea's cheek as she listened to his cries of pain, and she ached to hold him, to comfort him, but there was nothing she could do to alleviate his suffering.

"I'm sorry. I'm sorry. It's okay, I'm here. No one's hurting you."

"Please…just leave me alone," he begged.

She was reluctant to leave him like that, but it was clear she wouldn't find what she was looking for that day, and after another moment of hesitation, she turned and left him.

~~~☼~~~

"No luck?" asked Varg.

Halea only shook her head.

"You tried. At least your grandfather will be here soon to help."

"You're right. Even if he can't do much, I just need someone else to talk to who understands what's going on. Grandfather has studied the Chaos Dimension and worshiped Tiamet his whole life. He's the most learned cleric alive. I could really use that kind of help right now."

Varg was reluctant about the prospect of Halea's grandfather coming to live in the lycan territory at first, but he would endure anything for the sake of his mate. With so many other Tiamet worshippers coming to live within their lands for an indeterminate amount of time, what was one more at this point?

Though a gathering of the high council was not required, Varg still announced the news to his entire pack that soon, the Tiamet worshippers would be coming to seek refuge from the servants of the Chaos Dimension. Some were averse to the idea of so many humans coming to their lands, but most were supportive of Varg's decision. Those who feared the Chaos Dimension and worried about the fate of their people took comfort at the thought of having such powerful allies on their side. Many of their best warriors had hunted demons alongside the priestesses of Tiamet, and few hadn't seen their remarkable power to purify the evil of the dark weapons. There was also the fact that many were simply becoming more used to humans than they realized. Halea's presence had changed minds and challenged their preconceived notions about humans, and though most lycans still disliked the idea of strangers infiltrating their tight-knit community, at least their aversion wasn't entirely based on prejudice.

For the past few days, everyone had been setting up a large campground north of the den. It was far enough away that the Tiamet worshippers would not make the lycans uncomfortable but still close enough to be safely guarded. A rotation of lycan sentries would stand watch over their camp to ensure that no shade mimics could make a sneak attack, and if any of the devotees wanted to venture away from the camp, they would have to take a wolf with them for protection.

Batsuba took it upon herself to oversee the campground's formation and ensure that Halea's people would have every comfort and precaution that they could afford them. The temporary living arrangement would be fine for the warmer seasons but would probably be inadequate with the coming of winter. Hopefully, by then, a better arrangement could be made after everyone had enough time to get used to each other.

Varg and Halea could not stay to greet the arriving refugees, they had already made arrangements to claim Halea's grandfather from Antherose before this crisis arose and couldn't alter their plans, but Batsuba would see to everything while they were gone.

As Varg and Halea made their way out to the northern area beyond the den to survey the progress on the refugee camp, howls rang out in the distance.

"She's here," Varg explained, and Halea grew excited as she strained her eyes to see into the distance.

Sure enough, approaching from the west and flanked by several lycan escorts, two white-robed priestesses appeared.

"Mama Dragon! Kalee!" Halea cried as her friends approached, and she quickly embraced them.

With a nod, Varg dismissed the lycans who escorted the priestesses into their lands, and they took off back towards the den, undoubtedly, to spread the word that the first priestesses had arrived.

"We'd have been here a day or two earlier, but since we received your permission to come and stay, we had to notify as many others as possible. Rufus is still out there, spreading the word, and Samesa knows where more of our people are located than anyone else. If he can get the message to her, it's only a matter of time before the rest arrive," explained Mama Dragon.

"I'll spread the word to anyone I can find in Antherose or if we encounter any devotees on our way there or back," promised Halea. "I'm so glad you're finally here. I was so worried about you both. Rufus told me Samesa was attacked."

Varg left Halea to have a moment alone with her friends, and Halea showed them around the campsite that would be their temporary home and explained the precautions made for their safety.

"There's a hot spring for bathing over there and a latrine in that direction. We're actually overstocked on meat at the moment, thanks to all the hunting that happened during the recent festival, but lycans don't keep much non-meat food around, so you may have to forage for anything else you want to eat until the traders arrive."

"We'll manage," offered Kalee. Most priestesses were used to living off the land, and with spring in full bloom, they had plenty of time to forage.

"Once everyone's here, we'll pool our funds to help pay for supplies from the traders," promised Mama Dragon.

"Don't worry. We have it more than covered," Halea promised, but when Mama Dragon tried to argue, she wouldn't hear of it. The lycans had a mountain of gold, and Varg did not mind offering a few extra nuggets that would not be missed to ensure that the Tiamet devotees would have everything they needed over the coming months.

Now that Mama Dragon had arrived and would be guarding the den against demons and tears in their absence, it was time for Varg and Halea to set out on their journey. Varg would accompany Halea beyond the lycan territory, at least through the wilds, but not all the way to the human city. With the dragon contained, he felt less concerned about her safety when not within his sight, and he also had no desire to ever set foot within a smelly human city again. Once was enough.

Batsuba would stand in as alpha, and Lyall would guard the den and lead the hunts while Varg was away. Everything was ready.

Halea shouldered her travel bag, and together they set out northwest through the western lycan territory and beyond. It was a two-day journey at their speed, though the return trip would undoubtedly be much slower due to bringing back an elderly human. Along their way, Varg remained vigilant for any signs of danger and any traces of priestesses or clerics. By chance, they encountered two priestesses and one cleric as they neared the city, and Halea gave them the message about the danger of the shade mimics and that they should head for safety among the lycans. Varg remained hidden during this exchange to ensure the humans wouldn't become nervous or distrustful of his presence. Thankfully, they all knew and recognized Halea and had no reason to not heed her warning, and so they set out for the southeast, towards the lycan lands.

When Varg and Halea reached the edge of the forest that lay before the main road that led towards the city, they stopped.

"Hopefully he's ready, and I'll be back soon," said Halea.

"I hope so too, but if you need more time, I'll be waiting," Varg promised, and they embraced and kissed each other goodbye.

A few hours later, Halea entered the city and was struck by how different it seemed since the last time she was there. Rangers patrolled the streets that had once been much livelier, and everyone seemed to be keeping to themselves. Normally, there were at least a few clerics or priestesses coming or going on their way to or from the castle, but all she saw was townsfolk who looked at her with distrusting eyes.

When Halea reached her grandfather's house, she knocked and waited until she heard footsteps creaking on aging wooden floorboards, and the door flew open.

"Halea, you're here!" cried Favion.

"What, do you live here now?" Halea asked with a laugh before greeting her friend with a hug.

"Almost. Please, come inside."

"Where's grandfather?" she asked.

"He should be home from the market soon. I've been helping him clear out the house and organize his books and maps. He'll be so happy that you're finally here. He's been waiting for you."

Halea was surprised at how different her grandfather's house looked without all his clutter. Crates were stacked neatly against the walls, the books had been taken from the shelves, and even the kitchen was empty. A few spare pieces of furniture were still out, so she took a seat, and Favion joined her.

"How is he?"

"He's ready, as I'm sure, you can tell. I won't say he hasn't been a bit nervous, but he's been preparing for this since you were last here. He's sold off most of his possessions except for a couple of bags he's kept packed for when it's time to go. He even bought a horse. He was hoping you wouldn't mind. He's a bit arthritic these days, and it'll be a long journey."

"No, of course not. It's sort of strange to think of my grandfather parting with so much of his old junk. Even after losing everything in Ruinac, he still managed to clutter up this place," she laughed.

"Yeah, let's hope that horse has a strong back, 'cause those two bags aren't light."

"Favion…is there anyone left?"

"A few clerics are still at the castle, but it's getting pretty inhospitable for Tiamet worshippers right now. For ages, everyone just took us for granted, but now that things are getting out of hand, everyone's looking for someone to blame. The rangers are pissed that they've been asked to help fight demons. Despite Senior Priestess Gwen's best efforts, word has spread that Lord Anshar's gone, and people are starting to get scared about what will happen with the next convergence. There have always been those who distrusted Lord Anshar for being a therian, and now they're gloating as if that's the single cause of all this trouble. They don't have a clue but explaining what's really going on isn't going to make anything any better, and few would understand it anyway. We're kind of on our own."

"No. We're not alone. We have allies. The lycans will help us." Halea went on to share all the news of the new dangers, her work with Lord Anshar, and the offer of sanctuary.

"Our people are already gathering in the lycan territory? I scarcely know what to think, but for the first time in ages, I almost feel good again." Despite his words, Favion's expression darkened. "What about Kalee? Is she there?"

"Yes, she's with Mama Dragon."

"Would you mind if I made the trip with you? I was going to head north, past Westvear, but if we're regrouping, I want to be where our people are. There's also something I have to tell Kalee."

"We'd love to have you with us. It'll be safer with the lycans. What about the clerics at the castle? Can they come too?"

Favion knew the truth about Halea's mother, but Uro had sworn him to secrecy. Edmond would never leave Dean behind, and he had been tasked with looking after Theia too, and Codeon would not want to leave Edmond.

"It's just Codeon and Edmond. I'm not sure they'll want to leave, but at the very least, I'd like to let them know what's going on in case they decide to come along later. I'll run up there and give them the news, pack a travel bag, and meet you back here in a few hours."

"We'll wait for you," she promised.

With that, Favion jumped up and made for the door, but just as he was leaving, Uro arrived.

99

"Favion, where are you going?" Uro asked as Favion wedged past him through the door.

"Halea's here. She'll tell you everything. I'll be back later!" he called over his shoulder before disappearing out into the street.

Uro closed the door after him and turned to find that Halea had got up to greet him.

"Grandfather," she cried while wrapping her arms around him, and he returned her embrace.

"Halea, I'm so happy you're finally here," he exclaimed before cautiously looking all around. "I don't see that shifter with you."

"Lycan, grandfather. Please don't use that term in front of Varg. It's not very nice. As for him, he's waiting for us at the forest's edge, and he'll meet us on our way back. Favion told me about what's been happening in Antherose. He's coming with us. Please, sit down, and I'll tell you everything."

~~~☼~~~

The sun had set before Favion returned, alone, with a light travel bag and news that Codeon and Edmond would not be joining them right away but that they may come along at some point later. Halea and her grandfather had spent that entire time catching up and preparing for the journey.

"I still have your stipend. Are you sure you don't want me to fetch it for you?" Uro asked.

"No, grandfather, I don't have any need for money with the lycans. Can't it be donated?"

"I have written final instructions for my estate. I'll add directions that your funds are to be passed on to the Weldison asylum. There are many who suffer from Chaos Madness these days."

It pained Uro to think of leaving Theia behind, but there was no hope for the poor woman, and if Halea knew that she lived, she would be devastated. The most he could do was see that Theia lived out the rest of her life with the best care and pray that Halea never found out.

"The horse is saddled, packed, and ready," said Favion as he came back inside. "That poor beast."

"Oh, leave off. My bags aren't that heavy," grumbled Uro as he rose from his armchair with a slight protest from his aching joints. He grabbed his staff and paused to take one last look around the old place. It was bittersweet. It was the home Lord Anshar gave to him and Halea when they both lost everything after the destruction of Ruinac. He'd especially miss his comfy old armchair. He imagined spending the rest of his days sitting on rocks and logs and gnawing on twigs and berries to survive, but anything was better than being around the rangers, even living with a bunch of wild animals.

"It'll be okay, grandfather," Halea promised.

"Of course, it will, my child. And if not, well, I'll be dead soon anyway."

~~~☼~~~

Halea had to run ahead as they approached the forest.

"Varg?" she called.

"I'm here," he replied, springing up suddenly and startling her.

"Don't do that!" she shouted and swatted at him, but he caged her in his arms in relief that she was back, and she quickly calmed.

"Sorry," he laughed. "Where's your grandfather?"

"He's coming. Favion is coming too. He'll be traveling with us. Grandfather's on a horse," she explained.

"I always wanted to try horse," Varg mused.

"Yes, about that. You can't go spooking that poor beast. Grandfather's too old to get thrown from a horse. You might have to hang downwind and give us some space on the way back."

Only specially reared horses could tolerate the apex predator presence of a therian. Lord Anshar had a horse-drawn carriage, but those horses were conditioned to his scent from their birth. Most other animals were instinctually afraid if they picked up his scent and avoided him.

Varg growled low in frustration but didn't argue; it was partly a relief. He had no idea of what to discuss with an elderly human, especially one who clearly did not like him. It probably would have been an awkward journey anyway.

With the recent full moon's waning, there was enough light for the party to travel a few more hours into the night before they stopped to set up a camp. The two clerics were relatively silent, either from being out way past their regular sleeping hours or being uncomfortable with the dark and knowing that a wolf was silently lurking somewhere beyond their vision.

It took about four days to make the journey back with Favion on foot and the horse being walked at a gentle pace to suit Uro's aging body. Favion spoke to Halea about all the other remotely exciting news since she left human civilization, and Halea answered all his questions about what life was like living among the lycans. Her grandfather mostly listened in silence and occasionally interjected a scoffing sound of disbelief.

Halea sounded like she was doing quite well for herself among the shifters, but Uro suspected she was exaggerating the level of the wolves' civilization to not worry him. She seemed to describe a well-organized, yet primitive society attuned with nature. He hoped she was not just trying to convince herself that her situation was better than it really was. Out beyond the trees, that brute was lurking around, and he could occasionally feel his horse jitter beneath him if the wind made an abrupt change of direction. He did not know what to expect when they arrived, but he prepared himself for the worst.

CHAPTER 13 - PRIMITIVE

Samesa had already warned several priestesses to beware the shade mimics, but it felt so pointless. How could they even defend themselves from an enemy that could be disguised as anyone they knew?

As Samesa came down from the coastal hills, she thought she heard a falcon in the air, but disappointingly, she did not see anything. She hadn't heard from Mama Dragon in a while, and she struggled to bite back the fear that somewhere, out there, she could be losing her friends.

"Hey," a man's voice called, and she nearly jumped out of her skin, but when she spun around, she was surprised to find that it was Sufur.

"You again?"

"Aw, is that all the greeting I get?" he asked with a smirk.

"Where did you come from?"

"I was tracking you. It took me a while to find you. I've got a message from a priestess who said her name was Mama Dragon."

"Mama Dragon?" she asked in confusion. Something didn't add up. He may have tracked her, but that didn't explain his sudden appearance; unless she was really starting to lose her edge, and why would Mama Dragon send a ranger with a message instead of Rufus?

"Prove it," she demanded while eying him with suspicion.

"Huh?"

"Prove you're really here with a message from Mama Dragon and not one of those *things*."

"The last *thing* you encountered, a shade mimic as you called it, disguised itself as your deceased mentor cleric. This was an event that happened after your mind was breached, am I correct?"

Samesa visibly relaxed and let out a sigh.

"I'm sorry, Sufur. It's just – I don't know who to trust right now. I think I'm getting really paranoid over every little thing, and this whole situation is starting to get to me."

"It's okay, Samesa. You know, you're quite beautiful when you smile, and I hate to see you so worried…"

"All right, Mister Smooth. Can I have that message now?"

Sufur only laughed as she deflected his flirtations.

"Fine. Fine. Can't blame a guy for trying. When I found Mama Dragon, I gave her your message to beware the shade mimics. I also mentioned that the mimic demon stunk, and that's when she had an idea. She said that every priestess and cleric should gather in the lycan territory. I guess you have an ally among the wolves?"

"Halea?" Samesa cried. "Of course! The lycans can smell any demon, and I guess they're kind of on our side. Hey, wait a minute. How can you be sure it was Mama Dragon you were really talking to and not another mimic?"

"Well, she didn't try to kill me, and she was with another priestess with bright red hair, and they weren't trying to kill each other. I'd say the lack of murderous intent was a pretty good sign."

"Fine. Fair enough, though I don't see why she'd send you instead of her falcon."

"She had to send him into the lycan lands to ask for sanctuary before every Tiamet worshipper in a hundred miles started barging in on the wolves. I told her I could find you and let you know what the new plan is. Supposedly, you know where more priestesses are hidden than anyone else."

"That's true," Samesa admitted.

"You know, if you're worried about those things, I'd be happy to come with you – for protection."

Suspecting his offer wasn't entirely altruistic, Samesa decided to remind him of the obvious.

"I happen to be a highly trained super-powered priestess of Tiamet. I could snap you like a twig, and don't forget it. If you really want to help me, we should split up to spread this message. We'd cover more ground and find more of my people that way."

Sufur looked disappointed at her rebuke but was surprisingly undaunted.

"You couldn't make use of a fire-caster? I could teach you some elemental magic," he offered.

Samesa paused as temptation crept into her eyes but eventually shook her head.

"Maybe I'll let you show me a thing or two once we're done spreading this message."

"In that case, until we meet again," he said with a smile and a hopeful gleam in his dark reflective eyes.

~~~~◯~~~~

Eerie howls rang out through the trees the moment they passed into the wolves' land, and Uro had to suppress the shudder that rolled up his spine.

"Between the shade mimics and that attack on the den, our warriors have been on high alert. Plus, they're expecting us. I can sense that Varg has gone off to greet them and probably warn them not to approach and spook your horse," Halea explained, though Uro didn't know what she meant when she said she could sense what her shifter husband was doing.

When they passed through the tall oak trees, they entered a windswept plain. In the distance, a jut of land rose above the bank of a river, and beyond that, the looming mountains. Uro surmised that the base of these mountains was the hub of their primitive civilization. The den, as Halea called it. The old cleric tried not to cringe at the idea of living in some smelly animal hole, but it was too late now.

Uro's one comfort was knowing that the devotees would be gathered nearby, and he looked forward to having communion with the fellow members of his faith. This wolf's den would probably be a far cry from the splendor that had been the Citadel of the Sun or the stately abode that was Lord Anshar's castle.

"This is as far as we should go with the horse," Halea mentioned while offering her grandfather a hand as he stiffly climbed down from his steed.

Favion passed Uro his staff and stared off towards the mountains.

"Well, it looks the same as the last time I was here," Favion commented. He had been one of the clerics appointed to the mission of defending the lycan territories back when Halea had still been a priestess. The wolves hadn't been particularly friendly, but neither had they been hostile, and that was good enough for him. In the distance, he could make out the elaborately carved caves and statues along the mountainside, the trees adorned with wooden structures, and smoke rising from outdoor fires.

"I can't see a blasted thing," Uro grumbled as he took off his glasses and wiped them with the hem of his robe before returning them to his face.

"You will when we get close," Halea promised.

Halea and Favion removed Uro's bags from the horse, Favion taking one and Halea the other.

"Is this full of rocks?" Halea asked. Even with her superior strength, she could tell the bag was inordinately heavy.

"See, I told ya," Favion said with a grin, which was quickly wiped from his face after Uro clunked him on the knee with his staff.

"Halea, please, don't let that wolf eat my horse," Uro implored after turning his attention back to his granddaughter, who had set down his bag and was removing the tack from the animal.

"I knew you would ask," she laughed while giving the horse a gentle pat in reward for its service. "I told Varg to leave it be last night after you two went to sleep. Much to his disappointment. He won't let anyone else eat it either, providing it doesn't hang around here for too long." She doubted that would be the case as she gave the horse's rump a slap and sent it galloping back towards the west. Varg would be waiting to spook the beast and send it running the rest of the way to human civilization. She hated to think of scaring the poor creature, but it really would be at risk of being eaten if it tried to hang around within the lycan lands, and so it was for its own good.

"He's been like a ghost this whole trip. Are we going to see him?" asked Favion, who hadn't seen Varg since the castle's incident.

"He'll catch up before we reach the den," Halea promised while shouldering her grandfather's bag and leading them forward.

As they neared, Uro finally made out signs of habitation, and what he saw stunned him into silence. It wasn't a city or a town. It was like nothing he had ever seen before, a strange village with homes in trees and ornate caves that looked man-made rather than naturally occurring. More howls pierced the air, and before he could make out what caused the commotion, a deep voice spoke from behind him.

"It's good to be home. That was the slowest trip of my life," Varg grumbled to Halea, who offered him an apologetic grin.

Favion nearly jumped out of his skin. He hadn't even heard the lycan approach.

"Oh, hey. Hi, it's you," the younger cleric mumbled while offering his hand to shake, but Varg only looked at it in confusion before Favion awkwardly tucked it into his robe pocket.

Varg merely offered him a curt nod of greeting before turning his attention to Halea's grandfather.

"This will be your home now, Uro. My people were told of your coming. Don't expect a big welcome."

"I was not," replied the old cleric.

"Speaking of big welcomes. Favion, do you see that smoke way out past the north end of the den?" Halea asked, and Favion nodded. "Mama Dragon is there. Kalee too. Probably many of our people have gathered in the time that we were gone. Not that I don't want to invite you to the den..."

"I get it. You don't have to worry about me. I'll meet up with the rest of our people and talk to you later. Take care, Master Uro. Good luck!"

Favion handed Halea the bag he was carrying, and though she easily hoisted it onto her shoulder as if it weighed nothing at all, Varg insisted that she hand over both of her grandfather's bags.

Uro gave the younger cleric a farewell pat on the back, and he almost wished that he could join Favion at the human camp instead. It felt like ages since he was in the company of more than a handful of devotees, but it was best to get the worst of it over with now, and he was ready.

When they arrived, Halea noticed that the den seemed unusually empty upon their return, but they were not wholly without welcome. Many of the warriors who had grown accustomed to the presence of the Tiamet worshippers were there, as well as those who were comfortable with Halea's presence, and now the human woman Jance. A few came to greet them just out of curiosity as most lycans had never seen an elderly human before and were curious to know what a mortal looked like towards the end of its short life.

The aged human was unlike anything they had ever seen. He seemed frail, with thin, white hair, thick spectacles that magnified the size of his eyes to an absurd degree, and skin that hung in loose folds. He reeked of anxiety and decay, and it seemed hard to believe that such a creature could be of any relation to Halea.

Many greeted Varg and Halea with warm embraces and bright smiles of relief to have their supreme alphas home, though no one approached the old cleric who stood back and nervously watched the accumulating crowd of shifters.

One lycan took Uro's two bags from Varg and carried them away, despite Uro's protest.

"It's okay, grandfather. He's just taking them to your cave."

"Cave?" he cried in shock, but Halea ignored his outburst as Varg drew her attention.

Having been gone for much longer than he would have liked, Varg gave Halea a quick kiss before letting Lyall and the rest of his warriors drag him off for reports on hunts, the arrival of the Tiamet worshippers, and their surveillance efforts against the demons.

Halea didn't mind, she would have no shortage of duties to catch up on herself once her grandfather was settled, and she looked forward to getting back to her apprenticeship with Batsuba. To her delight, the old healer also appeared to welcome them home, with Marrok in tow.

"Fenris made a full recovery and set out for the eastern territory a few days ago," reported Batsuba after hugs and greetings were exchanged.

"I'm glad to hear it. I hope Fenris won't be too resentful of Otsana," Halea replied.

"I know he had his hopes up and was disappointed by his loss, at first, but he knows to respect a true alpha. Otsana still must prove herself as a leader, but she's very much like both her parents. She'll earn everyone's respect in no time."

Uro silently watched the conversation between his granddaughter and the young white-haired shifter with curiosity as they seemed to be discussing a political matter that he couldn't really understand.

"Well, what have you brought us this time?" the old healer asked.

"Batsuba, this is my grandfather, Uro, Master Cleric of Tiamet," Halea introduced.

Unlike the others, Batsuba had seen elderly humans before, though not this close, and it had been many years ago.

"So, you're Halea's kin. Welcome. Halea has been my apprentice since the fall, and I take it, she learned the ancient language from you."

At first, Uro was a little stunned to be addressed by the wolf woman, but she appeared harmless enough, and he quickly found his tongue.

"Why, yes, young lady. I personally taught her the language of the gods. Halea has always been an excellent pupil. She gets her intelligence from my side of the family."

Batsuba's eyes peeled open, and she sputtered in indignation at the old cleric's words.

"Young? You impudent pup, I have herbs older than you are!"

Marrok doubled over, laughing so hard he had to wipe the tears from his eyes.

"Now, now, Batsuba, grandfather hasn't met many immortals that aren't priestesses or Lord Anshar," Halea quickly offered in apology, but Batsuba only crossed her arms over her chest with a harrumph and stomped off to her tree-dwelling to stew over her perceived slight.

"Well, that was a terrible first impression," Halea bemoaned.

"It was marvelous," Marrok argued while still gasping for air and cackling in amusement. Once he was more composed, he introduced himself. "I'm Marrok. Batsuba and I are elders, though we may not quite look it to a mortal. I think I'm going to very much enjoy having so many humans around. Things are far more interesting here in the west."

106

"The west?" asked Uro.

"I'll explain the different packs to you later, grandfather. For now, I'm sure you're tired, so let's get you settled," Halea offered.

Uro was more than happy to move away from the scrutinizing eyes of so many wolf shifters who regarded him as some sort of rare curiosity. Thankfully, he wasn't met with hostility, which was the best he could hope for, though he would have been more than happy to teach those wolves a lesson if they dared to try anything.

Marrok shooed away the remaining onlookers, who quickly returned to their business, leaving Halea alone with her grandfather.

Uro looked around as Halea led him up a trail that wound up the side of the mountain. Below, lycans clustered around strange outdoor recessed fires in both humanoid shape and in the forms of massive wolves. Many dwellings were built into trees and connected by rope bridges, and remarkable stone-carved statues of lycans and wolf-headed gods exhibited an impressive amount of craftsmanship. The path was a little steep for his liking, but he compensated by leaning heavily on his rune-carved staff. They stopped before a large iron door, above which was a small window, and when opened, it revealed the foreboding black maw of a cave.

"Sorry, lycans can see in the dark, so they sometimes forget to light the lamps," she explained before slipping inside. Uro waited as a soft glow appeared from within the cave, and Halea returned to usher him into his new home.

He was utterly speechless at what he found. The cave was quite large, with a high ceiling covered in glittering stalactites and oil lamps mounted along the rock walls where they emitted a warm glow. The air was refreshingly cool but not cold, and there was an unlit wood-burning stove with a pipe leading up along the wall and that fed out through the front of the cave. A stone bath was carved into the cave's back wall where water trickled in from a spring and trickled back out again into some unknown crevice. The space was sparsely but comfortably furnished. There was a cozy-looking bed piled high with furs and cushions, a chest of drawers, an empty wooden shelf, and, most surprisingly, a desk and chair.

"I figured you wouldn't come empty-handed, so I asked Varg to make this bookshelf for you. He was doing a lot of woodwork this winter anyway, so a few more pieces weren't a big deal. He made the desk too, though I had to explain it to him. Some lycans use tables, but they usually prefer to do their work outdoors while hanging around with friends and family at the fire pits, or while sitting on the ground, though they do use chairs on occasion."

Uro admired the desk. The wood still smelled fresh and was polished to perfection. It had a single drawer and a built-on top shelf for extra storage. The chair was constructed well enough, with a cushion added to the seat for extra comfort, though he couldn't help but longingly think of the comfy armchair he had left behind. All things considered, his accommodations were far more hospitable than he could have ever imagined, and he realized he owed his granddaughter many thanks and an apology.

"To be honest, this is a far nicer abode than I was expecting."

Halea looked at him quizzically, and he went on.

"I imagined something a little more…primitive."

"Ah! To be fair, I made the same mistake when I first met Varg, and then he showed me the den through your old telescope…"

"Is that why you ran off with that rusty old thing?"

Halea nervously laughed, but her grandfather was not actually angry. Too much time had passed for it to matter anymore.

"Thank you, Halea, for bringing me here to share the last of my days with you. I don't want to be a burden to you, but I've been so lonely these past few years, and I can't begin to express how happy I am that you've welcomed me into your new life. These wolves are strange, but I think I'll manage as long as you're near."

Halea hugged her grandfather as her heart flooded with warmth. They hadn't always understood each other, but she was glad to have his acceptance and that there would no longer be any secrets between them.

"I suppose I must give my thanks to your husband as well."

"Mate," she corrected with a smile.

"Oh, fine. Whatever," Uro conceded with a sigh. "He seems to be treating you well, as far as I can see. If this is your life, it doesn't look so bad."

"You'll like him…eventually. Varg is a good man. Lord Anshar isn't the only decent therian to ever exist."

Uro's lips pursed into a frown at the mention of his lord, and he knew that it was time to ask.

"How is he, Halea?"

"He has good days and bad days. He saw something within the Chaos, I'm sure of it, but it's so hard to keep him grounded. I know Tiamet entrusted him to me, but I'm also afraid that my presence is bringing out the worst in him. I could really use your help right now. I don't know where else to turn."

Uro wrapped his arm around Halea's shoulders and nodded his head at the news.

"Then, I will do everything in my power to help you."

CHAPTER 14 – TOKEN OF LOVE

Mama Dragon stared into the west. Out in the distance, she saw a few moving specks of red and white, and she knew more clerics and priestesses were about to join them. The lycans let out howls whenever Tiamet devotees crossed the borders into their lands. She was starting to get used to that particular call, and it filled her with hope. It felt like ages since their people had last all been together, and though the circumstances were not ideal, there was comfort in numbers.

Lycan sentries guarded the refugee camp day and night, and no priestess or cleric went out to hunt or forage without a wolf accompanying them. Their hosts had ensured their safety and comfort, and in return, at the slightest detection of demon activity, the Tiamet worshippers would set out with their new allies to eliminate any threats.

Favion had arrived the day before, and Mama Dragon was happy to see the young cleric again and learn that Master Uro was now safely among the wolves. She was expecting a visit from the senior cleric in the evening and was looking forward to discussing the pressing issue of the new demons with him.

Kalee approached and stood beside Mama Dragon.

"Eighteen priestesses and forty-two clerics in just this past week, that's pretty good. I wish Samesa were here, though."

"She'll come as soon as she finishes spreading the message," Mama Dragon assured. "She knows where more of our people are than anyone, and it will take time for her and Rufus to get the word out. Providing the worst hasn't happened, we should be a few hundred strong within a few more weeks."

"So few," Kalee lamented. Once there were hundreds of priestesses and thousands of clerics, but after the devastation of the convergence that happened nine years ago and Lord Anshar turning on them, their numbers had dwindled with little to no hope for recruitment. It seemed as if their time was at an end.

"Favion's been looking for you."

"I don't want to see him. I don't want to hear anything he has to say," Kalee bitterly replied.

"It's not what you think. He has something important to tell you. You deserve to know the truth."

"Fine," Kalee relented with a sigh before heading back towards the camp. She had been dodging the young cleric since he arrived the day before, but if they were going to be living in the same place, she couldn't avoid him forever. It was best to get it over with.

She found Favion sitting outside among a cluster of other clerics on roughly constructed wooden benches surrounding a campfire. It didn't take long for him to notice her and get up to approach her.

"Kalee, you're here. Mama Dragon said you've been out on scouting missions since I arrived," he exclaimed while extending his arms for an embrace from which she shied away.

"Please, Favion, if there's something you need to tell me…"

"Right! Look, not here. Can we take a walk?"

Kalee nodded, and they headed for the small grove at the edge of their campsite.

"Do you want me to call for an escort?" asked Aatu as he noticed them leave.

"We're not going further than those trees," Kalee promised. It was as far as they could go before they were out of earshot of calling for help if a shade mimic attacked. The lycan nodded in agreement, but there was still concern in his eyes as he watched them walk away from the camp.

Once they reached the grove, Favion met her gaze with a serious expression, and Kalee waited as he seemed to struggle to express himself.

"I'm sorry to have to tell you this - Joanie's gone," he eventually blurted.

Kalee stared at him silently for a moment, and then one by one, the muscles in her face twitched, her lips trembled, and a gut-wrenching sob tore from her throat as she buried her face in her hands.

Favion wrapped his arms around her, and this time she didn't shy away, leaning into his comforting embrace as her tears quickly soaked into his robe.

"I'm alone. I'm alone," she wailed while gasping for breath between sobs.

He held her close and rubbed her back as she poured out her grief.

"No. You still have me," he promised.

"That's not true!" she shouted while breaking free from his arms. "You're going to die! Everyone grows old and dies, and I get left behind. Don't you understand that we can never be together? Do you think I want to watch you wither before my eyes, like my sister, like Joanie? I can't do it anymore! I can't watch any more people I love fade away!"

"Kalee…" he tried to plead as she crushed his heart beneath every word that fell like a hammer.

"Just leave me alone," she tearfully begged before turning and running back towards the camp.

~~~☼~~~

The next few weeks became somewhat of a routine for Halea. In the morning, she would do field research with Batsuba, who taught her the medicinal properties of every plant they found. There were so many herbs and roots that could do so many things that she had to start taking notes and drawing pictures of the different plants just to keep all the information straight. Despite the challenge, she loved being outdoors with the old healer, and even Marrok would occasionally tag along, though he had no interest in medicine.

Every afternoon her grandfather would come down the winding path from his cave and join her for tea and lunch at the fire pit. Most lycans still avoided him and

110

gave him space as he hobbled along with his staff while they obtrusively stared on. Thankfully, not all lycans were shy. One by one, some of Halea's closest friends among the wolves began to introduce themselves to her grandfather and ask him all sorts of questions, such as: "Does your face hurt from all those cracks?" or "Have you always looked this way?" and "Will you be dead soon?" His face would turn beet-red at such interactions, and once, he nearly choked on his tea. It took all his self-control not to start swinging his staff.

Much to his relief, the curiosity eventually died down, and overall, he found life among the lycans to be quite peaceful. He was shocked to discover that outside of his fellow Tiamet worshippers, another human woman named Jance was living among the wolves, and like his granddaughter, she had a lycan for a mate.

Jance was thrilled with another human's presence, and she took it upon herself to lavish Uro with pastries and sweets for his afternoon tea breaks, for which he was most delighted. The fact that a whole camp of priestesses and clerics was not far from the den filled Jance with glee, and Alf could barely keep her from pestering the Tiamet worshippers, though they didn't seem to mind all the baked goods she kept making for them.

Varg still didn't know quite what to discuss with the old man, who continued to regard him with a disapproving and insolent air that came perilously close to challenging his alpha will. If not for Halea's gentle coaxing, he probably would have snapped and put the old man in his place, but he had to think of his mate's happiness, and so despite the subtle slights, he kept the peace.

Uro had expressed his thanks to Varg for being allowed to stay with the lycans and for his comfortable accommodations, though in a somewhat terse manner. He still was not quite sure how he felt about Halea's choice of a mate. The wolf shifter seemed devoted to his granddaughter, but he appeared stern and commanding to everyone else. Perhaps that was the requirement of his leadership, but Uro wasn't used to anyone, especially anyone so young, bossing him around. No matter where he went or with whom he lived, he was still a Master Cleric of Tiamet, and he wasn't about to let some brutish wolf intimidate him.

After the afternoon meal, Halea would attend to her other alpha duties and accompany her grandfather out to the devotee's camp, where they would rally around maps and plan demon hunts. Every day more priestesses and clerics arrived, but things were taking a turn for the worse despite their growing numbers.

There hadn't been any new attacks from shade mimics since the Tiamet worshippers took refuge among the wolves, but almost as if in retaliation, tears were beginning to appear, and as far as they could tell, only within the western lands.

"This is coordinated," Mama Dragon observed.

"They've always been random before," Alec added. The young cleric had only recently arrived and was often clutching his bow in anxiety. His nerves were frayed between the erratic behavior of Chaos and the unnerving presence of the wolf shifters.

"If Chaos can't reach us with deception, then its next option is to overwhelm us with sheer force. We cannot let these tears get out of hand," cautioned Uro, who hadn't stopped tracking tear and demon activity since arriving in the lycan lands. He didn't like the look of the data he had collected, but it was still too soon to come to any firm conclusions.

Halea felt a sinking sense of dread with every new tear and demon sighting. Inside, she knew that time was running out.

In the evenings, Halea waited patiently at the base of the tree where the dark mirror was safely stored while her grandfather would sit within, attempting to speak to Lord Anshar. His first few tries at making contact with the Dragon Lord had been unsuccessful, but eventually, Lord Anshar responded.

"Uro? Is that you?" came Lord Anshar's voice, though the mirror remained dark.

"Yes, Lord Anshar. I am here now."

"Why are you here? Where is Halea? Why doesn't she come anymore?"

"I am here to help you, my Lord," he replied while ignoring his inquiry of Halea's whereabouts. "I understand that someone contacted you while you were within the Chaos. Who?"

"I don't know."

"Please," Uro begged.

"A voice…it told me the convergence must happen, that we are preventing the way things should be, that the world can be remade."

"Lord Anshar, you must know that you've been deceived."

"By who? The voice or Tiamet? I don't trust either. Nothing is right. None of this has ever been right! What if everything we know about our world is wrong? What if Tiamet really is trying to prevent something that should happen?"

"And what do you think this voice wants? What is there to gain by our suffering and destruction?" questioned Uro.

"Where is Halea?"

"It must want something, Lord Anshar."

A long pause of silence followed, and just when Uro was about to give up, the Dragon Lord's voice returned.

"I saw into its eyes. When the voice was in my head, I pushed back, and then I saw them."

"Whose eyes?" asked Uro.

"Where is Halea?"

"Lord Anshar…"

"Where is she? I want to see her!" he growled, and then the conversation promptly spiraled out of control, with Lord Anshar becoming disjointed and confrontational and eventually falling into incoherent ramblings of things that haunted him in the dark that weren't there and the tormenting evil voice from his memories.

Night after night, Uro would question the former head of his faith. Some nights Lord Anshar would respond, though no amount of interrogating could bring forth any new information, and other nights, he refused to speak at all. Real memories and things that only happened in his mind were confused within his thoughts, but one thing was always consistent - if he spoke at all, he would always ask for Halea.

When Halea's grandfather slowly descended the spiral stairs of Lord Anshar's prison, he always looked remorseful. Every night she asked if there were any breakthroughs, but Uro would only regretfully shake his head.

~~~~☼~~~~

One morning, Halea sat up in bed and wiped the sleep from her eyes. Varg had already risen and begun his duties for the day. At first, she felt idle in comparison, especially when Varg managed most of their domestic responsibilities. He was surprisingly tidy, tidier than her, but when she began to feel guilty, he assured her that he just had a little more time on his hands. Most lycans only slept a few hours a night if they felt like sleeping at all. The day was for hunting and work, the night for relaxation, hobbies, or pleasure.

She pulled off her thin summer nightdress and opened the chest of drawers and pulled out a clean green robe when a glint of white caught her eye. She moved aside a few things and found her old priestess robe neatly folded at the bottom of the drawer and lovingly stroked the red hem and sash. Though she was not really a priestess anymore, the Goddess still called to her. The desire to stare into the west where the Citadel of the Sun once stood among the ocean waves was always present, and her hand still itched to grasp her spear as if it were a missing part of her. Though she hadn't used it much since her battle with Lord Anshar, her old weapon remained propped in the corner, and the threat of Chaos still consumed her thoughts.

As Halea finished lacing her boots, howls of danger pierced the air. Without a second thought, she snatched her spear from its resting place and raced down the stairs and out towards the den.

"Halea!" Varg called as she neared the common area, which had erupted into lycans running for cover. "The sentries have found a massive tear on the northwestern edge of the hunting grounds."

"I'm going," Halea replied, but as she turned to take off, Varg grabbed her arm to stop her.

"Halea, the refugee camp is closer. Let them handle it. It's their job," he reminded with a look of reproach.

"It's my job too. Priestess or not, this will always be my fight. Please, Varg. I can't escape it. I can't," she implored with eyes that weakened him with their conviction.

Even without her spear and white robe, no matter how much he tried to convince her that theirs was no longer her fight, he could never change who she truly was. For as long as he had known Halea, she had been one of them, and he was forced to concede that she always would be. Her fate was undeniably bound to the Dragon Goddess's service, just as much as she was bound to him through their bond. She was as much a part of her people as he was a part of his, and though it pained him to share her, to risk her life by associating it with those who might be doomed, he could no longer deny her the calling to which she had been born. Whatever the outcome, he would love her and stand by her, just as she had always stood by him.

He pulled her close and wrapped her in his arms.

"Then, I fight with you."

"I'd like that," she replied while looking up at him, her eyes glistening with relief. He placed one loving kiss on her soft lips before they ran out to face the danger together.

When they reached the refugees' camp, they found that Mama Dragon and Kalee had already set out with Favion, Alec, and a few other clerics and several lycan guides. Varg picked up their scent trail, and Halea followed him until they caught up with the clerics who were being escorted by Aatu. The faster priestesses had gone on ahead to seal the tear, and the clerics would help eliminate any demons attempting to escape.

Before Varg and Halea could leave the clerics to their duty, a raucous horde of demons appeared through the trees and fell upon the clerics in overwhelming numbers.

Varg drew his sword as wraiths surrounded them, and soon the clash of steel and stench of black blood filled the air. The clerics used their rune-carved weapons and sutras of purification to fight back the demons as Halea's charged spear glowed like a bolt of lightning within her hand, slaying every servant of Chaos that dared to approach. Aatu shifted into his wolf form and leaped into the fray, biting off heads and limbs and spraying black gore across the forest with his ferocious attacks.

Alec wasn't sure what frightened him more, the demons or the menacing wolf in their midst. Favion seemed unperturbed by the massive shifter's presence as his rune-blessed daggers slashed into wraiths cutting them down left and right. Emboldened, Alec nocked his bow and released arrows carved with purification runes along their shafts into some of the more bestial demons, which burst into white light while letting out ear-splitting shrieks.

Halea deflected the dark sword of a wraith. Before it could rebalance itself, she kicked its legs out from under it and stabbed it where it fell upon the ground, causing it to burst in purification. If things were this bad here, further ahead, her friends were in danger.

"Varg, I have to reach the tear!" she shouted over the din.

Varg snarled as he locked swords with another wraith. He could not unleash the Fang's true power without harming their allies, who were scattered everywhere, battling among the many demons. As he was about to try and break away to join his mate, a monstrously large form broke out through the trees with a roar that stilled the air. A bestial demon with a behemoth body and an eyeless face of writhing tentacles charged towards them.

Now, there was no choice. Varg gave Halea a single glance, using the bond to convey his encouragement, and with a nod, she broke away from the wraiths and sped out through the trees to find the tear while he raised his sword and charged the massive beast.

~~~◇~~~

When Halea broke through the trees, the gigantic purple vortex of a tear loomed above her friends. Mama Dragon and Kalee were struggling to reach the dimensional rift, while Hemming and Daciana, their lycan escorts, valiantly tried to defend the priestesses.

114

"Get a barrier up. Hurry!" Halea shouted as she leaped into the fray, spear blazing as she tore down every servant of Chaos that got in her way.

Kalee chanted in the ancient language while Halea moved in to help defend her and Mama Dragon, who was already calling upon her powers to seal the tear.

"Daciana, Hemming, get within the barrier," Halea called, and the two lycans drew close to be encircled in the protective ring of purification just as Kalee finished her spell.

Halea stabbed one last demon through the barrier with her spear before planting the tip of her weapon into the ground and turning with Mama Dragon and Kalee to raise her hands against the tear. Daciana and Hemming stood close, claws at the ready as demon after demon threw themselves against the purified circle and burst into white light while shrieking.

"Tiamet, give us your strength," the devotees prayed in unison, and their hands glowed as the Goddess heard their prayer. The white light of Halea and the priestesses slowly began to engulf the dimensional rift, which pulsed in protest, until with one final thunderous roar, it snapped shut. The demons shrieked and howled in rage to be shut off from the Chaos source before fleeing into the forest.

"We have to go after them," Halea called while pulling her spear from the ground. "Each of you take a lycan," Halea ordered the priestesses. Mama Dragon and Daciana took off in one direction, but before Kalee and Hemming could chase a trail into the north, they stopped.

"Halea, what about you? We can't leave you without a lycan! What if one of those demons is a shade mimic?" asked Kalee.

"I'll follow the demons that fled back towards Varg and the clerics. I shouldn't be too far from help if I need it," she assured. "Now, hurry before they get away."

～～✧～～

Approaching the monstrous demon was impossible as its tentacles latched into anything that came within range. Varg had managed to slice off several tendrils only to be caught and pulled in towards its gaping maw. With one hand, he gripped his sword, which was buried in the beast's jaw, and with the other, he was using all his strength to hold its mouth open, preventing its razor-sharp teeth from chomping him to pieces.

Beneath them, Favion and several other clerics, having defeated the last of the wraiths, were hacking into the creature's colossal legs with their weapons, but the demon's limbs were so thick and sturdy their purified weapons could not pierce its iron-like hide.

Alec released arrow after arrow, but they all bounced uselessly off their target, and his quiver was running low.

The massive wolf fighting alongside them shifted back into its humanoid form and called out to him. "Shoot into its mouth!"

The shifter who wielded the sword must have heard as well because he strained with all his might to pry the beast's mouth open even further, and Alec knew this was his chance. He nocked another arrow and aimed into the gaping dark abyss of the creature's throat.

115

"Tiamet, bless this arrow. Let it fly true!" he prayed and added a few more words in the ancient language. His arrow blazed with the white light of purification as it shot from the bow and straight into the demon's gullet. The beast faltered for a moment before white light erupted from its mouth.

As the creature gagged, Varg pulled out his sword and managed to slice off a few more tentacles and leap away before the purification caused the monstrous demon to explode in a mass of black blood, chunks of flesh, and gigantic shattered bones which littered the ground. There was no escaping the gore as it rained down with a horrible stench, completely splattering all over the clerics and lycans who cried out in disgust.

"Holy shit, we did it!" shouted Favion, and several clerics joined in with whoops and hollers.

"How did you know that its throat was its weakness?" Alec asked of Aatu.

"I'm an archer too. Some game is too hard to kill by going through the hide, so you have to aim for the soft spots. Usually the eyes, but these disgusting demons don't even have eyes. I figured its throat would do."

Alec was surprised and impressed. Clerics did not hunt demons the way an animal was hunted for food, nor did he have any idea that a lycan could be so adept at his weapon of choice, but he figured he should have known that wolves would be expert hunters. He wondered what kind of technique the lycan used, but before he could ask, the larger sword-wielding shifter interrupted their celebration.

"Something's wrong. Halea had a moment of relief, so I'm sure she sealed the tear, but now I sense more danger. Aatu, stay with these clerics and escort them back to the camp," he ordered with red seeping into his eyes before taking off into the woods.

The clerics all looked at each other before their lycan escort noticed their confused expressions.

"What?" asked Aatu.

"What the hell is he talking about? Halea's not even here," asked Favion.

"Don't human mates get into each other's heads?" Aatu asked, but he was only met with more stares of confusion.

~~~⭑~~~

Halea tore through the trees. Something was moving ahead of her, but to her dismay, it was leading her further away from Varg and the clerics than she wanted to go, and she was forced to skid to a halt.

"*I better let it go. It's not worth getting separated. I'll find Varg first, and he can help me pick up its trail,*" she thought. As far as she could tell, two demons had fled towards the south when the tear was sealed, but she had already lost track of one, and it was too dangerous to go on alone.

Halea turned back towards the south and made her way through the brush while keeping an eye out for any signs of the other demon's trail when she noticed strange markings on the ground. She tightened her hand around her spear while fighting the temptation to pursue, and her blood seethed at the thought of these evil creatures evading her, but she could not take risks with her life. With a grunt of defeat, she started moving again when suddenly Varg's voice called to her through the trees.

116

"Halea?"

"Varg! I'm over here," she replied and was relieved as he stepped out from the thick brush and approached. "Thank the gods you're here. You're just in time. There's a trail over there and another one further that way. We can't let these demons escape. Let's go."

"Wait. We'll catch up. I just want to know that you're okay first," Varg pleaded while extending his arms towards her.

Warmth bubbled within Halea's chest to know how much he always worried about her, and she longed to reassure him, but as she neared, she noticed something strange about his emotions.

"You still seem pretty worked up. Are the clerics okay?"

"They're fine. I was just worried about you," he promised while taking a step towards her, and then she noticed something else.

"Varg, did you lose our crystal?" she asked. He had worn it every day since she gave it to him at the festival, but now it was gone.

"Our crystal? No, it's with you," he replied, but as he took another step, she moved away.

"You're not Varg!" she shouted while brandishing her spear.

When the white light from her weapon shined into his eyes, he let out a shriek unlike anything she had ever heard and covered his face. She lunged forward, but he leaped back, and when he revealed his face again, it was distorted and gruesome as his mouth cracked open and snapping mandibles shot out.

Halea twirled her spear in front of her as the creature jumped into the air to avoid purification, but with perfect aim, she launched her glowing weapon after the shade mimic, which burst into white light. With a horrible sound, it writhed into oblivion. A disgusting green smoke rose from its remains and seeped into the forest, where it disappeared among the trees.

"Halea, where are you?" called Varg's voice yet again.

"Varg?" she asked, though now her heart was pounding with fear. What if it wasn't Varg? What if it was another trick?

As Varg appeared through the trees, she swiped her spear at him in warning.

"Stay back!"

"Halea, what are you doing? What's wrong?" he asked.

He was covered from head to toe in black demon blood, and there was a faint trace of rage in his eyes, but she couldn't make out their crystal.

"Is it you?" she asked.

"Of course, it's me. Are you okay? Something attacked you again, didn't it?"

She slowly lowered her spear as he accurately sensed her emotions.

"A shade mimic. It tried to trick me into thinking it was you, but it wasn't wearing our crystal."

"But I am," he assured while raising the token of her love above his chest and wiping away some of the demon blood to reveal the shining blue beneath.

"Oh, Varg," she cried while leaping into his arms, causing his eyes to return to normal.

117

"I'm a bit messy at the moment," he said with a smirk, though he welcomed her embrace. He was relieved that she hadn't been harmed because he could now see the charred remains and smell the slain demon's stench not far from where they were. His chest clenched in horror as he realized how close she had just come to danger, and anger burned within him at the thought that Chaos would use his image to destroy her. Maybe she really was being singled out.

"I tried to come right back to you," she offered in apology.

"Shh, don't. I know. I could sense you coming, and then something went wrong. I came as fast as I could."

"Where are the clerics?" she asked as he released her.

"Heading back to camp. We should get back too. Where are the priestesses?"

"They split up to hunt the demons that escaped when we sealed the tear, and there's also another that went that way," she explained while pointing over her shoulder back towards the trail. "If we hurry, we can catch it."

"Are you sure you're up for it?"

"I'm always up for it," she replied with a feisty grin that made him want to sweep her off her feet and kiss her senseless.

"Puny human, I love you."

"I love you too, you mangy wolf."

CHAPTER 15 - A PEST IN THEIR MIDST

Halea paced beneath the tree that housed the dark mirror. She hadn't spoken to Lord Anshar since after the festival two months ago. Since then, her grandfather had been interacting with Lord Anshar in her stead, but little progress was made.

Lord Anshar had revealed that he saw something, someone, within the Chaos, but there was no way to be certain if that was true or if it was just more of his distorted memories playing tricks on him. Was there even a voice, or had it all been in his head? Some manifestation of his darker emotions personified and running wild?

"That can't be it," Halea thought. *"There is something in there. It used him to hunt the priestesses in its place and stole his blood to make these new demons. It used him for information. Something is in there, and now it knows about me."*

With a final sigh of resolve, she climbed the stairs and entered the darkened room, and lit a few candles.

"Lord Anshar, it's me."

The mirror's surface did not stir, but she waited patiently, and to her relief, his voice called out.

"Halea? Is it you?"

"Yes, Lord Anshar. I'm here."

"Where have you been? Why don't you come to me anymore?"

"I'm sorry. It's just… There's something I need to ask you," Halea prompted, and when she was met with only silence, she continued. "I was attacked the other day."

"Attacked?" he asked with concern in his voice.

"It's not the first time. I'm used to Chaos trying to kill me for being a priestess, but the thing is, I'm not a priestess anymore. I'm not in uniform. I don't even carry my spear that often, yet the demons keep singling me out. They've been resorting to deception. There are these new demons, shade mimics," she explained, then recounted all of her strange encounters and the unusual behavior of Chaos's newest servants.

"Since I got into a scuffle last year, I've kept close to the lycans," she went on while avoiding going into details about her battle with Rafe. "I'm usually with a pack of warriors, or our healer, or…. I'm always with someone," she faltered as she skipped over mentioning Varg in fear of inciting Lord Anshar's anger and jealousy.

"Here, I'm guarded – safe, and I think that's the only thing keeping me alive. It knows. Whatever is within the Chaos, it knows who I am. It knows that I was the last chosen sacrifice of Tiamet, and it discovered that information through you because it got into your mind. It wants to kill me more than anyone."

119

"Halea...I'm so sorry," Lord Anshar spoke, and she could hear that he was weeping. "Forgive me. This is my fault. My weak mind!"

"LIAR!" he suddenly roared, causing her to start. "Bastard! Damn you, I believed your lies! You promised me she would be spared. I knew I was being used, but I wanted to believe. Gods...I wanted to believe."

"Lord Anshar..."

"I wanted it to end. I wanted all of it to end."

Halea blanched at his words as she blinked hot tears from her eyes.

"Did you know the risk? Did you really think there was a chance that your sacrifice could end it when you threw yourself into the Chaos?"

"Yes, I knew the risk. A sacrifice was needed, and I hoped I would be enough, but I knew the risk of my failure, and I chose to die anyway. I couldn't go on. Forgive me. I risked damning the world because I was too weak to go on. I knew what I was doing."

"Oh, Lord Anshar," she wept as the weight of his true decision crushed her heart. He would have sooner let the Chaos destroy their whole world and everyone in it than to perpetuate the cycle. He had gambled with all their lives, and now they were lost.

"I made my choice," he continued. "And I don't regret it."

She gasped in horror at his outburst, but he went on.

"I risked everything, even your life, but I had to. I can't be the one to kill you, Halea. I won't. Let the world burn. Let Tiamet weep! But I will never sacrifice again! Never! Let everything end. Perhaps in death, we may all be free from this torment."

~~~✧~~~

Varg gently rubbed Halea's back as they lay together in the still of the night. Without fail, the dragon would always make her cry, and it made him angry and frustrated because there was nothing he could do but try to comfort her.

Even though he did not need as much sleep as her, he stayed throughout the night, offering the warmth of his love and support with his presence. He would never leave her side when he knew how much she needed him. Sometimes she would wake, panicked and screaming and trembling in his arms, and only his voice could bring her out of her nocturnal terrors.

She wasn't the only one afraid. He needed her too. The ever-present fear of the swordmaster's prophecy would consume him as he lay awake at night, the only time when he could openly worry without Halea noticing. He could always tell when she was asleep by the gentle rhythm of her breathing and how her emotions would become vague and jumbled. When she was awake, he masked his fear. She was already worried to the point of making herself sick. Even her scent was taking on a new quality, and he knew the stress had to be getting to her.

Through their window, the moon rose above the clouds and cast pale silver light across her face. He placed a gentle kiss on her brow and ever-so-slightly tightened his embrace as she lay in his arms. She let out an adorable moan but never awoke. They had made love until quite late that night, and the scent of her passion still hung heavy in the air. But before his thoughts could turn to his usual nightly brooding, a faint sound disturbed the silence.

"Is that a mouse? A bird?" he wondered while listening to a small but rapid heartbeat somewhere within their tree. It seemed muffled, which made it hard for him to detect its location. Because wolves were apex predators, most other animals avoided making homes within their tree-dwellings. Even though a rodent was hardly of interest to such large and powerful hunters, most small creatures instinctively avoided coming anywhere near the scent of a wolf. It was unusual for lycans to experience issues with pests.

He tried to ignore it but eventually got up to sniff around and see where it was coming from. Oddly enough, he couldn't detect the scent of any small animals. It was not coming from the walls. Perhaps it was outside in the branches?

Night after night, this sound would plague him, but he could never find the source. He even once angrily threw one of Halea's boots out the window and into the branches to see if he could scare the annoying thing away, but despite almost waking his sleeping mate, it remained. He had to apologize to Halea the next morning when she woke up to find one of her boots missing, and he was forced to retrieve it from outside where it had fallen into the mud and gotten soggy in the night. There was no choice but to patiently accept her scolding after that.

As spring drew to a close, the traders made their bi-annual visit to the western lands. With so many human refugees, Halea made sure to get extra supplies to ensure the Tiamet worshippers had more food than just meat. She purchased sacks of grain, large quantities of dried fruits and other preserved foods, wine, the variety of tea that her grandfather preferred, and anything else the priestesses and clerics would need.

Mama Dragon had come to meet the badger therians with a list, but Halea snatched it away, insisting that she would procure everything they needed. The priestess fretted over the purchases the entire time Halea was with the strange-looking traders, and she again tried to offer whatever funds the devotees had to pay for their necessities, but Halea only pulled out a hefty bag containing a large sum of gold without even batting an eye.

"Are you sure we can't pay you back?" asked Mama Dragon.

"I won't allow it. You've always done so much to help us, and Varg said that I'm to get you everything you could want or need. So, stop worrying," Halea insisted before calling over several strong lycan males to help carry all the newly acquired supplies back to the refugees' camp.

As Halea was finishing up with the traders, Batsuba approached.

"I'm done. We should still have some time to get some field research in before lunch," Halea offered in apology as Batsuba regarded her with a scrunched expression.

"Halea, there's something you should know."

"Know what?"

"Come up to my tree," said the elder, and together they left the common area and went back to Batsuba's home.

Once they were inside Batsuba's tree-dwelling, the old healer bade Halea to have a seat. The young woman regarded her in confusion but sat down and waited for Batsuba to explain their need for a private conversation.

"Halea, your scent has changed."

"Oh, Varg mentioned that. I guess I've been under a lot of stress."

"That's not stress. Have you been feeling ill at all?"

"Well, now that you mention it, my stomach has been feeling a little queasy lately."

"Halea, you're pregnant."

Halea froze, her mouth slightly agape and eyes wide in shock as the scent of fear burst from her skin with such force that it overpowered the potent herbs in the old healer's home. Batsuba could hear Halea's pounding heart but very little breathing, and she went to place a gentle hand on her shoulder.

"Halea, it's okay."

"No! No, it's not okay. Not now! I can't have a baby now! What if the world is ending?"

"We don't know that, Halea."

"A convergence will come. It's only a matter of time. If I don't find out how to stop it before it gets here, we're all dead. Or I'll be dead…I was Tiamet's last chosen sacrifice."

"Didn't you give Varg your word?"

"I did, and I mean to keep it. I can never sacrifice myself again. It would destroy him too. But what if something or someone else kills me? Lord Anshar swears he'd never sacrifice me, but he's not in his right mind, and then there are the demons. Whatever's in the Chaos knows who I am and has marked me for death. What if I leave my baby behind? What if I leave Varg behind? Oh, Batsuba, I'm so frightened!"

"Halea, get a grip on yourself! What's done is done. I understand your concerns, and you're right to be afraid. We're all afraid, but you must stay strong. We don't know when the end will come, and there's still hope."

"What will I do?" Halea asked as tears glistened in her eyes.

"Cherish every day. Every. Single. One. One at a time. Can you really say that this is all bad news?"

Halea sat thoughtfully for a moment, her hand absently gliding over her still flat stomach. She did want a baby. She wanted Varg's baby. She wanted to know the sort of love and happiness that she had once seen when Ralphina and Lycurgus were still expecting. When all the world was wrapped in the impending joy of knowing that their child would soon be with them. Perhaps it was meant to be. What if this was her only chance?

"No, it's not all bad. I want our baby. I want it more than anything."

"Then be happy. I'm happy for you too. Except for having to deal with Varg. That's going to be a nightmare."

"What do you mean?" Halea asked.

"If you thought Lycurgus was an ass when Ralphina was pregnant, you haven't seen anything yet. There's nothing worse than an alpha male when his mate is pregnant. They're simply unbearable."

~~~☼~~~

Rufus had scoured the wilds for months, and now it was almost summer. He delivered written messages with instructions to seek refuge in the lycan lands to every priestess and cleric he found, and occasionally, he would check in on Samesa, who was also spreading the word. She was so thoroughly on her guard, he didn't have to worry about a shade mimic getting the drop on her again, but he still didn't like her not being in the safety of the wolves' lands. He wanted to appear before her in his humanoid form again, but it was hard coming up with believable excuses for why she kept encountering the same ranger so much. Suspect or no, this was his last chance to talk to her before she went to join the other priestesses. Once she was within the lycan territory, she wouldn't be able to receive any more visits from wandering rangers, and there was no way to know how long the devotees would have to remain among the wolves.

He landed and transformed into his humanoid self before sitting down next to the one forest path that he knew Samesa would follow into the east. His sense of smell was not as strong as a wolf's, but he was downwind and could tell that she was not far.

"Sufur?" Samesa called as she came down the trail and sighted the ranger.

"Samesa! It's good to see you again," he exclaimed while getting up to greet her, but she halted him.

"Wait! What's the plan?" she asked while brandishing her spear.

"Plan? Oh, I get it. Your people are going to the lycan lands for safety, right?"

Samesa relaxed and lowered her spear. It was easy to question those she met about things that happened after her mind had been infiltrated as a way of proving who was a demon and who was not, but it was a little harder to be sure if it was someone she hadn't spoken to since before her encounter with the shade mimic. She had seen a few bestial demons, a couple wraiths, and sealed a single small tear, but thankfully, she had not run into any more disguised servants of Chaos. It made her wonder if perhaps the Chaos now knew that she was onto their tricks.

"Sorry. I just had to be sure," Samesa explained.

"I get it. You don't have to apologize. Any luck finding the others?"

"I finally spread the message to everyone I could find."

"They must have been pretty well hidden. I didn't find any," he said, but in truth, he was covering for the fact that he couldn't appear before anyone else in his humanoid form. It was safer to spread the message as a falcon, and it would have been odd if none of the other priestesses or clerics mentioned seeing a ranger.

"Well, thank you for offering to spread the word anyway. I guess now that that's done, it's time for me to join them. If we don't meet again, goodbye."

"Before you go, don't you want me to show you how to make fire?"

"I would like that, but won't it take a while?" she asked with temptation in her sparkling dark eyes.

"It's just one spell, so it shouldn't take long. You can practice it on your own time," he promised.

Rufus silently thanked the gods that after completing her priestess training, Sophia had thought to share some of her knowledge of the ancient language and a few basic spells with him. Elemental spells had always been of particular interest, and he had practiced for many years to achieve the tiny flames that he could produce. It wasn't much, not nearly as powerful as what a real ranger could do, but he was confident that Samesa could pick it up with ease.

He began with the first half of the spell, and Samesa's face grew crestfallen.

"I know this part, but it doesn't work for me," she explained after recognizing the ancient language's familiar words.

"There's more," he promised before adding a few unexpected invocations.

"Air?" Samesa cried in doubt, but before she could argue further, a flame came to life within his hands.

"See? Fire needs a little air to help it along. Just like when you're lighting a flame without magic, and you blow on it. Or when you use a fireplace bellows. Something about adding a small amount of air seems to help. I know it's not much, but it's enough to get you started. With practice, you can master the spell without having to speak the words aloud, and maybe in time, you can strengthen the spell and learn to bend it to your will. Why don't you give it a try?"

Sufur gave her a nod of encouragement, and mustering her resolve, Samesa opened her palms to the heavens and called upon the ancient elemental magic.

A tiny yellow spark ignited and flickered as she invoked the word for air, causing the struggling flame to burst forth from within her hands and burn bright and true.

"I did it!" she cried, and Sufur's heart thrummed within his chest as her lovely face glowed as much from her radiant smile as from the fire within her hands.

She was so beautiful. He had always given her shiny things to make her smile, but nothing compared to the joy the gift of fire had given her. He would have gladly spent an eternity finding new ways to make her happy to keep seeing that radiant look in her eyes.

"You're brilliant. The most amazing woman in the world," he declared, and though her complexion was too dark to reveal a blush, the bashful expression she wore at his praise told him that his words had touched something within her.

"It's a start, but I'm grateful. Thank you, Sufur," she said as the flame dwindled away within her hands. "I promise I'll practice every chance I get. Maybe someday I can wield fire with as much skill as a ranger."

"If you wanted to, you could be the best," he promised, and again she looked pleased but embarrassed by his open praise.

~~~◇~~~

Batsuba's diagnosis struck Halea like a bolt of lightning, and for the entire rest of the day, she struggled to come to terms with the truth of her condition, but most importantly, she had to tell Varg.

How would she tell him? When? She didn't know, and there was no hiding the confusion and anxiety within her. She couldn't block him all day. His concern reached out to her like a warm hand across their bond, and when he returned from the day's hunt, he immediately wanted to know what was distressing her.

"Halea, what's wrong?"

"I'm sorry. Something's come up, but please don't worry. I'm just not ready to talk about it right now."

"But what is it? You can tell me anything," he promised, but she avoided his eyes, and he detected the scent of fear. "Halea?"

"Please, Varg. I just need to gather my thoughts. Please understand. We can talk about it later."

A spark of dread rose within him. It had to be something terrible. Halea always shared everything with him, and now she seemed afraid to speak to him, and he wondered if he had done something wrong.

She detected his dark turn of emotions but rushed to reassure him.

"It's not you. I swear."

"All right. I'll understand if you're not ready, but please don't keep me in the dark forever. You're freaking me out."

Despite trying to brush it off, he was on pins and needles all throughout dinner, and an uncomfortable silence had fallen between them as they walked back to their treehouse at the end of the night, and still, she didn't seem ready to talk.

Once they were home, she changed into a thin summer nightdress, crawled into bed beside him, and laid her head on his chest. All he could do was wrap his arms around her and hope that she was okay.

"Varg, do you still hear it?"

"Hear what?"

"The little mouse. You said that some pest had moved into our tree, and you could hear its heart beating. Do you still hear it?"

He strained his ears to listen beyond the rustling of the wind through the branches of their tree and the steady beating of their own two hearts, and beyond that, still muffled and faint but ever-present, a small, fast fluttering.

"It's still here."

"It's our baby," she said.

A moment of silence stretched on into eternity. Eventually, Halea looked up into his face. His eyes were staring blankly at the ceiling, and the bond was open, but it was as if he couldn't grasp onto a single emotion, and so there were none.

"Varg?"

"Our...what?" he finally asked with strain in his voice.

"Batsuba told me today. My scent hasn't changed because of stress. It's because I'm pregnant. That little heartbeat, it's in me."

"Halea?" he asked as she rolled away from him onto her back, and when he met her gaze, she nodded. He sat up and looked at her where she lay before leaning over her and gently placing his ear over her abdomen.

Fast and strong and undeniable, he could hear the life of their unborn child.

The bond surged as panic, joy, fear, excitement, and confusion erupted within him, and Halea bit her lip in fearful apprehension of which emotion would finally surface in dominance. And to her disappointment, it was fear.

"Varg?"

125

He lifted his head and softly placed his hand over her stomach, his eyes clenched shut as the muscles strained along his neck and jaw.

Everything he ever wanted was finally his, and the moment was shattered by his secret burden.

The prophecy.

"She can't leave me. She can't die! Not now! I can't be left behind!" he thought in dismay. His only comfort in her inevitable fate was the knowledge that he could follow her, that even death would never keep them apart, but now he had to consider their child. If anything happened to Halea, he could not abandon their cub. No matter how much he longed for death, he would be bound to the life they had created together. The hand that was not resting on his mate's stomach clenched into a fist as he recalled his father.

His mother's death had destroyed his father's spirit, turning him into a shell of his former self. Cold. Withdrawn. Emotionless. He remembered all too well how his father couldn't bear to look into his eyes because they were his mother's eyes. As a child, he couldn't understand the depth of his father's grief, all he knew was that it felt as if his father cursed his very existence, resenting that he had to stay behind to raise his only son rather than join his mate in the next world.

Now, as a man, Varg knew his father's pain. Loving Halea and bonding with her allowed him to finally understand and even forgive his father for how he was treated after his mother's death. But that didn't change the fact that he had felt cold and unloved by the only parent that he had left.

What if he did that to their child? What if Halea died, and he resented being left behind? What if he took it out on their cub?

His heart thundered in his chest as panic and fear consumed him.

What if he was just like his father? What if he wasn't strong enough to get past his grief and raise their child with all the love and warmth that it deserved? The alpha in him roared possessively at the mere thought of any suffering being wrought upon the precious life they had created together, even if by his own hands. He couldn't bear the thought of turning cold against anything that was a part of his beloved Halea. He needed to protect it, cherish it, like the treasure that it was - the greatest gift his mate had ever given him. He could not make their child suffer as he had suffered, but the very thought of losing Halea, of being left behind, wracked him with unbearable sorrow.

He had no way of knowing how he would react if the prophecy came true while still raising their cub. Was he a stronger man than his father? He didn't know, but he knew losing Halea would destroy him. Of that, he was certain.

When he finally opened his eyes, he balked when he looked up to see that Halea was crying as she stared back at him.

"Varg…I…I thought you wanted this," she sobbed.

"Halea, it's not that! Don't even think it! It's just…like you, I'm afraid of the future," he said while sitting up and pulling her into his arms. "I'm afraid I'm not strong enough to protect you, to protect this child. I wasn't lying when I said I wanted to give you a cub…it's just, I didn't want to think of the consequences, and now that it's happened, it's finally hit me how precarious our situation is."

"I know," she whispered as fresh tears streamed down her cheeks. "I wanted to wait for a better time. If there ever would be a better time. I'm so sorry."

"No, Halea!" he demanded while pushing her back so she would be forced to meet his gaze. "Don't apologize. Not for this! No matter what dangers lie ahead, or what happens to our world or when, I want this! I want our baby. I want you! I love you more than anything, and I swear upon the gods, I will love our cub. I already do! Everything I've ever wanted is right here in my arms," he promised before kissing her passionately.

The bond shifted from fear and sadness to excitement, longing, and a love so intense it made her head swim. When he finally broke their kiss, her tears had dried, and her heart was thrumming in her chest.

"Varg, are you really happy?" she asked, hardly believing the shift in his emotions.

"Yes! You're pregnant! You're mine, and you're carrying my cub – our child," he huskily breathed while running his lips down her jaw and lower along her throat until he latched his fangs harmlessly but possessively over her mating mark.

His hands roamed lower along her body, igniting warmth in their wake, and she gasped as he pulled up her nightdress and trailed his fingers along her thighs.

"Varg, I love you so much," she professed as he slipped his fingers along her tingling folds, sending heat into her core.

The wolf within him stirred as the scent of her arousal permeated the air, and the red seeped into the edges of his eyes.

His.

His mate. His child. He'd fight the world for them both. Lay down his life for them both. Possessive need consumed him as he pulled her nightdress over her head and discarded it on the floor.

He always slept nude, so there was nothing between her and his hard, chiseled body. She feasted her eyes on him as he hovered above her, limned in moonlight through their open window. Faint scars could be seen all along his tanned flesh, but beneath the skin rippled powerful muscles that twitched as she ran her fingers over his body. His eyes glowed in the low light, revealing his lust, and he growled in need as her hands explored lower and along his pulsing shaft.

As much as Varg loved her touch, his inner wolf was taking control, and tonight the beast was impatient. He leaned over her but paused as he considered that perhaps he should start being gentler with her in her current state. With an encouraging nudge from him, she rolled onto her side, where he settled in close behind her and explored her voluptuous curves.

"Halea," he growled in a deeper bestial voice as he breathed in the intoxicating scent of her skin. She moaned as his hot mouth sucked and nipped along her throat while his fingers found the node between her legs and softly worked their magic.

When his fingers were coated in her lust, and there was no air but the scent of her arousal, he knew that she was ready. She cried out as he lifted one of her legs and inserted himself into her burning depths.

"Varg," she pleaded as he latched his fangs onto her mating mark. Through their bond, she could sense that his primal beast had assumed control. Dominance and carnal hunger raged within him as he thrust inside of her. The heat was building within her as the sharp prick of his fangs penetrated the surface of her skin, sending shivers up her spine and a shudder throughout her body. Sweet release washed over her as he claimed her, and she threw back her head in utter submission, causing him to emit a rumbling growl from deep within his chest as the red fully consumed his eyes as he came undone inside of her.

His arms embraced her possessively and lovingly from behind as the wolf within him receded.

"Halea?" he breathed as she was falling asleep.

"Hmm?"

"You've made me the happiest man alive."

CHAPTER 16 – THE MOUNTING DANGER

"But the God of the Dead refused to heed the call, and so Tiamet, in her infinite wisdom, stripped him of his sword and cast him…"

Edmond stopped reading as the shrieking from the patient down the hall became too distracting, and with a defeated sigh, he closed the sacred text.

"I'm sorry, Dean, it's a bit too loud to read in here, but don't worry, I won't leave you."

Dean didn't react to Edmond's futile act of altruism. He only stared blankly ahead of him into nothingness as a trail of spittle ran down his chin. At the other end of the wing, Theia lay sleeping in one of the infirmary beds. She no longer called out for her daughter.

Codeon walked in, and finding the usual state of her fellow cleric, shook her head in remorse.

"Did you send the raven?" Edmond asked as his friend approached.

"Yes."

They decided it was time to send a message to Senior Priestess Gwen to gather any devotees that she could find in the capital and head for the lycan lands.

"I'm not sure how long that will take. It's not going to be easy for her to break away from the king's council. I think we should leave too."

"No," Edmond quickly replied. "I can't leave him. This is my fault. I promised. He was so afraid of going on that mission, and I promised him I would look after him, that I wouldn't leave his side. He trusted me."

"Edmond, you've got to stop! You can't keep blaming yourself. Look…I know things were still kind of up in the air between you two, but it was clear how much he cared about you. He wouldn't want you to torture yourself like this."

Edmond's face darkened as unshed tears glistened in his eyes. "I can't. I can't turn my back on him. I know there's no hope, but I made a promise, and I won't leave him!"

Codeon placed a gentle hand on Edmond's shoulder as he shuddered in grief.

"Besides," he continued. "I also promised Master Uro that I would keep an eye on Halea's mother. I can't leave."

Codeon nodded in defeat.

"I had a feeling you wouldn't leave him behind, and while I hate to see you do this to yourself, I understand. Can you do me a favor? If my husband sends any messages to the castle, can you have a raven pass them on to me?"

"Does he know?" asked Edmond.

"Yes, I told him I don't know when I'll be back."

"Did you tell him that you love him?"

"Of course. I made a promise too. I told him if we can survive one more winter, I'll quit being a cleric and come home to him for good."

Edmond looked up in shock.

"That doesn't leave us a lot of time to save the world, but it's as much time as I can give," she explained with a sad smile.

"Is that really what you want?" asked Edmond.

"I wanted us to find a way to end all of this, but the way things are going, it looks like it will be our end instead. I know I haven't exactly been a good wife, but I don't want to go out with regrets when the end comes. You understand, don't you?" she asked, and Edmond nodded.

"Codeon?"

"Yeah?"

"I'm going to miss you while you're gone, and thank you for being such a good friend."

~~~☼~~~

Halea sat quietly at the fire pit, sipping tea while her grandfather prattled on, telling one of his old stories about his days as a younger cleric and his adventures across the sea. She had heard this one before, many times, but for some reason, he never got tired of retelling the same stories over and over again. She obliged him with her partial attention. It made her realize how depressingly lonely he must have been over the past few years, and she desperately wanted to make it up to him.

To her relief, her grandfather seemed to have settled into life among the lycans with surprising ease, but she supposed that was because her own experience among the wolves had paved the way. Most of the lycans gave him his space, but to her surprise, some had offered their friendship. One afternoon she had gone looking for Batsuba to begin their field study for the day when she happened upon her grandfather sitting with the old healer and Marrok, having a lively discussion entirely in the ancient language. The three seniors all turned on her with eyes that expressed irritation at her intrusion, and she quietly backed away.

She had been waiting all morning for the right moment to tell him, and now that they were alone, she didn't want to let the opportunity pass.

"I purified four wraiths before that stupid rookie would get off his ass and lend a hand. I hope cleric training isn't as lax over there today as it was when I was a lad. Alas, I'll never cross the sea again to know."

"I'm pregnant!" she blurted before he could continue.

Uro halted his cup of tea before it reached his lips and stared at her with slack-jawed surprise.

"With what?" he asked with unblinking eyes before shaking his head and correcting himself. "I mean…you are? How?"

"Gods, grandfather, don't ask me that question!" she begged as her face turned bright red.

The old man sputtered in mortification for a moment.

130

"I meant…well…he's not human. I just assumed…that wasn't something that happened."

"Apparently, it does happen – just not very often. Are you okay?" Halea asked as her grandfather's face went pale with shock.

"Gods, I'm old. You know you're really damn old when you're having great-grandchildren."

Halea couldn't help but laugh at her grandfather's shallow concern, but eventually, his face grew serious.

"When your parents told me that you'd been born blessed, I assumed my line would end with you. You'd swear the oath, and that would be it, and for the longest time, I thought that was what I wanted – a priestess in the family. I served all my life, only to lose your grandmother and all my children, including your father, and I felt as if Tiamet had abandoned me, but then you were born. I thought the Goddess had finally answered my prayers. I was wrong. A stupid old fool. I wanted you to be powerful, to be favored, but not to be chosen. Perhaps I was punished for my selfish wish. I can't make that up to you, but I want to see you happy before I die. Are you happy?"

"Well, aside from the unknown fate of our world, for this, I'm happy," she replied with glistening eyes and a warm smile.

"Then I'm happy for you. Maybe if I'm lucky, and the gods don't completely have it out for me, I'll live long enough to see this great-grandchild."

"You're not allowed to die. You're the only family I have left, and I need you. I just wish…I wish mother were alive."

Uro grew silent and grave for a moment, and without meeting her eyes, he gently patted his granddaughter's hand.

"I'm not the only family you have left anymore," he reminded.

"I guess you're right," she replied. She had Varg, and now their child, and living among the lycans and alongside the priestesses felt like having one big extended family, and it warmed her heart that everyone she loved and held dear was so close. She and Varg were overjoyed to know that they would soon have a child of their own, but at the same time, she was frightened. She had never had a baby before, and it occurred to her that maybe she didn't know what she was doing. Whenever the doubt began to creep over her, her thoughts would always turn to her mother. If she could be half the parent her mother was, everything would be okay. Even though it had been years since her death, Halea still mourned the loss of her mother. Her mother had understood her and loved her unconditionally, and there were times while enjoying her newfound happiness that she would think – *"If only you were here."*

Halea quickly wiped a tear from her eye. There was no helping it. Her mother was gone - forever.

"You won't mind having a half-therian great-grandchild?" she asked.

"I'm still in shock to have any kind of great-grandchild. These wolves are…interesting. Not what I expected. Some of their ways seem savage and wild, but they aren't very different from us in many other ways. I admit that in the past, there were times when I would forget that Lord Anshar wasn't just another human. He was so lordly, so civil and refined. I convinced myself that he was unlike any other therian, that he was uniquely sympathetic to humanity because he was of Tiamet's blood. I traveled enough in my youth to know that there are evil therians in this world who slaughtered humans out of nothing more than pure hatred, but I suppose they're not all like that. I don't know what to expect from a half-therian child, but at least a small part of it will be of my blood, and I don't want to make the same mistakes again."

Halea was glad to hear that her grandfather was coming around, but before she could ruminate much longer, howls echoed through the trees and were passed on until they reached the den. Excusing herself, she quickly jumped up and ran out to meet their warriors.

"Lyall, what is it?" she asked while skidding to a halt at the den's edge.

"A runner, from the north," he translated, and Halea sighed in relief that it wasn't another demon attack, though she wasn't entirely comforted. What could bring a runner from the north?

When the runner entered the den, Varg was already with him. The northern lycan stopped to offer his greetings to Halea and introduced himself as Sandalius, and once the formalities were out of the way, the three of them relocated to the alpha's pit.

Food and drink quickly arrived to refresh the tired runner, and from her peripheral, Halea noticed Alf and Jance observing from a distance, no doubt excited to see one of their fellow pack members.

After Sandalius had a moment to catch his breath and slake his thirst, he explained the reason for his visit.

"I bring grave news. Three tears have opened in the north."

"Three?" cried Halea, who was immediately suspicious of why Chaos was suddenly attacking outside of the western lands with such force.

"Please, you must send priestesses to help us. We slaughter any demons that come near the den, but we can't risk getting too close to those tears. If any of our warriors get injured by those dark weapons, we have no one to purify the wounds. Bertolf will not risk the lives of the pack, but the tears stand between us and our hunting grounds."

Varg shot Halea a knowing look, and she nodded.

"You're in luck! We've given refuge to the Tiamet worshippers since the gathering," Halea explained.

"I did notice that strange camp reeked of humans as I passed through from the north," replied Sandalius.

"I can send a few priestesses and some clerics to help you, but they must be guarded on the journey," Halea continued. "The reason they're here is they're being hunted by demons that can only be detected by scent. I'll bet Chaos is trying to lure the servants of Tiamet away from the safety of our den."

"I'll go!" announced Alf, who overheard every word and immediately flew into panic at the thought of his home and people being in danger. "Bertolf will need me, and I can help protect the Tiamet worshippers along the way," he offered as he approached the alpha's pit with a respectful bow of his head.

132

Jance ran up behind him. The color had drained from her face, and her eyes were wide with concern. "Alf?"

"Jance, you should stay," suggested her mate.

"What? I don't want to be without you."

"He's right," interjected Varg. "If Halea's suspicions are true, the journey will be dangerous, and Alf will already have his hands full guarding the priestesses and clerics without having to guard you too."

"Don't worry," Alf said while embracing his trembling mate. "We'll beat their asses, and as soon as the danger's over, I'll come back to the west. I'll always come back to you," he promised while placing a kiss on the top of his tiny mate's head.

"He'll be okay, Jance. We've got the best priestesses and clerics here to help. We better go over there and give them the news," Halea added before standing, and Varg got up with her. Jance, Alf, and Sandalius followed them out to the refugees' camp.

"Tears? Are you thinking what I'm thinking?" Mama Dragon asked Halea once their party arrived and explained the situation.

"Maybe Chaos knows that we've been protecting you," Halea confirmed, and Mama Dragon nodded.

"It could be testing the extent of our alliance with the wolves," added Samesa, who had rushed away from the clerics to embrace her former priestess friend.

"Well, who should we send?" asked Mama Dragon.

"I'll go," volunteered Samesa.

"You just got here this morning," argued Halea. "Stay and rest. Besides, if our theory about Chaos is right, we're going to be seeing more runners. You'll be back out there fighting again soon enough."

"I can take this mission," offered Kalee.

"I'm going too!" Favion declared while ignoring the reproachful glare of the redheaded priestess.

Eight clerics volunteered and two more priestesses, one of them being Pauline, who had arrived a few days earlier. After Alf bade farewell to his tearful mate, the devotees and their lycan escorts set out for the north.

Varg and Halea walked Jance back to the den, but the poor woman was inconsolable.

"I'm sorry, it's just, Alf and I are hardly ever apart," she explained through sobs and sniffles.

Halea wrapped a comforting arm around Jance's shoulder, and she sensed a pang of guilt from Varg.

Varg was often haunted with shame for the time he thought he was leaving Halea at the den for her own safety, and the moment his back was turned, Rafe, the previous southern alpha, attacked and nearly killed her.

"Alf is a good warrior, and the priestesses will help save your pack," Varg offered in condolence. "He'll return to you. In the meantime, you're safe here with us. The western pack is here for you."

"Aw, you're one of those sweetheart alphas, just like Bertolf," Jance exclaimed as her eyes brightened at Varg's kind words.

Halea stifled a giggle when she sensed that Jance's compliment had embarrassed her mate and caused his long, pointy ears to turn a little red.

"He's a total softy," Halea added and snickered when Varg shot her a look that said he was going to pay her back for the teasing the moment they were alone.

~~~☼~~~

Just as Halea suspected, there were more runners. A few days later, Ralph arrived on behalf of Raoul and the southern pack with news of tears and increased demon activity. Samesa, who had met Raoul and helped the southern pack the year before, volunteered to go again and took a handful of clerics and a few lycan warriors as escorts. It wasn't long before Fenris arrived from the east to also implore for aid.

Halea could not help her curiosity, and as supreme wolfmother, she had the right to ask.

"How are you doing, Fenris? I wasn't here to say goodbye when you left."

"Elder Batsuba is a skilled healer. I'm well."

"How are you getting on with Otsana these days?"

He looked a little shamefaced as he lowered his gaze, but eventually, he replied. "She is my wolfmother. I respect her. I'll admit it wasn't easy at first. I always envisioned myself as someone capable of leadership, and I had convinced myself that Otsana wouldn't rise to the challenge, but she did, and she's proven herself more than worthy. We all still mourn the loss of Alpha Ethelwolf and Wolfmother Úlfa, but I think the pack has handled their passing better because their daughter has succeeded them. She's a lot like them, and it's almost as if our old alpha pair is still there because not much has changed, and that's a comfort to most. I admit, if it had been me, I probably would have shaken things up, and perhaps in time, someone would have challenged me for it. I don't think anyone will ever challenge Otsana. She's where she belongs."

"I'm glad to hear that things are going so well," Halea said with relief.

"She asked me to tell you that you're always welcome to visit the eastern pack and that she looks forward to seeing you again."

Halea beamed at Otsana's thoughtful, personal message. She was so happy that they had set aside their differences and could finally be friends, and it was nice having another wolfmother among the lycans.

"I'll have some priestesses and clerics ready to set out with you by this afternoon. Please give Otsana my best wishes and tell her that I look forward to seeing her again too. Oh, did she have any messages for Varg?"

"No."

~~~☼~~~

Tears were even springing up in the wilds beyond the boundaries of the lycan territories, but still suspiciously close enough to where the lycans and devotees were made aware of their presence.

Despite their reservations about straying away from their lands, lycan warriors would still accompany the priestesses as far as the northern mountains and all the way to the edges of the ruined city to ensure their safety as they performed their duties. As soon as the demons were slain and the rifts closed, they would all quickly return to the safety of the western territory, but the situation grew more dire with every day. As the Chaos activity increased, more were injured, and there were many close calls with dark blades. In time, the lycan warriors and devotees were seen returning from missions carrying the bodies of the fallen.

Wails of grief were often heard among the den as news arrived of another loss. Someone's mate. Someone's parent. Someone's child. Several bond-broken lycans were soon to follow their fallen loves, and there were many funerals. Halea's heart ached as she would stand with Varg and Batsuba and pray over the graves while feeling helpless and afraid. If it wasn't a lycan funeral, it was a devotee's funeral. Clerics were usually the first to fall. As unblessed worshippers of Tiamet and mortal humans, they had no innate defenses against the evil poison of the dark blades. Even a few priestesses were slain, and their loss was the most devastating because they were the only ones with the power to seal the tears, and with every day, their numbers were dwindling.

Uro gathered reports on all the tear and demon activity brought back by the surviving priestesses and clerics, and soon his private cave was strewn with charts containing the accumulated data, and he did not like what he was seeing.

He didn't dare mention his findings to Halea. She was in a delicate condition, and the stress and grief of their situation and the recent losses had already upset her enough. Things were looking grim. It was still too soon to calculate when, but all signs pointed to the coming of another convergence.

Halea hadn't told anyone else about her pregnancy. It was hard enough telling Varg and her grandfather, but eventually, everyone would find out if only for the strange behavior of their alpha.

Varg had been volatile ever since learning that his mate was with child. He fluctuated between being ecstatic and pleased to hot-tempered and possessive.

Halea could sense that he was happy about the baby but also cripplingly frightened at the same time, and he was always on edge.

One morning Halea awoke and was surprised to find that Varg was still there. Usually, he was up before dawn, planning the hunts for the day and overseeing the sentries. But before she could question him, her stomach lurched, and she raced to the window, leaned out, and released the contents of her stomach.

"Halea, what's wrong? Are you okay? I'll get Batsuba!" Varg fretted with a panicky look in his eyes.

"No. No, it's okay," Halea argued. "It's just morning sickness. It's normal." This wasn't her first bout of morning sickness, but Varg wasn't usually home in the morning to witness the worst of it and blocking the bond had kept him from fretting and spoiling the hunts.

"Normal?" he practically shouted.

"Varg, calm down. Since becoming an apprentice, I've helped Batsuba care for enough pregnant she-wolves to know at least a few things about what to expect. You better get used to this. I…" But before she could continue, she had to lean out the window to be sick once more. She didn't usually get so violently ill straight out the window, but her nausea seemed particularly terrible this morning.

Apprentice or no, that was as much as Varg could tolerate, and as soon as Halea was done, he scooped her up into his arms and whisked her off to Batsuba's tree.

"Come on, Varg, I can walk," she argued.

"No!" he growled, and she could sense that he was in that alpha state of mind where he was not about to tolerate any argument.

When they finally reached the old healer's tree, Batsuba sighed at Varg's behavior.

"Out," she commanded Varg, and Halea was shocked when he snarled at the elder. He was usually so tolerant of the she-wolf's snappish behavior.

"Oh, save it. Unless you know how to brew herbs to cure morning sickness, you're just a big lump getting in my way. She'll be fine, now out!"

Halea heard his growl growing steadily louder, and she knew she had to step in.

"It's okay, Varg. I think we have it under control," she soothed, and reluctantly her irritated mate left them alone.

"I warned you. It'll get worse," Batsuba said as she poured hot water over some herbs in a cup. "Alphas are absolutely insufferable when their mates are pregnant. Their instinctual need to protect is at its highest. As if he wasn't already a hothead. Here, drink this," she said while offering Halea the mild medicinal tea.

"He seems worried," Halea replied while taking a sip and slightly burning her tongue on the hot liquid. "Ow."

"It's not entirely unwarranted. Pregnant females are more delicate and vulnerable, and that sets any lycan male on edge. He's going to be tiresomely overbearing until this cub is born, but if you want to make it as easy on yourself as possible, humor him. Though I hate to say it, that's the only way. Let him fuss. Allowing him to think he has some control of the situation, whether that's true or not, is the only thing that'll give him peace of mind."

Halea nodded her head before finishing her tea, which had finally cooled.

When Halea came down from Batsuba's tree, her nausea was gone, and she found Varg waiting for her.

"Weren't you going hunting?" she asked.

"I decided to let Lyall manage it for today. Are you okay? You were in pain."

"No, I...oh, that. The tea was a little hot. Varg, everything's going to be okay," she promised as she watched him sigh and press his fingers to the bridge of his nose.

"I'm sorry, it's just...I've been thinking - worrying."

"Yeah, I can tell," she said with a crooked grin.

"All these tears and demons. Things are getting worse. Every time there's a howl, you race out to the refuge camp. I know you haven't been joining the missions because of the risks, but you're always out there, and I don't want you getting so involved anymore. It's too dangerous."

"Varg..."

"Halea, I know they're your people. And I'm not saying to never fight Chaos again. I'm just asking you to take a break for a while, at least until after our baby is born. Your people are here, and our warriors are helping them. They'll handle it. You said it yourself; you've got a target on your back. Stay closer to the den, or at least don't go out to the camp without me, and let the runners bring you news of what's going on. Your grandfather and Mama Dragon can supervise the missions without you. Chaos knows who you are, and it knows you're here. Please, Halea. If you won't do it for me, do it for our cub," he begged.

Though she hated to admit it, he was right. She had avoided going on demon hunts within their territory since discovering her pregnancy, but she was still involved with almost all the other activities of the devotees, and continually running out there was not without risk. Chaos would do anything to eliminate her, and though she was used to risking her life, she now had to consider the life of their unborn child. As much as she wanted to help, as much as the Goddess still called to her, she had to put their baby first. With the progression of her pregnancy, her mobility would decrease, and it was not like she could fight in that condition anyway. All the other Tiamet worshippers were there to help. She could afford to take a break until after their child was born.

She sighed in defeat but wrapped her arms around his waist and laid her head on his chest, and he embraced her in return. "All right. I promise, I'll let Mama Dragon and grandfather manage the missions, and I won't volunteer for any hunts, at least until after the baby's born, and I won't go out to the camp without you, but I may ask you to take me out there a lot. Batsuba said treating the injured will be good field practice."

He instantly relaxed in her arms, and love surged across their bond.

"As long as I'm with you and you don't overexert yourself. I'll take you anywhere you want. Thank you," Varg whispered into her hair.

"Batsuba did say that I should humor you," she replied with a laugh.

"Wait? Since when does she ever take my side?"

"Never, she still said you're a hothead."

~~~☼~~~

One night before dinner, as all the lycans were still gathered in the common area, Varg rose and announced the news of Halea's pregnancy. Howls of joy and shouts of approval rang out, and ale flowed in celebration well into the night.

Halea abstained from the alcohol at Batsuba's behest, but she enjoyed the night just the same. So many of her dearest lycan friends came to wish her well and offer their congratulations. Ulrica, Daciana, and Ralphina were thrilled at the news, and each of them offered to give her any advice she could ever need to raise a lycan cub.

All the males teased Varg once they found out the true reason for his recent moody behavior. A few of those who had mates and children had suspected an announcement wouldn't be long, and some had even taken bets on whether his mate was pregnant or if he was just particularly annoyed by all the increased demon activity. He good-naturedly accepted their ribbing as everyone raised their tankards in congratulatory toasts.

The idea of a half-wolven child left a few in shock as they had never imagined that such a thing was even possible, and some secretly disapproved, though they would never dare say so aloud. Halea expected that a few would be less than pleased, and she noticed that Lyall was nowhere to be found during the celebration. She had to remind herself of Batsuba's words and try her best to ignore her disappointment.

As the night wore on, Jance approached Halea with distress in her dark eyes.

"Jance, what's wrong?"

"May I speak to you in private?" the diminutive redhead nervously asked.

Halea nodded, and they left the common area to find a quieter spot.

"I…I don't know what to say, I guess," Jance began. "I'm happy for you. Really, I am, but I'm also scared…and envious."

Halea was surprised, but she waited for Jance to continue.

"I couldn't carry our baby, and sometimes I wondered if it was because humans and lycans weren't meant to have children together. Elder Marrok swears that wasn't the issue. I don't know if he'd approve of me telling you this, but he once told me that he is half-wolven."

"What?" Halea practically shouted.

"Shh! Oh, I don't know if I'm not supposed to tell you about it, but I had to say something. Maybe it's true, but if it is, then…I guess it was just me. I'm weak…I…" Unable to continue, she broke into a sob.

Halea's heart wrenched in sympathy, and she quickly embraced Jance, who wept without restraint on her shoulder.

"I'm sorry. I'm sorry, Halea. I don't know what's wrong with me. You're just so lucky, you know…and…I guess I just can't help envying you right now. I meant what I said, though; I am happy for you. I was thinking that Alf and I should return to the north once he came back for me, but now…I want to see it - if you'll let me. I want to see a half-wolven child with my own eyes."

"Jance, of course. If that's what you want, then you're welcome to stay. You and Alf, and even Elder Marrok, are always welcome in the west. To be honest, I'm scared about this pregnancy. Even Batsuba's never delivered a half-wolven, and we don't entirely know what to expect, but I promised Varg I wouldn't go on any more demon hunts until after this baby is born. Until then, I can only pray to the gods that things will be okay."

Jance wiped her eyes as she recomposed herself. "I think you can do it. You're so strong. I've never met a woman as strong as you. You were even a warrior before you were an alpha."

"I don't know if that kind of strength has anything to do with pregnancy. For now, I'll have to rely on the strength of others. It's going to take some getting used to."

"I doubt I can be of much use, but if there's anything you need, anything at all – you can always come to me," Jance offered with sincerity.

"Thank you," Halea replied while resting a comforting hand on her friend's shoulder, and together they returned to the celebration.

~~~☼~~~

The next morning Halea arrived at the refugee camp with Varg and her grandfather. Varg had only accompanied her to ensure her safety while away from the den, and he left her to share the news with her friends in private while he went to check on the camp's sentries. Her grandfather also excused himself to speak with Samuel, who had just arrived with his acolyte, Jennifer.

Apparently, news of Halea's pregnancy had spread like wildfire and already made its way to the refugee camp. A few were stunned and didn't know what to think, but most had already accepted that Halea's new way of life among the shifters was far from conventional, but it suited her, and so they were happy for her. Those who disapproved remained silent and reproachful, but Halea had anticipated that some would hang onto their prejudiced ideas. It was enough that her closest friends were with her.

Mama Dragon approached Halea with Rufus perched on her shoulder. The falcon bobbed its head excitedly at the sight of Halea, and she suspected he was dying to say something but was maintaining his animal form for the sake of his anonymity.

"Wow, so, I heard the news," admitted Mama Dragon.

"I was hoping to wait until Kalee and Samesa got back, but lycans are a bunch of gossips," she confessed while suspecting that it was Aatu who had opened his big mouth before she had the chance to make the announcement herself. He was currently stationed as a sentry, and no doubt, Varg was giving him a scolding for spoiling her surprise.

"I'm happy for you, Halea," Mama Dragon said while offering an embrace. "You'll be a wonderful mother."

Halea returned her hug and felt reassurance at her words. Mama Dragon had always acted as a maternal substitute for her own mother, and it was comforting to know that she was near during her pregnancy.

"I'm nervous, though," Halea confessed. "It's not exactly a good time, and I don't know if I'm ready. I don't have a clue what I'm doing."

"Those feelings are all normal, I promise. Everything will be okay, and if there's anything you ever need, you can always talk to me. I'm the only priestess here who knows what it's like," Mama Dragon offered, and it was true. Most priestesses swore their oath when they were still young, before marriage or children, and thus would never experience motherhood, but Mama Dragon had not become a priestess until much later in life after losing her family. She knew firsthand exactly what Halea was going through, and sympathy poured through her eyes to see such uncertainty in the younger woman before her.

"I'd like that. Ever since I found out, I've been missing my mother so much. I know I can turn to my she-wolf friends and Batsuba for all kinds of advice, but I don't know. It feels different with you. You've been looking out for me since I was a child. You don't know how relieved I am that you're here."

"I'll always look out for you, Halea," Mama Dragon promised before leaning in to whisper. "Rufus is also very happy for you."

"Thank you, Rufus," Halea replied to the falcon on Mama Dragon's shoulder. Normally, she would have offered him a head scratch, but she refrained as she had to remind herself that he was actually a therian and that it might be awkward to be so forward with his animal form, but he bobbed his head and squawked when she smiled warmly at him.

As Varg reached the edge of the refugee's camp, he found Aatu at his post but was surprised when he also found Hemming and Faolan, who were not on assigned duty, and with them was the cleric they called Alec. They were standing around with bows and arrows, shooting at targets out in the distance.

"Is this how you spend your guard duty, Aatu?" Varg asked as he gave the beta male a stern look, causing Aatu to lower his head in apology.

Alec, quickly sensing an uncomfortable tension, decided to speak up. "It was my idea. Aatu has been keeping watch, and maybe it's not allowed, but I started keeping him company while he was out here."

"The human's a good shot with the bow. No harm getting a little target practice in, and if any demons try to get through our defenses, some long-range weapons will teach them a lesson," added Hemming, who, when made aware that Aatu and the cleric were practicing their archery, was not about to be excluded when it came to his favorite sport.

"I'm just here to make Aatu's life a living hell," added Faolan with a wicked grin. Hearing them go on and on about the skill of bow-hunting wasn't particularly interesting, but he enjoyed seeing the three archers compete, and he had done more than his fair share of encouraging and heckling.

"Just don't slack off. If so much as one demon gets through, I'll have your asses," Varg warned, but despite his threats, his friends were excited to see him there, and it wasn't long before everyone was showing off their archery skills.

Varg was pleased to see that his people were getting along so well with the humans, and he couldn't help but reminisce on how different things were the year before. It was hard to believe how much had changed, but unlike some, he did not fear change for the better.

He looked forward to the birth of their first child as the start of something wonderful and new, but always when his joy was at its zenith, the red-hot stab of doubt and fear would assail him.

What if something happened to Halea? What if he lost her? What if he couldn't go on and their child suffered the way his father made him suffer? He had to be strong to protect the ones he loved, and he hoped that perhaps this was all a part of the wolf gods' plans. They had blessed him with the skill to wield the Fang and chosen him to be the defender of his people. Surely that must include his mate and child? Was he being tested? He couldn't be sure, but one thing was certain; he could not fail.

CHAPTER 17 – THE EYES OF EVIL

Rufus delivered messages to Samesa from Mama Dragon about Chaos's increased activity and the losses they had sustained. Samesa was devastated by the news but not surprised. Subduing the tears and demons in the south had taken far longer than anticipated, and even her assigned party had lost two clerics before she was able to return to the western lands.

Upon her group's return to the refugee camp, Samesa was pleased to find that Codeon had finally joined them, and the two devotees shared a warm greeting.

"Is Edmond here, too?" asked Samesa.

"No, I couldn't persuade him to leave Antherose," Codeon regretfully replied with sadness in her dark exotic eyes.

Samesa shook her head. Edmond had always been quite sensitive, and his devotion to their fallen comrade didn't come as a surprise. Those two had once been very close.

"Mama Dragon kept me posted on all the casualties and Chaos activity while I was away. I'm so sorry I wasn't here. What else has been going on?" asked Samesa.

"Well, one interesting thing has happened. I suppose you haven't heard yet."

"Heard what?" asked the priestess.

"Halea is pregnant with that wolf shifter's child," Codeon exclaimed.

"Really? I can't believe such a thing is possible," Samesa said in surprise.

"Well, I guess it is. But Halea seems happy, and while these wolves are strange, they're treating us well, and they're treating Halea well. That big lycan male obviously loves her. You should see how he fusses over her now that she's with child," Codeon said with a chuckle.

"That doesn't surprise me. I once challenged him for Halea's life, and I know for a fact that he'd do anything for her. I can't wait to congratulate her."

Though still compelled by the Goddess, Halea had built an extraordinary life for herself among the lycans, and Samesa was genuinely happy for her friend. Samesa tried to imagine what it must be like, but the idea of ever having children was of no interest to her as she was content to live her life in obedience to her oath. There were many different types of happiness in the world, and she knew that one way or another, being a warrior was the life path that suited her and gave her all the sense of purpose she needed.

Mama Dragon appeared and warmly greeted Samesa, whose face lit up at the sight of the motherly priestess.

"Thank Tiamet that you've returned. Were you able to subdue the last of the tears in the south?" asked Mama Dragon.

"Yes. We had a lot more cooperation from the southern pack this time. They're still a bit standoffish, but I think their new leader has softened them to the idea of accepting our help. Some of them even helped us perform the funeral rites for Tim and Marie."

"I'm relieved to hear the wolves weren't giving you any trouble, especially considering there will be more missions. Don't be surprised if you end up having to go back. The frequency of these tears has Master Uro worried," Mama Dragon reported.

"He thinks it's coming again," confirmed Codeon.

"The last thing I wanted to hear," grumbled Samesa.

"The last thing any of us want to hear," added Mama Dragon.

The screech of a falcon drew Samesa's attention towards the sky, and she noticed Rufus circling down to land and extended her arm.

"Even Rufus is here to welcome me back," Samesa exclaimed as the sight of the falcon lifted her darkened spirits. "Is that for me?" she asked when she noticed that he was holding something in his beak, and when she opened her free hand, he dropped the object onto her palm. It was a smooth white seashell, but when she turned it over, the inside glittered with a rainbow of opalescence.

"Wow, thank you, Rufus. You always find the prettiest things. Good thing I'm a priestess, or this bag would be heavy," she said with a smile while tucking the precious gift into her travel bag.

Mama Dragon gave her feathered companion a sharp glare but said nothing.

~~~☼~~~

Summer came and went, and Halea did her best to keep up with her healer apprenticeship despite Varg's protests. Though she couldn't fight, she could help treat those who were injured by demons, and Batsuba was always with her to supervise as she applied her new skills. Halea left purifying the wounds inflicted by the dark weapons to the priestesses because she suspected it would be too much physical exertion for one who was pregnant, and Varg agreed. The bigger her stomach got, the more he fretted over her, and Batsuba was at her wits' end with Varg's overprotectiveness. He insisted on escorting them whenever they left the den, and the old healer often had to resist the urge to snarl at her hovering alpha. The elder knew it could not be helped. Halea's pregnancy, combined with the mounting danger of the Chaos, was enough to make any male paranoid and defensive, and so she endured.

"You've been out too long," Varg grumbled as the two women returned from foraging near the den for herbs.

"I'm fine, Varg," Halea promised as she handed Batsuba her herb collecting basket.

The old healer only groaned at Varg's scolding. It was a daily occurrence. He didn't want Halea getting too hot in the sun. He didn't want Halea walking too far and getting tired. He didn't want Halea to be out somewhere where she couldn't sit because it was getting harder for her to get up off the ground. The alpha had roared in her face the day Halea returned to the den with a slight backache from stooping to dig up roots.

As much as Batsuba hated to admit it, Halea's mobility was decreasing now that her stomach had grown. Soon, it would be better for the human woman to take leave from her apprentice duties. The old she-wolf knew that Halea would protest, but it was also for her own sanity because she couldn't handle much more of Varg's alpha temper.

Varg had many anxieties. Over the summer, the tears were a constant occurrence, and several more lives had been lost to demon attacks. The servants of Chaos were also disrupting the herds, which the lycans depended on for their food, and the hunters were beginning to have to spread out further and remain away from the den for longer to ensure they brought home enough meat for the entire pack. Priestesses, clerics, and many of the lycan's best warriors were often sent out on demon hunting missions, but no sooner would they return than more runners from the other packs would arrive, calling them back again. Eventually, many of the priestesses and clerics stopped bothering to return to the west and chose to remain in the other territories, but runners were continually sent to keep Varg informed about the status and safety of the other packs. The news was rarely encouraging.

Sometimes, between his alpha duties, and while Halea was busy with Batsuba, Varg would retreat to the lake closest to the den in solitude and practice his swordsmanship with the Fang. It would have been more beneficial to have a sparring partner, but even alone, he could focus on form and stance. The knowledge and skill bestowed upon him by the gods were still with him, and for that, he was grateful because he needed to be ready to challenge any foe that dared to take Halea away from him, be it demon or dragon.

The wolf gods had chosen him as their champion. They had a higher purpose for him, and when alone, he would pray for their guidance and strength. If he served their will and used the Fang to protect his people, he could perhaps avoid the threat of the swordmaster's prophecy. He tried not to get his hopes up about that possibility too much because Corbin's visions seemed so absolute, and the gods could be cruel, but inside, he wanted to believe that all wasn't yet lost, that he was still being tested. Prophecy or no, he had offered himself the wolf gods, and he would serve their will.

In a few more months, their child would be born, and Varg was filled with a mixture of excitement and dread. Everything he loved was at stake, and the thought of losing Halea and being left behind was nearly driving him mad. Thankfully, Halea only interpreted his terror and despair as nerves due to this being their first child and all the increased demon activity. He carried the burden of the prophecy alone, and only by forcing himself to focus on becoming stronger was he able to hide the extent of his fears from his mate.

The first time Varg felt the new life beneath his hand, he knew he could never give up. They were walking to their treehouse one night after an evening spent around the fire pit when Halea stopped and clutched her stomach with a pained expression. Before Varg could panic, she grabbed his hand and placed it over her stomach, and there, he felt the strong kick of their unborn baby. Varg's face lit up in exhilaration as he met the eyes of his mate.

"Ow! Kicks like a mule, and I'm blaming you for this," she teased. Together, they laughed and embraced. For that one moment, all the fears washed away, and there was nothing but joy and hope for the future.

His cub would be born healthy and strong, of that Varg was sure, but he was still concerned for Halea. Batsuba warned him that all pregnancies had risks, and he was aware that some women died in childbirth. Such a terrible thought had crossed his mind more than once - that perhaps the prophecy could be fulfilled through natural causes and not some foe. The possibility of Halea dying during childbirth terrified him worse than her dying by the enemy's hand. An enemy he could fight, but against the forces of nature, he was helpless.

Varg knew he was being obnoxiously overprotective, but he did not want Halea to take any undue risks. He couldn't bear the thought of something terrible happening and being left behind, because more than anything, he feared himself. He feared that his grief would consume him and that he would hurt their child the same way his father had hurt him. As much as he wanted to believe that he would never let that happen, he doubted his strength.

Despite the anxiety about the mounting danger, Halea had never known such love and support in all her life, not just from Varg but also from her pack and priestess friends. The long walk out to the refugee camp had become a tad exhausting, and Varg had insisted that Halea not exert herself more than necessary. Thankfully, Mama Dragon came to the den regularly to visit with Halea and offer her words of comfort and encouragement, and if they were not out on a mission, she would often be accompanied by Kalee or Samesa.

Kalee was beyond thrilled when she learned of Halea's pregnancy, but she was saddened as well.

"Maybe there's hope for happiness after abandoning one's oath after all," Kalee had commented.

"It's hard when you still feel the call," Halea admitted. "I can't help staring into the west at times. Tiamet never really lets us go."

"That's what I was afraid of," Kalee replied with a sigh as she rubbed her moist eyes. "Without Lord Anshar, I can't escape this immortality. Not without doing something drastic, and I'm too much of a coward for that. Believe me, I've thought about it. There's no point in abandoning my oath. I could never have what you have, and if I tried, eventually, I would have to watch the ones I love grow old and die. I've had more than enough of being left behind...alone."

Halea wrapped her arm around her friend's shoulders as she poured out her grief. She could only imagine how awful it would be to lose the ones you loved to the sands of time, and she unconsciously rubbed her hand across her stomach and gave thanks that her child would surely be immortal, and that time would never tear them apart.

~~~❊~~~

"It's coming, isn't it?"

Uro grew silent as they walked away from the common area and towards the tree where the dark mirror waited. A harvest moon hung heavy in the sky and illuminated the dry leaves that littered the forest floor.

"Everyone's talking," Halea went on. "The tears, the demon attacks, it's getting worse all the time. I know you've been tracking the tears since you came here. Always the cleric."

"Yes," he confessed. "I didn't want to frighten you – not now."

Halea sighed and stopped mid-step to place her hands on her aching lower back. To her surprise, her grandfather passed her his staff, but she waved her hand in refusal. He needed it far more than she did. The gesture's kindness was not lost on her, but it didn't do much to help her argument that she was not so fragile that she couldn't handle the truth.

"We're running out of time, aren't we?" she asked.

"That's why, tonight, I cannot fail," he replied.

Uro visited Lord Anshar regularly in Halea's place, but little progress was made. Some days Lord Anshar was incoherent with madness; other days, he was silent. Often, he called out for Halea, and when Uro refused to yield to his demands, Lord Anshar would become hostile and withdrawn. There were a few occasions when Lord Anshar seemed lucid enough to hold up his end of a conversation, but the more questions Uro asked, the more Lord Anshar's grip on reality would slip away as if the truth were too much to bear. He had seen something within the Chaos, of this, Uro was sure, but with every attempt to force the Dragon Lord to recall the encounter, the madness would grip him.

"If he doesn't talk, we're doomed," Halea lamented.

"I have a plan, but you may not like it."

"I suppose you're not going to tell me this plan?"

"No, because it may not work, but if it does, I may have to ask you for your forgiveness later," he explained as they finally reached the winding stairs that led up into the isolated tree.

Halea's brow furrowed at her grandfather's words, but she nodded her head as he ascended the stairs. She would agree to anything if there were even the slightest chance of getting the information they desired. Halea trusted her grandfather to interrogate Lord Anshar in her place, especially since her pregnancy began to show. She didn't dare appear before Lord Anshar in her present state for fear that it would drive him further into madness and speaking with him at the best of times had been upsetting enough.

"Lord Anshar, may I speak with you?" asked Uro after entering the room, lighting a few candles, and having a seat in front of the dark mirror. He gently removed a cloth-bound item from a leather satchel that he had brought with him.

Candles flickered, dancing light across the dark surface of the mirror as a slight breeze battered the branches of the tree against the dwelling, but there was no reply.

"You must be very lonely in there, Lord Anshar. Allow me to read to you from the sacred text," Uro offered as he unwrapped the cloth-bound item to reveal a well-worn tome. "I'm sure these holy words will comfort you in your…"

"Don't you dare," growled Lord Anshar from within the mirror.

"But Lord Anshar…"

"I will hear nothing of Tiamet!" he snarled.

"Then perhaps we can discuss something else," Uro offered as he rewrapped the tome and placed it back in the bag.

"You waste your time by tormenting me with your repetitive questions."

"No questions," Uro replied. "I just thought you'd like to hear about what's been going on since you've been gone."

"I don't care!"

"That's a shame. I was going to tell you about how Halea's been doing, but if you don't care…"

"Halea?"

Uro picked up the satchel and rose from his seat and went to grab his staff when again, Lord Anshar's voice rose from the mirror.

"Wait! Where is Halea? Is she okay?"

Uro stood with his back to the mirror, his hand reaching for the door as a sly smile slid across his craggy face. "I thought you didn't care?" he asked over his shoulder.

"The only thing I do care about is Halea. I want to see her again. Why doesn't she come to me anymore?"

Uro propped his staff against the wall and turned back to the mirror, reclaiming his seat.

"She doesn't come because you will not help us, and it breaks her heart. But perhaps I can persuade her to come see you again. I am an ailing man, not long for this world, and I'm sure she would humor the request or her poor old grandfather. That is if I should choose to ask her."

"Then ask her!"

"No. I think not. You've made it abundantly clear that you wish for the convergence to come and swallow us all. If you will not help us, then why should I help you?"

"What do you want, old man? Do you want me to kill her? Is that what you would ask of me? A sacrifice? Your own flesh and blood! I thought you loved her?" growled Lord Anshar.

"I do love her, and I don't want her to be the sacrifice. That's not what I'm asking. All I seek is knowledge. You have heard things, seen things, from within the Chaos. You said you saw eyes. The eyes of who? I must know what lies within the Chaos. Even before you threw yourself into the convergence, you once believed that there was a sentient entity controlling the rift between our dimensions. You were right, weren't you? Tell me what you saw!"

Flashes of darkness and terror clouded Lord Anshar's perception at Uro's words, and he snarled in anguish. "No!"

"Then I will tell Halea that there is no point in ever seeing you again," Uro threatened as he again rose from his chair.

"No! Stop!" Lord Anshar roared.

"Lord Anshar, I know you're in pain, but please, you must remember what you saw. Tell me!"

Reluctantly, Lord Anshar sighed in defeat before closing his eyes as darkness swirled around him, and the voice from his memory boomed from within.

You must remake the world, or you will never be free!

He remembered fighting his way past the voice and into the deepest folds of the void that lay beyond, and there within, he saw the eyes of a dragon.

"A dragon!" Lord Anshar cried. "I saw its eyes. The red eyes of a god! I felt his presence!"

"A god? A dragon god?" Uro gasped.

"The false god. It can't be anything else," Lord Anshar lamented.

"Zernebog," Uro uttered the cursed name with a shudder. "So, he has been trying to break through the dimensions to reenter our world."

"But why? Why didn't he kill me? If he wants to end the sacrifices, then my death would have been the answer," cried Lord Anshar.

"Maybe he wants more than just to return. Maybe he wants revenge against Tiamet for casting him out of heaven. You are her most beloved. Corrupting your mind and soul and turning you from Tiamet would inflict unbearable suffering upon the Goddess. Maybe that's what the false god wants."

A growl rose from within the mirror, causing it to shake upon its stand.

"Tiamet, that bitch! She must have known that this was Zernebog all along, but why wouldn't she tell me? Why would she keep this from me?"

"I don't understand it either, Lord Anshar. She must have had her reasons. I must reflect upon this information, but I will return," Uro said as he rose and gathered his things.

"No! You promised that I would see Halea. I want to see her now! I have given you what you want. Keep your word!" Lord Anshar snarled.

"I will keep my word and ask her to visit you, but not tonight. Convincing her to come may take some time, but I promise she will be the next person you see."

Uro could hear Lord Anshar growling and cursing in rage as he closed the door behind him, but he ignored it as he descended the stairs.

Halea looked up at her grandfather with hopeful eyes, but her face darkened when she noticed his pained expression.

"Grandfather, are you okay?"

"Lord Anshar has finally given us the answer we seek, but it's grave news indeed."

"He actually told you? But what is it? What's wrong?"

"It seems we are up against a god," he replied.

"A...god? Who?"

"Zernebog, the black dragon. The god of death," Uro explained. Zernebog was known to the worshippers of Tiamet as he was the god who had proven to be false and unjust, and after committing some insult upon Tiamet, she had cast him out of heaven. When the convergences first appeared, Zernebog had been suspected, but Tiamet had remained silent, even to her own grandson, and so the devotees were

147

forced to dismiss the possibility. After all, how could Tiamet fail against any lesser god? Surely, if it were another deity, the Great Dragon Mother could have easily used her power to cast them out for good. If the convergence was a threat from another god this whole time, why would the Goddess hide the truth from her followers? Uro had his suspicions that maybe another god challenging Tiamet and her creations would cause people to question the absolute nature of the Goddess's powers. Perhaps that was precisely what Tiamet wanted to avoid.

Halea stood in stunned silence as her heart collapsed into despair. A god? How could they fight a god? It was impossible. Like her grandfather, the possible reasons behind the Goddess's silence sickened her. Was Tiamet truly not all-powerful enough to save them? She couldn't bear to believe it, lest all her final hopes be dashed.

Halea's brow furrowed as a thousand new questions surfaced in her mind, but one question stood out to her above all the others, and she wondered why she had not thought of it before.

"I remember all the old dragon gods, but it just occurred to me...Morigan is the God of Death now, isn't he?"

"The Great Crow? Yes, but he wasn't the first god to hold that title. It was given to him by Tiamet after Zernebog had proven unworthy," Uro explained.

As it was told in the sacred text, Zernebog was malevolent and jealous. All that the gods created, he wanted for himself, and if he couldn't have it, he sought to destroy it. He relished chaos and death and was a bringer of suffering upon all that Tiamet loved, and so she stripped him of his sword and his title and cast him out of heaven, and that was why he was known as the false god.

"The legend is that Tiamet passed on the sword to a more worthy god, one who was impartial and fair and who had respect for the living and the dead, the Great Crow, Morigan. But, as devotees of the Goddess, we generally don't concern ourselves with the duties of the lesser gods," Uro continued.

"Abaddon," Halea said.

"What?"

"Varg said the name of Corbin's sword was Abaddon. Corbin is the son of Morigan, and that sword was entrusted to Corbin by his father, the God of Death. Corbin guides the lost souls of the dead to purgatory where the gods may claim them, and if they're not claimed, it's Morigan who leads them to oblivion. Abaddon must have once belonged to Zernebog!"

"I know nothing about the progeny of the lesser gods. And how is it that your shifter husband has such knowledge?"

"Corbin was Varg's swordmaster. He once took Varg to purgatory so that he could visit the heavenly realm and speak to the wolf gods."

Uro stared at his granddaughter in opened-mouth shock.

"Yeah, I guess I should tell you all about that. Better yet, let Varg tell you. It's his story."

Uro shook his head and sighed. "I must pray to Tiamet on all this. You must pray, too, Halea. The Goddess has spoken to you before. Perhaps she will listen to you."

"Tiamet hasn't spoken to me since she helped me capture Lord Anshar," she replied, then paused. "How did you convince Lord Anshar to open up to you?"

Uro nervously looked aside and cleared his throat. "I had to bargain with him. I suppose I must now ask for your forgiveness."

"What did you do?" she asked in a stern tone as her eyes narrowed.

"I promised Lord Anshar that if he told me the truth about what he saw within the Chaos, that I would convince you to visit him. I told him that you would be the next person he sees."

"What?" she shouted. "Grandfather, how could you? Look at me! He'll go mad! More mad! I can't see him like this!"

"I'm sorry, Halea. Forgive me. You were the only thing he wanted. The only thing that drew his mind from his madness. We're running out of time, and it was the only advantage I had. If we wanted answers, there was no other choice. Please, I know you don't want to go to him right now, but I gave him my word, and if I break it, we may never be able to save him. We need his trust."

Cold sweat dripped down Halea's back at the mere thought of revealing herself to Lord Anshar during her pregnancy, but her grandfather had given his word, and she had been willing to pay any price. Now, there was no choice.

"I'll go to him," she said in a defeated voice. "But you better be really nice to Varg after this. And stop calling him a shifter!"

CHAPTER 18 - VALRIA

The moment she said, "don't be angry," Varg knew he was going to be angry.

When Halea shared the news of her grandfather's latest visit with Lord Anshar and the discovery that was made, Varg was overcome with a sinking sense of dread. What hope did they have against a god? What could they possibly do to stop the next convergence that would not cost Halea her life?

And then she told him about the bargain that was made to gain this dismal information.

"No!" Varg growled as red seeped into the edges of his eyes. "Not now! You will not go to him."

"We promised," she argued.

"No, your grandfather promised, and it's not his place to offer you up to that monster. And for what, to tell us that we're doomed? We knew that much! You don't owe that bastard anything. All he does is make you cry. No matter how much you try to block the bond, the moment you lift it, I can sense that you've been upset. I always smell the dried tears. Always. And if you go to him now, it will just be the same. How do you think he's going to react once he sees that you carry my cub? He's just going to hurt you again, and I will not have you getting upset in your condition."

"There's nothing wrong with my condition, and I won't get upset," she said in as calm a tone as she could manage despite her irritation.

Varg scoffed as he paced their bedroom. It was late, but there would be no sleeping until this was settled.

"Varg, please," she pleaded while reaching out and clasping him by the wrist, causing him to halt mid-step. "Batsuba says I'm too sensitive, and she's right. I can't help that, but just because my emotions run deep doesn't mean I'm weak or fragile. Lord Anshar makes me cry, not so much because he says things that hurt me, but because there's nothing I can do to stop him from hurting. He wasn't always this way. Once, he was kind and good and did everything that he could to save our world. If he's a monster, it's because Chaos made him this way, and Tiamet has asked me to save him. That means there's still hope. Someway, somehow, there must still be hope. Saving Lord Anshar is the answer, I know it, but I can't save him by breaking his trust."

Varg sighed while frustratedly running his fingers through his hair before sitting beside his mate on their bed.

"Promise me, you won't let him make you cry. The moment he starts mouthing off, you'll leave. The agreement was that he'd see you. Nobody stipulated for how long, and if he gives you any shit, you walk out."

"I promise," she said while resting her head on his shoulder and sensing the ebb of his anger but not of his anxiety.

~~~⚬~~~

The next night, Halea stared up into the tree where the dark mirror awaited and shivered as the cold autumn air whipped her cloak around her ankles. She hesitated at the foot of the stairs while attempting to steady her nerves. No matter what happened, she could not break her word to Varg, and with a determined breath, she began the climb.

When she entered the single-room structure, she contemplated not lighting the candles. Perhaps her voice would be enough to appease the dragon, but something inside her wanted Lord Anshar to see her. Maybe if he finally saw the proof that she was Varg's, he would relinquish his unrequited affections and accept that she was happy.

"Lord Anshar, it's me, Halea. I came to see you," she called out after lighting the candles. The chair before the mirror was low, so she decided to remain standing to avoid any awkward attempts to get back up again. It would be easier for Lord Anshar to see her this way.

"Halea? Is it you? Sometimes I hear your voice, but you're not really there. I don't know what to believe anymore."

"It's me, Lord Anshar. Grandfather asked me to come and visit you. Can't you see me?"

The mirror's dark surface shimmered like a mirage before shifting to reveal Lord Anshar from where he stood within the other dimension. And then their eyes met, and she heard him take in a deep breath.

"Halea…you're…"

"Yes," she confirmed while refusing to look away as his face darkened and his hands trembled as they balled into fists at his side.

"I see. So, this is why you've stayed away," Lord Anshar growled.

"Partly. I am the supreme wolfmother of the lycans and an apprentice to a master healer, and I've been helping the priestesses battle the Chaos, though more strategically than physically at the moment. So much is happening all at once, and I figured…you would hate me if you saw that I'm pregnant with Varg's child."

"You're wrong," he said, and her eyes widened in shock. "I hate him, not you. I hate him for touching you. I hate him for claiming you. And I hate him for giving you the child that should have come from me. But I don't hate you. No matter how many children you give him, you are still you. That will never change, and it's you that I love."

She placed a hand over her protruding stomach and struggled to fight back the engulfing sadness and disappointment from his words, but remembering her promise, she steeled her nerves and met his gaze once again.

"You once told me to be happy. I guess that doesn't matter to you anymore?" Halea asked, and he turned his head in shame. "Well, I am happy. I love Varg. I love our child. Here, I have a home, a people - family. I've thought about what my life would have been like if I had never met Varg when we were children. Would I have loved you instead? I don't know. I wanted to be close to you because you always seemed so lonely, so sad. I wanted you to be happy, but there was always that distance you kept between us. If your hatred for Varg hadn't sparked your jealousy, I don't think you would have ever confessed your feelings for me. You would have kept me at an arm's distance and fulfilled your duty and struck me down – and none of us would be in this mess."

"That's not true!"

"It is!" she shouted. "If Varg hadn't stopped you, you would have completed the sacrifice."

Lord Anshar tried to shut his eyes and block out the past, but unbidden memories resurfaced. The sound of the barrier being disrupted as the wolf broke through. The Blade That Cuts Through Worlds raised high to strike Halea as she knelt before him, and then the battle that ensued as her lover fought for her life, just as he fought to take it. He remembered her crying over the wolf's fallen body as his life's blood pooled onto the ground and the haunting sound of her voice as she begged him to live. He remembered looking down on her, where she lay over the lycan, and how his heart constricted as he watched her suffering. She had thrown herself in front of his true form to save that wolf, and he had wished to know what it felt like, if only for a moment, to have that kind of love. Her love.

He clasped the sides of his head in torment as he tried to fight back the memories, but he couldn't block them out. He remembered Halea standing before him, offering her life as the sorrow in her eyes overwhelmed him and the way his hand shook as he raised his sword. He could see into the depths of her soul as she stared back at him, sacrificing herself, not to save their world, but to save her fallen love.

And that was when he knew – he loved her. He loved her more than anything, and he couldn't take her life.

Lowering his sword, he had reached out and caressed her beautiful face, her tears warm beneath his fingertips. Her heart did not belong to him, but he wanted to forget all that. For just one moment, he wanted to pretend that she was his, and so he stole a single soft kiss from her heavenly lips.

"I died for you!" he cried out as he forced his eyes open, and the painful memories once more receded into the shadows of his mind. It wasn't the whole truth, and he knew it. He wanted his torment to end, and he had hoped his sacrifice would be enough to free them. Being forced to kill the one thing he loved was the final burden to break him. He had risked everything and failed.

Halea took a deep breath. Varg was right, Lord Anshar knew just how to make her cry, but as much as she wanted to, she couldn't – not this time.

"I know, and that's why I want to save you. I owe you so much. Every happiness that I have now, I have because you chose to sacrifice yourself instead of me. I know what that choice has cost you, how much you've suffered on my account, and I know you did that for me. I never had the chance to say it before, but thank you."

"Halea," he breathed as her words sent him to his knees.

"I will find a way to save you, and nothing you say is going to make me give up," she promised, and with that, she blew out the candles, and Lord Anshar's image faded from the mirror.

<center>~~~☼~~~</center>

As the chill air of winter blew in from the north and stripped the last of the autumn leaves from the trees, Halea was forced to relinquish the last of her apprentice duties. Walking had become a slow and arduous task, and her back was often killing her. By the end of the day, her feet were swollen, and she was almost always tired. The baby kicked the fiercest at night, and when it wasn't kicking, she constantly had to get up to relieve herself or satisfy some craving. Varg rarely left her side anymore, and aside from demon hunts, he had delegated as many of his alpha duties as he could to spend as much time caring for Halea as possible. Halea's comfort and happiness had become Varg's utmost concern, and she did her best to indulge his overprotective nature because Batsuba had warned her that he needed to maintain some semblance of control for the sake of his sanity.

With every day that passed, Halea grew more and more impatient for their baby to hurry up and be born. Her own emotions were in a continuous tumble, shifting from anxiety, to sadness, to joy, to grumpiness, and back to being happy again. Sometimes she would burst into tears at the silliest things, and even with their bond, Varg couldn't always sort out what was going on inside of her. Halea could tell that he felt helpless and concerned, which in turn made her feel guilty for putting him through so much turmoil. But despite their combined volatile emotions, there were quiet moments when they were alone together when everything seemed perfect, and they could not help but dream about what the future would hold for their precious baby.

The coming of winter brought changes to the den. It was getting too cold for the refugees to remain in tents, so several caverns were cleaned out and furnished within their mountains to provide the Tiamet worshippers with more adequate shelter. In another month, the snow would begin to fall, and even the lycans would be forced to retreat from the harsh weather. This new arrangement brought the human devotees even closer to the lycans' den, and though some complained, most had accepted the necessity of their alliance.

Rarely was there a day when a runner did not arrive from one of the other packs or the howls of danger were not carried on the wind. Varg was regularly torn between his duty to protect the den from the demon invaders and his need to be with his pregnant mate. Priestesses and clerics fought alongside the lycan warriors whenever danger appeared, and tears were always swiftly eliminated, but it had become painfully evident to everyone that the Chaos was only growing worse.

Halea felt helpless and frustrated because she couldn't fight alongside Varg and her friends in their time of need. Being vulnerable and weak was an alien experience for her, but she couldn't take any risks with their unborn child.

153

Uro took pity on his poor granddaughter and would do his best to bring her news about all the tear and demon activity, so she didn't feel entirely left out, though he knew her mate disapproved. Varg had been particularly angry with the old cleric after Halea was made to visit with Lord Anshar, and though Uro had promised to be nicer to Halea's mate, it wasn't easy. Uro didn't consider Halea to be as fragile as her mate was making her out to be, and so they were constantly at odds about what was best for her and what was not. Halea wanted to be kept in the loop about the activity of Chaos, but Varg didn't want her to worry about such things while she was with child.

After Halea's last visit with Lord Anshar, Varg had sought out Uro and made it expressly clear that the old cleric was no longer to upset Halea with news about the dragon until after her pregnancy was over. Uro was not about to be intimidated by that big brute, but it didn't matter. Lord Anshar had slipped into incoherent madness once again, and while he still had many questions for the Dragon Lord, he doubted he would be receiving answers anytime soon.

It was easy to assume why Zernebog had a personal vendetta against Tiamet, but at the same time, it also seemed odd that a god would go to such great lengths to torment Lord Anshar and destroy the world that Tiamet had built. Uro knew that the gods could be petty, but there was something unusually personal about Zernebog's methods of manipulation. He suspected that there had to be something else, some other reason behind the false god's behavior. And most importantly, did Tiamet know the truth? If so, how was she incapable of once again banishing the former God of Death? Blessing priestesses and offering sacrifices to fight the convergence seemed beneath the abilities of one who should be as all-powerful as the Great Dragon Mother.

Something didn't add up, and though Lord Anshar wasn't in his right mind, when he did have moments of clarity, he seemed to share Uro's suspicions. Often amidst his ravings about invisible claws and memories of dark voices and shouting for Halea, he would interject accusations at Tiamet for hiding things from him and continually asking, "Did she know?" and "What isn't she telling me?" If Uro dared to pose any further questions, the Dragon Lord would deteriorate into repeatedly cursing the Goddess's name. It was hard for the devoted old cleric to hear such talk, but what if it was true? What if Tiamet was keeping something from them? If that were the case, he couldn't blame Lord Anshar for feeling betrayed.

Though Halea kept her word and hadn't let Lord Anshar drive her to tears during her last visit, she hadn't made any further attempts to speak to him. She was content to let her grandfather interact with Lord Anshar in her place, at least for the remaining duration of her pregnancy.

Varg was also relieved that Halea had chosen to avoid the dragon. It was one less stress for them both.

As the winter days grew ever shorter and colder, the time for Halea to go into labor was fast approaching, and Varg was already at the limit of his patience. He snapped and growled at everyone but Halea and had left the last few demon hunts to his warriors and the priestesses. Even Batsuba was going out of her way to avoid him as his temper had become intolerable.

One day, Halea was standing at the alpha's pit, warming her hands before the fire, and listening to Daciana as she explained what the first few months were like after Fillin was born. She often sought the advice of any woman who had more experience with children or pregnancy than her, as it helped her feel more prepared. Ulrica arrived carrying hot drinks, and the three women sat down and huddled up in front of the fire to enjoy each other's company.

"Where's Daisy?" asked Halea.

"Pestering Fillin," Ulrica replied with a laugh. "I'm grateful that Jance is here to help me keep her out of trouble these days. Without a mate, she's a lot to handle on my own."

Jance was sitting at a fire pit on the other side of the common area, surrounded by several small cubs who were listening as she told them stories. Occasionally, she snuck in a few symbols of the lycan alphabet while drawing illustrations on a bit of slate with a talc stone. She had an amazing way of teaching the cubs to read and write without them knowing it, and because listening to the human woman didn't feel like a tutoring lesson, the little ones didn't mind giving her their undivided attention. Even Daisy and Fillin, once bored with their play, went to join the others near the fire where they could listen to Jance tell an amusing story about a fox and a mouse.

From a distance, Halea could tell that it was actually a disguised arithmetic lesson, and she smiled at the redhead's cleverness. It was a shame her own grandfather was not half that entertaining. As a child, she would have much preferred to have been tutored by someone like Jance.

"I smell Varg," Daciana said as she nervously jumped to her feet and was joined by Ulrica.

"Call us if you need us, Halea," added Ulrica before the two she-wolves scurried away.

Daciana's sense of smell proved accurate as soon Varg appeared at the pit.

"Halea, is everything okay?"

Halea sighed as he took a seat beside her and wrapped an arm around her shoulders.

"You've developed such a reputation for being grumpy these days that everyone's avoiding you. You just scattered all my friends."

"I'm sorry," he said with a look of remorse. "I just can't help but feel tense and on edge all the time these days. I even left the hunt to come and check on you."

"I noticed. I'm fine, by the way," she said with an exasperated laugh. As much as she loved Varg, he had become smothering during her pregnancy, and she had rather hoped he would not abandon the hunt so she could have some time to herself.

"I'm annoying you again, aren't I?" Varg asked with a slightly unapologetic grin. He was more than aware that he was driving her nuts, but with an extraordinary degree of patience, she had, for the most part, humored him, and he loved her all the more for it.

"Gods, yes! If this baby doesn't get here soon, I'm going to kill you!"

Varg laughed before rising to his feet and offering her his hand.

"Come. Out of the cold," he gently ordered.

Halea pouted and crossed her arms over her distended stomach. "No."

"Halea," he said in a somewhat more commanding voice. "I don't want you catching a chill."

"I'm perfectly warm here in front of the fire," she argued while pulling up the hood of her fur-lined winter cloak. "And I'm tired of being cooped up inside all day. I'm going to be trapped indoors all winter. I want as much fresh air as I can get while I can get it."

Before Varg could argue with her, her face twisted into an unmistakable expression of pain that the bond confirmed.

"Halea? Is the baby kicking again?"

"No," she replied with disconcerting breathlessness. "Maybe I should go lie down after all."

Varg gently helped her to her feet, and they slowly walked back to their treehouse. Whatever discomfort had seized her seemed to have passed, but Varg was still ill-at-ease.

"Do you want me to call for Batsuba?"

"It may be nothing," Halea replied as he helped her up the stairs and into their home. "It's too soon to tell. Let me just lie down."

He didn't like it, but Halea did have medical training and had served as a midwife alongside Batsuba on many occasions, so he decided to let it go but keep a close eye on her.

Halea curled up in their bed, and he could sense that she wanted him to stay and comfort her.

"I see you don't mind me smothering you all of a sudden?" he commented while nestling into the bed beside her.

"Don't leave," she affirmed while rolling onto her other side to face him.

"I won't. I promise."

No sooner had he uttered those words than Halea let out a hiss of pain through clenched teeth and clutched her lower abdomen.

"I guess you better call for her," she finally managed to say after the worst of the spasms passed.

Varg leaped up and left their room, and from just outside, Halea could hear him howling, presumably to summon Batsuba. In the distance, more howls rose, and she knew the message was being passed along.

When he returned, he looked almost frantic, and the bond was a cacophony of intense emotions.

"It's okay," Halea said in an attempt to soothe her mate.

"Is this it?" he asked after returning to her side.

"Probably."

"Probably!" he nearly shouted, but after hurting his own ears, he lowered his voice. "I'm sorry. What should I do?"

"Call for Mama Dragon, please."

He quickly got back up and went outside. Soon the relay of howls would reach the refugee's guards, who would translate the message. Batsuba usually worked alone or with Halea, but Halea had begged the old healer to permit Mama Dragon to assist during the labor. Batsuba had once worked alongside the maternal priestess, and Mama Dragon did have some knowledge of midwifery. Most importantly, she would be a stand-in for Halea's own mother.

When Varg reentered their room, Batsuba was already with him, her bag of supplies ready at her side. With no preamble, the old healer went to Halea and checked her pulse and felt along her abdomen. Though Halea was due, there was still the possibility of false labor pains, but only the durations between the spasms would reveal the true nature of her condition. In the meantime, she would have to wait and observe, but Varg did not hesitate to voice his complaints.

"Well, do something! She's in pain," he growled.

"Are you in pain, Halea?" the old healer asked while ignoring her alpha.

"No," Halea replied. "Not at the moment."

"Then we wait, and you," she said, turning back to Varg. "Do something useful and start a fire, and another in your cooking station's stove too. I'll need somewhere to boil water. This can take hours, sometimes days."

With a huff of helpless defeat, he stepped out to fetch more wood and watch for Mama Dragon's arrival.

"You'll have to keep him calm when the time comes," Batsuba warned.

"But who's going to keep me calm?" Halea cried. Now that the time had finally arrived, she found herself trembling from nerves.

"Halea, you'll do just fine. Don't be scared. You're not alone."

Halea took a deep breath and did her best to think soothing thoughts, both for her sake and Varg's. Just as she was about to take in one more deep inhalation, another wave of pain seized her, causing her to groan and clench Batsuba's hand. If the old healer weren't a lycan, the bones in her hand would have been crushed in Halea's grip.

"How far apart are they?"

"I think they're getting closer," Halea replied once she was done writhing from the pain, and Batsuba nodded, feeling somewhat more convinced that this was no false alarm.

They waited together in silence until they heard footsteps running up the stairs and a knock at the door.

"Enter," Batsuba called, and Mama Dragon came in, her arms loaded with towels, blankets, and an extra water pail supplied by the she-wolves of the den who all heard the howls and quickly went to work gathering the items.

"I think everyone's going to make an event of it. When I passed through the den, everybody was gathering around the fires, and some of your lycan friends asked me to bring these to you."

"It's not every day that alphas bring new cubs into the den," Batsuba mentioned. "You wait. In a few hours, they'll break out the ale and wine and start feasting in your honor."

Mama Dragon handed the supplies to Batsuba, who excused herself to go into the main structure to see if Varg managed to get the stove lit. Now that the priestess was there to watch over Halea, she could begin brewing medicine to relieve some of Halea's pain and a few other concoctions that would be useful to have on hand.

"How are you feeling, Halea?" Mama Dragon asked.

"Scared. Nervous. I gotta pee," Halea confessed, and the two women chuckled.

Varg entered the room again, his arms laden with firewood, and he quickly set to work on getting a fire started in the fireplace. Once he was done, he returned to his mate's side and gently brushed the hair away from her brow. He could sense she had recently been in pain, but despite his screaming instincts, he had forced himself to stay focused on the task Batsuba gave him. He only wished there was more that he could do.

Time moved slowly with Batsuba or Mama Dragon passing from the bedroom structure and into the main dwelling space, carrying towels, buckets of hot water, and things that smelled like medicine. Varg wanted to ask if they needed anything, but he also knew that if they wanted his help, they'd ask. Instead, he focused on comforting his frightened mate. Though Varg couldn't physically feel her pain, the bond made it clear that she suffered, and he felt helpless as all he could do was offer her his hand to squeeze and gently stroke her back after the contractions passed.

As the sun began to set, Ulrica arrived with food. Varg wasn't interested in eating, and Halea could only muster a half-hearted attempt at trying some of the light soup that Ulrica had made. Mama Dragon and Batusba were thankful for the repast as they expected a long and tiring night ahead. After wishing Halea the best, Ulrica gathered up the serving trays and left.

Hours rolled by, and the moon had risen by the time Halea's water broke. As the labor pains came closer together, Batsuba instructed Varg to help Halea out of bed and position himself behind her for support as she was lowered into the squatting position.

"It's all right, Halea. I have you," he promised as she trembled in his arms from exhaustion.

Mama Dragon helped to wipe the sweat from Halea's brow with a dampened cloth as Batsuba monitored her patient's progress.

"You're doing fine, Halea," Batsuba promised after noticing that the baby had begun to crown.

Waves of pain and unbearable pressure passed through her as Batsuba instructed Halea to push down, but after several more agonizing minutes of strain mixed with screaming and a fair amount of cursing, her baby was caught by the old healer's waiting hands.

"It's a female," Batsuba announced, and both Halea and Varg burst into tears. A shrill wailing rent the air as the infant protested her first breath of life.

Batsuba cut and tied off the umbilical cord while Mama Dragon helped her clean and wrap the squalling baby before handing her into her mother's waiting arms.

Halea could barely see her child's face for the tears clouding her vision, but it didn't matter; her new daughter was beautiful, and even Varg was speechless in his joy as he gently touched the baby's teeny hand, which instinctively wrapped around one of his fingers.

"Look at her cute little ears!" cried Mama Dragon, who had never seen the pointy ears of a therian on such a tiny baby before. "What will you name her?"

"Valria," Halea replied. Halea had thought to use her own mother's name, but it was a name that carried a tormenting sadness for her. Instead, they had decided that if it were a girl, it would share the name of Varg's mother, and if it were a boy, it would have been named after Halea's father, Perion.

Though Batsuba was smiling at the joyous occasion, she carried a secret weight in her heart. She detected a faint but worrying scent. It was too soon to tell, but she would have to watch the cub closely and pray that she was mistaken.

CHAPTER 19 - ESCAPE

When Halea placed the squirming baby into Uro's arms, there was a tense silence before a single glistening tear escaped from beneath his spectacles and rolled down his wrinkled face. The young mother stopped holding her breath as her grandfather lovingly embraced the infant, who looked confused to be in such unfamiliar arms but vocalized no complaints.

Uro was pleased that the child was named Valria. Even though it came from Varg's side of the family, it wasn't a typical lycan name, but a name derived from the ancient language that meant "beloved." It seemed appropriate as even Theia had chosen to be sentimental and name Halea after the sun.

The old cleric reached into his robes and pulled out a small rune-carved medallion, and dangled it before the baby, who reached up to clutch the shiny object in her tiny hands. The talisman did not glow.

Tiamet had not blessed the child.

Uro wasn't surprised. It was just a precaution. He had not expected a half-wolven child to be blessed by the Dragon Goddess, and, also, Tiamet's blessings were always random and not something that could be passed along by lineage.

Halea and Varg were both relieved that their daughter was not blessed. Valria's life would be complicated enough by her unusual lineage without having to get the Goddess involved.

With that matter settled, Uro went back to coddling and cooing over the new baby.

Varg was standing nearby, protective to the last, as he observed the tender moment between the two kin separated by several generations. Great-grandparents were nothing unusual among immortals, but according to Halea, they were rare for humans. A silent ache filled him as he reflected on his own parents. Would they have loved his cub? His mother, and child's namesake, for sure, but he doubted his father would have approved. His father hated humans and had even eaten a few in times of scarcity, and if he had known that as a cub, Varg had befriended a human and even grew up to take that same human for a mate, he would have certainly disapproved. This thought saddened Varg at first, but then it occurred to him that hadn't Halea's grandfather faced his own prejudice to their union at first? Yet here the old man stood, living in peace among the wolves while cradling and cooing over his half-lycan progeny with undeniable love in his eyes. Couldn't his own father have changed? Change was never easy, and many were set in their ways, but hearts and minds could be swayed. He had seen this for himself as he watched his people slowly learn that

Halea was not a threat but an ally, and then a friend, and in time, a part of the pack, a member of the family. His father had not lived long enough to get the chance to know the woman he loved, but somewhere in Varg's heart, he could not help but believe that if his father had only known her, he would have come to see why Halea was the perfect mate for him.

"Just when you think you've lived long enough to see and experience everything. I give thanks to Tiamet for keeping the breath of life in me long enough to be here for this moment," Uro said.

"You like her?" Halea asked with hopeful eyes.

"I love her. Thank you for giving an old man one last gift," he replied before turning his eyes to Varg and offering a nod before continuing. "Thank you both. I know I'm not always a pleasant person, but you have my sincerest gratitude for allowing me to come here and enjoy my last days with the only family I have."

Uro had begrudgingly offered thanks in the past, but this time, it was different, this time Varg could sense the sincerity of his words, and it shattered the last of his own animosity. Varg realized that even if a human as old and as set in his ways as Halea's grandfather could learn to accept people who were not his own and love a child of mixed blood, then surely his father could have too. That thought brought him peace as he returned Uro's nod and accepted his gratitude with a gentle smile.

The next day, Uro returned to his cave for an afternoon nap after having tea with some of the lycan elders in the common area, only to find an unexpected addition to his room. Sitting before his lit and waiting stove was an armchair and ottoman of similar construction to the one he left behind in Antherose, but somewhat different. Instead of old, musty, moth-eaten fabric, it was upholstered in fine soft leather, giving the chair a luxurious scent. It was sturdy and made of beautifully polished hand-carved wood but comfortable and stuffed adequately in all the right places. When Uro sat in it, it felt as if the weight of all the years was lifted from his aching bones, and he sighed in delight as he raised his feet before the warmth of the stove, and before long, he was fast asleep.

From that day on, Varg and Uro were family.

Despite the ever-increasing threat from the Chaos Dimension, Halea managed to experience some of the joys of new motherhood. Her body quickly recovered thanks to Varg's lifeforce, which allowed her to rapidly heal, though she did give herself a few days of rest if only to enjoy the newfound bond between mother and daughter.

Like her father, Valria's ears came to a point, and though somewhat dull in her infancy, it was clear that with time, her tiny fingernails would sharpen into powerful claws. Most lycan cubs, like many babies, were born toothless, with Batsuba being one of the rare exceptions. It was too soon to tell if Valria would have sharp fangs to match her claws and ears, but it seemed entirely likely.

Despite her lycan qualities, Valria shared one glaring early resemblance to her human mother, her eyes.

Halea had hoped for a baby with Varg's brilliant blue eyes, but within a few days, the pigmentation developed to reveal a shade of bright hazel-green, much like her own eyes and her mother's eyes before her. Halea was not disappointed, though. She liked seeing the blend between herself and Varg. No matter what color her daughter's eyes or if she grew fangs or not, she was beautiful and perfect.

Even Varg was in awe of his tiny, helpless cub. Her little hands could barely wrap around his larger fingers, but when she was ready to be fed or changed, she could wail with impressive volume. She was strong, healthy, and lively and always squirming about and looking at everything with curiosity. He was terrified the first time Batsuba placed her in his arms. Valria was so small and delicate, and he simply stood frozen for fear that he could break her or drop her or upset her in any way. To his relief, her cries of protest quickly stilled as she looked up into her father's face and smiled a toothless grin that instantly melted his heart. She was a part of himself and Halea, and he would do anything in the world to protect her, but a silent ache stirred his heart as he dreaded the thought of what could happen if he ever lost Halea. He couldn't hurt his daughter the way his father hurt him. He couldn't. Somehow, he had to prevent such a fate from ever befalling his precious child.

Halea sensed the sadness and fear from Varg at that moment, but the lovesick look in his eyes as he gazed at their child told her that it was not for any disappointment on the part of their baby. Something was deeply bothering Varg and had been for a while. Whenever she asked him about it, he brushed it off as just the stress of being an alpha or the constant threat of the Chaos Dimension. To be fair, she, too, was afraid about the fate of their world. The reality of their predicament hovered like a cloud over anyone who knew the severity of the situation, and many of the devotees were losing hope.

Shade mimics had begun to attack the devotees on lycan lands despite the wolves guarding the Tiamet worshippers. Their shade mimic scent was harder to detect than a regular demon, and because of that, there was more than one close call. Thankfully the lycans had managed to stop the deceptive servants of Chaos before any lives could be taken, but one thing was clear; the danger was mounting.

Now that Valria was born and Halea felt more like her old self again, the Goddess was once more calling her to fight. Her conflicted heart was tearing her in two as one half longed to never be parted from her child, and the other half burned with an unbearable need to charge out and face the coming storm. Halea did her best to ignore the aching insistence of the Great Dragon Mother and focus as best as she could on her daughter. Valria needed her. Her first priority had to be her child.

Thankfully, Halea did not lack for help. After feeding Valria, if she was stubborn about not falling asleep, Varg would gently rock her in his arms while walking the floors of their home. This gave Halea a chance to catch up on some much needed rest and seeing Varg with their daughter warmed her heart. At first, he was unsure, but with every day, he proved more and more skilled at caring for their child, and Halea found something about that to be unbelievably sexy. There were times when she would just watch him holding their sleeping baby draped over his shoulder, and her heart would melt. He would meet her eyes at those times, and love flowed between their bond until they couldn't help but reach for each other.

Getting the hang of breastfeeding was a little tricky at first, but Mama Dragon was there to coach her until she was comfortable and sure of what she was doing. The

162

she-wolves of the pack would often visit and make sure that Halea and Varg were eating and sleeping enough and to offer Halea any advice she needed. Several pack members came by just to help with the household chores so Halea and Varg could enjoy their first week with their new cub in peace.

Jance, in particular, was thrilled to visit and behold the half-wolven child, with her recognizable lycan features but the gentle eyes of her human mother.

"A half-wolven baby, so it is possible. And she's so beautiful! Thank you for letting me stay to see her," Jance said to Halea, and though she was genuinely happy for mother and baby, a sad regret still tugged at her heart.

Alf, who had since returned to the western lands, quickly embraced his pleased yet heartbroken mate.

Many lycans were happy for Varg and Halea, but a few were not entirely comfortable with the idea of a half-wolven, though they kept their disapproval silent. It may have been one thing to mate a human, but to mix blood with one seemed to be tantamount to tainting their godly lineage. Halea suspected that her child was not beloved by all. Some of the devotees had voiced their disgust, but they were quickly silenced by Samesa and Mama Dragon, who were not about to let anyone speak ill of their friend and benefactor. Halea could only pray that with time, more people would come around to the idea of accepting her half-wolven daughter or at least get used to her, but inside, she knew her child may forever carry the burden of being a part of two worlds. The more Halea thought about it, the more a burning question plagued her.

One cold winter day, Batsuba was waiting patiently beneath her tree-dwelling. Halea and Valria would soon arrive for one of the baby's early-life checkups, of which the old healer insisted. The elder she-wolf had prayed that she was wrong in her suspicions, but with every day, the truth became undeniable, and the burden of her discovery wore heavily on her spirits. Batsuba chose to wait outside that day because Marrok was currently sitting inside her tree-dwelling being a nuisance again, and she preferred the cold to another minute of his pointless chatter.

When Halea finally arrived with Valria abundantly swaddled against her breast, Batsuba was surprised when the human wolfmother fell to one knee before her.

"Halea, what are you doing?"

Halea bowed her head and raised her infant before the elder, and it occurred to Batsuba that this was a ritual she had once performed many times long, long ago, but those days were forever gone.

"Halea, I can't. I'm not a wolfmother."

"Yes, you are. In your heart, you know you are. One doesn't stop being an alpha. I don't believe that. You told me once that a supreme wolfmother shouldn't bless their own child, but that it didn't matter because not all cubs are born to packs with wolfmothers. But it does matter! It matters to me! I created a life when our world is coming to an end. I brought my poor baby into an existence where she may never be accepted for what she is. Don't you see? She needs all the help she can get. Surely, you're closer to the wolf gods than I? I can't pray to Tiamet for her, not after breaking my oath. Not for a personal favor. Please, I'm begging you."

"Oh, go ahead, Batsuba. The gods won't mind," Marrok called down from Batsuba's tree before descending the spiral stairs.

"Says you!" the old healer grumbled as the northern elder reached the tree's base.

"She's right," Marrok continued. "You've never stopped being a wolfmother. Don't think the gods aren't aware of that. Give the poor little cub its blessing. Don't be stingy!"

Batsuba sighed in defeat. Though she hated to admit it, Marrok was even older than she was, and when it came to matters of the gods, there wasn't a lycan alive with a clearer insight into the will of their deity ancestors than him.

Halea hopefully watched, as at last, Batsuba relented and accepted the offered cub into her arms. A trace of remembrance flashed in the old healer's eyes as she cradled the squirming infant, and a rare smile revealed her gleaming white fangs.

Batsuba began her prayer and called upon the wolf gods in the ancient language, and though Halea held her breath, something passed through her like the wind, but warm and reassuring, and somehow, she knew the wolf gods had answered the call.

Batsuba must have felt it too because her dark eyes glistened, and her hands trembled slightly as she offered the baby back to its mother.

But to both their surprise, Marrok swooped in and scooped up the child.

"I shall offer a blessing as well. After all, she is like me."

His blessing was short but sweet as he prayed for the gods to bestow health, love, and joy. Halea thanked him with tears in her eyes as he handed back her daughter, who was beginning to fuss at the unfamiliar contact.

"Elder Marrok, what do you mean; she is like you?" Halea couldn't help but ask. She had meant to question the elder ever since Jance mentioned his past.

"I, too, am a half-wolven. I'm sure Jance has mentioned it to you," he explained with a knowing twinkle in his eye. Halea stood speechless for a long moment before eventually looking to Batsuba, who nodded her head to confirm the northern elder's words.

"Of course, Batsuba has always known. She's one of the few still alive who remembers my brother. I've lived for so long that most lycans have no idea that my father was a human man. They're content to assume that I am as fully lycan as they are, and I see little reason to bring it up. For over two ages, most have been blissfully unaware that a half-wolven has walked among them."

Batsuba looked troubled as Marrok spoke, and Halea recognized the familiar expression as when the old healer remembered something tragic from her past. She often wore the same look when her thoughts wandered to her lost mate.

"Explain what happened to your brother, Marrok. Please, I think there's something Halea needs to know," Batsuba implored.

Marrok nodded and went on. "My mother fell in love with a human man. Supposedly, he was quite intelligent. I wouldn't know. He died shortly after my brother and I were born. You see, it is the lycan male who must forge the bond with his bite. My mother couldn't share her lifeforce with the human man she fell in love with, and so she was left behind when he died. He was her chosen, though. The loss didn't kill her, but she suffered unbearably for hundreds of years until she couldn't anymore, and…well, then she wasn't with us anymore."

Halea nodded with grave understanding before the elder went on.

"My brother and I were twins, though we didn't look anything alike. I resemble my human father, both in appearance and mannerisms. I'm sure you've noticed that I don't quite have the average lycan muscular form. On the other hand, my brother looked like your average sturdy lycan male and was every bit a wolf, except for one thing, he had been born mortal. I don't know why my mother's godly gift of eternal life was passed onto me, but not my brother. I suppose a half-human lineage can manifest differently in various individuals," Marrok explained as his ancient eyes grew moist with remembrance.

"He did live a long time," Batsuba added. "A full-human wouldn't have lived that long, but he grew old, and it was strange to see an aged lycan. When I first met him, I thought he had some terrible condition until I recognized the scent of his decay, so unusual to detect in one of our kind but unmistakable in a mortal creature. I could scarcely believe it when Marrok explained the truth of their lineage. That is how I knew that humans and lycans could produce offspring and that wolves had chosen humans in the past. Halea, there's something I've meant to tell you…about Valria."

Without a further word, Halea's heart raced, and her pulse pounded in her ears, nearly drowning out the impending truth before it even left the healer's lips.

"She is mortal," Batsuba explained. "I couldn't be sure at first. The scent of decay is almost imperceptible in the newly born, but it's there. I'm sure of it. I hoped that I was wrong, but with every day that I have examined her, the scent has grown stronger. Valria was not given the gift of Varg's godly lineage. I'm so sorry."

Halea trembled in devastation as tears rolled down her face, and she sensed Varg flying into panic across their bond.

What was the good of being an immortal if you had to watch your children grow old and die before you? That was not the way of things for humans. Parents were not supposed to outlive their children. She imagined her precious daughter growing old and frail just like her grandfather, and a sob rose from her chest that nearly strangled her on the way out.

"Halea, it's not like regular humans don't…" Batsuba began, but Halea cut her off.

"I know, we die! Humans are mortal, but I'm not! It's me! I don't want to be left behind without her. I don't want to watch my baby grow old and die, no matter how long a life she gets. She can live a thousand years. She's still my child," Halea cried.

"Perhaps she will find a therian mate to share his lifeforce with her," offered Marrok in sympathy. "My brother never chose a mate, and no female could have saved him anyway, but for Valria, there is hope. Don't let one potential future spoil everything for you. Besides, we're not sure any of us are going to survive if the convergence comes again. Let's face just one disaster at a time."

Halea nodded her head, gleaning some comfort from the truth of the northern elder's words. He was right. The future was uncertain for everyone now, and Valria, being raised among lycans, would most likely find a lycan mate. But there was one thing she knew for sure, and at that moment, she decided it with finality - she would have no more children. She couldn't bear the possibility of creating another life that may grow old and die before her, and if she were to have a son, his fate would be sealed for sure. She couldn't take that risk, and the weight of her choice was enough to make her heart bleed. She and Varg had been dreaming of filling their home with so many children, but one would have to be enough.

"Varg is undoubtedly on his way. We'll pick up your lessons tomorrow," Batsuba said before she and Marrok retreated back up into her tree.

Halea tried her best to dry her eyes as she clutched her now sleeping baby tighter in her arms. It wasn't long before Varg appeared and approached her through the trees with evident worry written on his face.

"Halea, what's happened?"

<p style="text-align:center">~~~☼~~~</p>

A week later, Halea was sitting outside at the alpha's fire pit for lunch and tea. The sky was clear, and much of the snowfall they received overnight had melted away by the time the sun reached its zenith. The air outside almost felt warm, but it wouldn't last, and the lycans were already preparing to move all their communal activities indoors for the remainder of the winter. Her grandfather had finished his tea before her and offered to hold Valria while Halea finished her lunch. Uro was greedy for any opportunity to cuddle his precious great-grandbaby, and it warmed the young mother's heart to see how close those two had become. As was often the case, by the time Valria was napping, so was her grandfather.

Uro's chin tipped down to his chest, where Valria lay swaddled and warm, and both were snoring ever-so-gently. Halea couldn't help but smile in fondness.

Varg was devastated at the news of their daughter's mortality, and they both shed tears of grief at the possibility that they might someday outlive their only child. And an only child, she would remain. To Halea's surprise, Varg had agreed with her decision to not have any more children, at least not for the time being.

As much as it pained him to give up on their dream of having a big family, like Halea, Varg couldn't stomach the idea of bringing more cubs into the world if there was a chance that he would have to watch them grow old and die. Varg had seen age and mortality in Uro, and as a therian not used to seeing people die that way, he couldn't bear the idea of any of his children suffering such a fate. Perhaps it was natural that mortal creatures should die by the ravages of time and decay, but it was not normal for lycans to watch such a thing happen to their own children. For Valria, he could maintain hope that someday his daughter would grow up to find a lycan mate who would share his lifeforce with her, but even that was an uncomfortable gamble because not all lycans chose mates, and that possibility frightened him.

The thought that not all lycans chose mates had crossed Halea's mind, but she could not allow herself to fall into further despair. Elder Marrok's words were still with her. At the moment, the convergence was the number one threat to their world, and if she didn't find a way to vanquish the false god, then no one would have a future.

Lord Anshar was the key. Halea was not sure how but saving Lord Anshar from his madness had to be the answer. Zernebog was attacking their world for a reason. He wanted something, either from the Goddess or her grandson, and if only Lord Anshar were in his right mind, then surely, they could find the clue to the answer that they were seeking.

Perhaps Tiamet only wanted Halea to save Lord Anshar so that he could continue the cycle of sacrifice, but it was evident that the Goddess was hiding something from both her followers and from Lord Anshar.

Halea had been so lost in her thoughts that she almost didn't hear the howls of danger, but she snapped out of her stupor when Varg appeared before her.

"Halea, there's been an attack. A shade mimic tried to break into the refugee camp. Aatu was barely able to catch its scent in time, but he stopped it before it could kill anyone."

Uro had awakened to hear this news, and his withered face grew pale.

"It sounds like Chaos is getting desperate to try such a stupid thing when it knows we're protecting the devotees," said Halea.

"There must be a tear somewhere nearby. I must go out to the camp," Uro said as he passed Valria back to her mother and struggled to rise despite the protest of his aching joints, which had stiffened from the cold and his nap.

"I'm coming too!" Halea declared.

"Halea, we can manage without…" Varg started, but Halea cut him off as fire sparked in her eyes.

"No, I've waited long enough. I'm not pregnant anymore, and I can fight, and so I will."

"But what about Valria?" Varg argued.

"I can watch her!" came a voice, and the alpha pair turned to find that Ralphina had just arrived at the pit with more tea to refill their cups. "I'm still nursing Bardolph, and I have plenty of milk to spare."

Halea smiled at Ralphina's brilliant solution. Of course, everyone in the pack was family, and it was common for she-wolves to nurse each other's children when mothers needed a break or had other important matters to attend to. With Ralphina's help, she could rejoin the demon hunts.

Varg suppressed a growl of protest. As much as he disliked it, Halea had only promised to abstain from the hunts until after their child was born, and with Ralphina's assistance, there was no reason why she couldn't rejoin the fight.

"Oh, Ralphina, thank you!" Halea cried as she hugged her friend and handed her Valria at the same time.

Valria fussed at being placed in unfamiliar arms, but Ralphina managed to soothe her as she watched her alphas and the elderly human cleric set out to face the danger.

Lycurgus had been listening from a nearby fire pit where he was waiting for Ralphina's return with Bardolph on his knee. The moment his alphas were out of earshot, he approached his mate.

"Ralphina, how could you? You can't nurse that *thing* alongside our son!" he growled as anger reddened his face. Accepting Halea as his wolfmother was one thing; she was strong and worthy, but this half-breed child was an abomination, and he did not want it anywhere near his mate or their cub.

"Don't start, Lycurgus. Halea and Varg are out there fighting for our pack, including our son. I don't care what you think about this cub. Valria is a part of this pack, too, which means she's family, and it's my right to support my pack and my alphas however I choose. Bardolph will be fine. I have plenty of milk for both," she asserted before walking past her irate mate and returning to their fire pit.

Lycurgus felt sorry for upsetting his mate, and if it meant that much to her, he wouldn't bring it up again, but inside, he still disapproved of the half-wolven.

~~~☼~~~

Awakened by the jostling carriage, Maven looked out the small, barred window and squinted at the daylight. A couple of rangers guarding the rear on horseback were quietly conversing, and Captain Mark was undoubtedly riding somewhere ahead.

"Where are we?" Maven asked, but her throat was so dry it came out as barely more than a whisper, and the guards didn't hear her. Her wrists and ankles ached from the thicker than average iron shackles biting into her flesh, and she was shivering. It had taken a long while for them to figure out the safest way to transport her to Westvear, where she would eventually stand trial for assisting Lord Anshar in the murder of her fellow priestesses. The carriage was heavily armored, so she couldn't use her strength to escape, but it did nothing to keep out the cold.

Lifting her shackled arms, she reached her hands through the bars as far as they would go and waved them to get the guard's attention. Thankfully, one of the rangers noticed her and rode up to the back of the carriage.

"Water, please?" she begged, and with a begrudging sigh, the ranger reached for his waterskin and passed it through the bars.

"Where are we?" she asked as soon as her thirst was quenched.

"About halfway between Antherose and Westvear," the ranger replied as she passed the waterskin back through the bars.

"When will we stop again?"

"What is she on about?" a man's voice barked from beyond her vision, and her guard nervously backed away as Captain Mark appeared on his horse.

"Can't we stop? Please, I'm going to be ill."

"There's an abandoned village just up ahead, we'll stop on the outskirts as soon as we get there, but we're not staying long in that accursed place."

Maven tried to recall the villages between Antherose and Westvear when suddenly an idea came to her.

"Is that the village that was raided by demons late last fall?" she asked.

"That's the one. Nobody will return because you, Tiamet worshippers, never got rid of that tear. It's still there. Nobody wants to go anywhere near that thing."

"I can seal it. We're passing through anyway. Please, let me perform this one last service. I'm in irons, and you've got plenty of guards, so it's not like I'm going anywhere."

Captain Mark fell silent, and Maven nervously watched his stony face, her stomach clenching in knots as he internally debated her proposal.

168

"I suppose there's no harm in it, but don't think you'll get any extra consideration when you go to trial for doing what your kind was already supposed to be doing."

She only nodded her head and thanked him, and with that, he rode on ahead once more.

For the past year, she had been rationalizing the events that unfolded at the castle. Lord Anshar had suffered terribly within the Chaos and was obviously unwell, but he wasn't so unwell that she didn't still have absolute faith in him. He said more sacrifice was needed, and she believed that. Sacrifice had always been the way. Tiamet had probably only trapped him within the mirror to save his life. Lord Anshar had been so horribly wounded. It was not a fair fight when Halea's dirty shifter attacked him. Somewhere out in the wilds, Lord Anshar was their prisoner – trapped, and it was up to her to save him.

She needed to escape. She had to find Lord Anshar, or everything would be lost, and she desperately began thinking of some way, any way, that she could use this situation to her advantage. Though much stronger than the rangers, she was unarmed and could barely move in her restraints. She had tried using her powers on the iron chains, but they only glowed to no effect. If only she could break her chains while sealing the tear, she could run, but how?

"Tiamet, please. Help me," she silently prayed.

When they neared the outskirts of the burnt-out remains of the abandoned village, the guards opened the carriage and helped Maven out. The clanking of her heavy chains disturbed the silence and sent crows into flight.

The cold air stung her cheeks as she walked with short, awkward steps, a ranger holding onto each arm as they guided her towards the northern end of the village. Captain Mark patiently led the way, and it wasn't long before the swirling purple vortex of a tear loomed before them.

"Don't try anything," Captain Mark advised with a curt nod towards one of the other rangers who held his crossbow at the ready. "Just get it closed so we can get out of here."

Maven nodded in agreement, and her two escorts let go of her, allowing her to move towards the tear on her own.

As she inched closer towards the dimensional rift, a jolt of purification energy struck her with such force that she was thrown back onto the ground in searing pain.

The rangers were shouting, but she couldn't hear them past the ringing in her ears, and her eyes watered from the smell of smoke rising from her body. Rough hands lifted her from the ground where she swayed, and it felt like her hair was sticking up on end.

"Damn him," she thought. *"Uro must have reinforced this barrier."* The Master Cleric could construct a far more powerful barrier than any other cleric alive, and most priestesses too. This barrier was designed to contain the tear and purify anything that should try to get in or out. Serving as a High Priestess for almost an age had made her rusty when it came to basic field experience, and she hoped that her blunder had not caused the Captain's faith in her abilities to waver.

"What happened?" asked Captain Mark.

"It's a barrier. I didn't sense it fast enough, but I can get through it. Just give me a moment," Maven explained.

This time she approached with more caution; her hands stretched out before her like someone groping in the dark. She felt the crackling charge at her fingertips and slowly worked her way around the barrier, removing sacred runes one at a time. Their red marks were painted here and there, and when the last rune was found and broken, the barrier snapped and was gone.

"Tiamet, please. You must help me," Maven prayed as she scrambled to think of some way to get away from the rangers. She couldn't run. She couldn't break her chains. The Goddess was her only hope.

She stood before the tear and averted her eyes from looking directly into the void beyond as she raised her hands high and called out loud to her deity. "Tiamet, give me strength." The white light of purification surged forth from her hands and clashed with the tear's pulsing purple glow. As the rift began to shrink, the unmistakable sounds of demons interrupted her, and all hell broke loose as the servants of Chaos swarmed out.

Noise and confusion were everywhere, mixed with the screams of the rangers as the demons attacked them with dark blades killing on contact. Some of the rangers managed to call upon their elemental spells using fire to consume their foes or cracking open the ground that swallowed the demons, crushing them within the earth. Some of the servants of Chaos were launched into the air by air-casters with such force that they impacted into trees and buildings where the water-casters then drew moisture from the air and soil to pummel them where they lay.

Maven put up her hands, still glowing with Tiamet's light, and purified any demons that dared to come near, but there were too many, and as she tried to run, she was tripped by her shackles. The moment she struck the ground, a hideous demon with a bulbous body, long spindly legs, and snapping mandibles sprang for her. She shrieked in terror as the creature pinned her to the ground, and then the world turned dark before her eyes.

The first time she saw him: tall, fair, with shining eyes of silver that weakened her knees. Perfect. A god. A congregation of devotees praying to the Dragon Goddess for salvation. A sword that gleamed above a mantle. A sword coated red with blood. Centuries of sacrifices. Centuries of watching him save their world time and again. A convergence looming in the sky and sails billowing in the wind. The Citadel aflame. A wretched child, annoying and intrusive. A castle that became a home and an opportunity to be nearer to him, but he only slipped further away – because of that child. Her simpering face that drew his silver eyes without fail. The defiant child, refusing to bow before their Lord. Addressing him with such familiarity. And then, betrayal. Betrayal of Tiamet. Betrayal of him.

The darkness wavered before her eyes, but something was choking her. A green miasma was seeping into her nostrils and open mouth as she tried to cry out, but no sound escaped. Something flickered within her mind, eyes elliptical and red, then gold and pleading, then red again before a searing pain tore through her head, and finally her scream rent the air before she fell still.

The shade mimic slowly retreated from Maven's prostrate form only to be struck with a ball of fire that singed its barb-like hairs. It hissed as it turned its attention to its aggressor.

"Hey, ugly! Fight me!" shouted Captain Mark as he wielded another flame that roared before his outstretched hands. The mimic charged, but the ranger released his inferno, which engulfed the spindly-legged demon that writhed and shrieked as it blackened and burned. But as the creature crumbled to ash, a noxious green smoke rose from its foul remains and floated back into the tear.

Before the Captain could process the horror he had just seen, a searing pain tore through his chest, and when he looked down, a blood-coated dark blade was protruding from his ribs. The sword withdrew with a sickening squelch, and then his life was over.

CHAPTER 20 – SPURNED LOVE

Halea used her knife to penetrate the frozen earth until she found the roots Batsuba requested. She wasn't far from the den, and since the recent demon attacks, lycan guards were even patrolling her preferred foraging grounds. Her grandfather was watching Valria, and she hoped to be back in time for her daughter's noon feeding. If not, Ralphina would make sure that Valria was fed, but Halea preferred to be the one to nurse her baby because missing too many feedings would cause her breasts to feel painful and heavy.

It was difficult balancing new motherhood, her apprenticeship, her duties as a wolfmother, and her persistent need to join the priestesses in their fight against the Chaos Dimension. Between stress, fear of the mounting danger, and the needs of her child, she could barely sleep at night, and Varg had begged her to ask Batsuba for a break or to delegate more of her wolfmother duties, but stubbornly, she refused. She worked so hard to get to this point, to be respected by the pack, to contribute, to be a good mother and mate, and to heed the call of the Goddess, but Varg was right. It was too much.

As she knelt on the cold ground, her hands aching from pulling roots out of the soil, her breasts leaking milk into her robe, and another howl of warning in the distance – she broke. She gasped and sobbed in defeat and did nothing to hold back the tears streaming down her face.

"Mother. Mother, I wish you were here," she cried while sitting there feeling like a tired mess and a failure. She should have been with her baby. She should have been helping the priestesses. But there she was, crying in the dirt and wishing that her mother was there to help her, to tell her what she should do, to comfort and reassure her.

Varg, sensing her turmoil, was frantically reaching for her through their bond, but she did her best to send soothing emotions, though she couldn't entirely mask her melancholy. Varg had been so wonderful and patient with her since Valria was born. Even though he had plenty of his own duties, he would drop anything to help her if she asked, but that just made her feel guilty for burdening him. She had hoped her moods would become more stable after giving birth, but that didn't seem to be the case, and she was constantly fighting the despair that maybe she would never entirely feel like her old self again. Mama Dragon assured her that such feelings were normal for new mothers and that it wouldn't always be so hard, but Halea had difficulty believing it. Most new mothers were not former priestesses who had to stand by helplessly as the world was literally coming to an end all around them. Everyone was counting on her to get through to Lord Anshar, and though they had discovered the source of all their troubles, they were no closer to understanding the cause.

Her grandfather suspected that the false god wanted vengeance against Tiamet for casting him out of heaven and banishing him to the Chaos Dimension. Destroying the world that the Goddess helped create, her people to whom she had given the breath of life, and her only kin, Lord Anshar, were all a means to hurt and punish Tiamet. It seemed simple enough, but Halea suspected that there had to be more because there was something that Tiamet didn't want her followers, or even Lord Anshar, to know.

"I thought I smelled tears. What's wrong, Human Wolfmother?" asked Elder Marrok, who approached through the trees. He would often take strolls around the den, usually looking for Batsuba, who would go out of her way to avoid him. Noticing Halea's mournful face, he sat on a nearby fallen tree, his long spindly legs stretching awkwardly in front of him for being too low to the ground.

"Elder Marrok, do you know much about the gods?"

Marrok gasped, his face red with indignation before he blurted his ire. "What? You think just because I'm old, that I've literally been around since the days of the gods? What kind of a relic do you think I am?"

"Oh, Elder Marrok, I'm so sorry! I didn't mean..." she tried to apologize, but before she could finish, the old lycan laughed. He clutched his aching sides in mirth and nearly slid off his log.

"Elder Marrok?"

He laughed a while longer, occasionally drawing long gasps of air before falling into another cackling fit. Eventually, he recomposed himself and wiped the moisture from his eyes.

"Forgive me, Wolfmother. I can't make jokes like that with other lycans. They can smell when I'm full of shit."

Halea gave him a sharp glare. She wasn't exactly in the mood to be the butt of a joke, but after a while, the northern elder regained his dignity and replied to her original question.

"All jokes aside, I am old. Very, very old. I remember the world when it was still new when the gods and their first descendants still walked among us. Oh, and I met a few. It wasn't so uncommon back then, and the ones I never met, I heard about them. Especially the world dragons. Everyone knew when they walked upon the earth. They reigned over all, even over the other gods."

"Are you even older than Lord Anshar?" Halea asked.

"Only by about fifty or sixty years. I was practically still a cub when he was born, but I remember hearing about it because the Goddess herself came down from the heavens on the day of his birth. Tiamet had not walked upon the earth for over an age, but she returned when her daughter Lahamu delivered a son. It was said that the Goddess wept tears of joy as she cradled her grandson in her arms."

"She loves him," Halea softly interjected as she recalled the way her grandfather doted upon Valria. She knew just how strong such familial love could be.

"Oh, yes. The clouds parted, the seas were calm, flowers bloomed in every field and meadow, and birds took flight to sing in celebration of his birth. From that day on, Anshar was the apple of Tiamet's eye. She loved him above all others and blessed him and placed him as lord over her domain. Her hand upon the earth and the voice of her will. And so, he served her."

"If Lord Anshar turned against Tiamet, it would break her heart," Halea lamented. "I'll bet that's why the false god didn't just kill Lord Anshar when he had the chance. At least in death, Lord Anshar's soul would have been with Tiamet, but now that may not be the case because he hates her, and it's all Zernebog's fault for poisoning his mind."

Marrok nodded his head in understanding. Uro had mentioned the discovery he made with Lord Anshar to him and Batsuba, and it had not come as much of a surprise to the northern elder.

"I'm sure the black dragon wants to break Tiamet's heart the way she broke his."

"What do you mean?" asked Halea.

"Tiamet is the dragon of heaven, the keeper of the breath of life, and Zernebog wanted her for himself, but she rejected him for she had already chosen Abzu, the dragon of the earth, to be her mate. This sent Zernebog into a terrible rage, and he tried to destroy the world."

"I know the part about how he tried to conquer heaven and earth by bringing death and war into our world, and so Tiamet cast him out of heaven. That's in our sacred text, but I never heard the part about him being a spurned lover," Halea explained in shock.

"That is surprising. Why wouldn't Tiamet want her followers to know the truth about why Zernebog revolted?"

"Grandfather thinks she didn't want anyone questioning her power," Halea explained.

"So, the all-powerful Dragon Mother cannot defeat Zernebog? That puts us in a rough position."

"She either can't defeat him, or she can, but she won't," Halea spoke with anger rising in her voice as she got up from kneeling in the dirt.

"Where are you going, Wolfmother?"

"To get some answers," she replied over her shoulder while making her way towards the tree that housed the dark mirror.

~~~~☼~~~~

Samesa raised her hands to the swirling purple vortex as all around her, the piercing shrieks of demons being slain and the snarling and howling of wolves permeated the air. Her heart thundered in her chest, but she did her best to not let the chaos around her break her concentration as she called upon the Goddess.

Varg locked blades with a four-armed, black-eyed demon, and in each of the demon's hands, it wielded a weapon forged from the evil of the Chaos Dimension. The Fang's metallic sound could be heard in its war song as Varg charged the servant of Chaos without fear. Even though the beast had four arms, it did not have one-fourth of Varg's skill with a sword, and the wolf king found no trouble in battling back his foe in a series of lightning-fast strikes before severing the demon's head from its body.

174

Somewhere Halea was in turmoil, her heart aching, and it caused him to flinch as he desperately reached out for her. Every fiber of his being screamed to race home to his mate. She had undoubtedly heard the howls. He could sense that she was overwhelmed and frustrated, and when he explored her emotions, she tried to placate him, as was often her way of telling him not to worry or come running on her behalf. Despite her efforts, he was not pleased with the idea of his mate suffering. As an alpha male, he was a fixer. If there was a problem, it needed a solution, but when it came to their dire situation and the effect their predicament was having on his mate, he was helpless. He didn't like the feeling that he wasn't strong enough to help the person he loved the most, and he offered a silent prayer to the wolf gods as he begged them to stand with him, to give him the power that he needed to serve their will. He was the chosen protector of his people, and with every stroke of his blade, he could sense the will of the gods flowing through him.

Demons fell left and right as the Fang bit into foes without mercy while the tear snapped shut with a sound like rolling thunder, and before long, the last of their enemies were defeated.

Samesa wiped her brow as several clerics approached her in congratulations for successfully sealing the tear. One cleric had an injured leg, but thankfully it was a demon bite and not a cut from a dark blade. He would live. Samesa quickly went to work purifying a fallen lycan before their dark blade injury became fatal. It was a good day when everyone survived. They needed to feel like they had claimed at least one victory as the looming threat of the convergence drew ever nearer.

Varg watched as the devotees and lycans made their way back towards the den, but he remained behind. A familiar scent had attracted his attention. He had been noticing it a lot lately when the wind was just right, or, more particularly, when Samesa was available to join their demon hunts.

"You're not going to get anywhere that way," Varg called up into one of the nearby trees once he was sure that everyone else was beyond earshot.

A shadow leaped down from the tree with a fluttering of wings and quickly transformed to reveal Rufus looking embarrassed and unsure.

"I can't talk to her alone. She's always with the others," the falcon lamented as his dark reflective eyes stared out beyond the trees in the direction where Samesa had walked off with the other devotees.

"Oh, give it up already. Why are you still lying to her? Just tell her you're a damn therian already. She'll have to know the truth eventually."

Rufus's dark eyes swirled in horror as he envisioned the brilliant smile fading from Samesa's face the moment he revealed his true nature, and the fear of rejection made his stomach lurch.

Varg detected the scent of the falcon's fear, and he rolled his eyes.

"I don't know why you're hiding from anybody at this point. So, you're a therian? So what? Who cares? A few of the devotees maybe, but not the ones whose opinions matter."

"Samesa's opinion matters," Rufus added.

175

"Doesn't seem like she hates therians to me. I say to hell with secrecy and just talk to her."

"Well, maybe it's easy for you, you're an assertive alpha male, but it's not so easy for me. Almost my entire life, I've been the outsider looking in. Because of my secret, the only person I could really talk to was Sophia. I don't have much experience with people or women. I know everything about Samesa. I've loved her from afar for so long, but she doesn't even know that I exist, and if she knew that I was a bird this whole time, she'd probably think I'm a creep for having never said anything sooner."

"That's a good point. You are kind of creepily stalking her. You're also pretty awkward."

Rufus glared at Varg but couldn't argue because even though it was blunt and painful, it was the truth.

"I don't know how choosing a mate works for you birds, but when a wolf knows, they know. There's no going back. If you don't try, you can only lose," Varg offered with a note of sympathy and encouragement in his voice.

Rufus nodded his head. Perhaps Varg was right. It was better to take the chance, even at the risk of failure, than never try at all and fail for sure. At least he wouldn't have to live every day with doubt and regret. But even with this realization, Rufus felt his courage lacking.

Varg watched the cascade of readable emotions on the other male's face and sensed the nature of his hesitation. Courage was not something he had ever lacked, and it was hard for him to understand the situation from Rufus's perspective, but he knew one thing for sure; living with regret was unbearable.

"Look, you don't have to be an alpha male to let a woman know that you love her, and with the convergence coming, you may be running out of time. Isn't she worth it?"

Rufus's mouth drew into a stern line as his eyes gleamed in resolution. "She's worth it."

~~~☼~~~

Samesa arrived back at the camp to discover a bit of a commotion, and she could tell by the excitement that more of their people had joined them. It wasn't long before familiar faces appeared before her, and she was met with warm embraces of reunion. More than a hundred clerics and forty priestesses were safely escorted through the lycan's northern border. There had probably been howls to announce their arrival, but with the recent battle and her inability to decipher wolf calls, their appearance at the camp had caught her completely by surprise.

"Samesa!" cried Senior Priestess Gwen, who warmly hugged the younger priestess.

"Gwen! Senior Priestess," she quickly corrected in her enthusiasm. "You're here! I was beginning to think you'd never come."

"It took me forever to break away from the capital. The king and his council don't have a very high opinion of us right now, and when I realized there was nothing more I could do for our cause, I gathered every priestess and cleric from the capital and the neighboring towns that I could find, and we set out to find this place. Samesa, are you sure we're safe here?" she asked with a lower voice while leaning towards Samesa's ear.

"If you mean the wolves, they're fine. They've proven to be useful allies, and their kindness has kept what's left of our people alive during our exile."

"Are...are you sure?" the senior priestess questioned as her eyes darted around their camp while focusing nervously on the presence of their lycan guards. "They're not fattening us up for food?"

Samesa laughed at her senior priestess's paranoia. Gwen's reaction to their surroundings wasn't uncommon. Many of the priestesses and clerics who had never interacted with lycans, or any therians, were initially wary upon their first arrival, but in time, they all had learned that the wolves meant them no harm.

"Halea wouldn't let anything like that happen. She's not a priestess anymore, but she's still one of us, and she's one of the wolves too," Samesa explained, but before Gwen could argue further, a young woman ran up to the two priestesses and dropped to her knees.

"Senior Priestess Gwen? You are her, aren't you? They said you were her. Please forgive me for interrupting, but I've been waiting to meet you for so long. My name is Jennifer, and I'm blessed. I possess the light of Tiamet. I want to serve. I must serve! But there's been no one to make me a priestess now that Lord Anshar is gone. Master Uro said that you were the only one with the authority to speak on this matter. Please! Please, make me a priestess. I want to be one of you! I want to fight this darkness. Chaos has taken so much from me, and if I can't serve as an immortal, at least let me devote what life I do have."

Gwen looked stunned, but a softness eventually passed over her eyes. "And what has Chaos taken from you, my child?"

"My village was attacked, and I lost my twin brother and my mother. My father is still alive, and he's struggling to take care of all my other siblings. Cleric Samuel found me and told me I could help my family best by not adding to my father's burdens and fighting the evil that killed my mother and brother. I don't care about the risks. I would gladly lay down my life so that others will never have to know the pain and loss that I've endured. Please, can't you make me a priestess?"

Samesa's heart bled at the poor girl's sad tale, and the memory of her own losses to the evil of the Chaos dimension rekindled the fire of her own determination. No matter how much it cost, even if the price was her own life, she would not hesitate to fight until her last breath to save their world. It was the call of Tiamet, and it was undeniable.

"Sure. It's fine with me," answered Gwen with flustered nonchalance. Ordaining new priestesses was not her usual duty, but the girl had a point; with Lord Anshar gone and High Priestess Maven imprisoned, there was no one of higher rank. Other than the inability to bestow the gifts of Tiamet, there was no logical reason for her to refuse.

"Really? Oh, thank you! What must I do?" asked Jennifer, whose eyes shined with glee to hear the senior priestess's decision.

"You'll have to swear an oath, and you'll need a robe. I can't give you the immortality or the ability to heal quickly that usually comes with the job, but perhaps I can give you the title," Gwen explained before calling over a cleric who began a search among the other priestesses to see if anyone had a uniform to spare. A robe was quickly found, but nobody had an extra spear. Instead, one of the clerics was able to provide a rusty old sword. It was not much to look at, but it had the sacred runes of purification. It was better than nothing, so Jennifer accepted it with gratitude.

Word quickly spread throughout the camp that an oath was soon to be taken, and everyone prepared for a service.

Samesa went to fetch some water to wash up for the occasion. She was still covered in the gore of her recent battle and needed to use a spell to clean her robe, but as she was on her way to the edge of the camp, a shadow passed overhead.

Rufus squawked in warning that he was coming in for a fast landing, and she instinctively held out her arm.

"Hi, Rufus. Do you have a message?" she asked of the highly intelligent creature, but instead of having something tied to his leg, he carried something in his beak. When she held out her hand, he deposited a smooth piece of quartz before taking off in flight and disappearing into a sycamore tree just past the edge of their camp. Samesa laughed at the falcon's playful antics while tucking the stone into her bag before turning back to her task. Though given a nearby cavern as shelter for the night, during the day, they preferred to use the campgrounds they had initially been given as a hub for their daily activities and to not be as much of a burden to the wolves by spending too much time being close to their den. The clerics had set out a few pails of water for basic washing up earlier that day, and tossing down her bag and spear, she rolled up her sleeves when she discovered that her bag had accidentally dumped out onto the ground. While kneeling to scoop up the scattered contents, she noticed that most of the objects were small shiny gifts from Mama Dragon's bird. Shells, buttons, lots of rocks, a few smooth pieces of polished glass, but among all the gifts, one stood out to her above all the rest.

A small stone gleamed with flecks of green and orange that seemed to shine like fire.

"Sufur," she whispered to herself while plucking the stone out of the many other objects, and her eyes turned back towards the sycamore tree. "It...it can't be." Something inside her was calling for her to follow the falcon, and with a careful glance over her shoulder to be sure the lycan guards wouldn't complain that she was leaving without their supervision, she set out towards the tree where Rufus had landed.

"Rufus?" she called up into the tree, but he wasn't in the branches. Hearing something shuffling about on the other side of the tree's trunk, Samesa stepped around the base, and there, sitting at the roots with his knees tucked up under his chin and a forlorn expression on his face, sat Sufur.

"Sufur...how...how did you get here without the lycans stopping you?" she asked in shock.

"They know I'm here, Samesa," he explained while nervously avoiding her gaze and fiddling with his fingers.

"How?"

"They know what I am," he said before standing and leaning against the tree where his height towered over the dark-skinned priestess.

"What are you?" she asked with searching eyes.

"Didn't you think it strange that I was strong enough to pull you away from that shade mimic? Or how I could smell it? I could hear you leaving the camp and coming this way, even from all the way out here. My sense of smell and hearing aren't as powerful as the wolves, but my eyes can see further than theirs ever could. Don't you get it, Samesa?"

Samesa's eyes darted around her in confusion and doubt, but still, within her hand, she clutched the stone, and she knew.

"Are you…Rufus?" she asked while struggling to process the truth and cursing herself for not figuring it out sooner. His exotic accent was the same as Mama Dragon's, and she had never made the connection.

He nodded, and his eyes scrunched as if in pain.

"I'm sorry, Samesa. It's not that I wanted to lie to you. I just didn't know how to tell you the truth."

"It was you this whole time?" she asked with a note of irritation rising in her voice.

"Yes."

"You…you, big dumb jerk!" she shouted, and each word struck him like a stab to the gut, but before he could apologize further, she grabbed him by the collar and yanked him down into a kiss.

~~~☼~~~

"Lord Anshar?" Halea asked while taking a seat before the mirror.

"I'm here, Halea. I've been waiting for you," he replied, though he did not show himself. For days he had been drifting in and out of lucidity, but when his mind was not his enemy, he had dwelled on nothing but betrayal.

"There's something I need to tell you," they both spoke in unison, but after a pause, Halea continued.

"Is it true that Zernebog loved Tiamet? Is that why this is all happening? Did you know?" she interrogated with anger rising in her voice.

Silence.

"Lord Anshar, answer me!" she shouted, but to her surprise, his image revealed itself within the mirror.

"What do you mean, Halea?"

"Tiamet knew. She knew what was behind this all along, and she didn't tell us. Why?"

"Halea, I promise you, I don't know, but I've asked myself that same question over and over again since you were last here. This is the first I've heard of there being more to the story than what our sacred texts revealed. Where have you heard this? Has she appeared to you?"

179

Halea explained what she learned from Elder Marrok, and within the mirror, Lord Anshar's face grew dark with anger as he silently absorbed her words without doubt or question.

"Tiamet…you bitch," he finally growled.

"Don't!" Halea cried in shock to hear him use such language against the Goddess, but his wrath was far from over.

"She kept this from me, from everyone. What else is she hiding? Curse you, Tiamet! Why aren't you stopping this?" he shouted in anger to the Goddess, but if she heard him, she gave no reply, and Halea watched as he helplessly trembled in rage.

"Please. Don't curse her," Halea begged. "I've been asking myself the same question, and I'm afraid of the answer. Perhaps Tiamet deserves your anger, but don't you see? Zernebog wants this. He wants you to hate her because it will wound her in ways that he cannot. Haven't you already played into his hands enough?"

"I have been a puppet to them both. A pawn. Zernebog used me to do his dirty work. The demons were not powerful enough to kill the blessed, so he poisoned my mind and forced me to do his bidding. Their blood forever upon my hands. The fear and horror on their faces. But it's not any different than when I served Tiamet. It was all the same, even the way their eyes pleaded with me. I slaughtered priestesses for them both. I took the blood of the innocent for the false promise of salvation…or the false promise that someday I could build a world in which you could be mine. But there is no salvation, and I see now that it was always Zernebog's intent that once I was done with his dirty work, he would have slaughtered you and then me. I have been used and betrayed by both, but no more. Perhaps having me turn against Tiamet is what Zernebog wanted, but at least in this, he's right. She is not my Goddess anymore. I curse them both."

"Then what will we do? What's left? Is this the end of our world? Is it our fate to perish because we're all caught between the petty squabbles of two gods who don't really care whether we live or die?"

Lord Anshar mournfully avoided her eyes, and Halea bit her lip to fight back the urge to scream or cry.

It couldn't end like this.

"Halea, I can't save this world. That's what I've been waiting to tell you. I can't save you. It would have been better if you hated me. I've wronged you in so many ways, and I deserve your hatred. I tried to kill your mate and force you to love me, and when I knew I could never have you, I made threats because I wanted to hurt you the way you hurt me. Those things I said to you that day in the tower were lies. I wouldn't have been able to go through with such evil deeds. I could have never forced your love. I've already hurt you enough, but no more. If banishing the convergence means taking your life, then let it be the end of us all because I can't be the one to kill you. You're the only one I could never harm. I'm so sorry."

Tears spilled from Halea's eyes, but inside, the anger dissolved and gave way to warmth as she reached her hand towards the surface of the glass. Deep down inside, she had always known that he never meant all the awful things he said to her. He had lashed out in pain. He was always in pain. For as long as she had known him, he had

180

never been happy, and though they couldn't agree, even now, she only wanted to ease his suffering, and so she laid her palm over the cool glass of the dark mirror.

"It's okay, Lord Anshar. For the longest time, you did your best to save our world. I know that you meant well and that you deserve better than the life you were given. I really do want you to be happy. Someway. Somehow. I just want you to be at peace. I don't want you to suffer anymore. You may have been compelled to do some terrible things, and you may face judgment for it in this life or the next, but as for the things you did or said to hurt me, I forgive you."

From within the dimension beyond the dark mirror, he could see her entire form standing suspended before him like a pale reflection with one hand pressed against the transparent surface of the glass. Her beautiful eyes were weeping, but her face was soft and kind as she smiled gently as if suddenly unburdened from all his sins.

He reached out slowly, and though he could not feel her warmth, he laid his palm against the other side of the glass where their two hands would have been united if not for the barrier of the dimensions. And though she could not see him as he could see her, he smiled an achingly sad smile to know that she still cared for him just as she had always cared for him, even if he was a damned and undeserving monster.

~~~◇~~~

Maven rolled over and emptied the contents of her stomach onto the ground. Her head was pounding, and her limbs were shaking, and it took her a moment to realize that everything was quiet.

The tear was gone. Bodies of demons and rangers littered the ground, and her dingy prisoner's clothes were splatter with gore.

"What happened?"

Maven struggled to sit up, but her restraints were still biting into her flesh, and she was forced to slowly crawl along the frozen blood-soaked ground until she happened upon the fallen body of Captain Mark. The festering black wound in his chest told her everything she needed to know. She quickly rifled through his pockets until she heard the jingle of keys and offered up thanks to Tiamet while unlocking her manacles.

The flesh of her wrists and ankles were red and blistered raw, and she was shivering from laying on the frozen ground, but at last, she could stand and move without restraint.

"Thank you, Tiamet. Thank you," she prayed between sobs of relief. Truly, this had been a miracle.

And then the world spun, her vision went white as the gentle face of a beautiful therian woman with weeping red elliptical eyes appeared before her.

Release him.

"Tiamet, is that you? Help me, Tiamet, I don't know how!"

Instead of answering her cries, the face of the Goddess vanished, and suddenly Maven found herself standing within Lord Anshar's castle, in the infirmary. Screams of the mad echoed beneath the vaulted ceiling, and there, slouched in a chair, next to Cleric Edmond, who droned on from the sacred text, was an unfamiliar woman. She cautiously approached, afraid to be seen, but the nurses ignored her presence, and

181

though she drew nearer, Edmond never looked up from his tome. Something compelled her to observe the face of the woman beside him.

Her dark blond hair was streaked with grey, and her vacant eyes were hazel-green, but there was something familiar about the shape of her face. She felt as if she should recognize this woman, but she couldn't place where or how – and then the vision was gone.

"Who was that woman, Tiamet? What do you want me to do?"

A sharp pain tore through her head, and if not for her stomach already being empty, she would have retched a second time.

Go.

And without further question, Maven took off, running back towards Antherose.

CHAPTER 21 – TO PREPARE FOR WAR

The sun had set by the time Halea left the tree where she conversed with Lord Anshar, and she could sense that Varg was worried and upset as she made her way towards their treehouse. When she entered the main structure of their home, she found Varg seated at the recessed fire pit near the lit stove, rocking their sleeping daughter in his arms. He looked up as she entered and welcomingly patted the seat beside him, and she braced herself as she joined him by the fire.

"You promised you wouldn't let him make you cry again," he began, and the taut muscles of his face slackened to reveal his concern.

Halea unconsciously wiped her mostly dry face, but it was too late; he detected the scent of her tears the moment she walked through the door.

"I wasn't crying because I was upset."

"But you are upset," he argued as his brow furrowed in frustration. "I've been worrying about you all day. The last thing you need is him making things worse for you."

"He didn't make anything any worse. I was crying because Lord Anshar had a moment of clarity. I don't know if he's entirely well, but for the first time…it felt like I was talking to the old him. Before Chaos destroyed his mind. I forgave him…"

"Forgave him!" Varg growled but quickly regretted it as Valria opened her eyes and cried.

Halea reached for her fussing baby, and Varg gently handed her over, feeling genuinely sorry for how his outburst woke their child. Recognizing the warm and comforting arms of her mother, Valria quickly settled once more.

"Ralphina fed her while you were busy," he explained.

Halea sighed in anguish as she recalled the sense of overwhelming helplessness she had felt just that morning, and Varg was quick to scoot closer and wrap an arm around her shoulders.

"I know you still hate him, and I don't blame you, and I won't tell you how to feel, but there is still good in Lord Anshar. That's why I was crying. I was sad, yes, but relieved, I guess. It's hard to explain. But, as for being upset, well, he can't help us. No, that's not it. He won't help us. That much hasn't changed. We're on our own. The convergence is coming, and there's nothing we can do to stop it."

He watched her lips tremble, and the salty scent of her tears renewed as she looked down with despair at their sleeping baby.

"Then we'll fight," he declared while gently stroking the soft skin along her jaw, and she raised her eyes to see the sincerity in his face.

"How?"

"The last time the convergence came, we were unprepared. My people had no choice but to run. This time, we'll stand our ground, and you and I will fight together. We're a team, remember?"

Halea nodded her head in agreement. He was right. What other choice did they have? Even if they couldn't stop the end of the world, they would go out fighting – together.

Sensing her growing resolve, he leaned in and softly kissed her tear-soaked lips. Love and grief surged across the bond for them both as they parted and stared into each other's eyes with tender longing.

"You're right. We fight this together."

"Maybe this time, we can be ready," he offered.

"I think it takes time for the Chaos to build an army of demons," she mused. "Perhaps that's why it always used to take a couple hundred years between convergences. Maybe that's why tears and demons become more frequent the closer we get to the event. I don't know what will happen if the convergence tear actually manages to swallow our whole world. Nobody really knows. We've never let it get that far, and the worst it's ever gotten was the convergence that destroyed Ruinac. I don't think our chances are good."

"We're not giving up. I don't care what our chances are. We fight to the end. I will summon the other packs, and here is where we'll make our stand."

"The devotees will fight as well. I know they will. The lycans won't be alone this time," Halea replied while rocking their sleeping baby, the rising need to protect their only child kindling a flame within her.

That same fire burned within Varg. His mate, his child, and his entire pack were at stake. It would take an army to stand against the demon horde. The lycans would have to unite, and he would have to call them to battle.

"How long do we have? And where exactly will it happen?" he asked.

"I'll go over it with grandfather to be sure, but I think it will happen somewhere near the ruined city or the Citadel once again. Ever since the last convergence, I keep feeling the need to return to Ruinac. To look out once more upon the Citadel. All the priestesses have been feeling it. It's like we're being called to return to the sea. I don't think there's much time left."

"Then we can't wait."

~~~☼~~~

There was some debate among the priestesses and clerics about whether or not Senior Priestess Gwen had the authority or the right to conduct an oath ritual, but most set aside their qualms after Master Uro and Mama Dragon sided with her and reminded everyone that without their lord, they could quit or they could fight. For the priestesses, quitting was never an option. The call was too strong to deny, and though not blessed, most clerics shared their sentiments. If they did not fight the coming of the convergence, then who would?

Senior Priestess Gwen held forth a worn copy of their sacred text, and Jennifer, who knelt before her, placed one hand over the holy words.

"Will you swear upon this holy script that you will devote your life to Tiamet, and only Tiamet? Will you serve this world and all life upon it? Will you vanquish Chaos wherever it may be, and if asked of you, will you lay your life down if the Goddess wills it so?"

"I swear upon these holy words, my life and soul belong to Tiamet. I will go where she leads me. I will do as she wills. I will devote myself to the Great Mother Dragon, and I will defeat Chaos by her hand."

"Rise, Priestess Jennifer, servant of Tiamet."

Everyone came forward one by one and welcomed Jennifer into the fold with open arms and words of encouragement. Though it was a solemn occasion, tears of joy welled in the new priestess's eyes.

"She doesn't know what she's done," grumbled Kalee as Samesa appeared beside her with a radiant glow on her face.

By swearing one's life and soul to Tiamet, the Goddess would forever be their priority. Nothing else could ever be allowed to get in the way of their service to the Great Dragon Mother. To love and devote themselves to anyone besides the Goddess would be to break their sacred vow. Because of this, attachments that ran deeper than the bonds of friendship were strictly prohibited. Even sex, which they were not denied, was regarded as something to be experienced as no more than a bodily need and practiced with the utmost emotional detachment. Priestesses were expected to exercise caution when it came to contraception.

"She has no more choice than we did," Samesa argued without letting Kalee's bitterness spoil her good mood.

"And what are you grinning like an idiot for?"

"Nothing," Samesa answered, though her eyes betrayed a sense of guilt that Kalee immediately recognized.

"You lucky dog, did you get laid? Out with it! Which cleric was it? Hopefully, one of the cute ones."

Kalee was no stranger to the look of passion, and she had teased her friend about her dalliances in the past, but this look was different. Samesa's smile was brighter than she had ever seen before, and her dark eyes sparkled with an unfocused dreaminess.

"I wasn't having sex with anyone…yet," Samesa defended.

"Yet? You look awfully pleased with yourself, just the same. A little too pleased for someone not yet getting laid. And you didn't tell me who it was. Come on, don't keep me in the dark!"

"Shhh," Samesa implored as her friend's voice grew in volume. "I'll tell you later, I promise. Now isn't a good time, and besides, I'm…still processing it myself."

Kalee shook her head and prayed that her friend was not developing the sort of emotional attachment that would leave her heartbroken. Oath or not, the call would never let them go.

~~~~☼~~~~

It took Maven several days to make it back to Antherose. Travel was slow in her weak condition while also having to avoid the rangers who traveled along the main road and half of the more maintained paths throughout the wilderness. She had managed to salvage food, water, a sword, and a winter cloak from her fallen captors, though all their horses were slain by the servants of Chaos or chased into the woods. Undoubtedly the ranger's remains had already been found among the carnage of the burnt village. Demons often devoured their prey, leaving little behind, and she hoped that perhaps any rangers who came to investigate would assume that she was dead and consumed.

Despite her scavenged cloak, she shivered and longed for her priestess robes, which were confiscated by the rangers shortly after they arrived in Antherose and began interrogating her about Lord Anshar's whereabouts. She had insisted that Lord Anshar was trapped within the dark mirror and stolen away by Halea and her dirty shifter, but her story was too remarkable to believe, and they had laughed in her face and called her a lunatic. In place of her uniform, she was given a plain, dingy cotton dress that was so thin it was a wonder she had not caught her death of cold during her many months within the castle dungeon.

Returning to the castle filled her with apprehension, but she had no choice. The Goddess had shown her a vision of a mysterious woman in the infirmary, and she had to find out what was so important about this person.

As soon as the sun set, Maven moved stealthily beneath the cover of darkness along the path leading up to the castle. At the sound of boots crunching on gravel, she ducked behind some hedges as two rangers were on their way to the seaside city, and she prayed that the home of Lord Anshar would be deserted when she arrived, but there was no such luck.

The front doors were guarded by rangers and barred shut. She would not get in that way, so she decided to creep around back, through the courtyard, where perhaps she could gain entrance through a side door.

Her heart ached with regret and anger as she slowly slipped between the shadows of the crumbled courtyard walls. The fountain was smashed, and the once beautifully manicured garden was left to grow untamed, and weeds had overtaken the flowerbeds.

"*Lord Anshar's beautiful home - ruined. Halea and that filthy shifty. They did this! They ruined everything!*" she bitterly thought while passing unnoticed through the dismal remains of her lord's courtyard. To her relief, the back of the castle appeared to be unguarded. The inept rangers would see no reason for anyone else to want to come to the abandoned home of a dragon therian except for burglars.

"*They've probably already stolen everything that hasn't been nailed down,*" Maven thought while recalling many of the less-than-noble rangers she had encountered in her long life. The idea of anyone defiling Lord Anshar's home in such a manner made her blood boil. Lord Anshar had accumulated numerous irreplaceable artifacts over the many ages of his life, including priceless art and weapons.

She paused mid-step as the thought of weapons reached the forefront of her mind.

"*The sword! Oh, please, Tiamet, let it still be here,*" she prayed while trying the iron handle of a heavy wooden backdoor.

Locked.

Her eyes darted in all directions, but the coast seemed to be clear, and with one shove of her shoulder, aided by her super-human strength, she was able to break the bolt to force her way in. She paused, preparing to hear the shouts of guards and feet running her way, but one moment passed, and then another.

No one had heard, and she breathed a sigh of relief before closing the door behind her.

"Those lazy guards at the front are either drunk or sleeping," she thought with a smile of triumph before making her way through the familiar halls and corridors of the castle. Taking care to walk as softly as possible, she passed no corner without peeking around the edge first. Occasionally the voices of rangers echoed throughout the empty castle, but most seemed to be on their way out for the night. The few who remained occupied themselves in random rooms around tables with cards and tankards overflowing with ale, laughing loudly at bawdy jokes, and ignoring everything but their own companions. One ranger she passed was fast asleep on a chair, snoring loudly as he tipped precariously against the wall, but he did not stir as she crept past him and up into the high tower of the eastern wing.

At last, she reached it, the door to Lord Anshar's study. With a nervous gulp, Maven turned the handle, and by the grace of Tiamet, it was unlocked, and within, the room was empty.

Her heart ached as she stepped into the familiar study, once warmed by the roaring fireplace, but now dark and cold and somehow in even more disarray than she had left it. She groped blindly in the dark until she reached the desk and fumbled to find the oil lamp and some matches. Pawing through the untidy drawers, her hand brushed against a crumpled piece of parchment before eventually finding the matchbox and lighting the lamp. A soft glow illuminated the room, and she once again noticed the small scrap of paper as she was about to close the drawer. It was the last message she had received from Kalee before Lord Anshar returned to the castle.

It was clear that the rangers had searched this room, looking for valuables or important information of any kind, but this appeared to be nothing more than a crumpled list of herbs, perhaps an idly discarded recipe to an undiscerning eye.

As Maven read the instructions for the preparation of the strange concoction, one of her long-forgotten drunken memories returned.

"You must swear upon Tiamet's name that this information will remain a secret. It can't fall into the wrong hands. This knowledge is for priestesses only. Only the blessed. Swear it!" Kalee had pressed, and so Maven had sworn upon Tiamet's name that she would keep the secret of the potion that could be used to hide one's scent.

"This could be useful," Maven thought while stuffing the message into her dress before picking up the lamp and searching the room.

Many things were missing, but tears of joy sprang from her eyes as she held the lamp above the mantle, and there, glittered The Blade That Cuts Through Worlds.

Only Lord Anshar could unleash the true power of The Blade That Cuts Through Worlds. It was a holy weapon, and perhaps that was why it had remained untouched despite its obvious value. It was the one thing that even the rangers would be held accountable for if it ever went missing, as this was the only weapon they had that could fight against the Chaos. Without a master to wield it, they had left it in its place.

"Thank you, Tiamet. Thank you. Thank you!" Maven whispered in prayer as she reached for the sword but stopped short in fear.

She had never before dared to touch the holy weapon. Even the idiotic rangers were too reverent to attempt to move it from its resting place, but she was afraid that if she didn't take it that it would eventually fall into the hands of the king. They wouldn't leave it abandoned in the castle forever, and if she didn't take it, it could be lost to Lord Anshar forever.

Her hands trembled in uncertainty as fear squeezed her chest like a vice, but making up her mind, she reached up and grasped the hilt of The Blade That Cuts Through Worlds and pulled it down from the mantle. Even with her superior strength, the blade was so heavy it nearly came crashing to the floor.

It occurred to her that perhaps one of the reasons it had been left behind was because the rangers probably didn't even have the strength to lift it. Despite her perilous situation, that thought was nearly enough to make her laugh. No one could ever be as powerful as Lord Anshar. She had seen him wield the blade as if it weighed nothing more than a feather, and that knowledge only further assured her of her lord's magnificence.

"I'll set him free, Tiamet," she promised while wrestling the great sword into its sheath and hoisting it onto her back.

No one heard or saw her as she crept back through the castle and towards the infirmary. It was late. There would be no visitors, but she expected to find a few orderlies or nurses watching over the patients who suffered from Chaos madness throughout the night.

When Maven peeked beyond the threshold into the main infirmary hall, she noticed a single male orderly leaning over a desk with his back towards her. The echoing screams of the insane filled the room, and desensitized to the never-ending barrage of racket, the orderly didn't hear as Maven approached him from behind. Using Lord Anshar's sheathed sword as a club, she struck a blow to the back of his head, causing him to fall out of his chair with a thud upon the floor.

Maven's eyes quickly darted back towards the threshold, and she held her breath and waited for the sound of rangers to come running in and investigate the commotion.

But no one came.

She could have almost been relieved, but when she turned back to the fallen orderly, her stomach lurched at what she saw. She had only meant to knock him out, but he was dead. The sword had been so heavy and combined with her priestess strength, his skull had caved in like a mashed gourd.

Sobs wracked her body as tears flooded from her eyes. Though she played her part in helping Lord Anshar hunt and kill the priestesses, that was out of duty. They were necessary sacrifices, and their blood was spilled for the greater good, to save their world, and it had not been by her hand that they had met their doom. But this,

this was different. In all her long years, she had never murdered an innocent. Did this young man have a family? Did he even have a name?

Of course, he did, and she had robbed him of his life, and as a priestess sworn to protect all life, the guilt of her crime caused her to tremble with grief.

"Tiamet…Tiamet, I'm sorry. I didn't mean to. I'm so sorry. It was an accident. I didn't mean to hit him so…Ah!" she screamed as darkness seized her mind, and searing pain sent her to her knees and caused Lord Anshar's sword to crash to the floor with a metallic clang that echoed throughout the infirmary hall.

Go.

This single word from the voice filled her with a sense of urgency. Someone might have already heard her, and she still had to find the woman from her vision. Hefting the sword over her shoulder once more, she turned her back to the lifeless man and the way his blood seeped across the floor and took off running through the infirmary. She ran past locked doors and sparsely occupied rooms where patients wandered in confused states of hopeless madness. Some were cackling, and some were crying, and some were mumbling in incoherence or screaming as they rocked in lonely corners or clawed at the walls until their fingers bled. It was no wonder that nobody had paid any attention to the noises she made. The horrors within these walls were meant to be forgotten, locked away, and ignored where no one would have to hear or see or smell the true destruction that the Chaos could bring to those unfortunate enough to look into the heart of the darkness.

Every face she looked into was vacant, their mouths twisted and slack with eyes that stared into nothingness or a horror from which they could not escape. At last, she entered a room filled with cots where patients lay waiting in the dark, and there, sleeping as still as the dead, was a woman who appeared very much like the one she had seen in her vision, but because of the darkness, she couldn't yet be sure.

Reaching for the sword she had taken from one of the fallen rangers, Maven held the blade up high and called upon the light of Tiamet until a soft white glow illuminated the face of the sleeping woman.

It was her.

The strangely familiar face was unmistakable, but what now?

The question had scarcely entered her mind when she was brought to her knees once more by a searing agony that ripped through her head like a hot spike, and her scream soon mingled with the screams of the insane all around her.

Darkness passed before her eyes and gripped her with sickness until, at last, a vision appeared before her.

"It's alright, Halea. Everything will be fine. I'll be here waiting for you," spoke the woman with tear-filled eyes as she embraced the young girl who noticeably trembled with fear.

"I'm proud of you."

Maven's eyes snapped open, and once again, she was on the floor trembling and sweating as the intense sense of loss and longing hovered against the edge of her memories like a ghost that was slowly fading.

Tiamet had shown her the way, and she knew what to do.

189

Convincing so many lycans to gather alongside the Tiamet worshippers hadn't been easy, and many of the humans and wolves chose to stand as far apart from each other as they could as Varg and Halea stood waiting for silence.

Once the gathered masses had settled, Varg began. "We wouldn't have asked both humans and lycans to gather here together today if it wasn't a serious matter that affects us all. You who worship the Dragon Goddess can probably guess why this meeting has been called, but my people also have the right to know."

"Know what?" called a lycan.

"What is it, Alpha Varg?" cried another.

Varg could see the tense unease in the eyes of his people all around him. No doubt most had suspected that things were not going well with their battle against the Chaos. Even with the priestesses' help, many wolves had fallen in the fight against the encroaching dimension of evil, and softly spoken words had carried the mutterings of fear and uncertainty for the future. More than anything, Varg wished that he could comfort them and tell them that all would be well and not to fear, but the time for secrets and doubt was over. Everyone needed to prepare.

"The convergence is coming," he announced to the collective gasps and cries of terror from his people. Voices of panic rose both in fear and in anger.

"They were supposed to stop it!"

"Why is this happening?"

"Can't they make it go away?"

"This is their fault! We protected them, and they've done nothing but live fat off our lands while our people die!"

The devotees clutched tightly to their weapons as many of the wolves turned to them in accusation, but before the two sides could come to blows, a snarl of warning reverberated through the trees with such force that birds took flight and the ground beneath their feet shook.

Varg had called for silence.

Halea, standing beside him, placed a comforting hand on Varg's arm before stepping forward.

"The only person with the power to banish the convergence tear is Lord Anshar, and as many of you know, he has turned against us. What some of you don't know is that he's also turned against Tiamet. He has refused to ever perform another sacrifice, and without his help, no amount of wolves, priestesses, or clerics can stop the convergence. It will come, and it will try to swallow our world. The demons will swarm these lands just as they did once before, but this time the great convergence tear cannot be closed."

More voices rose in panic and horror, but she continued. "We don't know what will happen if the two dimensions converge. It has always been prevented in the past. But we do know that the demons are not an infinite resource for the evil that lives within the Chaos. Perhaps, this time if we're ready, we can make a stand."

"We'll be slaughtered!" shouted an angry lycan.

"We've seen what their hordes can do. Even with the help of priestesses, we're not strong enough to hold back an entire demon army," cried another.

"Enough!" roared Varg, and quickly the voices of anger fell. "You're right. As we are now, we would be overrun and defeated, but this time must be different. This time we must prepare. We must fortify our mountains for a siege, and we must call for the help of the other packs. If the wolves unite, we can make a stand."

The last time the lycans challenged the forces of Chaos, the western pack had fought with the help of the eastern and southern wolves, but they had been quickly abandoned to their fate by their southern brethren. The eastern and western packs had not been strong enough to withstand the onslaught of the demon horde and were forced to flee. This time, things were different.

"I will summon the other packs to war. The northern, eastern, and southern alphas have sworn their allegiance. This time we shall not fight alone."

"And we will fight with you," called the thickly accented voice of a woman, and all eyes turned to see that Mama Dragon had stepped forward with spear firmly clutched in hand and eyes blazing.

"This is our fight, as well. We are sworn to protect this world with our very lives, and we cannot rest until Chaos is defeated," added High Priestess Gwen, who was accompanied by nods and shouts of approval from the rest of the devotees who stepped forward to stand with her and Mama Dragon.

Among the lycans, a spark of hope grew as they beheld the determined faces of the devotees. Wolves were not cowards, and they weren't about to tuck tail and run where even a human refused to show fear. Their homes, their lives, everything they had spent the last ten years to regain and rebuild was at stake, and this time, they were not alone.

One by one, the voices of the lycans rose to shout.

"This is our home. I say we fight!"

"I'm not running!"

"If those devils from beyond the Chaos want a fight, then we'll give it to them."

"We're with you, Varg."

"If the humans will fight, then so will we."

For the first time in ages, even Halea's hopes came alive as she beheld the humans and wolves before her, pledging to stand and fight together against their common enemy.

It was time to call the wolves to war.

CHAPTER 22 – SECRETS

Day and night, the lycans were excavating a new tunnel system that would lead out into the north and east, providing an escape route in case their defenses could not hold. To fortify their mountains, the iron doors that sealed the entrance to many of their caves and caverns were reinforced, and supplies were stockpiled within. Below, some of the more open and vulnerable of their surrounding lands were fenced-off with timber barricades topped with sharpened spikes designed to deter demon invaders and send them into narrower paths through gullies and ravines where lycans and priestesses could get the upper hand by ambushing them from the higher ground. These barricades were also filled with dry kindling. If the spikes were not enough to do the job, they could be lit by a flaming arrow to buy their warriors extra time.

The clerics had thoroughly reviewed the maps and charts that Master Cleric Uro used to track the tear and demon activity, and all agreed; the convergence would strike again in the west just as it had the previous two times it appeared. Every priestess among the devotees sensed it since the last convergence. The remains of the Citadel were the heart of Tiamet and where the evil was determined to make its mark upon their world. Zernebog wanted to crush everything sacred to the Goddess, and the blessed were being called to war.

The priestesses and clerics were hard at work, setting as many barrier traps as possible throughout the surrounding lands. The larger the barrier, the more powerful the spellcaster had to be, so most of these traps were small, but with enough of them scattered throughout the western front, it would be difficult for demons to cross the lycan hunting rounds without severe casualties.

Varg stood at the vantage point, looking down at the barricades below as regret and anger burned him up on the inside. It was an ugly sight, and the loss of so many precious trees torn down to hold back the demon hordes made him curse the god that lived within the Chaos. If they somehow survived the war ahead, he would make it his mission to replant two trees for every one that gave its life for the sake of his people. Lycans were careful to only take timber when a tree was coming to the end of its life or if it had fallen by storm. They rarely chopped down trees in their prime, and if they had to, they always made atonement to nature for the sacrifice that was given, usually by planting something in its place.

"Varg, the northwestern barricade is near completion. Where should we place the archers?" asked Lyall with a curt respectful bow as he approached his alpha.

"I want one troop of archers stationed on the south ridge and another further up the western face of that ravine in case the first troop gets cut off."

Lyall nodded and turned to leave but noticing Halea as she made her way up the slope, he briefly stopped to acknowledge her. "Wolfmother."

"Hello, Lyall," Halea replied, but the old warrior said no more and went on his way. She paid him no mind and went to stand beside Varg, who instinctively wrapped his arm around her.

"I've secured the inner cavern on the northernmost edge," she reported. "It's not very high, but it has an easier escape route than the other caves. I figured we could keep the cubs inside with some of the nursing mothers and station guards just outside. Jance has volunteered to watch over Valria while we fight. Ralphina will be with her, but she'll have her hands full with Bardolph and several other cubs placed in her charge. Ulrica will be there with Daisy, and she'll mind Fillin while Hemming and Daciana fight with us. Lycurgus and Alf have asked to be given the assignment of guarding the young."

"Of course, they'll want to be there to protect their mates and the cubs. I'm sure you've already agreed," replied Varg.

"Well, yes, but I could take it back if you said no."

"But you knew I wouldn't."

"Damn right. I know you better than anyone," Halea said with a cheeky smile, and despite all the stress and anxiety he carried in his heart, his spirits felt a little bit lighter when her beautiful hazel-green eyes shined up at him. Wrapping her tight in both his arms, he rested his face in the crook of her neck and drew comfort from her warmth and the scent that he had known since they were children. His Halea had never changed. She was right, nobody knew him better, and he could trust her to make any judgment call in his place, but he also appreciated that she openly communicated with him despite already knowing his thoughts on the matter.

"You're the best thing that's ever happened to me," he confided as he raised his head to meet her gaze and heard the flutter of her heartbeat. "I love you, puny human."

"I love you too, you mangy wolf," she replied while reaching up to meet his lips with hers. The bond between them swelled with their love, and neither wanted to let the other go, but eventually, they had to break their kiss and come back to the devastating reality of their situation.

"I trust you. Just keep me updated on who will be posted where," he eventually said.

"Batsuba asked to stay with the cubs. I told her it was fine."

Varg nodded.

"Grandfather made a fuss about wanting to join the priestesses at the western front, but I begged him to stay behind with the mothers and cubs. Only for Valria's sake was he finally willing to agree, and I've also tasked him with moving the mirror at the first sign of attack. I know you don't want Lord Anshar close to the den, but we also can't risk having him fall into the hands of the demons. Grandfather agreed to retrieve and guard the mirror if the southwestern blockade falls."

Again, Varg nodded. The southwest wasn't likely to see much action, but it was a somewhat vulnerable stretch of their territory. If their defenses fell, the den would be open to invasion, and Uro was the only other person they had trusted with the dragon. Precautions to defend the southwest stretch of land had been taken, but it was unlikely to face the brunt of the demon horde because the thick, old forests would make for slow advance, and it was at a lower elevation. The grassy plains of their western hunting lands and northwest pass were hit the hardest during the last invasion, and it was safe to assume they would be the demon's preferred focus for attack once again.

Because of the vulnerability of the southwest, they had already abandoned their beautiful treehouse and moved back into the alpha's cave that they shared when they were first mated. Leaving their new home broke Halea's heart, but neither were willing to risk living so far from the safety of the den with a war on the way and a cub to protect.

Every day, Varg's anxiety rose as the ever-present fear of the prophecy loomed over his mate. His instincts howled and tormented him from the inside, warning him that the time would soon come for them to meet their fate, and he was powerless to stop it. He hadn't slept since they decided to summon the other packs, and it was wearing on his nerves, but he couldn't rest. Everyone was counting on him, and for the first time in his life, the stress was on the verge of breaking him.

"I sure hope the other packs get here soon," Halea continued. It had been a little over a week since they sent the runners. Winter was bearing down on them in full force with heavy snowstorms blowing in from the north, and the weather would undoubtedly delay the arrival of the other packs. Unfortunately, time was against them. On top of preparing their defenses against the demons, they also had to ready the den for the arrival of thousands of lycans, except this time, it would not be like the Spring Moon Festival.

"The southern pack should be here first," he assured. "The north gets heavier snow, but they're used to it, and they're the closest. It's the eastern pack that I'm worried about. I regret making them cross the mountains during the blizzard season. It's a treacherous journey at this time of year."

"Otsana will bring the eastern wolves. I'm sure of it."

"We'll just have to be ready," he said.

"Is that Rufus?" Halea asked as she noticed a bird flying straight for them from her peripheral vision.

Varg, who could see better, confirmed her suspicion, and prayed it wasn't bad news.

As Rufus circled down, he quickly transformed and sloppily landed, nearly skidding into them, and setting Varg's nerves on edge.

"What?" Varg growled, preparing for the worst.

"What? Is that any way to greet a friend?" replied the falcon therian.

Varg only narrowed his eyes in irritation.

"We haven't seen much of you lately, Rufus. Where have you been?"

"With Samesa," Rufus said with a sly grin that caused Varg to raise a brow in scrutiny and Halea to gasp before bursting into an ecstatic smile.

"I take it things went well?" Varg asked.

"Well, you said you wanted me to bring some good news. Does my good news count?"

"I don't care whose good news it is, as long as it's not bad news for me," Varg grumbled, but he could not hide the smile tugging at the corner of his lips. "So, you told her the truth?"

"Yep."

"And she didn't zap you?"

"I think she wanted to, at first, but no."

"Oh, Rufus, that's wonderful! I'm so happy for you both. Congratulations!" added Halea, who was warmed to know that two of her dearest friends had come together, and she was already itching to go find Samesa and grill her for all the details.

"And your mother?" Varg asked, to which the enthusiasm immediately fell from Rufus's face.

"I…haven't figured out how to tell her yet."

"Rufus, Mama Dragon loves you," Halea admonished. "She's only been disapproving because she didn't want you to get your feelings hurt if Samesa rejected you. I mean, she is a priestess. But if she's already professed her love for you, then the oath is broken, and you two can be together."

Rufus nervously cleared his throat as his dark reflective eyes swiveled between his two friends. "Well…there hasn't quite been any professions of love…just yet. I mean…what with the war coming. She's had a lot on her mind."

"What?" growled Varg. "Didn't you tell her how you feel?"

"I was trying to wait for a good time."

Varg and Halea exchanged a doubtful glance between each other and shared their exasperation across their bond.

"You've spent the past week with her, and you didn't tell her?" prodded Halea.

"I wanted to, but that oath, what if she doesn't want to break it for me? Accepting me as a therian and a lover is one thing. But what if Sophia is right? What if Samesa doesn't want to give up being a priestess to be with me?"

"I honestly don't even know if that oath is worth anything anymore," Halea replied. "Only Lord Anshar could give and take away our immortality, and right now, I can assure you, he doesn't give a damn about anyone's oaths. Immortal or not, we're still blessed, and Tiamet never lets us forget it," Halea explained. "The next time you have a chance, you should tell her that you love her."

Rufus nodded in solemn agreement. He had mostly spent the past week hovering close to Samesa in his falcon form and only chancing to meet with her in secret for a few moments at a time as the lycan guards were ever-present and vigilant because of the shade mimics. Whenever they came together, they fell into each other's arms and passionately kissed as if nothing else in the world mattered, and only when they were on the verge of being discovered would they part. He wanted to give up his deception and let the whole world know the truth of his form so he and Samesa could finally be together without shame, but the truth was, there would be shame. Though Samesa had accepted him for what he was, he knew many priestesses and clerics would not approve of him and Samesa. Nor of Sophia for having kept him hidden for so many years. He couldn't betray Sophia like that after she had raised him as a son and protected him. He did not want to cause trouble for the two women he loved most in life, and so he would remain hidden.

"A raven," Varg mentioned, as a tiny dark speck flew in from the northwest.

"It looks like it's heading for the refugee camp," observed Rufus, who partly eyed the inferior bird in hunger.

"I hope that's not the bad news bird," Varg added.

<center>~~~☼~~~</center>

Mama Dragon watched the raven as it flew in towards the devotees. The messenger bird was trained to spot the devotees' white and red uniforms, which was one of the reasons why their robes were designed to stand out. She had been watching the sky for Rufus all morning, but he was nowhere to be found, and it was starting to worry her. She had seen very little of him for the past week, and when she did see him, he seemed to be in a hurry and avoided taking his humanoid form even when they were alone.

The raven gracefully landed on the outstretched arm of one of the clerics, who quickly untied its message and offered it a handful of food as a reward for its service.

"What is it, Jim?" asked Mama Dragon.

"It appears to be for Master Uro."

"I'll take it to him. Make sure that bird gets some water," Mama Dragon said as she accepted the message. She sought out the elder cleric and found him on the southeastern edge of their encampment, going over maps and charts with some of the younger devotees.

"It's for you," Mama Dragon said once she found him, and when Uro saw the message, his face became noticeably pale. "Master Uro, are you all right?"

"Yes. Yes, I'm fine. I'll take it, Sophia, thank you," he said before dashing off with the message as fast as his legs could carry him back towards the den.

Faolan, who was on guard duty, spotted Halea's elderly cleric grandfather leaving the camp, and he quickly dashed out to join him.

"Wait, Halea's grandfather, you can't walk all the way to the den without an escort. Those mimics are still out there," Faolan reminded. The old man looked up at him with annoyance looming behind his thick spectacles, but eventually, he nodded in agreement, and Faolan accompanied him on his way back to the den.

As they walked, Uro tore open the sealed message and read, but something made him halt in his tracks.

Faolan did not want to pry. The old human had a reputation for being cantankerous, and he had enough of that from Batsuba. He knew better than to ask too many nosey questions, but he could tell something was seriously troubling the man.

"Are you okay?" he eventually asked when he noticed the human was shaking and looked on the verge of collapse. "Do you need a healer?"

"No. No, I'm fine. Thank you. Let's go," Uro curtly replied, and despite his obvious distress, he mustered his staff and walked onward.

196

Uro clutched the note within his fist as a million questions plagued his mind. It was from Edmond. Apparently, an orderly in the castle infirmary had been murdered. Both The Blade That Cuts Through Worlds and Theia were missing.

~~~~☼~~~~

Another week rolled by, and there was scarcely a moment when Varg was not scanning the horizon or perking his ears for the howls that would announce the arrival of one of the other packs. He had not slept for more than a few hours in the past two weeks, and he had become increasingly short-tempered with everyone who came near, except for Halea and their cub.

Halea knew he couldn't rest; she could barely sleep herself. Many a night, she would stay up beside him, and they would take turns holding their baby. Valria's tiny fingers were beginning to show the signs of budding claws, and her curious eyes always sought the faces of her parents. Her toothless grin lifted their spirits while simultaneously breaking their hearts.

What if help didn't arrive in time? What if they couldn't survive the convergence? What if this really was the end?

Varg had no way to comfort Halea as guilt ripped her apart. She still held herself responsible for bringing their daughter into a doomed world, and nothing he said or did could ease her pain. While he would not trade Valria for anything in the world, inside, he was frightened of what would happen to her if Halea died. Would he only be there for her in body but not in spirit, as his father had been with him? Those tormenting thoughts plagued him like phantoms as he wandered aimlessly through the mountain caverns on sleepless nights.

He desperately tried to think of some way to assure their survival and had even considered beseeching the swordmaster for his aid. This idea was quickly thrown out. He had seen the destructive nature of Abaddon for himself and knew that if the sword of destruction should ever fall, it would not discriminate between friend or foe. It had the power to scorch the earth until nothing remained. It was his sword, the sword of the earth, the Fang, that was the sword of protection.

Night after night, he would pray to the wolf gods for guidance, for strength. They were still with him; of that, he was sure. His skill with the Fang had not waned, but he wasn't sure how best to serve their will. Was he doing all that he could?

At last, as the sun crested over the western horizon, a lone piercing howl rang out over the trees.

The southern pack had come.

Varg gently woke Halea, who had begged to be told the moment any of the other packs arrived. He would have preferred she get more rest, but he knew she was just as eager for the arrival of the other packs as he was and that she would want to greet them as a proper wolfmother.

Bundling Valria in warm furs and carrying her in a sling near her breast, Halea joined Varg as they went down to the common area to greet the southern pack who were already being offered rest and refreshment after their long journey.

"Greetings, Wolf King," offered Raoul, who had arrived with even more pack members than when the Spring Moon Festival was held. With war on the way, every able-bodied southern lycan who could fight had come to the aid of their king.

"Raoul, thank you," Varg said, eschewing formalities as he exchanged a hearty embrace with his cousin, who reciprocated in kind.

"It's time the southern pack proved its allegiance to all our people and our king. You won't stand alone this time. We're with you," Raoul promised.

"Raoul, thank you so much. We've made room for you and your pack," Halea began, but Raoul cut her off when he laid eyes on Valria's chubby face peeking out at him.

"Is this your half-wolven cub?" he asked in a tone that was hard to read. News of Halea's pregnancy and the birth of their cub had been shared with the other packs. All of the alphas had sent runners with congratulatory messages, including Raoul, but neither Varg nor Halea were entirely sure if those sentiments were genuine or spoken out of polite obligation.

Varg was tired and tense and not in the mood to have someone hassle him and Halea about their daughter, and if he were in his wolf form, his hackles would have surely been raised.

"Her name is Valria," Halea introduced before Varg could become defensive. "Valria, look. It's your, uh…"

"First cousin, once removed," Raoul offered. Due to immortality, most lycans had extensive and complex family trees, and they were used to keeping track. "She can call me Uncle Raoul when she gets older. Can I hold her?"

The request did not make Varg any less defensive. If anything, it put him even more on edge. Halea sensed his qualms and shot him a confident and knowing glance before holding out their baby for the southern alpha, who accepted her with open and eager arms.

"Valria! You gave her your mother's name," Raoul said to Varg. "And my aunt. I like that. She looks lycan, but I see she has her mother's eyes. There doesn't seem to be anything particularly unusual about her. This is a strong cub."

"And loud, like her father," Halea added, and the two joined in laughter, to which Varg finally eased and smiled with relief.

"It's good to have more family," Raoul confessed as he rocked Valria, who looked up at him as if confused as to why her father's eyes were in a different face. "I'm happy for you both. I don't know if the gods will ever bless me with a mate or cubs of my own, so in the meantime, I hope you won't mind if I spoil yours."

"Get in line," Varg said with a grin.

"Why don't we all get out of this cold? We can gather in the communal cavern and tell you everything over breakfast," Halea offered.

There was much to discuss and even more to prepare for. Raoul had been told of the coming convergence, but he still had many questions and concerns.

He listened patiently as Varg and Halea told him about what they discovered from the Dragon Lord and the details on their preparations for the coming convergence.

"Like you, I don't know what hope we have," Raoul confessed. "A god! The one thing no wolf can fight. If we make our stand here in the west, the southern pack is with you, and let us pray our own gods are with us."

Halea and Varg spent the rest of the day going over their defenses with Raoul.

"If we're going to retreat to high ground and evacuate through the mountains, I suggest setting up a few rockslides. With these new tunnel excavations, you won't have to go far to find rocks and boulders," Raoul suggested, and Varg and Halea agreed that it was a sound idea.

That night, the southern and western wolves gathered in the communal cavern for an evening meal, but Halea was troubled because her grandfather had once again declined to join them. Her grandfather had proven that he would let no lycan intimidate him, so she knew he wasn't avoiding the southern alpha. If anything, it was her. For the past week, he had been distant and jittery. At first, she wondered if she should do something about his heart medication, but he assured her that he felt fine.

His odd behavior began on the same day the raven was seen delivering a message to the devotees at the refugee camp, and she knew her grandfather was there that day. When she questioned him about it, he had dismissed it as having been nothing of any importance, but she had her doubts. Something had shaken him up, but she also knew that her grandfather was stubborn and often kept many things to himself. That was just his way. She had no choice but to let him be.

As everyone did their best to relax and enjoy the company of their southern brethren, a howl echoed from somewhere outside. Halea listened carefully, and to her surprise, she knew that it was not a call of danger.

"It's the northern pack!" she cried before Varg had a chance to translate for her.

"Since when do you speak wolf?" he said with a laugh. All around them, the western and southern wolves rejoiced to hear of the northern pack's arrival.

"I don't know about speak, but I think I've listened to enough calls that I'm finally beginning to tell the difference."

"Next, you must learn to howl," Raoul added with a laugh as they all got up to go outside and greet the northern wolves.

"I've heard her howl. It's gibberish," Varg added, and Halea blushed.

If her hands weren't full with Valria, she would have swatted at him. The last time she howled in front of Varg, they were children, and she had asked him to teach her how. That lesson hadn't gone on for very long before her pitiful attempts had left him rolling on the ground with laughter.

Once outside, rather than go through greetings in the dark and cold, Varg and Halea quickly ushered the entire northern pack into the vast cavern that was just spacious enough to accommodate the three packs. By the time the eastern pack arrived, they would have to start spreading out into the other caverns.

The western and southern packs welcomed the northern wolves, and soon, the entire cavern was filled with boisterous voices as everyone celebrated their arrival by bringing out more food and drinks.

Halea and Varg welcomed Bertolf and thanked him for coming so quickly, and as they were seating themselves with Raoul at the alpha's pit, they heard someone shouting.

"Bert!"

Bertolf looked up to see Alf and Jance rushing over to greet him, and he jumped up to hug his brother and sister-in-law.

"We missed you," Jance confessed as the little family exchanged hugs.

"Stay and eat with us, you two," Halea offered. It was nice to see their family reunion, much like the one she and Varg had shared with Raoul, and she didn't want to break them apart. Halea knew just how much Jance had begun to miss her home in the north and all her pack friends and family. Alf had missed his pack as well, especially his brother.

Since Valria's birth, Jance had been torn about whether or not she was ready for her and Alf to return to the north. They had only asked to stay until Jance could see the half-wolven child, but in truth, Jance had become attached to many of the western cubs, especially Daisy, who reveled both in Jance's attention and her sweets. With the threat of the looming convergence, it seemed as if they would never return to their northern home, but at least they could be with their pack once again.

As everyone gathered before the fire, Varg and Halea shared a surge of hope and relief. They had more than doubled in strength, but they still could only pray that the eastern pack reached them in time.

~~~~⬦~~~~

The cold winds whipped Maven's cloak around her knees as she walked through the rubble of the ruined city. The howling winds and dark clouds rolled in from the sea, past the decimated remains of the Citadel of the Sun, warning her to hurry as she ran back to the ramshackle building where she had been hiding for the past few days. The freezing torrential rain began before she could reach her shelter, and by the time she pried open the rotten wooden door, she was soaked all the way through to her white priestess robe.

She had pilfered a new uniform before leaving Antherose, along with a horse and wagon that had belonged to the rangers and a couple of weeks' worth of food. She couldn't find any spears, and it was not a High Priestess's robe, but she had been in a hurry, and it would have to do.

Clothing and supplies had not been the only thing she had taken. There, slumped in a rickety old chair in the corner, sat the catatonic mother of Halea, and hidden beneath a loose floorboard, The Blade That Cuts Through Worlds.

Tiamet had tasked her with rescuing Lord Anshar, but not only that, there still had to be a sacrifice, and Halea was that sacrifice. She could lure Halea away from the wolf shifters with this woman, but first, she needed to find Lord Anshar.

For days Maven had prayed to the Goddess for another vision. She knew the mirror was with the wolves, but she didn't know where among the wolves or how she would be able to retrieve it. She had practiced making the potion that masked scents but couldn't be sure if it would work. Her nose was not sensitive enough to detect any

200

noticeable changes, and all she could do was pray that Kalee had not been raving nonsense.

Halea's mother never moved. Never spoke. She only stared into nothingness and drooled pathetically. Maven was not a nurse and caring for the woman who could do nothing for herself was a nasty inconvenience, but it would all be worth it if she could rescue Lord Anshar and help him fulfill the sacrifice that would save their world.

Imagining his gratitude, his joy to be freed, filled her moments of silence with hope and encouragement. Surely, he would see how much she loved him. How she would do anything in the world for him. For him, she would even break her oath to Tiamet.

As Maven settled on the cold hard floor before her pitiful fire to dry, a searing pain ripped through her mind with such intensity that she screamed and writhed on the floor in agony.

The world became a void before her, and trees sprang up from the ground. A swirling purple vortex pulsed in the sky, and another, and another, to the accompaniment of shouts and screams, and the howling of wild beasts. So many tears – and then the demons came.

Set him free. Now!

"Where is he, Tiamet? Where?" but instead of an answer, her pain only increased until she could only roll over and retch.

And then the vision was over. The voice was gone. Trembling with sickness, and pulse pounding with fear, Maven pulled herself to her feet before snatching up her sword, and the potion that masked scents, and running out into the storm.

CHAPTER 23 – WHITE WOLF

Between the arrival of the northern and southern packs and the many preparations for the coming convergence, Halea barely had any time to spend with the devotees. Mama Dragon and Senior Priestess Gwen would come to the den every day to report minor tear and demon activity and the devotees' efforts to set traps and barriers throughout the lycan hunting grounds. Halea wanted to talk to Mama Dragon about Rufus, who was nowhere to be found when the maternal priestesses arrived to make her reports, but she could tell that Rufus hadn't told Mama Dragon about revealing himself to Samesa just yet. It wasn't her place to be the one to break the news, but there was something she could do.

One early morning, Halea found Varg surrounded by the other alphas and the best hunters from the western, northern, and southern packs. With so many mouths to feed in the winter and their western hunting lands being prepared for war, many herd animals had fled north into the mountains forcing the hunters to travel further to find enough game to feed such a large congregation of wolves. Varg would be leading the hunt, leaving her to supervise the den, but she needed to have a word with him before he left.

She didn't have to interrupt the hunters because, as she approached, Varg quickly took notice of her and excused himself from the group.

"Is everything okay? Where's our pest?" he asked, using his favorite nickname for Valria.

"Valria's with Jance. I know you're about to leave for the hunt, but I was wondering if I could follow you guys out as far as the refugee camp? I've wanted to have a word with Samesa for days, but it's been hard to find the time to get away with everything that's been going on."

"Of course. Just make sure that when you're ready to head back to the den, that you get a wolf to go with you."

"I won't forget," she promised.

Halea followed Varg and the hunters until they reached the camp, and Varg escorted her to its edge.

"If you need me, use the bond to call for me. If there's any trouble, we can cancel the hunt," he reminded as he wrapped his arms around her.

Halea nodded in agreement before stretching up on her toes to kiss him goodbye.

After Varg returned to the waiting hunters, Halea made her way through the camp, where she noticed that the tents were covered with furs for extra insulation against the cold weather, and many campfires were surrounded by gloomy-looking clerics and priestesses. The devotees had been given a large cavern for shelter, but during the day, they still preferred to remain outdoors, monitoring the activity of Chaos, and staying well out of the way of the wolves. The arrival of the other packs, though expected and necessary, made the devotees acutely aware that the time was swiftly coming for them to prove their worth.

As Halea wandered the camp, the bright red of Kalee's hair drew her attention, and she called out to her priestess friend.

"Hello, Kalee. Is Samesa here?"

Kalee's face lit up at the sight of her old friend, and as she approached, her blue eyes took on a twinkle of mischief.

"Halea!" she cried with joy before gently pulling her aside and lowering her voice. "Samesa confided in me that Rufus finally revealed himself as a therian. Did he tell you?"

"Yes. Varg and I both know."

"Boy, was she mad when she found out that I knew he was a therian for almost a year and never told her. She's angry with you too."

"Me?" Halea cried.

"Oh, don't worry. She'll get over it. The person she really needs to be angry with is Rufus. It was his secret, though she technically wasn't the last to find out. Mama Dragon still doesn't know."

"Where is Samesa?"

"The northeast end of camp. Probably hoping the guards will take a break so she can sneak off and find Rufus again," Kalee said with a laugh.

Halea thanked Kalee before making her way through the northern end of the camp, where she found Samesa sitting alone by a fire sharpening her spear.

"Hi, Samesa. I've been looking for you."

"Hey, Halea," Samesa greeted, though she did not pause in her task.

Halea took a seat next to her friend, but before she could say anything further, Samesa looked up from her work with a frown.

"Oh, gods, what did Kalee say?"

"She said you were mad at me," Halea replied.

"Well, I'm not."

Halea was relieved to hear that her friend wasn't angry with her, but she could tell that something else was bothering her.

"So…a little birdy told me…"

"Okay, now I'm mad!" Samesa snapped while angrily tossing down her whetstone.

Halea only laughed as her friend pouted in indignation.

"Sorry. Sorry. I couldn't resist. I did come out here to talk to you, though. Rufus has a clumsy way of going about things – everything, but he's a sweet guy. Don't you like him? I hope so. You're both friends of mine, and I'd like to see you happy."

Samesa grew quiet as she twirled her spear between her hands. Eventually, she looked up again and sighed.

"I do like him. I like him a lot. When he first came to me as a man, I thought he was attractive and mysterious and weird, but not in a bad way. He grew on me. When he told me what he was, I was angry, not because he was a therian but because I hate being deceived. He did apologize, and now…"

"He did say you two have been sneaking away from camp to see more of each other," Halea mentioned with a raised and questioning brow.

Though Samesa's complexion did not make for a visible blush, her embarrassment was plain to see.

"We can't steal more than a moment or two alone together, what with all the lycan guards around. I know they're trying to keep us from getting killed, but it doesn't make for much privacy. I really would like to have more time alone with Rufus – to talk," she said with emphasis.

Halea looked up at the sky and surrounding trees.

"He's not here right now. I think he flew off to hunt, but he stays close to the camp when I'm here. I can barely look Mama Dragon in the eye. I feel like a teenager sneaking around behind my parent's back. I think he feels the same."

"Do you love him?" Halea asked.

Samesa chewed her bottom lip in contemplation.

"Samesa?"

"I don't know! I like him. I do! And I certainly wouldn't mind getting him alone for a bit more than just some talk, but the truth is…I don't know him that well. For years he's known me, but it feels like I've just met him. He's gorgeous and exciting and so, so sweet, but…I barely know him. Not enough to know if I love him. Not yet anyway. Maybe…in time."

"And your oath?"

"I don't know if that matters anymore, but I also know that I don't want to give up being a priestess. I love being a warrior for Tiamet. I love fighting for a good cause and making a difference in the world. Don't you regret giving that all up for Varg?"

Halea had to bite back her own anger as she wanted to defensively argue that Varg had taken nothing from her, but the truth was that she had made some sacrifices. She couldn't exactly expect that if another person were in her place, that they would want to make the same choice.

"I'm still a priestess," Halea argued. "I've never stopped being a priestess. Not on the inside. Just because I followed the man I love; doesn't mean I've given up the fight."

"I'm sorry, I didn't mean for it to come out that way," Samesa quickly amended after feeling remorse for her friend's wounded feelings. "Even if you're not technically a priestess, I know you haven't given up. Without you, we wouldn't all be here alive and preparing to make our final stand. Perhaps one can never really give up being a priestess, at least not on the inside. I know I don't want to stop. It's just…I don't know if that's what Rufus wants."

"He stuck it out with Mama Dragon," Halea added.

Samesa nodded. Maybe she would not have to give up her place in the world to follow her heart, but the truth was that she still didn't really know how she felt about Rufus. She felt drawn to him, and whenever they were together, everything seemed right, but was that love? Confusion clouded her thoughts, but one thing was certain, she would have to sort out her feelings soon. Time was running out.

~~~☼~~~

Aatu escorted Halea home from the refugee camp, but it was a quiet walk back to the den. The beta male could sense that his wolfmother was in a contemplative mood, and so he avoided forcing conversation, for which Halea was grateful.

Samesa and Rufus would have to figure things out for themselves, and all she could do was hope for the best for them, but something Samesa said was still gnawing away at her thoughts.

Did she really give it all up? At first, it felt that way, but she had convinced herself that Lord Anshar's sacrifice had banished the convergence forever and that their fight was finally over. But then it all returned. The sacrifice was a failure, and she was left shut out from the order that she had fought to be a part of for almost her whole life. Being a priestess had meant everything to her – once.

Halea entered one of the communal caves and found Jance sitting before a circle of cubs, giving another one of her covert lessons while cradling Valria in her arms. Daisy and Fillin were there with the other young ones, listening with rapt attention to the story of the field mouse and the fox that was meant to teach the value of hard work and perseverance. Halea approached and indicated for Jance to not interrupt the lesson on her account, and the redhead nodded and passed off the sleeping infant to her mother.

As Halea was leaving the cave, she noticed Batsuba and Marrok sitting among a circle of elders that had gathered away from the cold. Her grandfather was not with them because though the western pack had grown used to him, the arrival of all the other packs made him uncomfortable, and he was far too busy helping the other devotees to prepare for the coming of the convergence. Whenever she tried to get a moment of his time, there was always some task that needed his immediate attention, and she was beginning to worry that he was overworking himself. He hadn't left the den that day, and she suspected that he was still in his room poring over maps.

It was nearly time for Valria's feeding, and so Halea carried her daughter away from the crowded communal cavern to the alpha's cave. Once inside, Halea stoked the fire in the stove, lit a few oil lamps, and sat in a chair before the fire with her green robe pulled down to expose her breast, which she offered to her child who had awoken from her nap and was beginning to fuss. Once latched onto her mother, Valria quickly settled, and Halea gazed lovingly at her daughter's peaceful face.

"*No,*" Halea thought. She had not given it all up. Whether she had the permission of the Goddess or not, she would fight for their world. Her daughter was counting on her, and so were Varg, the lycans, the devotees – everyone. Their whole world needed to be saved, and as long as she lived, she could never back down until Chaos was defeated.

Once satiated, Valria went right back to sleep, and Halea gently lay her in the bedside cradle.

In the corner, gleaming in the low lamplight, sat the spear she had carried since she was a girl, and against the wall, the chest of drawers taken from their treehouse and relocated into the cave for safekeeping. With fists clenched in determination, Halea approached the chest and pulled open the drawer.

<center>~~~☼~~~</center>

It was still cold when the sun reached its zenith, and Ralphina carried little Bardolph in a bundle of furs as she walked up to the alpha's cave and knocked. It was approaching time for the mid-day meal, and the wolfmother would be needed to oversee the den with so many packs having to share the same space.

"Enter," Halea called, and so Ralphina let herself in, though she gasped at what she saw.

Halea was twirling her spear with speed and agility that was impressive to behold for the she-wolf who was unused to such weapons. Ralphina had seen Halea carry her spear when joining demon hunts, but she had never witnessed it in action.

"Wolfmother?"

"I'm coming, Ralphina," Halea replied with a final flourish. Valria was still sleeping when Halea handed her off to the she-wolf, but rather than leaving her spear behind, she carried it out of the cave.

"It's quite cold. Won't you need a cloak? And why are you bringing your weapon?" Ralphina asked.

"I can't explain it. Perhaps it's Tiamet calling me, but I just have this feeling that I need to be prepared."

"Prepared for what?"

And at that moment, a volley of howls rang out across the den, and there was no mistaking their message.

"For that," Halea replied.

"Demons!" Ralphina cried. "And there's smoke rising above the trees!"

"Where?" Halea asked as she looked out past the den, but it was no use. Her vision wasn't as powerful as Ralphina's.

"The border of the western hunting grounds, not far from the refugee's camp."

All around them, the den was erupting into panic and chaos as lycans ran screaming for cover, and Halea could sense that somewhere Varg was aware of their situation. She did not attempt to mask the worry consuming her, allowing her fearful emotions to call out to her mate.

"Ralphina, can you please watch Valria until I find grandfather? The den should be safe for now, but if anything happens, I want you to take Valria and Bardolph to the inner cavern on the northern end of the mountain, along with all the other cubs and mothers. Ulrica and Jance can help you if things get out of hand. Batsuba and the other elders have already set up a makeshift infirmary inside the inner cavern. If anyone gets injured, we're sending them there. It's the safest place."

"Yes, Wolfmother."

206

As Ralphina carried the cubs back up the mountain path, Lycurgus and Alf appeared.

"Tears! Several of them. They're calling for help," Alf reported.

"You two, pick out a group to help you stay and guard the den. I'm going to take everyone else that can fight. Now hurry."

As Halea ran down the path into the den, she found her grandfather struggling to wade through the frenzied lycans.

"Halea," he called, but thankfully she had already noticed him.

"Grandfather!" she shouted over the fearful wolves. "The mirror! Take the mirror to the inner cavern where the elders can keep it safe in case our defenses can't hold, then do me a favor and keep an eye on Valria. She's with Ralphina."

Uro nodded before quickly turning to make for the tree where Lord Anshar was kept within the mirror. The den should be safe, but Halea couldn't tell just how bad things were out beyond the barricades, and when it came to the safety of the mirror or her child, she was taking no chances.

As Halea pushed through the crowds, she managed to find Hemming and Daciana as they were passing Fillin off to Ulrica. The pair watched with tear-filled eyes as Ulrica led their son up the path by the hand while carrying Daisy on her hip.

"He'll be okay," Halea promised. "We need to gather all the warriors and hunters."

"We can't get this crowd under control without Varg," warned Hemming, and he was right. There were so many howls of danger filling the air and mixing with the screams of terror and the cries of lycans searching for kin amidst the chaos that it was impossible for any one voice to rise above the din. Varg could have calmed them, his howl could drown out an army of lycans and stand every one of them to attention with the power of its authority, but without him, it was up to Halea.

In desperation, she climbed atop one of the stone-carved wolf statues that adorned the common area around the den, and with a deep breath, she let out a howl like the one she heard Varg use on just such occasions. The call of the alpha wolf.

Startled by the unfamiliar sound but recognizing its message nonetheless, every lycan stopped in their tracks and looked up at their supreme wolfmother in shock.

Halea's face was bright red, but ignoring her embarrassment, she quickly called out over the den.

"Cubs, mothers, and elders are to stay here at the den. If the demons make it past our barriers, make for the inner cavern. Everyone else, if you can fight, come with me!" she shouted before leaping down from the statue and tearing off her green robe to reveal the white priestess robe beneath. Despite a few gasps of surprise, every lycan that could fight, regardless of their pack, rallied together before Halea, who led them out of the den.

Before they made it very far, Samesa appeared through the trees unescorted and in a panic.

"Eight tears, and they're massive!" Samesa cried as she skidded to a halt, and her eyes grew wide when she noticed that Halea was wearing her old priestess robe. "We're being swarmed. Mama Dragon rushed out after the first tear to stop it, but she

207

was trapped when the other rifts opened. There are too many demons. She can't go forward, and she can't retreat, and Rufus is with her!"

"We're on our way," Halea promised as she tightened her grip on her spear. Somewhere across the bond, she could sense that Varg was fighting already. With eight massive tears between them, she could only pray that they could make it to Mama Dragon and Rufus in time.

<center>~~~☼~~~</center>

Maven lay on her stomach beneath some brush just west of the river that flowed before a tall jut of land, and beyond that was the wolf shifter settlement. She could hear howls and screams in the distance. Something was going on, but she couldn't see from so far away. She needed to get closer, but fear froze her where she lay. The lycan civilization was larger than she imagined and far more populated, and she had no idea where to find the mirror. She could not fight her way past an army of wolves; it was impossible. Everything inside her was screaming to turn back, to run, but she could not. Lord Anshar needed her. She was his only hope. Tiamet had shown her that now was the time, and so with trembling knees, she forced herself to get up and move forward.

She followed the river around the jut of land until she could get a better look at the wolves' home, and it was hard to believe that savages could have built something so impressive. Not only was the den of the wolves built like a strange city, but it was also fortified with barriers, and even from a distance, she could tell that it was well guarded. Perhaps these beasts were not to be underestimated, but she had to find a way through. The closer she got, the faster her heart hammered in her chest. What if she was seen, or heard, or smelled? What if that scent masking potion was a lie?

A dark shadow leaped through the trees, and with a scream of horror, she raised her sword as a demon lunged for her. The blade glowed with the light of Tiamet, and the creature shrieked and jumped back in pain as if blinded, though it had no eyes. Maven pressed her advantage and charged with sword held high, but before she could strike the beast, a swarm of demons charged through the woods and pressed her back against the river. There was nowhere to escape.

Dozens of the servants of Chaos surrounded her, snarling, and lashing with claws like steel, and among them appeared a leader. A demon with eyes of black and a dark weapon clutched within its gnarled hand. It was not bestial like the creatures it commanded, and when it saw Maven, it sneered at her with rotten metallic teeth, but then its expression changed.

Maven stood with her blazing sword before her, ready to fight to the last if necessary, but to her utter shock, the black-eyed demon laughed a sickening inhuman laugh, and with a wave of its hand, the others lowered their weapons and claws and backed down.

Go.

Maven recognized the voice of Tiamet once more, and without hesitation, she ran towards the southwest, to where the forest grew thick and tall. Something inside her was urging her forward in that direction, and she knew that the Goddess's will was her guide.

208

As Maven ran, she kept looking over her shoulder, expecting to find a horde of demons in pursuit, but when she realized that she wasn't being followed, she slowed to a halt as she neared the border of the shifter civilization. High in the trees, she saw buildings built into the naked branches and, further in the distance, rose the snowcapped mountains teeming with activity as the lycans prepared for the coming attack.

"Did you hear something?" came a man's voice, and Maven quickly dodged behind a fallen tree.

"A demon?" asked a female.

"I don't smell anything," he replied.

"The tears and demons have probably spooked all the forest animals. Come on, we have to keep an eye out."

Maven held her breath as she peered out from where she crouched as two lycans leaped swiftly through the trees. The potion had worked, but she needed to hurry. Undoubtedly there would be more lycan guards patrolling the area.

Maven slipped out from her hiding place and dodged between the trees, moving ever closer until something red in the distance caught her attention - a cleric's uniform. The cleric was slowly climbing down from one of the lycan tree buildings, and as she neared, she recognized the staff, the white hair, and thick glasses. It was Master Uro, and under his arm, he carried a wrapped object. The shape of the item and the familiar cloth covering – it was the mirror! It had to be. She had sat beside that covered mirror in Lord Anshar's office long enough to be sure. And of all the people that could have had it, Uro was one.

This was her chance. She had to overtake him before he returned to the wolves' den, but as she was about to leap out and rush him, a voice from behind startled her.

"Priestess, what are you doing here?"

Maven gasped and nearly jumped out of her skin. She spun around to find herself face to face with a big brute of a lycan who was staring down at her. Her mouth hung slack as sweat poured down her body despite the biting winter cold, and her sword trembled in her fist, but to her surprise, the lycan sighed and took a step back.

"Sorry. I didn't mean to startle you," the lycan offered. It wasn't the first time one of the human dragon worshippers had looked distressed to be so close to a lycan. Some were less comfortable with the alliance than others, but he didn't detect the scent of fear and assumed she must have just returned from a mission to one of the other territories. "Tears have opened near the refugee camp, and demons are swarming all over this area. You better get out there. They'll probably need all the help they can get."

Maven said nothing but slowly nodded her head, and with that, the lycan guard shifted into his wolf form before her eyes and ran off to continue his patrol. Maven's heart thundered in her chest as the gigantic wolf tore off through the trees, and she struggled to stay standing as her knees threatened to give out beneath her.

When, at last, she regained her senses and looked back, Uro was gone.

As Uro reentered the den, he noticed that many of those who stayed behind were milling around in the common area waiting for news, and even he was anxious to know what was happening. He had heard from the lycans around him that multiple large tears had opened throughout the western hunting grounds, and he could only pray that Halea and the others could contain the Chaos, but until then, the mirror had to be kept safe.

"Did you get it?" Batsuba asked as she approached the cleric.

"Yes. Has there been any word?" Uro asked, but before Batsuba could reply, another voice called out for him.

"Master Uro," a lycan cried, and when Uro looked over his shoulder, he recognized the she-wolf Ralphina and the human woman Jance. Ralphina was carrying her infant son, and Jance had assumed the responsibility of looking after Valria.

"You two should come with us to the inner cavern until this situation is under control. It's too cold to be outside," Uro urged.

"We were waiting for news," Jance explained with an apologetic tone.

Before Uro could utter a reply, the sound of thunder cracked the sky, and a furious wind ripped through the common area extinguishing all the fire pits as a purple light cast its glow throughout the den. Screams of horror rent the air as the unmistakable clamor of demons were heard from within the massive dimensional rift, now blocking the main path up to the mountain.

Mothers scooped up their cubs in panic as the lycans who remained behind to guard the den sprang into action, but before anyone could decide where to run, the tear pulsed, and demons spilled out through the rift in alarming numbers.

Alf, Lycurgus, and the other guards leaped upon the demons, shredding them with claws and fangs, but the harder they fought, the more demons surged out through the tear, and there were no priestesses to seal it.

Uro held fast to the mirror and was torn between his desire to stay close and protect Valria and the pressing need to reach the tear. He could not close the dimensional rift, but perhaps he could put up a barrier until help arrived. Using the ancient language, he called upon the light of Tiamet to bless his staff as demons barreled past the guards and charged towards the mothers and cubs. To Uro's surprise, Batsuba appeared at his side, ready to fight as the servants of Chaos surged forward.

Bestial demons and wraiths with dark weapons led the attack, but they were met with resistance as Uro wielded his rune-carved staff with as much deadly skill as a priestess wielding her spear. With each strike of his holy weapon, the demons were touched by the light of Tiamet and burst into flames. Beside him, the red was slowly bleeding into Batsuba's eyes as she leaped onto the bestial demons and tore out their throats and snapped their necks with the sickening sound of cracking bones.

Behind them, the mothers did their best to shield their crying and frightened cubs from the danger as the demons crept ever closer. The guards were trying to help, but the demons were too many, and soon three of the lycans were slain. Lycurgus let out a growl of agony as a dark blade pierced through his thigh. Behind him, Ralphina let out a scream as she sensed her mate's pain and watched him fall, but before another demon could deliver a killing blow, Alf was at his side and fighting the demons away.

Jance watched in horror as her mate fought against the horde, and she held Valria close. Another demon broke past the guards and dove for the cubs, but one of the she-wolf mothers sprang forward, transforming into her wolf form mid-leap and tearing the beast limb from limb.

Many of the lycans who were stationed to guard the outside perimeter of the den had returned upon hearing the eruption of Chaos and quickly entered the fight, but still, the wolves were outnumbered.

Uro purified demons with all his might, but still, the tear released more. In desperation, he tried to break through a gap between the servants of Chaos, but a two-headed black-eyed demon appeared and swung its blade before the cleric could get out of the way. The vicious strike knocked the dark mirror from his grasp, but Uro had no time to react before the black-eyed demon was bearing down on him. The cleric raised his staff just in time as the creature brought down its dark blade with tremendous force, but instead of breaking, Uro's weapon blazed with the light of the Goddess until both heads of the demon were blinded, and using his advantage, the Master Cleric pulled a sacred sutra from his robe and lobbed it at the beast causing it to burst into flame.

Uro quickly ducked the attack of another demon and tried to find the mirror that had disappeared in the chaos, but as he frantically searched, from his peripheral vision, he saw a priestess in white. Just as his spirit was about to lift with the hope that they were saved, he noticed the priestess's face and saw that it was Maven, and within her hands was the dark mirror.

"Maven!" he shouted. "Stop!"

The High Priestess smiled in smug delight before turning and running back out through the trees, but before Uro could give chase, more screams of terror drew his attention.

The demons were pushing past the lycan guards, and the cubs and mothers were trapped with nowhere to run, and Valria was with them.

"Valria!" Uro cried. As much as he wanted to go after Maven, he couldn't leave his great-granddaughter, and at that moment, he made his choice and raced back towards the fight.

"Alf! Alf, where are you? Help!" Jance cried as a wraith broke through the guards and charged straight for her. With nowhere to run, she dropped to her knees to shield Valria with her body and braced herself for the end, but a high-pitched shriek caused her to look up in time to see the demon as it exploded into a flame of white. From behind where the creature once stood was Halea's grandfather with his blazing staff clutched firmly in hand.

Before Jance could even utter a word of thanks, Batsuba appeared.

"Priestesses and reinforcements are on the way, but we have to hold them off a little longer," the old healer announced. During all the fighting, the howls of distress had reached the rest of the packs, who, though facing their own battles, were quick to send aid.

"Then we keep these demons busy until the priestesses can reach the tear," Uro said, and with that, he and Batsuba pushed back against the demons once again.

Batsuba's eyes blazed red as the demons' black blood stained her claws and fueled her rage. She hated fighting. She hated killing, and she had hoped to never have to kill again, but when it came to protecting her children, she would show her enemies the true power of a wolfmother. Her face elongated as a howl of war tore from her throat, and many demons stepped back in fear as she transformed and grew, twisting until a gigantic white wolf stood before them.

Jance gasped in shock, and even Uro was surprised. The white wolf was far greater than any other transformed lycan they had ever seen. She was twice as large as Varg with fur so long it nearly touched the ground and glowing red eyes that hovered above a snarling mouth filled with fangs as big as a man and as sharp as swords. The demons shrank back, but she leaped on them and crunched the servants of Chaos between her teeth with such brutality that heads, limbs, and black blood sprayed the den.

As intimidating as the sight of Batsuba was in her true form, Uro could not let her fight alone. They had to protect the children. He had to save Valria, and with renewed strength, he charged into the fight with agility and speed that defied his years. His staff blazed like a bolt of lightning in his hand, and everywhere he struck, the demons shrieked in agony as the flames of purification consumed them.

The more Uro fought, the faster his heart beat until he was forced to clench his teeth against the pain in his chest. He couldn't stop. Just beyond the melee, he could see that help had arrived. More lycans were joining their battle, and four priestesses were charging past the demons to the tear with their spears aglow. He just had to hold out a little longer.

Only a little more.

CHAPTER 24 - MOTHER

The raucous clamor of demons and devotees echoed throughout the trees, and Halea's stomach clenched into knots as she led her warriors into the fray. A colossal tear loomed above, blotting out their view of the hill rising behind it, and beyond that, further up the slope, another rift. A few of the erected barricades and purification barriers were slowing the demons, but the servants of Chaos didn't appear to be interested in marching towards the den. It was almost as if their intention was to draw their enemies out to them.

Kalee and more than a dozen devotees were trying to fight back the servants of Chaos to reach the tear, but they were being overwhelmed by their sheer numbers.

"We'll split up here. Half of you stay to help subdue this tear, and the rest, come with me. We're going after that one up the hill," Halea commanded, but as her party divided, she noticed a falcon swooping in towards them.

"It's Rufus," Samesa exclaimed with certainty.

Ignoring the presence of both lycans and devotees, the falcon transformed as he landed with panic apparent in his dark reflective eyes.

"Samesa, Halea, thank the gods! Please, come quick. Sophia's trapped. The clerics who accompanied her are nearly wiped out, and that tear is too big for her."

"Let's go!" Halea called out, and her remaining band of warriors fought through the onslaught of demons standing in their way while Rufus returned to his bird form and flew back to Mama Dragon's side.

Through the bond, Halea could sense that Varg was in the throes of battle somewhere beyond the western hunting grounds and that he was treading perilously close to rage. Fear for her safety was nearly crippling him, as if her life were in mortal danger, though her situation could be no worse than his. She had no time to placate him with her emotions. Mama Dragon was in danger, and every step of the way, the servants of Chaos dogged them.

With her spear aflame with the light of Tiamet, Halea cut down demons and wraiths as they fought their way to the base of the hill. The ground was littered with the bodies of slain clerics and demons, but just ahead, Mama Dragon was holding back the forces of Chaos with her few remaining devotees. Rufus was fighting beside her, using his dagger and therian strength to keep the wraiths from overpowering them.

The lycans spread out among the melee and tore into the demons without mercy. Some shifted into their wolf forms, and others helped to clear the way for Halea and

Samesa as they charged their way up the hill, purifying every servant of Chaos that dared to come near their blazing spears.

"Halea! Samesa!" Mama Dragon called in relief as the rescue party broke past the last demons standing in their way. "We have to reach that tear."

Samesa was shocked to see how powerful Rufus really was as he leaped upon the wraiths, snapping necks and slicing into them with his dagger with such force that they fell like flies against his wrath. Even his once large, dark eyes were now tinged with a strange shade of orange. Lycans fought with fangs and claws, and though Rufus didn't possess such weapons in his humanoid form, he was far from helpless as his strength and speed were far greater than that of a human, and he was proving to be a force to reckon with. It was such a startling contrast from the usually awkward and gentle man that Samesa had come to know, but even as they all joined him in the throes of battle, she could not entirely ignore the way her heart fluttered at his bravery and strength.

With the help of Rufus and the lycans, Halea, Samesa, and Mama Dragon fought their way up towards the tear that glowed above the snowy hillside, but just as they neared, the rift pulsed as more demons spilled out, and among them was a black-eyed demon. Instead of arms, it had many long tentacles stretching out from its shoulders with frightening range.

The three women tried to fall back as the new wave of demons surged down the hill, but with the fight surrounding them on all sides, they could not evade the onslaught raining down upon them. Samesa attempted to lunge past the black-eyed demon to rush the tear, but it shot out one of its tentacle appendages and seized her by the throat.

Samesa gagged and fought as the creature dragged her in. She tried to purify it by laying her hand on the tendril, but the rubbery appendage resisted the conductive nature of her power. She couldn't cut herself free as another tentacle was wrenching the wrist of her spear hand. With desperation, she managed to force her weapon into the ground for something to hold onto as the tendril pulled her in with a strength surmounting her own. The harder she fought, the tighter it squeezed her throat, cutting off her air and making her vision swim before her eyes as the pressure in her head forced her to her knees, causing her to lose her grip on her spear. Her fingers helplessly raked into the snow-covered hillside but found no purchase, and with horror, she watched with darkening vision as the creature's chest split open, revealing a gaping maw filled with long, sharp, serrated, snapping teeth. There was no air, then everything went black.

Rufus acted quickly. His eyes burned orange as he charged past a cluster of wraiths and dove in with his dagger at the ready, slicing the tentacle holding Samesa by the throat and causing her limp body to collapse to the ground. Before he could reach for her, several more of the creature's tentacles seized him, but in his rage, his strength had doubled, and the back-eyed demon could not pull him in. The demon's severed appendage quickly regenerated, and soon the falcon therian was completely restrained. Rufus struggled against the creature's grip, but the black-eyed demon was losing patience, and with several of its tendril appendages, it managed to wrestle the dagger from the falcon therian's hand, and turning the weapon upon its owner, it pierced Rufus through the chest.

Mama Dragon and Halea had noticed Samesa and Rufus's peril but couldn't shake off their attackers in time. Mama Dragon let out a scream of horror as her adopted son collapsed into the blood-stained snow.

They managed one last push past the wraiths blocking their advance, and Halea jumped ahead to confront the black-eyed demon, her spear twirling in a blaze as she fought back each of the beast's tentacles. Purification had no effect on the creature's appendages, and she could not get close enough to strike its body.

"Rufus! Rufus, open your eyes," Mama Dragon begged as she rolled Rufus onto his back and pulled the dagger from his chest. The wound gushed uncontrollably until her hands and the front of her white priestess robe was soaked with his blood, and no amount of pressure could staunch the bleeding.

Rufus blearily forced his eyes open and looked up into the face of the woman that had been his only family since he was a boy. "I'm sorry, mother," he managed to say before his eyes fell shut, and his labored breathing came to an end.

Mama Dragon clutched her son to her breast as her long-battered heart shattered, and an uncontrollable sob tore from her throat as a scream.

Halea didn't have to look away from her opponent to recognize the cause of Mama Dragon's cry. More than once, she had heard the gut-wrenching wail of a grieving mother. Many lycans had lost children and kin to the devastation of the Chaos Dimension, and now as a mother herself, the horrifying reality of losing a child crashed over her in a way that chilled her blood and spilled tears from her eyes. Across the bond, Varg's panic increased, and she knew that somewhere he was fighting to reach her.

Mama Dragon forced herself to her feet, the blood of her son still warm upon her skin as she turned her attention back to the black-eyed demon as it fought Halea. Letting out a war cry that burned with rage and hatred, her spear burst into a flame of white as Tiamet's light coursed through her, and with lightning speed, she rushed the black-eyed demon. Its tentacles whipped forward to stop the onslaught of the priestess, but her glowing spear fought back every strike, and once within range, she unleashed the full fury of her power by stabbing her spear into the gaping chest of the demon. Its piercing shriek rent the air as it burst into the light of purification and was gone.

As Mama Dragon took down the black-eyed demon, Halea quickly rushed to Samesa, who had begun to stir, and fought back a wraith that was about to take advantage of the fallen priestess by stabbing her with its dark weapon. The wraith exploded from purification with one slash of her spear, and Halea was quickly at her friend's side.

"Samesa, please get up. We've got to help Mama Dragon," Halea pleaded as Mama Dragon continued her rampage, cutting down wraiths and moving ever closer to the tear.

Samesa's throat was burning, and her head was spinning as Halea forced her to sit up, but one look at the devastation around them convinced her that what she was seeing could only be a nightmare as Rufus lay lifeless in the snow.

"Rufus? Rufus!" Samesa screamed as Halea held her while she cried, but there was no time to grieve as once again, the tear pulsed, and a new surge of demons emerged from the dimensional rift.

"Get up, Samesa. Please," Halea begged as she dragged her distraught friend to her feet.

A group of monstrous black-eyed demons charged out from the tear and blocked Mama Dragon's advance up the snowy hill, but with burning hatred in her eyes, she charged without fear. She locked weapons with the twisted servants of Chaos, who struggled to fight her off, but soon the priestess was surrounded.

Samesa and Halea had to fight every step of their way up the hill, but they were too far away when the demons overcame Mama Dragon. They could only watch in horror as the servants of Chaos sliced into the priestess with their dark weapons. The first blade entered her back and sent her to her knees, but Mama Dragon raised her illuminated spear and cut down the black-eyed demon standing before her. As she struggled to get up, another servant of Chaos ran her through, then another, and another, until there was no more fight left in her, and at last, she collapsed, her blood spilling onto the snow.

Halea could barely see beyond the tears clouding her vision, but inside, the light of Tiamet blazed with her anger and pain.

Standing beside Halea, Samesa clenched her hands around her spear and grit her teeth as she fought to choke back the grief threatening to consume her. Rufus was gone. Mama Dragon was gone. And the demons were now turning their attention upon them as they charged down the hill. Something inside her was burning. Burning. And though she didn't know why, she cried out in the ancient language for fire, dropping her spear and raising her hands to the heavens as her palms burst into flames, not with the light of Tiamet, but with the unbridled force of her elemental spell.

Focusing the burning rage of her will, Samesa unleashed the fire that roared like a tornado up the hillside, melting the snow and searing every tree while incinerating every demon along the way. Bursting into flames, the servants of Chaos shrieked and flailed wildly before collapsing into charred heaps on the smoldering hillside.

"Run, Halea! Close it. I can hold them," Samesa yelled as she continued to exercise her power over the flames that were now creating a barrier that prevented any other demons from coming near.

Halea didn't know how it was possible, but seizing the opportunity, she raced up the charred hillside, leaping over the blackened bodies of the demons littering the ground and making her way to the massive tear that loomed above.

Halea had never sealed such an immense rift before. Ideally, she should have had the help of at least 3 or 4 more priestesses, but this was their only chance. Samesa could not hold back the demons forever, and there was no one else. Planting her spear in the ground, she raised her hands to the glowing purple dimensional rift and called upon the Great Dragon Mother.

"Please, Tiamet. Give me your strength, for Mama Dragon, for Rufus – help me!" she cried as the Goddess's light consumed her until her entire body glowed to rival the tear's illumination. The strain was immense, like a crushing boulder that threatened to rain down upon her as if her hands held up the weight of the dark dimension itself. She trembled with the effort of unleashing her power and prayed over and over for Tiamet's help as the tear above ebbed at an excruciatingly slow pace. Behind her, she heard Samesa begging her to hurry as the fire was going out. Halea roared under the effort of one final push as the Goddess's light surged forth with an intensity that consumed the tear between their worlds and swallowed the vortex with a thunderous crash.

Halea's last memory was of collapsing onto the cold hard ground, and the sound of Samesa's screams as everything faded.

~~~⚬~~~

Varg unleashed the Fang's power, again and again, to fight back the demon hordes that kept emerging from the massive tears that had cracked open all throughout the western hunting grounds. This was deliberate. Something was wrong. The dragon god of death that lived within the Chaos Dimension had launched a coordinated attack, and somewhere across the bond, he could sense that Halea was also fighting. He desperately needed to reach her. It would not have been the first time the being behind the dimension of evil launched attacks or sent demons to draw out Halea. She was the last chosen sacrifice of Tiamet, and the prophecy was hanging over her head. Every second felt like an eternity as his heart hammered in his chest with fear. As much as he wanted to rush to his mate, he couldn't abandon his pack or the others, but with every moment that passed, the red was slowly creeping into his eyes.

All around him, the other alphas did their best to lead their warriors against Chaos' servants, but it was only the Fang that could make a dent in the demon's numbers. Impatiently, Varg stood his ground, releasing the force of his holy weapon as he stood between his people and the tears, clearing the way for the priestesses. The dragon worshippers fought among the wolves who did everything in their power to shield the devotees from the onslaught until, slowly, one by one, the tears were sealed.

Halea was alive, but he could sense that things were not going well for her. She was in pain, in grief, and anger had seized her with such force that if she were not human, he could have sworn that she was in a blood rage. The alpha wolf within him was torn in two as it raged between wanting to protect the woman he loved and his people, but he believed in Halea. She was the strongest woman he knew, an alpha and a warrior, and as long as she was alive and fighting, he could hold on.

With the ebbing of the final tear and the elimination of the demon stragglers well within the hands of the other alphas and their packs, Varg howled for the western wolves and led them back towards the den, towards where Halea and the others were still fighting.

As they neared the scene of the devastation, they found lycans and a few scattered clerics being nearly overwhelmed but no sign of Halea or any of the other priestesses. The western pack was quick to help as Varg went on ahead to find Halea.

The sound of rolling thunder shook the sky, and he knew that a tear had just been sealed somewhere up the hill. As he raced up the slope, he noticed the snow had all melted away, and charred remains of demons littered the ground among the scorched trees. The burnt demons' rank smell made him sick to his stomach, but there was something else – Halea's emotions had stilled.

Ahead, Varg spied a form clad in white, and as he raced towards it, he could see that it was Halea's priestess friend Samesa. She was sobbing and holding her smoking hands stiffly in front of her as she knelt on the ground before Rufus's fallen body. The wind changed, and Varg could smell her burnt flesh and tears mingling with the demons' stench and Rufus's blood. Remorse filled him at the sight of the fallen therian and injured priestess, but with the western pack helping to eliminate the demon stragglers below and the tear sealed, he had to keep searching for Halea.

"Samesa, what happened? Are you okay? Where is Halea?"

"I don't…I don't hardly know. I think so. They killed Rufus and Mama Dragon. I was so angry, and then I called for the fire," Samesa replied in a shaking voice as she looked up with tear-filled eyes. "Halea sealed the tear alone. She's up there – somewhere. Find her, please."

Varg nodded in thanks before racing up the hill, but he could barely breathe as he imagined himself finding Halea's scorched body. Along the way, he saw the lifeless form of Mama Dragon lying beneath a pile of slain demons. She appeared unburnt, which was remarkable because all the demons around her were charred to a crisp, but Halea was nowhere in sight.

Just when his panic was reaching a frenzy, he found Halea lying on the ground near the top of the hill. She was unconscious, and the gore of battle coated her skin and white robe, but she appeared otherwise unharmed. Scooping her up, he clutched her to him and thanked the gods as tears broke free from his eyes.

The keening wails and howls of grieving lycans filled the air as the exhausted warriors slowly trickled back to the den carrying the bodies of the injured and the dead, and what they found made their blood run cold. The den had been attacked, and slain bodies of both lycans and demons littered the ground. Those who weren't crying over the fallen were working tirelessly with Batsuba to move and tend to the injured. Elder Marrok was with her and a few priestesses who were purifying the lycans wounded with dark weapons. Varg noticed that Lycurgus was among the injured. His leg was wrapped in bandages, and he was doing his best to comfort his distraught mate, who was crying over him while cradling their cub. His wound had already been purified, but Ralphina was still shaken from how close he had come to death.

Valria was nowhere to be seen, and as Varg carried Halea to Batsuba, terror renewed its grip on his heart.

"Batsuba! What happened? Where is Valria?"

"Calm down, Varg. She is unharmed. A tear opened and blocked our path to the safety of the inner cavern. Many women and cubs were trapped out here when the demons attacked. We did our best to hold them off until the priestesses arrived."

It was then that Varg noticed the stench and stains of demon blood on the old healer and northern elder. Marrok and several of the other elders were trapped above the path where the tear opened, and even they had been forced to fight to help defend the entrance to the inner cavern.

"You fought?" Varg asked Batsuba in shock. Batsuba hated killing, and he had never seen her raise a claw in all his life.

Batsuba's face clouded with anguish, and Marrok placed a comforting hand on her shoulder. Having known Batsuba longer than anyone, Marrok knew the cause of her pain, and for once, the old healer accepted the comfort of his friendship.

As a carnivore and a wolf, Batsuba accepted the necessity of killing, but as a healer, she disliked being the one to take the life of another creature, no matter how wretched that creature was, which was why she never participated in hunts. She was all for the extermination of demons. She hated them as much as any lycan. It wasn't killing demons that bothered her; it was the memories from her past that came rushing back to torment her as she fought. She had not wanted to ever live those memories again, but her cubs had needed her, and as a true wolfmother, she would endure anything to protect her children.

"Forgive me. I should have been here to protect you all," Varg offered.

"You were protecting us. This could not be helped," Batsuba replied as she chased the memories from her vision and looked up at her alpha. "Don't blame yourself. We are all in this fight, even Uro…"

Varg looked at her in confusion as she hesitated to continue.

"When Halea wakes up, you must tell her. His heart…"

"He's dead?" Varg asked with sinking dread as he imagined Halea's devastation.

"No. He lives. But he is not well. I did all that I could for him. The moment Halea wakes up, you must take her to him, if he's still with us. He's in his cave, and I posted a she-wolf to keep watch over him and call me the moment he stirs."

After Batsuba performed a quick check to ensure that Halea was uninjured, she instructed Varg to let her rest.

"Jance is looking after Valria. I can't howl for her, but if I find her, I'll have her bring Valria to you," Batsuba said.

Varg thanked Batsuba and gently lifted Halea once more, but as he passed through the common area, he couldn't see anything but the devastation of his home. Several tree dwellings were burnt to the ground, statues were smashed, and bodies were gathered to prepare for burial. Samesa sat beside the dead, her hands covered in bandages, and she was weeping over two shrouded bodies that laid together, and he knew that it was Rufus and Mama Dragon. There was so much to process, so much grief and suffering all around him that he felt like an utter failure as an alpha. Despite Batsuba telling him not to blame himself, he couldn't help it. These were his people, his friends, his family, and he was their alpha. Why wasn't he strong enough to save them?

Varg gently lay Halea on their bed in the alpha's cave and softly stroked her cheek, but his beloved did not stir. He needed her comfort more than ever. He needed to hear her voice because he was lost without her, but he also had to find Jance and their cub. With a whispered promise to quickly return, he rushed back outside to find their daughter.

Varg searched the den until, at last, he found Jance helping some of the she-wolves who were preparing bandages for all the injured. Valria was sleeping peacefully in a sling tied around the human woman, and Varg let out a sigh of relief when Jance noticed him and got up to hand him his cub.

It took all his remaining strength to not weep as he held his precious daughter in his arms.

"Is Halea okay?"

"She has been weakened. She may be asleep for quite some time," Varg managed to reply as his emotions threatened to overcome him.

"Oh, no. What about Uro? Is there any news?" Jance asked.

"Only that he isn't well. I can only pray to the gods that he lives long enough for Halea to say goodbye."

"I'm going to go sit with him. If he comes to, at all, I need to thank him. He saved our lives. Me and Valria."

Varg was shocked and horrified to learn that his daughter was so close to peril while he and Halea were away.

"What happened?" he asked, and Jance went on to describe how Uro and Batsuba fought to protect the mothers and cubs. Of how they were cut off from the inner cavern and surrounded while Alf and the guards were overwhelmed. And of how Uro narrowly saved them from a demon's attack.

As Varg listened to Jance's tale, he gazed down at his precious cub, who opened her hazel-green eyes and looked up at him in fond recognition, a toothless smile on her little face. He owed Uro for Valria's life, and there was nothing he could do to repay him.

"Alf is okay. He's gone to help dig the graves. If you're going back to Halea, I'll walk with you as far as Uro's cave."

Varg nodded and accepted Jance's company, and together they made their way back through the den and towards the mountain path. The wails and howls of grief still filled the common area, but as they made their way up, a faint sound stood out to Varg above all the rest.

A cub was crying.

He stalled mid-step, and Jance, who was walking just behind, nearly crashed into him. Her human ears could not detect what Varg's ears could, and she did not understand what had suddenly come over him.

Varg turned and moved back down the path, and to the side, hidden from sight by some of the mountain vegetation, he found the body of a dead she-wolf, and laying over her crying her eyes out, was Daisy.

Jance ran over to see what had drawn his attention and gasped in horror.

"Mama. Mama, wake up. Maaaaaa. Maaaaaaa. Wake up. Wake up," her little girl begged between sobs while prodding her mother's back, but Ulrica would never wake up. Her throat had been torn out by demons. Varg could smell their blood on her claws and saliva on her throat, and he knew that she must have died fighting to protect her cub.

"Daisy!" Jance cried as she rushed in to scoop up the distraught child, who continued to wail and beg for her mother.

<center>~~~☼~~~</center>

The sounds of the crackling fire inside their stove startled her awake.

"Varg!" Halca shouted as she struggled to move, but her entire body felt like lead, and soon Varg was there, placing gentle hands on her shoulders to keep her from thrashing about.

"It's all right, Halea. I'm here," he replied.

"My baby! Where's my baby?" she cried in half-delirious confusion.

"It's okay. She's sleeping. Ralphina stopped by a little while ago to make sure that she was fed. You've been asleep since yesterday."

"Varg...what happened? I remember..." she began while fighting to recall the last events that happened before she lost consciousness. Slowly the fog receded from her brain, and her heart shattered.

"Rufus...Mama Dragon...they..." she could not finish as she wept, and Varg gently sat her up so that he could rock her in his arms.

Halea poured out her grief as Varg did his best to comfort her. Rufus had been such a dear friend. He had helped them both so many times, and she could sense that even Varg was saddened by the loss of the falcon therian. But it was the loss of Mama Dragon that hit her the hardest.

Ever since she was a little girl, after the convergence had destroyed her home and took her mother's life, Mama Dragon had been there for her. Now she felt like a child again, stripped of the only motherly love she had left in all the world, but the pain was two-fold. Losing Mama Dragon was not only a blow in and of itself, but it reopened the wounds that she had always carried in her heart over the loss of her real mother. The grief and regret that never went away and tormented her dreams ever since the day she watched the convergence destroy the city that was once her home. The city where her mother had been waiting for her – alone.

Varg held her gently and rubbed her back until, eventually, she stilled.

"Is Samesa okay?" she dared to ask, though she feared the worst.

"She's alive," he assured, and her relief swept across their bond. At least he could offer her *some* good news, but it wouldn't be enough to compensate for the terrible news that he was waiting to tell her. He didn't want to upset her again, not in her fragile state, but time was running out. She had to know.

"Halea...the den was attacked," he began, and she looked up at him with puffy, red, tear-stained eyes, but before she could interrupt, he continued. "A tear opened within the den. It blocked most of the mothers and cubs from getting to the safety of the inner cavern, and Valria was with them. She's okay!" he quickly offered as she

221

paled before him. "But that's only because Uro fought to protect her and the other cubs. Halea, it's his heart. He's alive, but…he may not have long."

"Grandfather…" she said as her tears flowed once more. "Help me, Varg. I need to see him! Please."

"There's something else," he added before handing her a small scrap of parchment.

Halea struggled to read it through bleary eyes.

> *Halea,*
>
> *I have your mother.*
>
> *-High Priestess Maven*

"Maven? I don't understand. What does this mean? What is she talking about?"

"I don't know. It was found pinned to a tree with a knife. Our written language is different from humans', so Samesa had to tell us what it said. It's all the more reason why you need to speak with your grandfather."

Halea nodded, her brow pinched in confusion, and she struggled to move, but her body was drained. She was still too weak to stand, and even sitting up for too long was causing her head to throb and swim with an intensity that made her want to be sick to her stomach. To make matters worse, her breasts ached terribly. She had not fed Valria in over a day, and she was afraid that if she did not feed her baby soon, her milk would start to dry up, but she had to see her grandfather first.

Varg gently carried Halea outside and along the path until they reached Uro's cave. The door was left slightly ajar as there was always someone coming to keep watch, and even Batsuba came to check in on him as often as she could, despite having so many other patients to take care of.

A she-wolf looked up at their arrival, and with a curt, submissive bow, she stepped out of the cave to allow them to have a moment of privacy.

Halea did her best to choke back her tears as Varg helped her into a chair placed by her grandfather's bedside. Her grandfather looked so pale, and his glasses had been removed and set aside on a nearby table.

"Grandfather, I'm here," Halea called as she gently took her grandfather's hand. "Please. Please, wake up."

To their surprise, the old cleric managed to pry his eyes open and recognize his only grandchild's face.

"Valria?" he asked in no more than a whisper.

"She's safe," Halea promised.

"Halea…" he began through labored breathing. "The mirror…it's gone."

Halea gasped in horror.

"Grandfather, what happened?"

"Maven…it was Maven…she was here. This attack was planned. It wanted Lord Anshar. This was all to get to him."

"Grandfather, a note was found from Maven. She said she has my mother. What does she mean? Has she gone crazy? I can't understand…"

"I didn't want to tell you. Please forgive me," Uro said as tears streamed from his eyes.

"Grandfather, what is it?" she begged as his face scrunched in torment.

"Halea, your mother is alive."

Halea's eyes flew open as she went numb inside and out.

"No. What are you saying? That's not possible!"

"I don't know how Theia survived, but she was found abandoned on the Weldison asylum steps. Halea…she has Chaos Madness. I'm so sorry. I tried to do all I could for her. She was transferred to the castle infirmary in Antherose. When I last saw her, she was with Edmond, and I thought she'd be safe. You suffered so much. I didn't want you to have to see her that way."

"You…saw her?" Halea asked as she trembled all over, from anger, anguish, or despair; she could not tell. It seemed as if she felt everything all at once and yet nothing at the same time. "How long have you kept this from me?"

"A year. She had not been at Weldison for long, and nobody could tell me where she had been for all the years she was missing. That raven that came to the camp, it was a message from Edmond. Your mother went missing from the castle infirmary, along with The Blade That Cuts Through Worlds. It was Maven, and now she has the mirror. She has Lord Anshar. Please, Halea, don't go looking for her. That's what she wants."

Varg growled in anger. He had suspected the attack was launched for a purpose, but instead of being after Halea, the false god had been after the dragon. If the beast got out, Halea's life could be in danger, but he could already sense that she was thinking of her mother.

"He's right, Halea," Varg said. "You can't help her. If she has the madness, she's more dead than living, and nothing can bring her back." As he spoke those words, he could feel Halea's soul shattering once more. She had just lost Mama Dragon, and beneath all her pain and grief, he felt the undeniable spark of hope and longing.

It didn't matter. He knew Halea wanted her mother.

CHAPTER 25 – LOVE AND LOSS

The mirror would not break. No matter how many times she called to him, Lord Anshar never spoke or revealed himself. Maven had done everything she could think of to shatter the sacred object, smashing it onto the rocks, taking her sword to it, taking *his* sword to it. Nothing could even crack the surface of the dark mirror, and time was running out.

"Please, Lord Anshar, you must be in there. Tell me what to do. Tell me how to set you free," Maven cried to the uncovered relic where it sat upon a toppled statue. The icy sea breeze caused her to shiver and look to the west, where the Citadel shielded her eyes from the last rays of the setting sun just beyond the horizon. Maven ached to return to their holy temple, the home of Tiamet, but no one except Lord Anshar and a few mer-therians who had attempted to reconstruct the Citadel had seen it since its destruction. Without Lord Anshar to finish commissioning the repairs, the half-crumbled remains of the Citadel sat abandoned beyond the ocean waves.

"*I want to go home,*" Maven thought as a tear rolled down her cheek. Home – that's what the Citadel had once been, and she ached for the familiarity of the past, a time when priestesses still commanded respect, and the Chaos Dimension was kept under control. If she could only free Lord Anshar, he could put everything back to the way it had once been. The way it was meant to be.

"Tiamet, what do I do?" But only the echoing wind replied. With a forlorn sigh, Maven picked the mirror up from its resting place. She dreaded going back to that dilapidated building and facing the vacant face of Halea's mother again. Seeing that woman reminded her of the poor young orderly she had killed, and the guilt of what she had done kept her up at night. She was tired of watching over someone with Chaos Madness, but it was only a matter of time before Halea came to claim her mother, and that knowledge only increased Maven's anxiety.

"I need you, Lord Anshar. Please just talk to me," Maven begged once more as she stared at the mirror in her hands.

"Halea?" asked a voice.

Maven's heart leaped into her throat, and the mirror nearly slipped from her shaking hands.

"Lord Anshar! It's me. It's Maven. I'm here."

"Maven? That voice again. More lies. Get out of my head!" he roared.

"No, Lord Anshar. I'm here. I'm really here. I have you. You're safe, and I'm going to set you free."

The dark surface of the mirror rippled, and the image of Lord Anshar appeared. He looked well but weary and unsure as he stood within the dimension beyond the dark mirror dressed in his menacing blackened armor and blood-red cloak.

"Maven? Why are you here? Where is Halea?"

Maven couldn't help but wince as he asked for the very woman who had caused his demise.

"I rescued you from the shifters, my lord. I'm going to set you free. Please, just tell me what to do."

"Don't," he growled. "Leave me."

"I can help," she argued.

"You don't know what you're doing, you..." But before Lord Anshar could explain, the mirror slipped from the high priestess's hands and clattered to the ground.

Maven let out an ear-piercing shriek as darkness invaded her mind and blocked everything from her vision but a pair of menacing red elliptical eyes. An unknown force seized her body, filling her with an alien and unnatural power.

Lord Anshar could see nothing from within the dimension beyond the mirror except for an ominous purple light that slowly expanded where once his visions of the outside world had been.

"No! Get away!" he shouted as the dimension tore open, and he could feel himself being pulled as he tried to resist.

The dim light of the fading sun and stinging cold of the sea breeze caused him to collapse to his hands and knees upon the ground. Beside him lay the shattered mirror.

Maven stirred from where she had only a moment before been writhing in pain and could scarcely believe her eyes. Lord Anshar had returned.

"Lord Anshar," she whispered while drawing near, but he growled menacingly from where he knelt.

"What have you done?"

"I...I don't know how it happened. It must have been Tiamet. She's been helping me to set you free."

"Tiamet?" he snarled. "That makes no sense. She is the one who trapped me. What did you see? Did you see her?" he demanded as he grasped Maven by the arms with lightning speed and shook her.

"Only her eyes," the High Priestess replied as she trembled in fear of his increasingly painful grip.

"What eyes?"

"Dragon eyes. They were red, and I heard her voice..."

"Red? You fool!" he shouted while rising to his full height. "That is not the Goddess! It's the false god who lives within the Chaos. He's tricked you and poisoned your mind just as he poisoned mine. When did he get to you?" Maven hesitated in confusion, but he violently shook her again. "When?"

Tears streamed down Maven's cheeks as she struggled to break free from Lord Anshar's grasp, but his hands were stronger than iron, and she feared that she had let loose a madman.

"When did you start hearing this voice?" he pressed.

Maven ceased her struggling as she recalled the first time she heard the voice of the Goddess. The day she escaped from the rangers. The day that thing attacked her.

"Something…came out of a tear. A strange demon. It was like it could see inside my mind…and then…I don't remember much except that the Goddess must have saved me because I survived, and that's when I heard her voice begging me to save you."

Lord Anshar shook with rage, and the scent of Maven's fear was almost overpowering as he fought against the urge to lash out in frustration, but it wasn't her fault. He knew what it was like to be used as a pawn.

"Go. Leave this place," Lord Anshar commanded as he released Maven with such force that she nearly toppled backward. "You were deceived."

"I can't leave you, Lord Anshar. No matter how it happened, we need you. The convergence is coming. You're our only hope. I have your sword, and I found Halea's mother. She's here, and Halea knows and will come for her, and with her sacrifice, we can put an end to the Chaos."

"Never!" he roared.

Maven wept in anguish. Lord Anshar had been unwell before he was captured by Halea and her shifter and being trapped within the mirror had only worsened his condition. He wasn't making sense. She still believed the voice that guided her belonged to Tiamet and that it was her duty to ensure that Lord Anshar performed the sacrifice. She would help him whether he wanted her help or not.

"Please, just come inside, Lord Anshar. You've been through so much. You'll feel better if you rest and have a hot meal," Maven pleaded as she motioned for him to follow her back to her shelter.

He ignored her as he gazed out towards the Citadel, and after an uncomfortable moment of silence, Maven sighed and shook her head in resignation. She couldn't make him move, and she couldn't force him to listen. All she could do was hope that he would come to his senses or at least be more open to reason. They didn't have much time left. She doubted he had anywhere else to go, and she had his sword. He could easily follow her scent to the shelter when he was ready. As much as she hated to leave him that way, perhaps he needed a moment to reflect.

"Please consider it, Lord Anshar. You're the only one who can save us," she added before disappearing through the ruins.

Lord Anshar's eyes glistened as he dropped to his knees once more.

"Save us? I can't save anyone. Not even myself," he thought with bitterness. He didn't know what madness Maven was speaking about Halea's mother, and he didn't care. The last thing he wanted was for Halea to come anywhere near the ruins or the Citadel.

And then the darkness seized him. Not the dreamlike torment that his unstable mind experienced while within the mirror, but the undeniable presence of another entity as it tore through his memories, examining his thoughts, his fears, and everything he learned during his confinement. The false god could not reach him while he was imprisoned in the mirror dimension, but now, once more, he had unfettered access to Lord Anshar's mind.

Lord Anshar screamed in agony as he tried to force the presence of Zernebog out of his head, but he couldn't stop the visions and emotions that engulfed him.

Jealousy. Suffering. Rejection. Tiamet had chosen the love of another, and he hated her for it. He hated everything that she loved. He hated her world. He hated the living things that she had blessed with her breath of life. He hated the other gods who sided with her. He hated her mate, her daughter, and her grandson. He wanted to tear it all away from her. He wanted to make her suffer as she had made him suffer. He wanted to see everything that she loved torn away from her for all eternity. Destroyed. She possessed the power to strip him of his sword and banish him into the Chaos Dimension, but she could not keep him there without sacrificing a descendant of her bloodline. Only a being of her blood and light could ever seal away the dark dimension for all time. It was a price the Goddess would never willingly pay. She had come down from the heavens the day her grandson was born to hold him in her arms. Anshar was hers. Her blood. Her heir. Her legacy. Her hand upon the earth and the servant of her will, and she loved him above all else. He wanted to take Anshar away from her, not just to kill him. The separation of life from death meant little to a god because a soul was more valuable than a life. A soul was eternal. But even though killing Anshar would only deliver his immortal soul into the waiting hands of the Goddess, Tiamet would sacrifice anything to save the life of her precious only grandson. As long as Anshar lived, her will would be carried out, her name would be praised, and all life would know that she was supreme. And that was why Anshar had to be shown the truth. Tiamet did not create priestesses to save the world, she created them to save her grandson. The Goddess did not care how many died, as long as Anshar survived, and her legacy lived on.

"Curse you! Stop it!" Lord Anshar shouted as he fought with every ounce of his strength against the dark presence swirling within him. A sinister laugh was the last thing he heard as the dim light of dusk chased the last of the darkness from his vision, and then it was gone.

Lord Anshar trembled as he struggled to roll over from where he had collapsed upon the ground, feeling sick to his stomach and gasping for breath as his heart beat at a pace that would have killed a mortal being.

"Is it true? Tiamet, is it true?" he growled as he beat his fist upon the earth. "Damn you, Tiamet! Was this for me? You let them die for me? Ages of suffering and slaughter and fear and people begging me to save them, and for what? Because you couldn't let me go? Because you selfishly had to hang on to your only living kin? All the lives you let Zernebog destroy, and it was all for me?"

A shimmering light flashed before him, and he found himself staring into a pair of beautiful golden elliptical eyes that wept with such sadness, such remorse.

"Anshar," called an angelic voice.

"You bitch!" he snarled, causing the golden eyes to shrink back as more tears gushed forth. "It is true! Get away from me!"

And with that, the light was gone, and he was alone once more.

"Curse you, Tiamet. I will put an end to this. You will never have my soul. Never."

227

The crackling flames of the funeral pyre illuminated the faces that stood around in grief. Halea let the tears flow freely as she stood before the gathered and offered prayers to Tiamet for the safe passage of Mama Dragon's soul into the heavenly realm. When her prayer was over, she returned to Varg's side as Senior Priestess Gwen stepped forward and read from the sacred text.

Varg held Valria on one arm and wrapped the other around Halea's shoulders for comfort when she drew near. While Halea was recovering her strength, Varg had tended to the injured, the frightened, and the dead. Every pack suffered losses, and everyone was in mourning for friends and kin, and for those who lost mates in the attack, even more deaths had followed. The northern and southern packs would take their dead home to their own sacred burial grounds, but many prayers and mourning rituals had already been observed. The western pack had carried their dead high into their mountains to be buried in the hallowed ground of their ancestors. Halea and Varg had overseen the funerals of the western pack. The echoes of Daisy wailing for her mother haunted them both as Ulrica was placed into the ground. One by one, everyone approached to add dirt to the grave. There were many graves that day.

The worshippers of Tiamet did not bury their dead without burning the bodies first. Fire was the symbolic gateway to the Great Dragon Mother. The ashes could be buried or scattered, but for Rufus, nobody knew what to do.

Though his adopted mother was a priestess, Rufus was not a devotee. He had always shown reverence for Tiamet, if only for Mama Dragon's sake, but as a falcon therian, it seemed most likely that one of the great bird gods would claim his soul.

"I'm sure Corbin or Morigan will see that he is claimed in the afterlife. I'll pray for them to guide his soul," Varg promised to both Halea and Samesa.

Thanks to Corbin, Varg had been to the place between the living and dead and stood before the mighty wolf gods. He had seen the Great Crow in his true form, and he knew that if anyone could safely guide Rufus's soul into the next life, it would be Corbin.

"We don't really know anything about funeral rites for a falcon therian," Samesa lamented. "I wish there was something special we could do just for him."

Halea looked to Varg, who seemed devoid of ideas as he was only familiar with the ways of wolves, but as she regarded her mate, her eyes fell on the blue crystal pendant hanging from his neck. He had worn it ever since the Spring Moon Festival, and the sight of the gemstone reminded Halea of the way Rufus had often admired it. Just like a bird, Rufus had always loved anything shiny.

Halea's eyes suddenly took on the light of inspiration, and Varg questioned her with a raised brow.

"Varg, the lycans wouldn't have happened to have found any quartz while they were excavating the mountains over the ages, would they?"

"Yes, tons of it. We probably have more storage caverns filled with quartz than we do gold. But unlike gold, it's worthless for trade."

"Wait, you've got caverns filled with what?" Samesa cried in shock.

"That's perfect!" Halea cried. "Rufus loved shiny stones, and quartz crystals are beautiful but not so valuable that anyone would take them."

"You mean, bury Rufus beneath a grave of quartz?" Samesa asked. "You're right. I think he would have loved that idea."

"Rufus was not a lycan, but he helped me save your life," Varg said to Halea. "And he was a friend. A friend to us both. He'll be given a place of honor in our sacred burial grounds."

Early the next morning, the lycans and devotees ascended the mountain to stand before the freshly dug grave. Samesa watched with tears in her eyes as the shrouded form of Rufus was lowered into his final resting place. Halea, Varg, and Kalee stood close by her side for comfort, and even Batsuba was there.

Samesa looked down at her scarred hands in grief. The burns had healed, but pale marks marred her palms and the back of her knuckles and stood out in stark contrast to her naturally dark skin. If not for Rufus, she and Halea would have died that day. He had not only fought beside them, but he had taught Samesa how to perform the elemental fire spell that saved them from their enemies, though that spell was far from perfect. As an inexperienced fire-caster, Samesa had maintained little control over her spell, and her will had raged without restraint and burnt her hands in the process. A truly skilled fire-caster wouldn't have injured themselves with such a basic spell, but there was so much Samesa did not yet understand about the secrets of elemental magic. She suspected Rufus knew little more than what he taught her, but it was enough to make her thirst for more. Wielding fire magic was unlike anything she had ever experienced before, and she couldn't help but wonder what she could truly be capable of if she only had the right guidance.

"I did it, Rufus. I made fire. I wish you could have seen it," Samesa thought to herself.

News that Mama Dragon had secretly hidden a therian for decades had spread among the Tiamet worshippers, and almost everyone was shocked. The falcon that carried their messages had been a shifter for all the years they had known Mama Dragon. Some felt betrayed that she had dared to harbor a therian in their midst, but most were remarkably understanding. Many saw Mama Dragon as a close friend or a maternal figure who had fought beside them for years. If anyone could be credited for having the unconditional love of a mother, it was Mama Dragon. Perhaps spending so much time among the lycans had softened their hearts and opened their minds, but a surprising number of devotees had come to pay their respects to the falcon therian, even though most had never known him as more than just a clever bird.

A considerable amount of lycans had also come to pay their final respects, and it warmed Halea's heart to see such a large gathering of both humans and wolves who were willing to set aside their differences to mourn someone different from them all. It was just a shame that it had taken a tragedy to bring them together.

"Besides Mama Dragon, he was without kin, but he had friends. He was my friend," Varg began, and it was true. Though he and Rufus hadn't always gotten along when they first met, in time, the wolf and the falcon had learned to respect one another, and Varg couldn't help but feel a profound sorrow at the loss of his strange friend. "Most of you only knew him as a falcon, but some of us knew him as so much more. He was a good man, a loving son, and even though he was neither human nor wolf, he fought and cared for all people the same. He was on our side, and he never turned his back on someone in need. He helped me to save Halea's life. He watched over Samesa and Mama Dragon and me, and he even looked out for the rest of you when perhaps you didn't know it. He spread the messages that saved countless lives. I didn't always appreciate that, but I do now. I think we all owe him our gratitude and our remembrance."

"I'll never forget him," Samesa added.

"I'll remember him too," said Kalee.

Batsuba promised to remember as well, and all who gathered bowed their heads as Halea approached the grave.

"We'll remember you both," Halea said as she knelt and gently placed the pottery urn containing Mama Dragon's ashes in with Rufus. One by one, the mourners passed the grave and placed a quartz crystal inside until a glittering burial mound was formed.

Samesa was the last to approach, but instead of placing a quartz crystal upon the mound, she placed the gem that glittered with flecks of green and orange. The first present Rufus had given her in his humanoid form. It sparkled in stark contrast against the quartz. She still did not know if she had loved him the way he loved her. Their time together was so short, but she knew that she would forever feel the hole he left in her heart, and she would have to live out the rest of her long life with the regret of never knowing how it might have been.

~~~✕~~~

After the funeral of Rufus, Varg went to check in with the other packs, and Halea returned to the alpha's cave to feed Valria. After the battle and losing consciousness for so long, Halea had a terrible scare when she went to feed her baby, and her milk would not flow. Batsuba had given her some herbs and poultices that started the flow of her milk again, but the old healer gave her a stern warning to be careful to not go too long without feeding Valria, or her milk could permanently dry up. Ralphina was kind enough to ensure that Valria had not gone hungry while Halea was incapacitated, but Halea took Batsuba's warning to heart. She did not want to risk losing the precious time for bonding that she shared with her daughter, but it seemed as if everything was pulling her in all directions at once, and if something didn't give soon, she would break apart.

Even Varg was beyond strained by everything that was happening. He was riddled with guilt that as an alpha and a king, he hadn't been able to save more lives during the attack, and there was an underlying crippling fear that he seemed to be trying to hide from her. Whenever she asked him what was bothering him, he passed it off as general stress, and she could believe it, but this seemed to be something more. Halea was also keenly aware that Varg hadn't slept for more than an hour in almost three weeks. He had gone from irritable to nearly unresponsive, as if he did not even have the energy to feel anything more than grief and fear.

Even a therian as powerful as Varg had his limits, and once Halea was done feeding Valria, she decided she would have to find him. Halea tucked her sleeping baby into her cradle and called for a she-wolf nurse to watch over her. Halea promised to not be gone for long before throwing on her winter cloak and heading down the mountain path to look for Varg.

As Halea walked, she noticed Jance running up the path towards her, and she stopped to greet her.

"Halea, how is your grandfather? Is he doing any better?"

"He seems weak but stable. Batsuba says he's the stubbornest old goat she's ever met. I sure hope she's right," Halea reported.

Despite all odds, Halea's grandfather seemed to be hanging on to life, though he was in no condition to be moved and was under constant watch in case his health took a turn for the worse. Halea popped in to visit him periodically throughout the day, though he was rarely awake.

Jance tried to visit when she could, but with the funerals and looking after Daisy, she hadn't had much time to look in on Halea's grandfather, though she had kept him in her thoughts and prayers.

"How is Daisy?" Halea asked.

"Oh, Halea. I feel so terrible for her. She barely eats, and whenever she tries to sleep, she wakes up crying for her mother."

Halea had been older than Daisy when she lost her own mother, but she knew exactly what the little cub was going through. She also knew from experience that that pain would never entirely go away.

Since learning that Theia had survived the devastation of the convergence, Halea could scarcely sleep for lying awake and thinking about what must have happened to her mother for all the years she was missing. It just seemed so impossible to believe that her mother could have escaped the city. Halea had watched it crumble with her own eyes, but somehow it was true. Her mother had made it out alive against all the odds, but the Chaos had destroyed her mind. Where had she been for all those years? Someone must have taken care of her before she was found at the asylum, but who? Were they kind to her mother? Had she been abused? Had she been hungry? Neglected? So many things could have happened to a defenseless woman in all that time, and it made Halea physically sick to think of all the possibilities and to know that there would never be any answers.

To make matters worse, her mother was now in the hands of Maven, and for all she knew, Lord Anshar had already been set free from the mirror, and she could not begin to predict how he would behave if released from his prison. Would he keep his vow to never again perform a sacrifice? Or would he resume his jealous vendetta against Varg? What if the false god still held sway over his mind and compelled him to do evil again? It was all the more reason why she wanted to talk to Varg. Time was running out.

"At least she has you and Alf. I can't express how grateful I am that you two are taking care of her. To be honest, Varg and I don't know what to do about Daisy. She has no kin. Not even among the eastern wolves."

231

"That's what we heard. Actually, I was kind of hoping I would run into you for that reason. If…if Daisy has no one else to give her a home, would it be okay, I mean, with your permission and Varg's…can Alf and I adopt her? I promise we would love her like our own daughter. Oh, please, Halea. We've always wanted a child so much, and we love Daisy."

Halea's eyes misted over at Jance's heartfelt plea. If anyone could give Daisy a chance for a happy life, it would be Jance and Alf. If it were only up to her, she would have given Jance her blessing on the spot, but a decision as momentous as allowing members of the northern pack to adopt a child of the western pack could not be made by her alone. She at least wanted to discuss it with Varg, though she was sure he would have no reason to deny Jance's request; it felt wrong to not consult her mate on such an issue.

Someone from the western pack would have eventually offered to take Daisy, as no cub was ever left orphaned in a pack where all were treated like family. The thought had even crossed Halea's mind that she and Varg could have taken in the little girl, but it was clear that Jance's offer made the most sense. It felt right that Jance and Alf, who had always longed for a child, could give a loving home to a cub with whom they had already formed a bond. Halea had no doubts that Jance and Alf were perfect for Daisy.

"I'll have to talk it over with Varg, but I will certainly plead your case. I know you love Daisy, and you and Alf are exactly the kind of family she needs right now. I'm sure Varg will see it that way too, but as wolf king, he should get the final say on the matter. I'm on my way to go find him now."

"Thank you, Halea. I'm sure if anyone can convince him, it'd be you," Jance exclaimed with hopeful, shining eyes.

The two women parted, and Halea made her way down to the common area. It was mostly deserted except for a few lit fire pits. Most lycans were seeking shelter inside the caverns, away from the cold, and were no longer taking meals outdoors. A few of the hunters and sentries kept the fires burning to allow themselves to warm up as they came and went from their patrols, and as Halea approached, she noticed that Varg was among them. Even from a distance, she could tell that he was giving orders for guard duty shifts. The western territory was on constant alert since the last attack, and warriors were stationed not only around the den but throughout most of the vulnerable western hunting grounds.

The attacks came so suddenly and strategically that their numbers had taken a significant hit, and morale was low. If three packs could barely fend off a series of tears, what hope could they have against the force of an entire convergence? It seemed as if the winter storms were plotting against them as well because the eastern wolves had not yet arrived, and every day they worried that help would not come in time. Despite the doubts of those around her, Halea maintained hope that Otsana would bring the eastern wolves.

When Varg noticed Halea, he excused himself from the guards and greeted her with his usual warm embrace. No matter how stressed or busy he was, Halea was his greatest comfort. Her warmth and scent eased his tension, and the love that flowed through their bond gave him the strength to soldier on, even in the face of his crippling exhaustion and stress. But as reassuring as her love was, he could sense that she had come with a purpose, and Halea immediately sensed the spike in his anxiety.

Since the moment Halea learned that her mother was still alive, Varg's greatest fear was that Halea would want to go to her, and every instinct within him was howling for her to avoid that obvious trap at all costs, but he also knew that this was the one thing he couldn't deny her. He had known Halea since they were children, and he knew how much she loved her mother and how devastated she had always been since the convergence. Thanks to the bond they shared, he had felt her loss, the tormented dreams, the guilt, the regret, the longing. It was the one pain that he could never wipe from her heart. The one hurt he could never heal. He loved Halea with every fiber of his soul, but when faced with the chance of relieving the pain that had plagued her every waking moment since the convergence that divided them, he knew it was the one risk they might have to take.

"Shh," she said with a sad smile. "You act like I came all the way down here to beat you up."

"Please just beat me up and get it over with," he pleaded only half-jokingly.

"You feel beat, and I haven't even done anything to you. You're not fooling me. I know exactly how tired you are. Have the other alphas take charge for a while and come get some rest."

"I can't."

"Varg," she said in a tone that would brook no argument. "If they need you, they'll call. You're going to rest or so help me; I'll knock you out myself, you mangy wolf."

He sighed in defeat. For the moment, it was quiet, and even in sleep, he could hear the howls of warning if something were to happen, and he couldn't deny just how much he wanted to rest, to forget his worries, if only for a short while.

"You win this round, puny human."

He broke away from her just long enough to tell one of his beta males to inform the other alphas that they would be in charge for a while and to call for him at the first sign of danger. With that settled, Halea took him by the hand and escorted him back up the mountain path and to their cave.

"She's still sleeping," the she-wolf nurse reported at the sight of her two alphas.

Halea thanked her and sent her on her way, but despite the assurance, she couldn't help but peer into the cradle to see her peacefully sleeping child for herself. Once satisfied, she returned to Varg, who had removed his winter boots and armor and sat at the edge of their bed.

"Lay down, you," she commanded.

"Only if you lay down with me."

Halea smiled despite shaking her head at his request. She could use some extra rest herself, and so without argument, she kicked off her boots and crawled into bed. Rather than lying next to her, Varg laid his head over her breast, where the soothing beat of her heart played a gentle rhythm to lull him to sleep. Just as he was getting comfortable, her voice drifted to him through the hazy exhaustion of his mind.

"Jance and Alf want to adopt Daisy. I told Jance, I'd ask you first."

"And what does the wolfmother want?" he asked in a low mumbly voice as he struggled to stay awake.

"I think they love Daisy and that they'd give her a good home and be the family that she needs."

"If that's what you want, it's fine with me. I'd do anything for you, Halea...anything you want," he promised before drifting off with a gentle snore.

CHAPTER 26 – LAST CHANCE

Varg stretched out his hand but found only air.

"Halea?"

"Shh," came Halea's voice. "She's almost back to sleep. I was afraid she'd wake you," she explained while tucking Valria back into her cradle. Halea had snapped awake at the first sounds of their baby fussing and quickly got up to feed and change her before her cries could wake Varg.

"I should get up," Varg said with a groan, but before he could sit up, Halea was at his side and pushing him back down again.

"No, you don't. It's the middle of the night. You're going to get at least one full night's sleep."

"I already slept through half the day. I think I'm good." But he regretted arguing when he saw the worry on Halea's face and felt the sadness through their bond.

"Please, stay," she pleaded. "The others have things under control, at least for tonight. You slept through dinner. Aren't you hungry?"

"Now that you mention it."

"I can fetch some food," she tried to offer, but before she could run out of the cave, Varg grabbed her by the wrist and pulled her back onto their bed.

"I didn't say I was hungry for food," he explained in a deep voice that sent a jolt of excitement into her core.

Halea quickly melded into his arms and reveled in his warm embrace. Things had been so hectic and stressful that it felt like ages since they last made time for one another, and the way Varg was grazing his lips along her jaw and throat made her easily compliant. It felt so wonderful to rake her fingers through his thick dark hair, and when he found her lips, she blissfully surrendered to the hunger of his kiss.

"Is she asleep?" she asked after reluctantly breaking away.

Varg paused as his hands were slowly roaming down Halea's body and carefully listened. He could tell by the gentle rhythm of Valria's breathing that she was sleeping peacefully in her cradle.

"Our little mouse is fast asleep. We'll just have to be quiet," he confirmed as he nibbled Halea's ear, causing her heart to beat excitedly.

Halea tried not to giggle at the pet name Varg had given their baby. He had taken to teasingly calling her *little mouse* or *the pest* because he had once been so convinced that a rodent had moved into their tree before discovering that what he was hearing was the sound of their unborn daughter.

"I've missed you so much lately," she quietly confessed as he opened her white robe, and his exploring lips left a trail of heat on her skin that simultaneously sent shivers down her spine.

Her aroused scent was already calling to the beast in him as he gently scraped his fangs along her heated flesh, and the tremble of her breath sent the blood racing to his already throbbing erection.

The need was too great for either of them to wait, and soon they were joined. Halea desperately struggled to suppress the sounds of her desire for fear of waking their baby. It was difficult to not let go and entirely surrender to the waves of pleasure coursing through her body as the bond nearly drowned her in sensation. There was a frantic, desperate longing mixed in with the love and desire she felt from Varg. A possessiveness mixed with fear and a primal urge that begged for her affirmation.

"I love you, Varg. I promise I won't let you go."

"Swear it, Halea. Promise you'll never leave me," he begged as he slowed his pace inside of her, drawing back and denying her the relief she so desperately craved.

"I promise," she said while gently reaching up to sweep his wild locks behind his long, pointed ears, and when she met the piercing gaze of his ice-blue eyes, she caught a glimpse of the anguish tormenting him from within. "I'm never going to leave you, Varg. We'll always be together. Nothing will ever tear us apart."

Varg sighed with some relief as the weight of his anxiety eased across their bond, and he leaned forward to capture Halea's lips in a deep and sensual kiss that stole her breath and caused her to writhe against him in desperate need. With no further holding back, they surrendered to their deepest passion before collapsing against each other, spent, and glowing from the warmth of their lovemaking.

As much as Varg didn't want to spoil the mood, he knew it was time.

"I meant it when I said I'd do anything for you. I'll help you get your mother back. I know you haven't been able to stop thinking about her."

A silent tear rolled down Halea's cheek, and she breathlessly nodded. "I didn't know how to ask you. I was afraid you'd say no."

Varg gently wiped the glistening bead from her face and replaced it with a kiss.

"I know. I'm sure you've noticed how on-edge I've been lately. How frightened I am that something could tear you away from me. You were the last chosen sacrifice, and for all we know, the dragon has been set free. I know you believe that he'll keep his word never to sacrifice you, but the wolf inside me won't rest." He paused as he struggled with the weight of his inner burden. He hated keeping things from Halea. A part of him wanted to tell her the truth about the prophecy, but Corbin had warned him that the knowledge was for him alone, and he didn't want to tempt fate by angering the gods. Bitterly, he swallowed his secret before continuing. "I don't trust him. I can't. Not after everything that he's done to you, to us, and after everything that the Chaos has done to him. You've said it yourself many times that his moments of clarity come and go. What he swore to you in his right mind, he could take back in his madness. That's why we have to do this together, and we have to do it now before the convergence appears. I can protect you while you get your mother to safety. The gods are with me, and I swear on my life, I won't let him take you."

Halea wrapped her arms tightly around him and buried her face in his neck. He could feel her tears moist against his skin.

"I'm so sorry I brought all this trouble on you. I'm frightened too. If anything took you from me, I'd go mad. I can't forget what it was like when Corbin took you into the next world, and our bond was broken. It doesn't matter if I'm human. My soul is as much bound to yours as your soul is bound to mine. I don't want to risk your life any more than you want to risk mine...it's just...I can't..." she tried to explain but only broke into sobs of grief. "Oh, Varg, what happened to her? Where was she? I thought she was dead all these years, and she was somewhere out there needing me, and I wasn't there for her. I didn't know. I didn't know."

Varg gently stroked her back and rocked her in his arms as his heart shattered alongside hers. Every ounce of her anguish and grief tore through him like a hot knife, and he knew that no matter the risks, he had to take away this pain. He loved her too much to see her suffer.

~~~☼~~~

Samesa woke up crying from a nightmare. Even when awake, she couldn't close her eyes and not remember the death of Rufus and Mama Dragon. Since losing her family as a child, she thought she had outgrown what it felt like to be lonely. She cared about Rena, but Rena had shown her to be brave and independent, and as a Priestess, she had accepted a solitary life. Though she didn't want to believe it, her brief relationship with Rufus had awakened a longing for something that she didn't dare define. Now, it was gone, and a sense of abandonment haunted her, even in her sleep.

With a sigh of defeat, Samesa rolled out of her cot. She couldn't possibly go back to sleep, and as silently as possible, she pulled on her robe and gathered her spear. She shared a large cave with many other female priestesses and clerics. It was not fancy, but it was comfortable, with running water and a hardy stove glowing in the corner from where it had no trouble heating a space already filled with so many warm bodies. The lycans had kindly given them shelter in one of their northernmost caverns. It was closer to the den than their outdoor camp, but not too close. The soft sounds of her fellow devotees breathing and snoring around her made her extra cautious as she walked past them, but she did take note that Kalee's cot was also empty.

The devotees often took shifts to stand outside at the camp and keep watch for danger alongside their lycan guards because demons and tears appeared day and night, and they could never let down their guard.

Samesa almost regretted coming outside the moment the freezing night air tore right through her double-layered robe and even her thickest winter cloak. She could only be thankful that it wasn't snowing again.

"Fuck, it's cold!" she cried to no one in particular before jogging out to the campfires of the night's watch.

As she neared the center of the camp, several devotees and a couple of lycans who were standing around the warmth of the fire socializing greeted her. It was still remarkable for her to see humans and wolves in such a companionable alliance. The very idea, only a year before, would have been inconceivable, but in that time, even she had changed, and once again, her thoughts returned to Rufus.

"I've got something to warm you," called Kalee, who held up a flask that glinted in the firelight, and Samesa quickly sat down beside her and accepted the drink. Kalee knew just how much her friend hated the cold.

"Thanks, I needed that."

"I can think of something else I need," Kalee added with a smirk before winking at a cute young male cleric who sat across the fire, and everyone laughed.

"Is that why you're out of bed? It's not your turn to be on guard duty," Samesa asked.

"It's not your turn either, but here we are. How are you doing?" Kalee asked as her tone grew low and serious. Around them, the others carried on with their own conversations.

"I don't know. I can't stop thinking about him."

"Break your oath?" Kalee asked.

"I don't know. Maybe. What about you? You're not fooling me. You broke yours ages ago."

"I did not!" Kalee defensively cried. "It wouldn't do any good anyway. I'm still an immortal, and he's not. He's better off without me."

"I don't think he sees it that way."

Before Kalee could prepare her next argument, the sky cracked with lightning, and the wind picked up, and somewhere in the distance, a wolf's howl pierced the air.

"Tears outside the barricade," Faolan translated.

"How many?" asked Samesa.

"Two," he answered before yet another howl rose in the distance. "Four, and they're growing fast."

Kalee had already sprung up and was racing back to the cavern to summon the other devotees.

<div style="text-align:center">~~~✧~~~</div>

At the familiar sound of warning, Varg and Halea gathered their weapons and raced outside into the cold night air.

"Shit! Tears outside the barricades separating the western hunting grounds from the refugee camp," Varg translated.

They raced down to the common area, which had erupted with lycans screaming and running in panic, and Varg quickly howled to bring everyone to attention.

"Cubs and mothers to the inner cavern. Half of the warriors will stay here to guard the den, the rest with me."

Halea quickly found Ralphina, who agreed to take Valria to the safety of the inner cavern with the other cubs. When she returned to Varg, she also found Raoul, Bertolf, Lyall, and a regiment of lycans, with nearly a thousand wolves from each of the three packs. Without further delay, they raced out to the refugee camp, and upon arrival, the frantic guards briefed them on the situation.

"A company of over a hundred of the Tiamet worshippers has already set out to defend the barricades. It's bad, Varg. These tears are huge, and a horde of demons is on its way to the northwestern barricade. They'll be here soon," Faolan explained, as all around them, more devotees raced out to join the fray. The northwestern barricade was their largest defensive structure between the refugee camp and the lycans' western hunting grounds.

"Why didn't a tear just open within the camp?" Varg wondered aloud.

"With so many priestesses right here, we'd seal it in a second," Halea replied.

"Do you think we're being lured out?" Samesa asked as she joined them.

"I'll bet that's exactly what this is," Halea said with anger rising in her voice. "The last time Chaos attacked, it made sure to scatter us before hitting the den. It was trying to draw us out so that Maven could get in and steal the mirror. Now it's here for us, the priestesses. Priestesses are a threat to the false god, and with the convergence soon to appear, he wants to eliminate every single one of us who's blessed."

"And we're all conveniently together," Samesa added as she unconsciously tightened her grip on her spear.

"There's a horde of demons between us and those tears, but if we can't reach them to seal them, the demons will keep coming and overwhelm us. It'll only be a matter of time before they breach the barricade," said Halea.

"Then I'll cut a path," Varg declared as he instinctively drew the Fang that glinted in the low light of the campfires.

"We're with you, Varg," promised Raoul, and Bertolf nodded his head in agreement.

"We'll take two of the packs to fight beyond the barrier and half of the devotees. One of the packs and the rest of the Tiamet worshippers will stay and guard the barricade. Our charge won't stop the rest of the demons from trying to break through to the refugee camp. If the barricade can't hold them back, light it."

"But Varg, that barricade was supposed to hold us until the convergence," argued Lyall.

"If we don't stop that horde, we may not even live to see the convergence. We can rebuild, but let's pray to the gods that it holds."

They agreed that the northern pack would stay to guard the barricade along with Aatu and Hemming, who were the western pack's best archers. They would be more useful fighting from behind the barrier. Daciana chose to stay with her mate, and Faolan was granted permission to fight alongside his friends.

All of the clerics would stay behind, they couldn't seal the tears, and their lives would be too much of a liability during the charge. Senior Priestess Gwen would command the devotees who remained behind the barricade.

Favion was surprised that Kalee would not be joining the offensive movement.

"Staying behind?"

"Priestesses will be needed behind the barricade, too," she explained. Though she was frightened for Halea and Samesa, who would be at the head of the charge, she didn't dare mention that she was even more frightened for him.

"I'm glad you'll be here, Kalee. There's nobody else I'd rather fight beside."

Kalee's face burned as red as her hair, and she quickly turned away not to be caught, but Favion recognized the look in her eyes, and he knew that she stayed for him.

They opened the massive wooden gates to the barricade, and Varg led the way. Far in the west, they could hear the approaching demon horde, and he offered a silent prayer to the wolf gods. If they failed to cut a path through to the tear, they would be slaughtered, and it would not be long before the demons broke past them and stormed the barricade, which had now closed behind them. If the barricade had to be lit aflame to keep the demons at bay, they wouldn't be able to retreat the way they came. The river cut them off to the south, and the northeast was a steep slope up into the mountains. They could climb to higher ground if they had to, but they would undoubtedly be hampered by demons every step of the way.

It wasn't long before the demons appeared in the distance. The plains of their hunting grounds were now teaming with thousands of the servants of Chaos.

Halea's heart sank into her stomach. They were greatly outnumbered, and they had a long distance to cross before they could reach the glowing tears beyond the western tree line.

"Hey," Varg called to her, drawing her attention away from the horror storming their way. "Don't be afraid. You know I'll protect you."

"I'll protect you too," she replied with a reassuring smile.

With a war-howl, Varg led the charge with the rest of the packs and devotees following close behind in a V formation. As soon as they neared the raucous swarm, Varg swung his sword, releasing a blast of light so powerful that it sent demons and wraiths flying into the air and cutting a huge section out of their enemy's advance. The lycans and devotees surged ahead, and the battle was soon underway from all sides as the demons crashed against them with overwhelming force. The light of purification burned from the hands and spears of every priestess, and the lycans fought with claws and fangs, as humanoids and in their wolf forms.

Halea's spear twirled and crackled with the power of the Goddess that flowed through her as she struck down wraiths, black-eyed demons, and lower bestial monstrosities. All around her, priestesses and wolves were fighting and dying. The fire of Tiamet burned like hot rage within her as she slashed through a wraith before it could pounce on Lyall in his wolf form and run him through. The old wolf acknowledged her with a nod of thanks before tearing another servant of Chaos apart with his powerful jaws.

Varg used the Fang to cut their path again and again, but their advance was slow, and it wasn't long before the demons had them surrounded.

Samesa flinched as she watched Pauline take a dark sword to the back from a black-eyed demon and collapse. The yelps of lycans in wolf form as the demons swarmed over them, tearing them to pieces and devouring their flesh, made her sick to her stomach, but she fought on with determination.

"Varg, they're breaking past us and making for the barricades," Raoul warned.

"We can't turn back. I can see the tears just ahead!" Varg roared over the chaos.

It was true, the dimensional rifts, massive and imposing, loomed in the distance, but everyone could see the demon hordes as they continued to emerge from within the Chaos.

"We can't make it. There's too many," cried Samesa as she cut down yet another wraith. Even her superior strength seemed to be waning.

"They're between us and the northeastern slope too," added Lyall, who shifted back into his humanoid form to speak.

Trapped on all sides and vastly outnumbered, Varg called upon the wolf gods.

<center>~~~✦~~~</center>

Behind the barricade, the devotees waited in dread. Even the humans could hear the demons storming towards them, and like a tidal wave, they crashed against the heavy wooden gates. The massive wooden structure groaned under the strain of the onslaught but held firm.

Archers launched barrage after barrage of arrows over the barricade, taking down countless demons. Still, the servants of Chaos pressed forward, producing makeshift ladders, and launching grappling hooks over the spiked fortification. Despite the deterrents, many crossed over, and once the bodies piled up outside the gate, they started throwing their own dead over the spikes to shield their crossing.

While some demons climbed over, others chopped down a large tree that was quickly being fashioned into a battering ram.

The clerics, priestesses, and lycans fought every demon that crossed the barricade, but it seemed nothing was slowing their advance.

Kalee and Favion fought back-to-back as they guarded each other against the never-ending onslaught of wraiths and black-eyed demons, but their foes continued to press in on all sides. Kalee's spear burned with the white light of Tiamet as she cut down every servant of Chaos that came near, and Favion fearlessly charged with his rune-carved daggers into a pack of wraiths.

"Favion!" Kalee cried in horror as they quickly swarmed him, but with speed and strength almost unbelievable for a non-blessed human, he slashed his blades through his enemies, causing them to explode in purification with ear-splitting shrieks.

Just as he seemed to be gaining the upper hand, another wave of demons surged over the barricade, and before Favion could fall back, a wraith leaped forward with a dark spear and attacked. Favion dropped one of his daggers to grapple with the demon's weapon, but the wraith had the superior strength, and with tremendous force, it pressed down on him, causing the bones in his right arm to snap against the strain.

Favion buckled under the pain, but before the wraith could finish him, Kalee broke past her enemies and threw her charged spear through the demon, sending it into oblivion.

"Favion, your arm! Let's move back. You can't fight like this," Kalee cried as she moved in to defend him from more approaching demons.

"I still have my left arm," he struggled to argue as the pain shot up to his shoulder.

"Don't be stupid!" Kalee barked as she cut down another wraith that charged towards them. "I'm not going to let you risk your life."

241

"I can't leave you," he pleaded while picking up his dropped knife with his good arm and clenched his teeth as he quickly regretted that simple motion.

"Look, I'll be okay. Just go!"

"Okay but stay safe. I love you," Favion confessed, causing Kalee to nearly miss putting up a block with her spear before a wraith with a sword could cut her down.

"Hurry," she begged, and with a final nod of agreement, Favion moved back while Kalee held off their attackers as something warm rolled down her cheeks.

The battle raged on as more and more demons surged over the barricade, and soon it became necessary to set the structure ablaze.

"What if it's too soon? If we light it up now and Varg and the others haven't reached those tears, then when the fire's out, they'll keep coming, and next it'll be the den," Aatu bemoaned to his fellow archers. Beside him, Hemming and Alec continued to release arrows over the barricade and even within as demons crept ever nearer. Daciana and Faolan had shifted into their wolf forms and were doing their best to defend the archers.

Seeing the growing predicament of the archers, Codeon, Samuel, and Jennifer rushed in to help defend them as the lycans continued to debate if it was time to enact Varg's plan.

"Maybe we can call the den's defenses to come to our aid?" Hemming asked.

"The den can't afford to be vulnerable again. That's why Varg insisted they stay where they are. This is up to us," argued Faolan.

As their enemies pressed in all around them, the barricade shook, and they heard a boom and the splintering of wood as the demons battered at the gate.

"Light it!" shouted Bertolf as he led his pack forward against the next wave of demons pouring over the barricade. "It won't hold much longer anyway."

The archers lit their arrows and aimed for the straw bales packed against the base of the massive wooden structure and released. The flames spread slowly at first, but the archers continued to launch their lit arrows until the fire spread through the internal structure of the barricade, and before long, billows of black smoke rose into the sky.

Just as the barricade fire was roaring to life, another wave of demons spilled over the top, shrieking as their black robes caught fire and frantically flailing as they continued to stumble towards their targets.

Jennifer was fighting to get back when a black-eyed demon sailed over the smoldering barricade on bat-like wings and landed on top of her. Before she could even raise her sword or call upon her power, the beast unhinged its jaw and bit down over her head. Samuel and Gwen cried out in horror, but they couldn't reach her before the demon's teeth crunched through the bones in her neck and tore Jennifer's head from her limp body.

Samuel screamed in anguish as his acolyte crumbled, and her blood gushed out over the frozen ground.

The archers quickly aimed, desperate to slay this terrifying demon, but it was remarkably fast as it shot back into the air. The smoke and light from the burning barricaded blocked out the stars above, making visibility almost impossible as the black-eyed demon swooped in once more and pounced on Aatu, who yelled in pain as the beast sunk its claws into his chest and shoulders. Again, the demon's jaw unhinged, and Aatu could see deep into its blood-stained maw as it loomed over him. Before the servant of Chaos could bite down, it released the frantically struggling lycan and let out a shriek as Alec shot a rune-carved arrow through the creature, causing it to burst into the white light of purification.

Aatu turned to thank his human cleric friend, but before the words could escape his lips, Alec let out a strange sound, as if gulping in a bad breath of air before he collapsed with a dark blade buried in his back. Aatu charged the demon, who threw the dagger with rage in his eyes and tore it limb from limb as hatred and anger burned within him. Nothing could assuage his inner wolf, and soon he had forgotten his bow and was mercilessly tearing into every demon that came near.

<center>~~~☼~~~</center>

Varg heard the howls rising from behind them, and he knew the barricade had been lit.

"Shit, we're out of time," he called as he swung down the Fang once more, sending yet another blast through the demons that continued to block their way to the tears.

Halea's spear and fists glowed as she purified every demon within range, but if they did not reach the tears soon, she and the other priestesses would not have any strength left to seal them. As every moment grew more desperate, she could not escape the fleeting thought filling her with despair. *"What if I never see my baby again?"*

Just as all hope seemed lost, the howling of wolves once more pierced the night air, but this time it was not the call of the western or southern pack or even the northern pack behind the barricade. Halea looked up towards the howls, and there, charging down the northeastern slope, was the eastern pack with Otsana leading them into battle.

Nearly four thousand lycans poured down the mountainside like a cascade and overtook every demon that dared to stand in their way.

"It's Otsana! I knew she'd bring the eastern pack!" cried Halea with relief.

Enheartened, Varg and Halea fought on, pressing ever closer to the tears waiting just ahead. With the eastern pack's reinforcements, they soon reached the massive dimensional rifts that pulsed their sickening light.

Every priestess who could break away from the battle sprang forward and raised their hands to call upon the Goddess as the lycans protected them from the onslaught of the continually emerging demons.

Each tear was challenged by over a dozen priestesses, who slowly began to overpower the dimensional rifts, and even Halea was doing her part by lending her powers. Varg decimated the demons who spilled out from the Chaos with the Fang, but their enemies that had already emerged were still many. All around them, the sounds of pain and death rent the air.

As Halea struggled to help seal one of the tears, a black-eyed demon with a dark whip lunged forward. Its weapon crackled with the evil purple light of Chaos, and

243

with blinding speed, it lashed out towards her, but with her spear planted and her hands in the air, she couldn't react in time as the sizzling crackle of the whip tore through the air straight for her.

Almost faster than Halea could see, a form sprang up before her and took the brunt of the evil weapon, and Halea cried out in horror as Otsana was struck down by the force of the dark whip.

The she-wolf let out a scream of unbridled pain as the dark energy zapped through her body, and abandoning the tear, Halea took up her spear once more and launched it into the black-eyed demon who erupted from purification on contact.

"Otsana!" screamed Halea as she dropped to her knees beside the fallen eastern wolfmother. "Otsana, get up!"

But Otsana did not move.

Halea placed her ear over the she-wolf's chest and listened for the sounds of a heartbeat or breath, but all was still. A glance confirmed that the other priestesses were overcoming the tear without her, and so drawing upon her healer knowledge, Halea quickly began to do chest compressions on the fallen wolfmother.

"Wake up!" she shouted before tilting Otsana's head back, pinching her nose shut, and sealing Otsana's lips with her own before breathing into the she-wolf's mouth. Again, Halea began a series of chest compressions as the chaos of the battle continued all around her as the priestesses slowly overcame the tears. But no matter how much of her breath she forced into Otsana's lungs, or how furiously she fought to make her heart beat, the eastern wolfmother would not respond.

"You're not dying! I'm a healer. I can save you. Wake up!" she shouted again before giving the she-wolf a furious slap to the face, hoping to provoke her into life, hoping to kindle some semblance of the eastern wolfmother's feisty nature, but to no avail.

Tears streamed from Halea's eyes as she buried her face in her hands, and she remembered how Úlfa had asked her to look after her daughter. With renewed resolution, she began to perform chest compressions on the fallen she-wolf once more.

"I'm not leaving you. Not this time. Please, Otsana, breathe!" Halea pleaded after filling Otsana's lungs with more of her air, and then a thought occurred to her that she had never considered before. With nothing to lose, she called upon the Goddess while furiously pressing into the eastern wolfmother's chest, sending a jolt of energy straight to Otsana's heart. At first, there was no response, but after one more zap, Otsana's eyelids twitched, and the she-wolf drew in a ragged breath. Beneath Halea's hands, Otsana's heart came to life once more.

CHAPTER 27 – PROPHECY

Lord Anshar felt the warmth of the rising sun on his back, but his eyes never left the dark horizon where the Citadel in the sea met the sky. For the first time since he cast himself into the Chaos, his mind felt free and clear from Zernebog's torment. Delusions no longer clouded his thoughts. No more was he deceived or coerced by the taunting voice from the darkness. Everything was clear.

He was a murderer.

The truth of what he had done at the behest of the false god tore his heart asunder and rent tears from his silvery eyes. He could scarcely recall what was going through his mind as he slaughtered the innocent priestesses or as he threatened the woman he loved. He had behaved like a monster, and though he knew his mind had not been his own, and that he had been tricked by lies his crimes were unforgivable.

He refused to eat the food that Maven brought him or join her in the shelter. In a desperate attempt to coax him away from his perch upon the ruins, she had even brought his sword out to him. He watched her dejectedly leave it on the ground and head back to where she was supposedly keeping Halea's mother. He had no interest in verifying if the woman she was keeping was Halea's mother or not. In the end, it didn't matter. Halea would come, or she would not.

If she did not come, it would be best for her. She was Tiamet's last chosen sacrifice, and thanks to him, Zernebog knew it. The false god would want Halea dead just as it wanted him dead. Soon the convergence would appear, and any who posed a threat to the Chaos Dimension would be hunted, but above all, he would be Zernebog's main target. Lord Anshar had tried to warn Maven that as a priestess, it was not safe for her to stay with him in the ruined city, but she refused to leave him. He could not make her understand that all their problems were because of him.

Now that Lord Anshar knew the truth and had utterly and completely severed all ties to Tiamet, his soul was destined for the oblivion of hell. It pained him to give the false god the satisfaction of denying Tiamet his immortal soul, but his own grandmother had betrayed him to the loss and detriment of countless lives. He couldn't forgive Tiamet for her selfish choice to shield him from his fate. If he had only known, he could have set everyone free from the Chaos Dimension's grip long ago.

No matter what happened, his life would be the price, but there was one hope. Perhaps Halea would come, and if so, she would undoubtedly bring her mate. He needed the wolf to challenge him just one more time.

~~~☼~~~

Halea stood cold and numb as she silently observed yet another funeral pyre. How many had there been? Too many. It was morning, and the attack targeting the refugee camp had ended only a few hours earlier. Since then, she and Batsuba had worked tirelessly to help the wounded that were carried back to the den for care, and the dead were swiftly prepared for their final rites. Devastated mates were lost, and everywhere people were grieving for friends and kin. In a few more hours, she and Varg would have to lead the funeral services for the lycans who also lost their lives. Their graves were still being dug. It felt as if she had no more tears left to cry as the flames slowly consumed the bodies of Pauline, Jennifer, Alec, and the many other devotees who died in the night. There were so few of them left now, so very few.

Senior Priestesses Gwen did her best to comfort Samuel over the loss of his acolyte, but he was unresponsive with grief.

Aatu, Hemming, and Faolan had also come to pay their respects. Alec, though human, had made a lasting impression on them. It had taken Aatu quite a while to satisfy his blood rage, but no amount of vengeance against the servants of Chaos could ever return his human archer friend.

Halea turned away from the heat of the fire and was shocked to find her grandfather sitting on a log next to Batsuba. His face looked weathered and pale and tired.

"Grandfather, you shouldn't have, not in your condition," Halea started to argue, but Batsuba waved her hand to stifle the wolfmother's panic.

"This stubborn old goat. He insisted on coming, but I only allowed it under the condition that I accompany him. It was the slowest walk of my life. He's weak, but the exertion and fresh air could do him some good."

"It's my fault," Uro spoke, his mouth trembling as he fought back the tears forming in his eyes. "That poor girl."

"Who?" asked Halea.

"Jennifer. She wanted to fight so much. Tiamet was calling her, and I encouraged her to serve. I shouldn't have let her. I should have forbidden her from following the path to the Goddess. She was so young. So young."

Halea placed a comforting hand on her grandfather's trembling shoulder. She worried that his grief would send his health into another downward spiral.

Samuel overheard the lament of the Master Cleric and approached before Halea could say more.

"Don't blame yourself, Master Uro. You couldn't have stopped her. Even if Senior Priestess Gwen had refused to let her take the oath, she'd have been out there fighting just the same. I know. I knew her better than anyone. Priestess or not, she'd have fought."

Uro thanked Samuel with a nod, but there wasn't much comfort. It was still as if the blood of the young priestess were on his hands, and nothing could ever wash it away. But it was more than Jennifer's blood; it was the blood of his granddaughter too.

"I've made many mistakes. You're going to look for her, aren't you?" Uro asked Halea after Samuel returned to stand among the mourners.

"No," Halea lied, knowing that he was asking about her mother. "It's not that I don't want to, but you're right. There's nothing I can do for her. So, please, go back and rest. It's so cold out."

Uro nodded, and with Batsuba's help, he rose to his feet and, leaning heavily upon his staff, he set back towards the den.

Batsuba looked over her shoulder as she led the master cleric back to his cave and noticed Halea's apologetic gaze. She had detected the scent of the young wolfmother's lie and now knew that both she and Varg would soon, once again, be facing off against the dragon.

"Great wolf gods, please watch over my children," Batsuba silently prayed.

~~~☼~~~

Darkness had fallen by the time the last of the dead were buried, and the lycans assembled within the caverns of the western mountains for a somber evening meal. Before joining the others, Halea carried a tray of fresh meat to the private cave where Otsana was recuperating. Batsuba praised Halea for using her medical knowledge combined with her powers to save the eastern wolfmother's life but cautioned that Otsana would still need rest.

"I brought dinner," Halea announced upon entering the cave and finding Otsana sitting up in bed. The she-wolf looked to be in good health, but there was a strange air of discomfort about her that Halea couldn't quite understand. "Are you okay?"

"I'm fine, thanks to you," Otsana replied in an almost breathless and subdued manner.

Halea set the food tray next to Otsana's bed before pulling out her stethoscope, causing the eastern wolfmother to look at her in confusion.

"Humans can't hear things as well as lycans can," Halea explained before gently pressing the strange device to the she-wolf's chest. Otsana's heartbeat was strong but unusually fast, and Halea frowned in concern. "Your heart is really pounding. I better get Batsuba."

"No! No, please. Don't. I'm fine. Well, I was until you came in. I don't mean that in a bad way! Sorry. Um," the she-wolf babbled as her face grew redder and redder to the point where Halea was seriously becoming concerned, but Otsana clasped her by the hand to prevent her from leaving. "Don't go."

"I think you could at least do with a hot cup of tea to help you relax. Let me make you some," Halea offered, and Otsana reluctantly released her hand.

Using the cave's stove, Halea boiled water for the tea, which she mixed with some additional herbs to help the anxious she-wolf sleep. As Halea worked, she could feel Otsana looking at her, and every time she glanced over her shoulder, the she-wolf would lower her eyes and purse her lips as if she wanted to say something but couldn't.

As Halea was handing Otsana her tea, the door to the cave opened, and Varg entered. He was curious to see how Otsana was doing and hoped to walk Halea back to the communal caverns because they were both late for dinner. The moment Varg entered the cave, he detected the same scent from Otsana that he noticed the day she said goodbye after the Spring Moon Festival, and he narrowed his eyes at the she-wolf who quickly lowered her head in shame.

Halea sensed a strange emotion from Varg and looked at him with curiosity.

"I'd like a word alone with the patient," he said while also sending his mate a sense of comforting reassurance. Halea nodded her head in agreement before wishing Otsana goodnight and exiting the cave.

Otsana braced herself for the worst, but to her surprise, Varg sighed regretfully before sitting on the bedside chair and looking the nervous she-wolf squarely in the eyes. It wasn't the threatening stare of an alpha but a look of remorse.

"How did this happen?" he asked.

Otsana burst into tears before burying her face in her hands. "I don't know. I don't know. It just happened. I'm sorry. I'm so sorry."

Varg waited patiently for Otsana to collect herself as she desperately tried to dry her eyes but to no avail.

"I suppose you never could choose anyone less than an alpha," he remarked, and the she-wolf smiled sardonically.

"When we sparred together, she once asked me to pray to the wolf gods, and I did. I told them what I wanted. I wanted to be a wolfmother, no matter the cost...and they answered me. There was a voice. It said I could have what I wanted, but there would be a price – my heart. At the time, I didn't understand it. It didn't make any sense at all. I almost thought I imagined it. But now...I'm paying for it."

Varg shook his head in commiseration. He truly felt sorry for Otsana. No matter what differences they may have had in the past, he would never wish the suffering of a lycan's unrequited love on anyone. Otsana would have to carry that pain and emptiness for years beyond count, and if the gods willed it so, perhaps forever.

~~~☼~~~

"Is she okay?" Halea asked when Varg joined her in the communal cavern with the other alphas around the fire.

"She's not ill," he replied before swiftly changing the subject by greeting Raoul and Bertolf.

Halea wanted to question him further but now was not the time.

"We'll have to work quickly to rebuild the northwestern barricade before the convergence comes. How much more time do you think we have?" Raoul asked Halea.

"Nobody can say precisely when. It doesn't help that the Chaos Dimension is behaving differently from its previous random nature. One thing is certain - it's growing in strength. It can't be much longer."

"Different, how?" asked Bertolf.

Halea explained her theory about the motivation behind the two most recent attacks, and an uncomfortable silence followed. If her suspicions were correct, the false god could send the convergence at any moment, and after their last two encounters with the forces of Chaos, many lives were lost. Even with the eastern pack's help, it seemed unlikely that they would have the numbers to survive a full-on offensive attack from a convergence.

"We'll rebuild the barricade with what time we do have and hold them back for as long as we can, and if we must, we can evacuate through the northwestern mountains," Varg explained. "Let's pray that it doesn't come to that. There's something Halea and I must do, and we have to do it now before the convergence opens. Before sunrise, we're setting out for the ruined city. We need to discover if the dragon has escaped his prison, and Halea must retrieve her mother, who's being held captive by a traitor priestess."

Bertolf and Raoul had heard that the mirror, the sacred object of Tiamet, had been taken by a betrayer of the devotees, but they did not know that Halea's mother was being held captive.

"What if the dragon has escaped?" asked Raoul.

"Then I will fight him – again," Varg replied with his lips set in a firm line of determination.

"Let us fight with you," offered Bertolf.

"No. If that dragon is loose, I won't risk more lives than I have to. If he hasn't been set free and the gods are merciful, we may be able to quickly retrieve Halea's mother and be back before mid-day."

"And if something does happen to you two?" asked Raoul with worry evident in his vibrant blue eyes.

"Then I'm counting on you two and Otsana to lead the fight against the convergence. Batsuba can lead the western pack until a new alpha is chosen," Varg replied.

"Try not to worry," added Halea. "Lord Anshar swore he wouldn't perform another sacrifice, and I know Varg has his doubts, but I believe he was telling the truth. We'll both be back before anyone even notices we're gone."

Halea didn't dare mention that since the last attack, she could scarcely keep her eyes from turning to the west. The Goddess was calling to her, and she knew the reason why. The convergence would happen soon, and with every moment, the anxiety was rising within her. They had to rescue her mother before the Chaos Dimension tore their world apart. She was certain that if she and Varg didn't leave before long, she would lose her only chance to ever see her mother again.

~~~✵~~~

Before sunrise, Halea and Varg kissed their baby goodbye before entrusting her to Ralphina with a promise to return soon. Batsuba said nothing when Varg told her of their plans. She had already guessed what they were going to do, and though Varg could sense her disapproval, the old healer only watched her two alphas set off into the west.

Halea carried her spear and wore her white cloak over her priestess robe to ward off the cold as they sped through the trees. Varg kept pace with her but suddenly skidded to a halt as they neared a familiar landmark – their old tree forts.

Patches of snow covered the one fort that still had remnants of its old roof, but it felt strange to see them decayed and abandoned in the stark branches of the trees as the sunlight was only beginning to crest over the horizon in the west. Aching loneliness passed through Halea as she looked up at the rickety wooden structures, and she could almost imagine the laughter of their youth. Suddenly Varg clasped her hand, and when she turned to meet his piercing blue eyes, the ache went away. The years of pain and loss and fear faded as he softly caressed her face, and she couldn't help but lean into him to feel his warmth and the beat of his heart and know that he was there with her.

"I don't want to ever lose you again," she confessed.

Varg struggled to fight back the wolf within that was warning him of the danger. It had never stopped howling since the day he learned of the prophecy, and he was at war with every instinct inside himself. All he could do was silently pray to the gods to not take her away from him.

"You'll never lose me. I'll always be here for you," he promised.

"I love you, Varg."

"I love you too, Halea," he breathed as the bond flared with warmth between them, and their lips found each other, locking in a frenzy of passion and promise. No matter what lay ahead, their love would never die.

With newfound resolve, they continued out beyond the forest to where the ocean waves crashed upon what remained of the ruined city.

Halea's heart thundered in her chest, but not from their run through the forest. Her mother was out there, in that city, waiting for her. Returned from the dead after all these years. Anticipation mixed with dread as she and Varg scouted from the tree line. They had to be careful. This was, after all, a trap.

"There's smoke on the southside. Can you see it?" Varg asked while pointing into the distance. The sun was still rising behind them, and the morning light hadn't yet reached the darkened coast.

Halea strained her eyes, but sure enough, there was a column of smoke wafting from somewhere within the ruins and being swiftly carried off by the sea breeze.

It was obviously there to garner their attention, but they had to anticipate an ambush.

"Go ahead and see if you can find her. I'll cover you," Varg offered as he unconsciously clasped his hand around the hilt of the Fang. He would not let the dragon or the traitor priestess get the drop on them.

Halea nodded and stepped out from beneath the trees and out into the open. She approached slowly and with caution, warily scanning her surroundings for any signs of danger, but as she made her way into the ruins of the city, everything was eerily quiet.

~~~☼~~~

Maven lay atop the fractured roof of a tall building split in half during the devastation and strained her eyes against the rising sun to stare out into the trees. For days she had watched for some sign that Halea would come to claim her mother, and she was beginning to give up hope. The rotting ceramic tiles of the roof were uncomfortable as she struggled to adjust her position, and she could feel them coming loose beneath her, but with caution, she settled once more and continued her watch.

Lord Anshar had accepted his sword and warned Maven to flee because he feared the Chaos would soon come for him, but she couldn't leave. If Lord Anshar was in danger, he would need her help, and she didn't want to give up hope that he could come to his senses and do the right thing if Halea should arrive.

A sudden movement caught Maven's attention, and she strained her eyes to see out beyond the crumbled walls of the old city. Someone was coming - someone in white.

Maven's heart leaped into her throat while she scrambled on her hands and knees to move further along the roof for a better look as the brittle tiles slid and clacked haphazardly beneath her.

There was no doubt. It was Halea.

Maven slipped inside the split open gap in the roof and climbed down through the inside of the building before making her way onto the deserted street below and taking off to where Lord Anshar was waiting on the northern end of the city.

Maven breathlessly tore past the crumbled remnants of homes and scattered pieces of rubble until she found Lord Anshar perched unmoving atop a broken statue of Tiamet in her dragon form. The dragon's head was missing, and one of the wings was shattered, but it was a tall enough fixture to allow Lord Anshar to see above the city's remains and out into the sea where the first rays of dawn were beginning to illuminate the water.

"Lord Anshar, she's here! Halea came for her mother. Please, come quick."

At the sound of Halea's name, Lord Anshar stirred and looked down on Maven.

"And the wolf?"

"I...didn't see him."

"He won't be far behind," Lord Anshar surmised. "Leave this place, Maven. Run as far as you can. The convergence is coming. I can feel it."

"I'm not leaving you!" she shouted, causing him to leap down from his perch in frustration.

Terror seized her as he approached with anger in his silver eyes, but before he could reach her, a crack of thunder reverberated through the air, and the wind howled as it rushed through the empty remains of the city.

A tear opened, spilling forth its unnatural purple light, silhouetting the inhuman shapes dwelling within.

Lord Anshar tore his attention away from Maven as an army of black-eyed demons poured out into their world, and he remembered how the tears opened to attack and slay Priestess Ami on the day that she was to be sacrificed.

"The false god has finally made his move," Lord Anshar spoke to himself as he drew The Blade That Cuts Through Worlds.

"Lord Anshar!" Maven cried in horror as the demons surged towards them in numbers she had not seen since the Citadel was destroyed. Most had black eyes, and some were wraiths, but all were monstrous in form.

"Maven, run!" Lord Anshar shouted, but there was no time as the demons attacked.

~~~✧~~~

Varg waited until Halea safely reached the crumbled walls of the city before emerging from the forest to follow. The human civilization was as unsettling to

251

behold as it had been the last time he was there. Nothing but shattered structures, hungry rats scrounging the barren streets, and weeds and vines overtaking the ruins. He moved cautiously with sword in hand, following Halea's scent, but a sudden sound drew his attention.

A rotting tile had fallen from the remains of a roof in the distance. Varg couldn't see anyone, but as he approached to inspect the shattered tile, he narrowly ducked another as it slid out of place from above and fell to the ground, where it shattered to pieces on impact. He discovered the fresh scent of a human female trailing towards the northern end of the city, and he knew he had to follow it.

Across the bond, Halea was still searching the city and didn't seem to be in any danger. If the traitor priestess was fleeing away from Halea, undoubtedly, the dragon had been freed, and the traitor priestess was going to summon him.

Varg snarled in anger as he chased after the source of the scent. He would not let that bastard dragon anywhere near his mate. Past toppled buildings and shattered statues, he ran until somewhere in the distance, he heard the roll of thunder and the unmistakable sounds of a demon horde. As Varg rounded the corner of yet another fractured building, he witnessed a massive tear pulsing as black-eyed demons spilled out by the hundreds. Within the middle of the conflict, he saw the dragon and the traitor priestess fighting the servants of Chaos, who attacked them from all sides.

Maven's sword glowed with the light of Tiamet, but the demons were many and stronger than any she had ever encountered. Wraiths surrounded her, snarling with silvery, jagged teeth, but the blade in her hand was unwieldy compared to the familiarity of a spear. Against so many foes, she was quickly overwhelmed. So many centuries of serving as a High Priestess had dulled her combative skills, and seeking protection and relief from the onslaught, she tried to fight her way closer to Lord Anshar.

Lord Anshar charged fearlessly, slaying black-eyed demons with such speed and fury that his eyes became elliptical with rage. The servants of Chaos were no match for him as their black blood sprayed the ground and crumbled ruins all around them, and their shrieks pierced the air. An explosion of white light shook the ground and tore through hundreds of the demons, and when Maven looked up to find the source of the blast, she recognized Halea's shifter mate.

"Lord Anshar! Lord Anshar, the wolf! The wolf is…" Her cries were cut short as a three-armed black-eyed demon cut her in half with a massive dark ax.

Lord Anshar looked back in time to see Maven's stricken face as the top half of her body separated from the lower half and collapsed upon the ground only to be beset upon by several of the demons who quickly devoured her entrails and flesh.

Lord Anshar was sickened to his stomach by the sight, but there was no time for remorse. In the distance, another blast was unleashed from the wolf's divine weapon as he fought to make his way through the sea of demons.

At last, the time had come.

Just as Lord Anshar tore through the servants of Chaos to meet the wolf in combat, the tear snapped shut with a crack of thunder.

Every demon stilled and looked out to the Citadel, where blackened storm clouds rolled in faster than the ocean waves. Another roll of thunder shook the earth, and several buildings collapsed under the force of the boom, and the rush of the wind as the mighty purple vortex of the convergence split open the sky.

With the demons distracted, Lord Anshar halted his advance on the wolf and turned to face the colossal expanding rift that revealed the Chaos Dimension as it loomed above the Citadel. Without fear, Lord Anshar gazed into the heart of the madness, and there within, glowed the red eyes of the black dragon.

~~~☼~~~

Halea frantically searched the ruins, peering into every dilapidated building along the way to be sure that someone wasn't waiting to jump out and ambush her until, at last, she reached the source of the smoke. A depressing little shack with boarded-up windows sat across from an empty courtyard. Halea's palms were sweating, and she could feel her pulse pounding in her ears as she approached. Was her mother inside? Would it really be her?

With her spear at the ready in case she should come face to face with Maven or Lord Anshar, Halea kicked in the door as thunder rolled overhead.

It was empty, but it was apparent that the room had been lived in recently. Someone had made a bed, there was half-eaten food, and the fireplace contained the smoldering remains of a fire. Beside the hearth sat an empty rickety chair.

Halea fought back the tears of disappointment as she turned her back to the shabby little hovel and stepped back outside into the fresh morning air. The last shadows were being chased away by the rising sun, and it was easier to see her surroundings. The wind howled and whipped her cloak around her ankles as she stepped through the courtyard, but a dark form crouching on the ground between the remains of two buildings caught her attention. It was a woman huddling in fear, her face obscured by her disheveled hair.

"Hello. Who are you?" Halea asked as she slowly approached the trembling form. "What are you doing out here in a place like this?"

When the woman looked up, Halea's breath hitched in her throat as thunder shook the air and drowned out the sound of her spear as it slipped from her hand and clattered onto the broken pavement. Hazel green eyes stared out from a familiar face ravaged by time and suffering, but she would know that face anywhere.

"Mother? Is it really you?" Halea managed to ask in no more than a whisper that was carried away by the howling winds as dizziness nearly sent her to her knees. She froze in shock as her mother rose and slowly stepped out from between the crumbled buildings as another boom of thunder shook the ground beneath them, causing Theia to cower in fear.

Halea looked up in horror as black clouds gathered over the Citadel, and the unmistakable purple light of a convergence tear split open the sky as panic seized her. She had to find Varg and get her mother out of there and return to the den's safety. If they stayed any longer, they would all be destroyed, but as Halea took a step towards her cowering mother, Theia shrank back in fear.

"It's okay, mother. It's me, Halea. Please, I won't hurt you," Halea implored. Theia looked up before cautiously rising to her feet, and it broke Halea's heart to see how frail and broken she appeared as she slowly shuffled forward with an unsure fear in her eyes as the menacing convergence expanded overhead. Theia met Halea's tearful gaze as she neared and stalled, her vacant eyes searching until they dilated in recognition.

"Halea."

"Mother," Halea sobbed. "Mother, you do recognize me!"

"Halea," Theia repeated once more as she took another cautious step forward.

With tears streaming down her face, Halea threw her arms around her mother and poured out her sadness and her joy. "Oh, mother, I'm so sorry. I didn't know you were alive. I didn't know!"

"Halea," Theia said once again as her chest split open and a barb shot out, piercing Halea through the chest.

Halea choked as blood filled her mouth and soaked her robe with its warmth.

Theia stepped back as her face distorted, and her body bent and split further open, revealing a bulbous black form covered in barb-like hairs. Long spindly legs tore out through the flesh and clawed into the earth as it tore off towards the north end of the city, leaving Halea to collapse - lifeless.

~~~✕~~~

Varg watched in dismay as the convergence split open the sky above the Citadel, causing the sea to rage and the wind to howl. Something massive, dark, and sinister was moving within the vortex, and he had to avert his eyes as panic seized him. He could not be sure if he was feeling his own emotions or Halea's, but he knew she was watching the same horror somewhere within the city.

The demons froze for only a moment to witness their god's coming, but with emboldened vigor, they soon resumed their attack. As much as Varg wanted to slay the dragon, his chance was lost. He had to go back and find Halea and get her away from the ruined city as fast as possible. The demons who were swarming him would soon reach her, and with the convergence looming in the distance, they would quickly be overwhelmed.

Varg unleashed another blast from the Fang, which decimated the demons that had resumed their attack before reluctantly turning his back on the dragon, who appeared to be looking into the heart of the Chaos without fear. Sheathing his blade, Varg raced back to Halea, but he could sense something strange and profoundly sad through the bond, and he knew that Halea had found her mother.

Varg followed Halea's scent through the city as the convergence continued to expand overhead. He could only hope the demons would keep the dragon busy enough for them to escape, but as he neared a courtyard, he skidded to halt as he saw Halea embracing a strange woman in the distance, and then he felt it – an unspeakable pain.

She was gone.

The bond shattered, and in its wake, Varg roared to the heavens as his soul tore asunder. He watched his beloved collapse to the ground as the shade mimic attempted to escape, but it chose a poor route, and Varg pounced with burning eyes of red, shredding the servant of Chaos with his claws before it could get away. He rushed to his fallen mate and scooped her up, but the demon had pierced her heart. Her warm blood coated his hands as he desperately clasped her to him, but she lay limply in his arms.

"You promised you wouldn't leave me. You promised," Varg choked out as hot tears burnt his eyes. "I need you. I need you. Don't leave me behind. I love you."

As the convergence spread in the sky above, the black god emerged.

<hr>

Lord Anshar could feel the malevolent will of the false god as it emerged through the great convergence tear, but the madness of the Chaos no longer had the power to affect his mind. Hatred and anger burned hot within him as he cursed the names of both Zernebog and Tiamet until his uncontrollable rage erupted in a roar of defiance as the wings sprouted from his back. The demons shrank back in terror as the white dragon barreled into them, shredding them with its claws and breathing fire that incinerated them on contact until the remaining few were forced to scatter.

Flames consumed the remains of the buildings caught in the blast of the dragon's breath, and smoke wafted in great billowing clouds as the raging winds tore in from the sea before Lord Anshar resumed his humanoid form. He had to work swiftly to create a barrier before the black-eyed servants of Chaos could regroup. The false god had to be stopped before he fully entered their world, and this was his only chance.

Reciting spells in the ancient language, Lord Anshar erected a barrier that would be strong enough to keep the demons at bay but not so strong as to deter the wolf. He had no ink, but he wouldn't need it as he shed his blackened armor and red cloak until he was naked from the waist up. Extending his razor-sharp claws, he etched the sacred runes of sacrifice into his flesh until rivulets of blood stained his skin and soaked into the ground at his feet. The searing pain reminded him of the torture he endured while within the Chaos, but he continued, cutting runes in the ancient language over his old scars until every part of his upper body was marked except for his face.

Using The Blade That Cuts Through Worlds, Lord Anshar drew a circle around himself in the dirt and etched more runes while overhead, the dark shadow of the black dragon stretched out its mighty wings and blotted out the last stars still glowing in the western sky. The remains of the Citadel collapsed into the churning sea, and the deafening wind howled as lighting continued to crack the sky, illuminating the horror breaking through into their world.

The false god was almost free.

"Do you really think you can stop him?" asked a strange voice, and when Lord Anshar looked up from carving the final rune into the dirt, he saw someone that he never thought he would meet.

"Son of Morigan, have you come to my aid?"

Corbin stood before him with his inky black wings spread wide from their recent flight.

"I don't concern myself with the living unless the gods will it so."

"You're here for my soul?" asked Lord Anshar. "Piss off! I'll let no god have me. Especially not Tiamet. And I can assure you; I know the way to hell."

Corbin laughed grimly and shook his head.

"I came here today for Halea's soul. She's in my hands now."

"You're lying!" snarled Lord Anshar, but once again, Corbin shook his head.

"Halea?" Lord Anshar gasped before buckling to his knees as hot tears streamed down his face.

She was gone – the only thing he ever loved. He was too late.

Corbin cocked his head in interest as Lord Anshar wept without restraint while his claws dug into the earth.

"I'm here because it's my job to carry her into the next world, but I won't because you can save her. There is still time," the swordmaster explained. "You don't have to cast your soul into the oblivion. Give yourself to Tiamet. Tiamet owes you, and you owe Halea. If you truly love Halea, you will save her."

CHAPTER 28 – THE FINAL SACRIFICE

Varg sat unthinking, unfeeling, unseeing as he cradled Halea in his arms. Everything was numb. He had been dead once before, but this was worse, unimaginably worse. He remembered the first day he met her, a lonely little girl with a dirty face and messy hair, but there was no one like her. Memories of growing up with her as the years rolled by, the anguish of losing her during the convergence, the years of emptiness, and then the day she came back into his life. He vowed he would never let her go. He would never stop loving her. He would never give her up. He promised to protect her – and he failed.

He longed to join her in the next life. That one thought soon consumed him more profoundly than any blood rage. He needed to feel her soul once more. Nothing else mattered, and his eyes turned to the Fang as he lingered on the precipice of indecision, but Valria suddenly invaded his thoughts. Their sweet little pest. She was a part of Halea and a part of him. The symbol of their love. He could not leave his daughter behind, but as he grasped the Fang, his hand trembled. Would it be worse for her to suffer with a living shell for a father as his father had made him suffer? Would she be better off without him? It hurt so much, but Halea would not want him to abandon their child. He could not save Halea, but perhaps he could still protect his daughter. Valria needed him, but the pain of Halea's loss was all-consuming.

"Before you do anything stupid," came a voice.

At first, Varg barely heard it against the raging winds, but a dark figure appeared before him, and some part of him assumed it was a demon, but he couldn't bring himself to care. At that moment, if a servant of Chaos wanted to kill him, he was not even sure if he could fight it.

"The prophecy has been fulfilled, but there was also a prophecy that I was given that I couldn't reveal to you until now. Varg, you must slay Lord Anshar."

It was only then that Varg looked up and recognized the swordmaster standing before him.

"I don't care about the dragon."

"It's because of him that all this is happening. The dragon god of death is coming into our world once more, and he will destroy everything that Tiamet helped to create. If you have any love for your child, your pack, or Halea's immortal soul, you will slay the dragon and put an end to all this."

"I can't leave Halea," Varg argued.

"I will watch over her body just as I am now watching over her soul. Hurry. We're running out of time."

With great reluctance, Varg kissed Halea's cold lips before leaving her with the swordmaster and setting off to challenge the dragon one last time.

With every step as the convergence continued to grow above, demons sprang out at him only to be slaughtered in his anger. The rage within him grew until the red consumed his eyes, and the Fang blazed within his grip. If he could not join his mate in the next world, then he would have blood. He would make the dragon pay.

Lord Anshar could hear the wolf fighting his way past the remaining demons. The blast of the earthly sword shook the ground, and out from the dust and debris, Varg charged towards the barrier with eyes of blazing red. With the flick of his wrist and a few words in the ancient language, Lord Anshar quickly lifted his protective barrier just long enough to allow the wolf to enter before letting it snap shut once more and trapping them both within.

Varg wasted no time, charging the dragon and unleashing the power of the Fang with explosive force. The blinding light of the blast kicked up dust and debris that mixed with the smoke of the burning ruins, but the tearing winds quickly revealed that Lord Anshar was still standing. He had raised The Blade That Cuts Through Worlds just in time to block the assault of the Fang.

Varg snarled as he charged the dragon with sword in hand, but Lord Anshar was ready and blocked his attack. The metallic clang of their clashing weapons rang out above the thunder and wind as the convergence menacingly expanded above them, and the shadowy form of the black god loomed in the distance.

Rage burned in Varg's eyes as he bared his elongated fangs and locked swords with Lord Anshar. His every strike was calculated and ruthless, but the dragon outmaneuvered him at every turn and effortlessly resisted the brunt of his assault.

But Lord Anshar was not on the offensive, he was only holding the wolf off, and this only increased Varg's rage.

"I can't let you kill me this way, wolf. That won't do any good."

Varg growled as he continued his attack, combining brute force with every swordsmanship skill bestowed upon him by the gods until it was all that Lord Anshar could do to hold him off. Varg had challenged the dragon before, but this time it was different. It was as if the fight had gone out of him.

With every moment growing more dire as the convergence continued to spread, Lord Anshar could hold back no longer. His silvery eyes sharpened into slits, and it was as if the dragon within had finally awakened. Shifting his stance, Lord Anshar attacked with such speed and force that Varg struggled to avoid the bite of the dragon's blade, which moved so fast it could barely be seen. Despite his best efforts to withstand the brunt of Lord Anshar's assault, the Fang was knocked from Varg's grasp and sent clattering into the rubble.

Sword or no sword, Varg was not ready to back down, and he lunged forward once more only to have the dragon narrowly dodge his attack before leaping up high onto the broken statue of Tiamet. To Varg's shock, the dragon threw down his weapon.

"If you want to kill me, then make it count. It's I who must die to banish the convergence. I'm the only sacrifice that can seal the false god away forever. Only my blood can do this - the true blood of Tiamet. But it must be done right this time, and I need someone with the Strength of the Divine who can wield a holy weapon. The son of Morigan won't help me, so that leaves you. Take up The Blade That Cuts Through Worlds and strike me down. Banish the black dragon back into the Chaos Dimension where he belongs, and in exchange, I will trade my soul for Halea's life."

With nothing to lose and the massive form of the black dragon god emerging from within the Chaos Dimension, Varg picked up The Blade That Cuts Through Worlds. The unfamiliar sword was feather-light within his grip, but he immediately sensed the immensity of its power.

Lord Anshar leaped down before him with profound sadness in his silver eyes, a resignation to a fate from which he could not escape, and for the first time in Varg's life, he felt pity for the dragon. For all his faults, Varg knew that Lord Anshar genuinely loved Halea to make such a sacrifice, and that was something he understood all too well. With a nod of thanks, Varg stabbed Lord Anshar through the chest with The Blade That Cuts Through Worlds. The dragon slumped against the sword and drew one final breath before dropping to the earth, his silver eyes closing for the last time.

Varg withdrew the blood-soaked blade, which blazed to life with a blinding light. The divine strength of the gods took hold of him as he raised the sword towards the heavens. Lightning rained down from the sky, and the sea churned with the raging wind as a mighty vortex appeared and fought against the black dragon god, who roared in anger as the convergence began to be swallowed up by the true power of Tiamet's blood sacrifice.

Unable to withstand the might of the vortex, the false god was forced back into the Dimension of Chaos as the massive purple tear was consumed. Suddenly the thunder was silenced, and the sea grew calm as the last of the grey clouds dissipated, leaving only the clear blue sky of the bright morning's dawn.

The convergence was gone.

Varg dropped The Blade That Cuts Through Worlds and retrieved the Fang before rushing back to Halea. Corbin was there waiting, but as soon as Varg drew near, the swordmaster smiled and then vanished, leaving behind only a single black feather.

Before Varg could reach for his mate, a brilliant golden light consumed Halea's fallen body and faded. He knelt beside her as she drew in a ragged breath, and their bond burst to life. The wound in her chest was gone. Halea opened her hazel-green eyes and looked up at him with an indescribable expression.

"Varg."

"Halea!" he exclaimed with tears in his eyes while scooping her into his arms and kissing her with unrestrained passion as he reveled in the joy of feeling her soul joined with his once more. She parted her lips, now warm and soft, and accepted his fervent love as she buried her fingers in his thick, dark hair.

When they finally broke their kiss, they were both crying from the rush of their emotions, but the only thing that mattered was that they were together again.

As Halea embraced Varg in the early morning light, she looked over his shoulder towards the sparkling sea. What remained of the Citadel was gone, but for the first time in her life, the call of Tiamet was not there beckoning her.

As if carried on the wind, she heard the familiar sound of a man's voice, and it said, "*Be happy.*"

CHAPTER 29 – RUN WITH ME

Edmond awoke in the night to a booming roll of thunder and screams of terror as the convergence was spotted just southwest of Antherose. Everyone in the seaside city grabbed what they could carry and fled in panic. People were trampled in the streets and shouting for order amid the chaos, and rangers were dispatched to defend the city. Before anyone could get very far, the convergence vanished just as mysteriously as it appeared, leaving everyone in disarrayed confusion. Seeking guidance, Edmond immediately set out for the castle of Lord Anshar, but when he arrived, there was a strange commotion. The rangers were rushing about, and when Edmond asked them what was happening, one of them said that the patients were talking.

Before the ranger could even fully explain, Edmond rushed into the castle infirmary and was shocked to find nurses and healers speaking with patients and that the patients were speaking back. The vacant look was gone from their eyes, though they seemed confused as to why they were in an infirmary. The shrieks of madness were replaced with echoes of wonder and pleas from the formerly mad, asking for kin or their friends and wondering when they could go home.

Edmond sped through the halls until he entered the room where Dean usually slept, but he wasn't there.

"Where's Dean?" Edmond asked of a startled-looking nurse.

"Have you checked outside?" was the only response he could get from her.

Edmond ran back outside and around to the back of the castle, where the patients were sometimes permitted to sit and get fresh air. Sure enough, the grounds were filled with roaming lucid patients and rangers and castle staff trying to figure out what was going on. And then he saw Dean.

"Dean?" Edmond cried as he sped over to where the young man sat on a cracked marble bench, looking up at the clouds with his flaxen hair glowing in the sunlight. Edmond ceased to breathe when Dean heard his name and responded.

"Edmond? Is it you?" he asked before struggling to stand on wobbly legs weak with atrophy.

Edmond quickly moved to steady Dean before he could stumble and was rewarded with Dean's warm embrace.

"Edmond, you're here."

"I promised I wouldn't leave you," Edmond replied as he held Dean close, and warm tears of joy obscured his vision.

~~~☼~~~

Shrouded in his red cloak, they buried Lord Anshar beneath a temporary cairn, and Halea erected a barrier to ensure that no demon stragglers could defile the Dragon Lord's remains. Halea wept as they worked. No words would ever be enough to thank Lord Anshar for his sacrifice.

Though Varg did not want it, Halea insisted they retrieve Lord Anshar's sword for safekeeping. It felt wrong to abandon it in the ruins. The blade was useless to anyone who did not possess the Strength of the Divine, but that did not mean it could not fall into the wrong hands.

The moment the convergence was banished, the remaining demons fled the ruined city. They would have to be tracked down before they could do harm, but Halea suspected that they no longer had the power to summon tears.

Varg carried the dragon's sword on their way back to the den, and Halea was eager to get home. More than anything, she longed to hold their baby in her arms and never, ever let her go. Yet, after nearly losing everything, Halea's sweet relief for their salvation was tinged with the sadness of Lord Anshar's death and the bitterness of the truth that her mother was truly gone.

Varg walked beside Halea with a comforting arm around her shoulder. It was the most he could do. He knew how much she had hoped to find her mother alive and finally mend the wounds of the past, but some wounds could never be healed.

Sensing Varg's growing concern, Halea halted them as they neared the den.

"Ever since the day the convergence destroyed Ruinac, I've lived with the guilt that I left her behind, that I wasn't there to save her. I can't help feeling disappointed. When I thought she was alive, I imagined all the things I could finally tell her. I wanted to show her the home you've given me - that I was okay and happy. The last thing she told me was that she was proud of me, and I just wanted her to know how much I loved her, how much I've missed her every day. I'll never have that chance," Halea explained as tears poured from her eyes.

"She knew," Varg assured Halea while encompassing her in his embrace. "Sometimes love is spoken with more than just words. When I was a cub, I thought my father didn't care about me anymore after my mother died, but now I know how incredibly much he must have loved me to endure the pain of a broken bond and stay behind to be there for me when I was young. He may not have been the person he was before my mother died, but he was there. Through immense suffering, he did his best. Your mother knew how much you loved her, Halea, and being proud was just another way for her to express her love for you. What more is left to say after that?"

"Nothing," Halea replied as Varg's words sank into her soul with comforting finality, and for the first time since that black day, she felt ready to let go of the past because ahead of them was the future.

Howls rang out across the trees as they neared the den, and Halea could understand their message without Varg's interpretation – they were being welcomed home, and her heart swelled with joy.

Batsuba and the other alphas were the first to greet them, and everyone was quick to explain what happened at the den during their absence.

The sky had split open in the west with a thunderous roar, and every pack had rushed out to the barriers to await the demon invaders while the vulnerable were ushered into the inner caverns for protection. The remaining devotees had joined the lycans as the convergence loomed in the distance, and everyone was ready to make their final stand.

"When you two hadn't returned, we thought we'd lost you," Raoul confessed.

"We waited for what seemed like forever, but the demons never came, and then just as swiftly as it appeared, the convergence was gone," Otsana continued after embracing Halea in relief for her safe return.

"It's over," Varg promised to the shocked and confused crowd. "It's a long story."

Everyone was eager to hear their tale, but Varg and Halea were quickly drawn away from the gathered throng by the one sight they had longed for above all others. Ralphina had brought Valria out to meet her parents, and everyone watched as Varg and Halea wept to be reunited with their cub, and no one dared to interrupt their moment of joy.

~~~~☼~~~~

Word soon spread of how the Dimension of Chaos was finally banished, and at first, it seemed almost impossible for the devotees to believe, but many strange things were soon discovered. The lycans could confirm that the scent of decay had returned to the priestesses, and a few minor injuries soon proved that they had lost their ability to rapidly heal. They were no longer immortal.

"We're free," Kalee exclaimed with tears in her eyes. "We don't have to live forever anymore!"

"At least Tiamet didn't take everything from us," added Samesa, who was not as happy for the changes as her friend. The former priestesses still maintained their speed and strength, and even their powers for purification, though they seemed somewhat weakened, but the gifts bestowed to them in exchange for their service to the Goddess had been stripped away. Samesa was overcome with a crippling sense of loss. What was she, if not a priestess? Being a warrior with a just cause was the foundation of her identity, but without the Chaos Dimension, the Goddess no longer needed them.

"You do seem to have the knack for making fire," Halea had reminded, and Samesa's eyes lit up with inspiration.

Perhaps it was time to choose a new vocation, and Samesa liked the idea of continuing to fight for something. Rufus had given her the spark, but it was up to her to carry the flame. There was still much to learn, but Samesa was ready for a change, and she knew that someday, she would be a ranger.

Kalee wasted no time in confronting Favion with the news of her discovery.

"What will you do with a mortal life?" he asked.

"Did you mean what you said that day when we were defending the barricade?" Kalee asked while shyly avoiding his eyes.

A brilliant smile spread across Favion's face as he exuberantly embraced Kalee with his unbroken arm.

263

"I love you, Kalee. Let's get the hell out of here and go make babies and grow old together."

Kalee could only nod in agreement and excitedly giggle as Favion took her by the hand. She no longer had to be afraid to be left behind.

The devotees did not know what to do with Lord Anshar's sword. It was a sacred artifact of Tiamet, but no one among them had the power to wield it, and like Halea, they feared what could happen if it fell into the wrong hands. The decision ultimately fell to Senior Priestess Gwen, who begged Halea and her mate to keep the sword hidden within the lycan territories. If The Blade That Cuts Through Worlds returned to human civilization, it would only be a matter of time before it was confiscated in the name of the king, and none of the devotees wanted the sword to be taken from the true practitioners of the faith. Halea was the only person they could trust who possessed the devotion, power, and resources to protect the holy weapon of Tiamet.

Many of the devotees now looked at Varg with a newfound respect and admiration. Never in all their years of serving the Goddess could they have imagined that anyone other than Lord Anshar could possess the power to wield The Blade That Cuts Through Worlds. If the wolf king could banish the convergence, it only made sense that he and Halea should be its new guardians. With that decision made, The Blade That Cuts Through Worlds was carried deep into the caverns of the western pack's mountains and hidden where only Varg and Halea would know where to find it.

The few demons left behind from the last tears before the convergence were hunted down and swiftly eliminated, but the task was easier than expected. With no access to the Chaos Dimension, the evil servants of Zernebog were withered and weakened. Their kind was over.

With the demons eradicated, several clerics returned to the ruined city, where they found Lord Anshar's remains buried beneath a cairn next to the headless statue of Tiamet. His body was eventually returned to the castle in Antherose and entombed because no amount of fire could cremate a dragon. Even in death, Lord Anshar was immune to fire. A marble statue in Lord Anshar's image was erected before the tomb so that all who prayed to the dragon Goddess could give thanks and remember the man who saved their world.

As time went on, the former priestesses and clerics slowly left the lycan lands and set out for new adventures and new lives. Codeon had received a raven from Edmond explaining that everyone afflicted with Chaos Madness had miraculously been cured, and he also passed on a message from her husband, who was asking when she would return home. For the first time in Codeon's life, she was able to reply – "I'm on my way."

Lyall was pleased to finally see the human dragon worshippers go away. He could admit that his people would have been lost without them, but with the power of the humans no longer needed, it was best for the wolves to be on their own. Accepting Varg's mate and her strange ways was already as much human interaction as he could stomach. Halea's arrival into their lives had forever changed his people and his home, and change was hard for him to accept.

With the threat of the convergence finally over, it was also soon time for the northern, southern, and eastern lycan packs to return to their homes. The southern pack was the first to leave, but before parting, Raoul promised that if ever needed, they would always come to their king's aid. Varg and Raoul shared a warm farewell hug and a promise to see each other again soon.

Halea couldn't help tearing up when it was time to say goodbye to the northern wolves. Even Batsuba seemed a little sorry to see that Marrok would be returning to the north with the rest of his pack.

"We'll take good care of Daisy," Jance promised.

"I know you two will. Please bring her for gatherings on occasion so we can see her again," Halea asked before giving Daisy a goodbye kiss on the cheek. The little cub was contentedly waiting in Alf's arms. Losing her mother had given Daisy a melancholy air, but it was apparent that since then, she had also come to rely on Jance and Alf for their loving support. Halea knew that in time, Daisy would learn to smile and be happy again.

Fillin had already said goodbye to Daisy, but it was a sad sight because the little cub could not understand why his friend had to go away or why he could not go with her. Daciana and Hemming could do little to console him as they carried him away while his cries pierced the air.

Halea could not help hugging her own baby just a little tighter as Jance and Alf bid farewell to the other packs.

"I'm grateful for what you've done for my brother and Jance," added Bertolf, who was genuinely happy to see that his brother and sister-in-law finally had a cub of their own. They had both endured so much trial and sadness in their lives, and he had only ever wanted the best for them. He was particularly grateful to Varg and Halea for allowing them to adopt Daisy. "She will be treated as one of our own, a member of the northern pack."

"We know that she'll be safe with you," Varg replied.

"I'm happy for you two as well," Bertolf said while reaching out and gently touching Valria's tiny hand, eliciting a gurgle of interest and a toothless grin from the squirming infant. "Take good care of her. Every cub is a precious gift."

Varg and Halea thanked the northern alpha, who shifted into his wolf form before leading his pack home.

When it was time for the eastern wolves to leave, Otsana could barely speak as Varg and Halea offered their safe travels. The eastern wolfmother's face was grave and stony even as Halea embraced her in farewell. There was nothing Otsana could say except for goodbye. The wolf gods had given her what she wanted, the eastern pack was hers, and she would have to pay the price. If she told Halea the truth, it would only make her sad, and Otsana did not want pity. If she could have nothing else, she wanted to know that Halea was happy, and as the supreme wolfmother waved goodbye next to her doting mate with her baby in her arms, it was easy to see that she was.

<center>~~~⚬~~~</center>

A year and a half had passed since the convergence was banished from their world, and not a single child had been born blessed in all that time. There were still those who worshipped the Goddess and served as clerics, but without anything to fight, their roles were only that of spiritual devotion. All those who had once been priestesses had relinquished their service and settled into their new mortal lives. They no longer felt the call, and, at last, Halea folded up her white robe and placed it away for the final time.

Samesa visited the lycan lands every other season between her training as a ranger, and she would bring news from the outside world to Halea. Kalee and Favion were happily married and had already had their first child, and the rangers had eventually relinquished control of Lord Anshar's castle back to the devotees. There were no longer any traces of activity from the Chaos Dimension.

Halea sat in a fern patch by a stream in the forest and refilled her water bag. It was a warm summer day, but a cool breeze rustled the ferns all around her. She had been out foraging for herbs for most of the morning, and somewhere across the bond, she could sense Varg's joy, and she knew that their baby had awakened from her nap and that he was playing with her in their treehouse. Valria was growing like a weed, already walking, and becoming quite a handful with her lycan speed.

Halea silently thanked the gods that her grandfather was still living to see Valria grow, though, in her heart, she knew that he would not survive another winter. His soul would join the Goddess in the next world, of that she was sure, and it made her consider her own fate. She had no memories of her short time in the afterlife. Corbin had not taken her to the in-between, but if she had gone, she wouldn't have given her soul to Tiamet. She was a wolfmother, and her soul was bound to Varg. If there were a place for her in the afterlife, it would be among the wolf gods where she and Varg could be together.

Valria's mortality still weighed heavily on Halea's heart, but she could not fall into despair. Her daughter's future was not yet decided. For the time being, the only thing that mattered was that their little mouse was happy and loved.

A hot tear rolled down Halea's cheek as her thoughts drifted to Lord Anshar. Without his sacrifice, she would have lost everything, and her daughter would have had no future. Nobody would. Not a day went by that Halea didn't silently offer her thanks for what Lord Anshar had given to save their world – to save her.

Halea was startled from her moment of sorrow by strong arms encircling her from behind and Varg's hot breath next to her ear.

"What can I do to make you happy?" he asked.

Even after all these years, he never tired of sneaking up on her, but Halea welcomed his presence by turning in his arms to gaze into his icy blue eyes, a smile tugging at the corners of her lips. He was still wearing their crystal, and the memory of the day she gave it to him in that same spot so long ago jumped to the forefront of her mind.

"I am happy. As long as I have you, I'll always be happy. I love you, Varg."

"I love you, Halea," he replied before seizing her lips in a deep and hungry kiss as their bond thrummed with warmth and desire. Every sadness faded, and every painful memory from the past was replaced with hope for the future – their future.

"Our little pest was asking for mommy. Are you going to keep her waiting?" he asked after breaking their kiss and leaving Halea in a state of breathless need.

"I suppose we should head back," she replied while arranging the last of her herbs into her medicine bag. "I'm sure Batsuba will chew me out for taking so long."

"You are pretty slow."

"What?" she cried in indignation.

"She should really give you some slack. You are just a puny human, after all."

"Listen, you mangy wolf, you're just bitter because you know damn well that I'm faster than you."

"Ha!" he scoffed. "Prove it."

"You're on," she challenged before bolting off through the trees, but Varg was right there with her.

~~~THE END~~~

J.M. Riddles (aka Your Humble Author, aka J) is an avid fantasy and science fiction lover. Some of her writing also features romance, paranormal, horror, and surrealism. Some of her interests include heavy metal, food, art, makeup, nature, and all things nerdy. For other writing projects, social media links, and additional information, you can visit her at

jmriddles.com

www.ingramcontent.com/pod-product-compliance
Lightning Source LLC
Chambersburg PA
CBHW070103030726
47506CB00002B/572